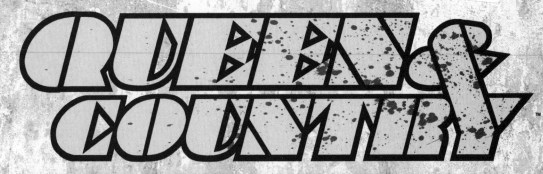

OPERATION: CRYSTAL BALL

Report of Proceedings

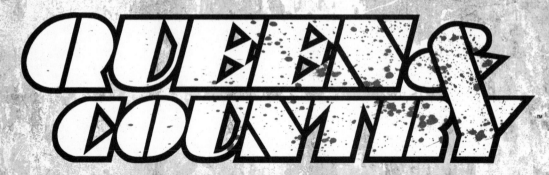

OPERATION: CRYSTAL BALL

Report of Proceedings

compiled by **GREG RUCKA**

illustrated by **LEANDRO FERNANDEZ**

lettering by
JOHN DRANSKI

introduction by
JUDD WINICK

book design by
KEITH WOOD

collection edited by
JAMIE S. RICH

original series edited by
**JAMIE S. RICH &
JAMES LUCAS JONES**

Published by Oni Press, Inc.
JOE NOZEMACK, publisher
JAMIE S. RICH, editor in chief
JAMES LUCAS JONES, associate editor

Original Queen & Country logo designed by
STEVEN BIRCH @ Servo

This collects issues 8-12 of the Oni Press comics series *Queen & Country*.

ONI PRESS, INC.
6336 SE Milwaukie Avenue, PMB30
Portland, OR 97202
USA

www.onipress.com

First edition: January 2003
ISBN 1-929998-49-X

3 5 7 9 10 8 6 4 2

PRINTED IN CANADA.

INTRODUCTION
by JUDD WINICK

To begin we need full disclosure. Greg Rucka is a buddy of mine. A good buddy of mine. He, his wife Jen, and their son attended my wedding; we honestly delight in each other's presence; we share a love of *The West Wing* that, if we allowed it, could morph into fetish; our politics both fall into the "liberal Jew" category (*proudly* falls, I must add); we hate the same people; we conspire, and we share the lies we tell to others. So there. We're pals, I love him like a brother, I'm biased.

Be that as it may, Greg Rucka is one of the best writers in comics. He's easily one of the most *powerful* writers I know. "Powerful" isn't a word I use lightly, but it fits. Greg can write more that anyone I know. In a day, he can pound out more than most produce in a week. "Must be easy for him," you say? Fuck no.

Have you ever seen the "strongest men in the world" competitions? They're the televised contests between these monstrous pituitary cases that were born a thousand years too late. They *should* be walking the land with a battle axe and ruling a nation, but instead they pull trucks from chains wrapped around their waists on ESPN 2. Go watch these guys. Look at them as they dead-lift boulders. See them throw cinder blocks the size of steamer trunks. Do they make it look easy? Fuck no, they appear like they're having aneurysms while passing a bowling ball. They are working, grunting, fighting, giving it *everything* they have. Just because the big boys can hurl twenty to thirty times more than the rest of us mortals, doesn't make it a breeze. They are merely exerting themselves at their own level. That's Rucka. Sitting at his keyboard, he's ripping up tree trunks four at a time and killing himself to get there.

Which brings us to *Queen & Country*, or as many of us—friend or foe—see it: Greg doing his best work in this medium. *Q&C* brings together all his passions, demons, and windmills. Spies, terrorism, war, flawed characters weighted down with conflict, assassins on both sides of the table, international intrigue, and just some real pain-in-the-ass office politics. Everyone in this book has a very bad job to do and they really don't seem to like it.

Plus, this li'l world just stinks of realism. Uncomfortably so. Greg's a student of world politics and history. He also has a comprehensive knowledge of the military (which is only rivaled by his knowledge of police work). This book blends fact and fiction so seamlessly that as a reader you want footnotes that say, "That one's real" and "Nah, I made it up" and "Well, made *that* one up, too, but it's *so* close to the real thing, you'd just shit yourself." It's all in here.

And now we come to our artist for this arc, Leandro Fernandez. This guy *kills* me. I love the compositions. I love the angles. I love the shadows. I love the choices he makes. Brother likes to draw a big fucking nose and I love seeing it. Every character is just that—a *character*. No one looks similar and they each have their own visual language. A lot of folks can draw a pin-up, or a gun battle, or a fist fight—these are the meat and potatoes of comics. Leandro pulls off each and every one of those in style, but what really gets me are the *conversations*. You want to separate the men from the boys art-wise? Have your illustrator draw people sitting and talking. The words coming out of their mouths are only half the ball game, you need it to look great. And here? It *does*. If Greg and Leandro put out a double-sized issue consisting only of watching Crocker bitch and smoke a pack cigarettes, I'd be there.

So, congrats. You hold in your hands the meeting of two powerhouses as they deliver us another tale of Tara Chace in her role as a *Minder*. It will not be the last. As you sit here right now, the big man puts on a fresh pair of work-out gloves and eyes tree trunks. Always lift with your knees.

Judd Winick
(who never watches ESPN)
San Francisco, December 2002

Judd Winick is the highly acclaimed creator of the comic books Road Trip, Frumpy the Clown, Pedro & Me, *and the hilarious* Adventures of Barry Ween, Boy Genius, *whose fifth volume is currently in the midst of being created. In addition to his own creations, he has dabbled with those of others, including* Green Lantern *and* Green Arrow *for DC Comics and the* Exiles *title for Marvel Comics. Oh, yeah, he also used to be on TV, when that show* The Real World *touched down in San Francisco—but it's been long enough that maybe we should stop bringing it up.*

CHAPTER 1

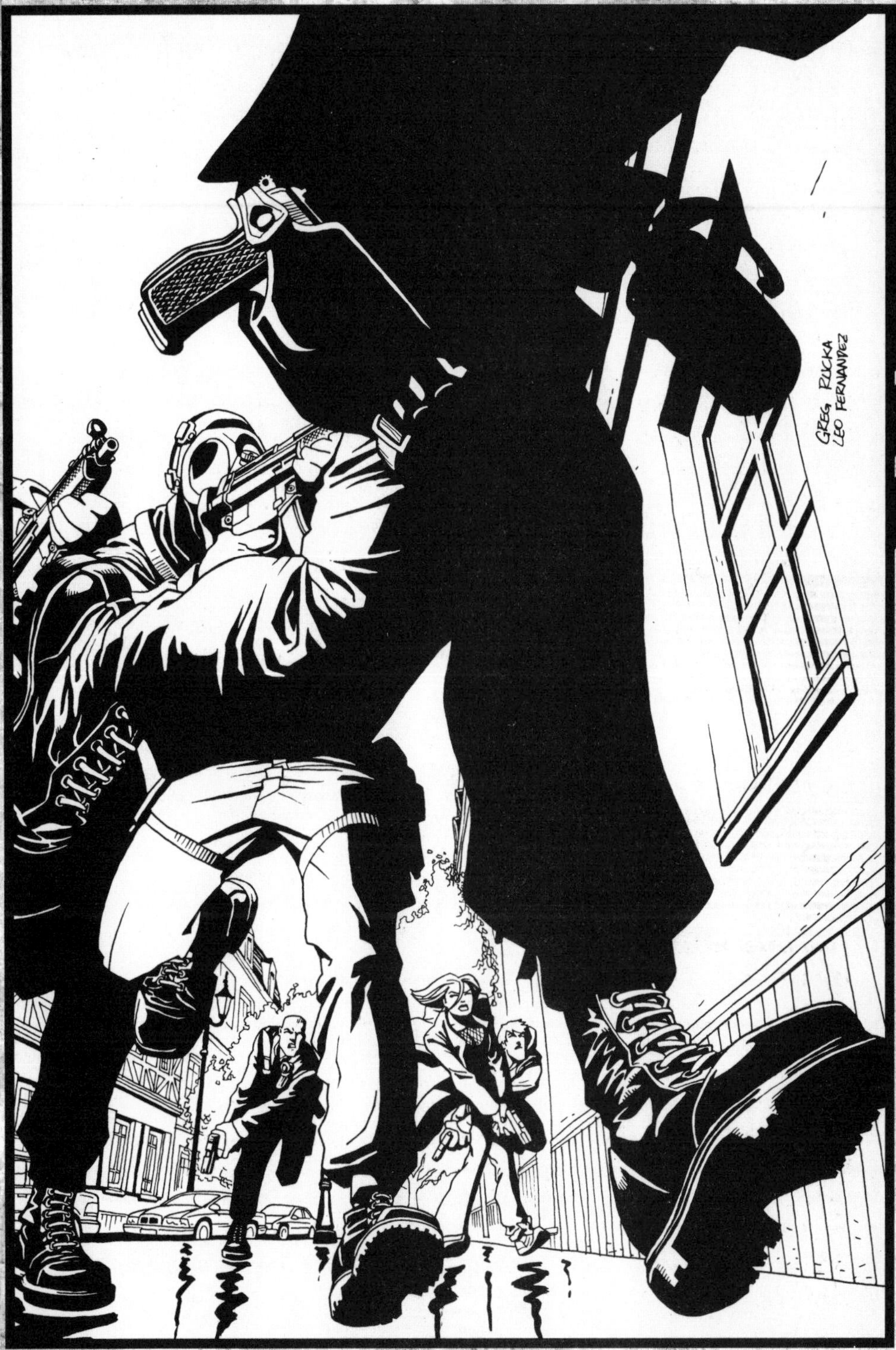
GREG RUCKA
LEO FERNANDEZ

ROSTER

C

Ubiquitous code-name for the current head of S.I.S.. Real name is Sir Wilson Stanton Davies.

DONALD WELDON

Deputy Chief of Service, has oversight of all aspects of Intelligence gathering and operations. Immediate superior to Crocker.

PAUL CROCKER

Director of Operations, encompassing all field work in all theaters of operations.

In addition to commanding individual stations, has direct command of the Special Section—sometimes referred to as Minders—used for Special operations.

TOM WALLACE

Head of the Special Section, a Special Operations Officer with the designation Minder One. Responsible for the training and continued well-being of his unit, both at home and in the field. Six year veteran of the Minders.

TARA CHACE

Special Operations Officer, designated Minder Two. Entering her third year as Minder.

EDWARD KITTERING

Special Operations Officer, designated Minder Three. Has been with the Special Section for less than a year.

OPS ROOM STAFF:

ALEXIS

Mission Control Officer (also called Main Communications Officer)—responsible for maintaining communications between the Operations Room and the agents in the field.

RON

Duty Operations Officer, responsible for monitoring the status and importance of all incoming intelligence, both from foreign stations and other sources.

KATE

Personal Assistant to Paul Crocker, termed P.A. to D.Ops. Possibly the hardest and most important job in the Service.

OTHERS:

ANGELA CHANG

CIA Station Chief in London. Has an unofficial intelligence-sharing arrangement with Crocker.

SIMON RAYBURN

Director of Intelligence for S.I.S. (D. Int), essentially Crocker's opposite number. Responsible for the evaluation, interpretation, and dissemination of all acquired intelligence.

DAVID KINNY

Crocker's opposite number at M.I.5, also called the Security Services, with jurisdiction primarily confined to within the U.K.

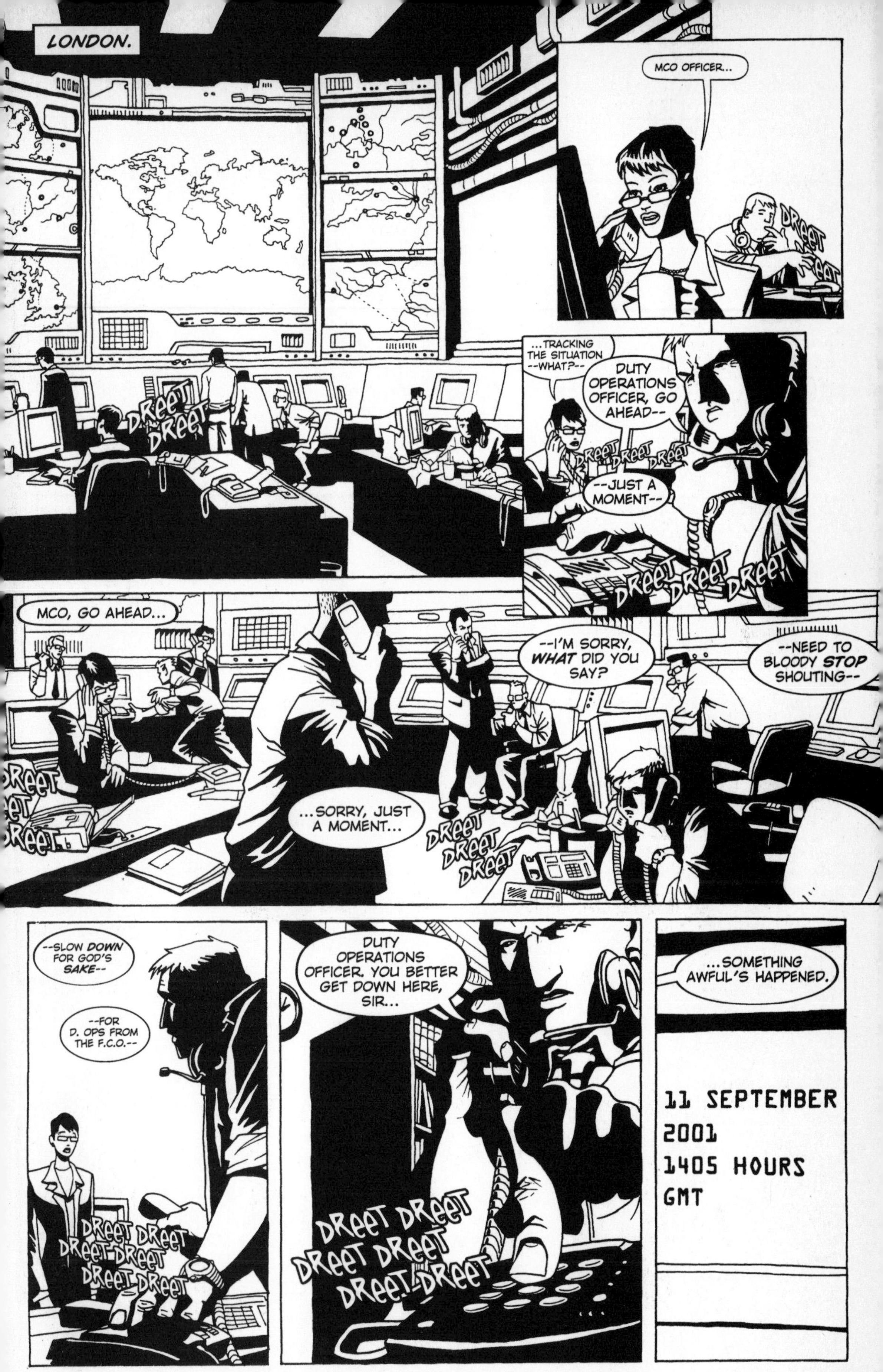
LONDON.
MCO OFFICER...
DREET DREET
DREET
DREET
...TRACKING THE SITUATION --WHAT?--
DUTY OPERATIONS OFFICER, GO AHEAD--
DREET DREET DREET
--JUST A MOMENT--
DREET DREET DREET
MCO, GO AHEAD...
--I'M SORRY, WHAT DID YOU SAY?
--NEED TO BLOODY STOP SHOUTING--
...SORRY, JUST A MOMENT...
DREET DREET DREET
--SLOW DOWN FOR GOD'S SAKE--
--FOR D. OPS FROM THE F.C.O.--
DREET DREET DREET DREET DREET DREET
DUTY OPERATIONS OFFICER. YOU BETTER GET DOWN HERE, SIR...
DREET DREET DREET DREET DREET DREET
...SOMETHING AWFUL'S HAPPENED.
11 SEPTEMBER
2001
1405 HOURS
GMT

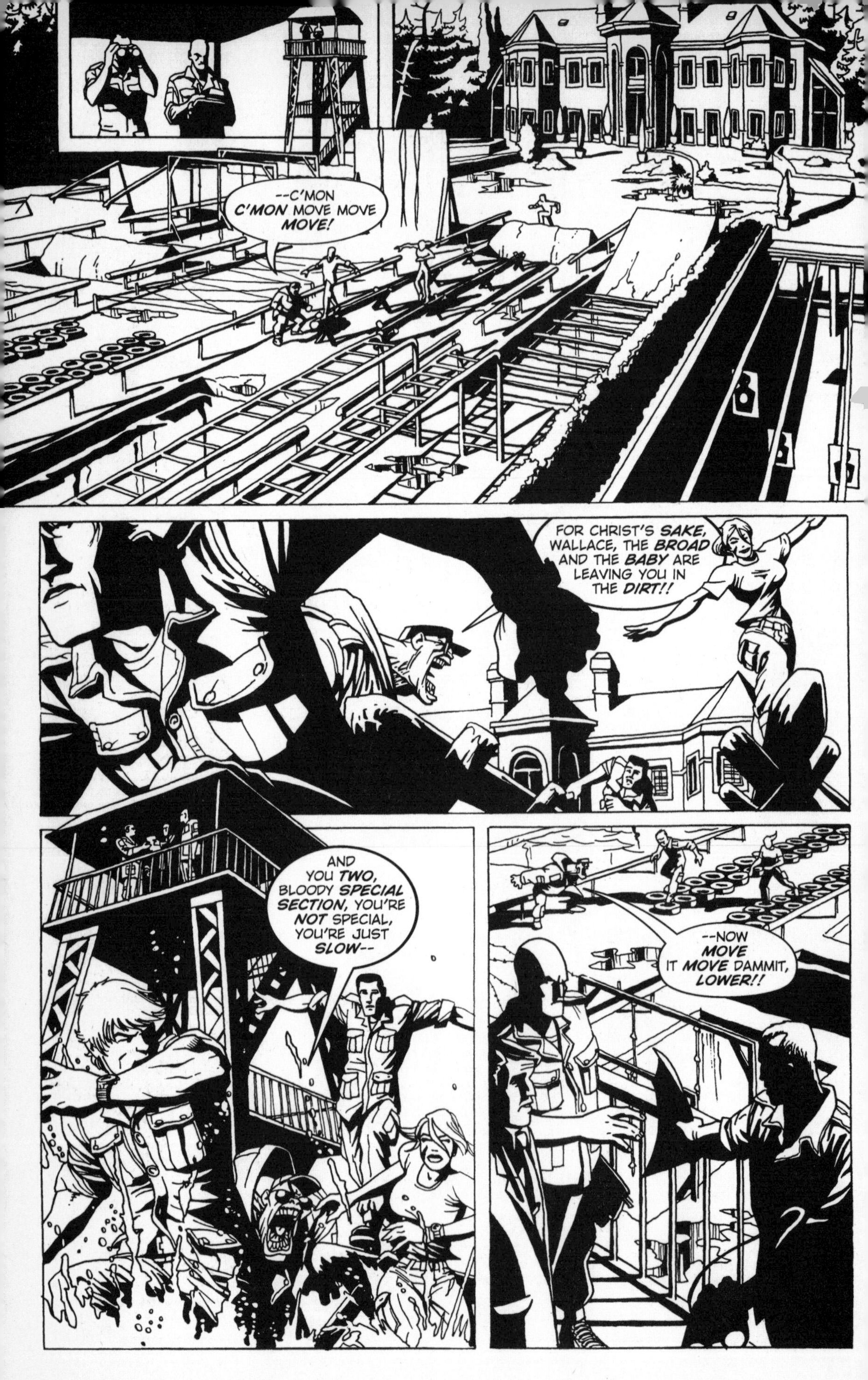
--C'MON
C'MON MOVE MOVE
MOVE!
FOR CHRIST'S SAKE, WALLACE, THE BROAD AND THE BABY ARE LEAVING YOU IN THE DIRT!!
AND YOU TWO, BLOODY SPECIAL SECTION, YOU'RE NOT SPECIAL, YOU'RE JUST SLOW--
--NOW MOVE IT MOVE DAMMIT, LOWER!!

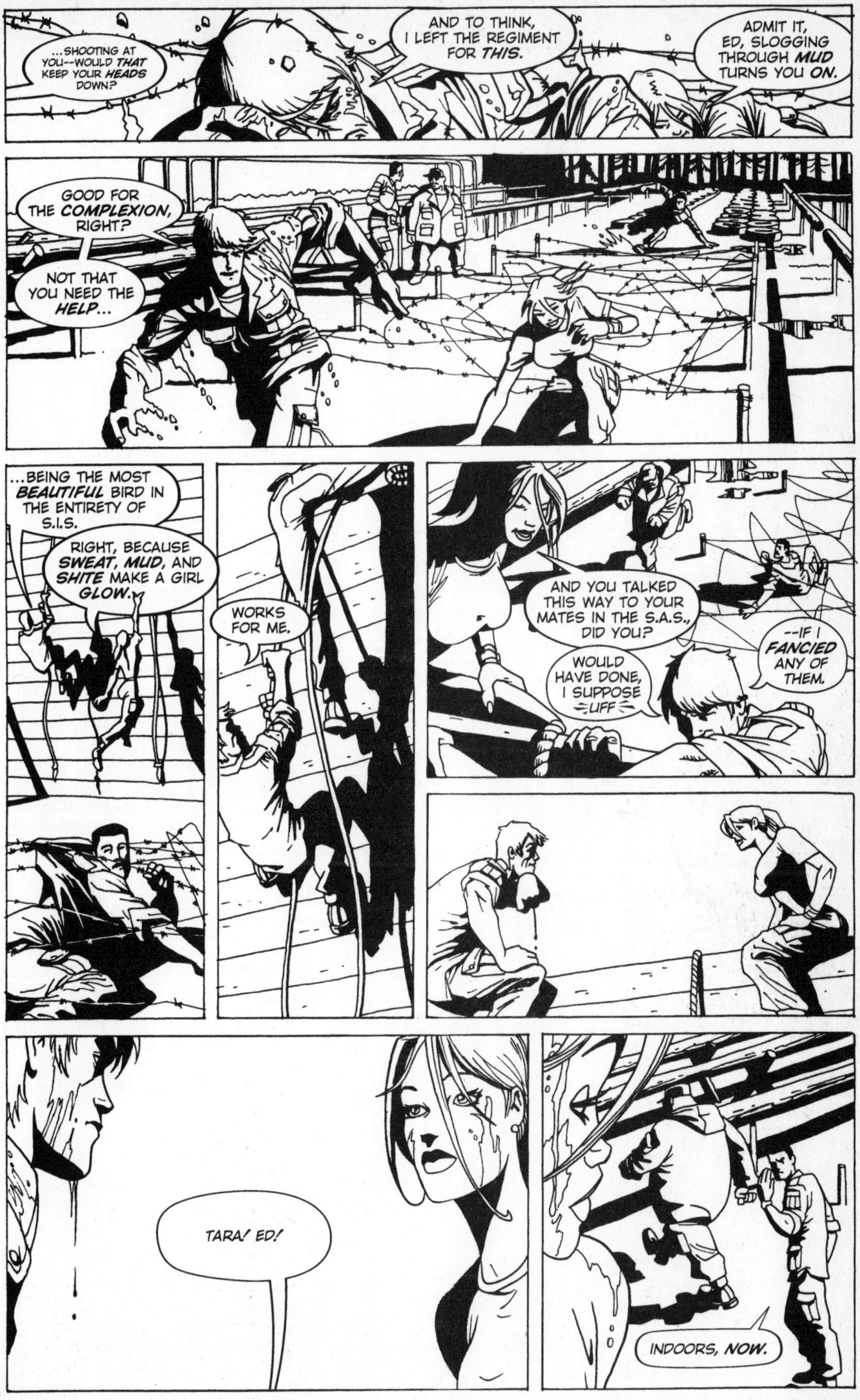
...SHOOTING AT YOU--WOULD *THAT* KEEP YOUR *HEADS* DOWN?
AND TO THINK, I LEFT THE REGIMENT FOR *THIS*.
ADMIT IT, ED, SLOGGING THROUGH *MUD* TURNS YOU *ON*.
GOOD FOR THE *COMPLEXION*, RIGHT?
NOT THAT YOU NEED THE *HELP*...
...BEING THE MOST *BEAUTIFUL* BIRD IN THE ENTIRETY OF S.I.S.
RIGHT, BECAUSE *SWEAT, MUD,* AND *SHITE* MAKE A GIRL *GLOW*.
WORKS FOR ME.
AND YOU TALKED THIS WAY TO YOUR MATES IN THE S.A.S., DID YOU?
WOULD HAVE DONE, I SUPPOSE
UFF
--IF I *FANCIED* ANY OF THEM.
TARA! ED!
INDOORS, *NOW*.

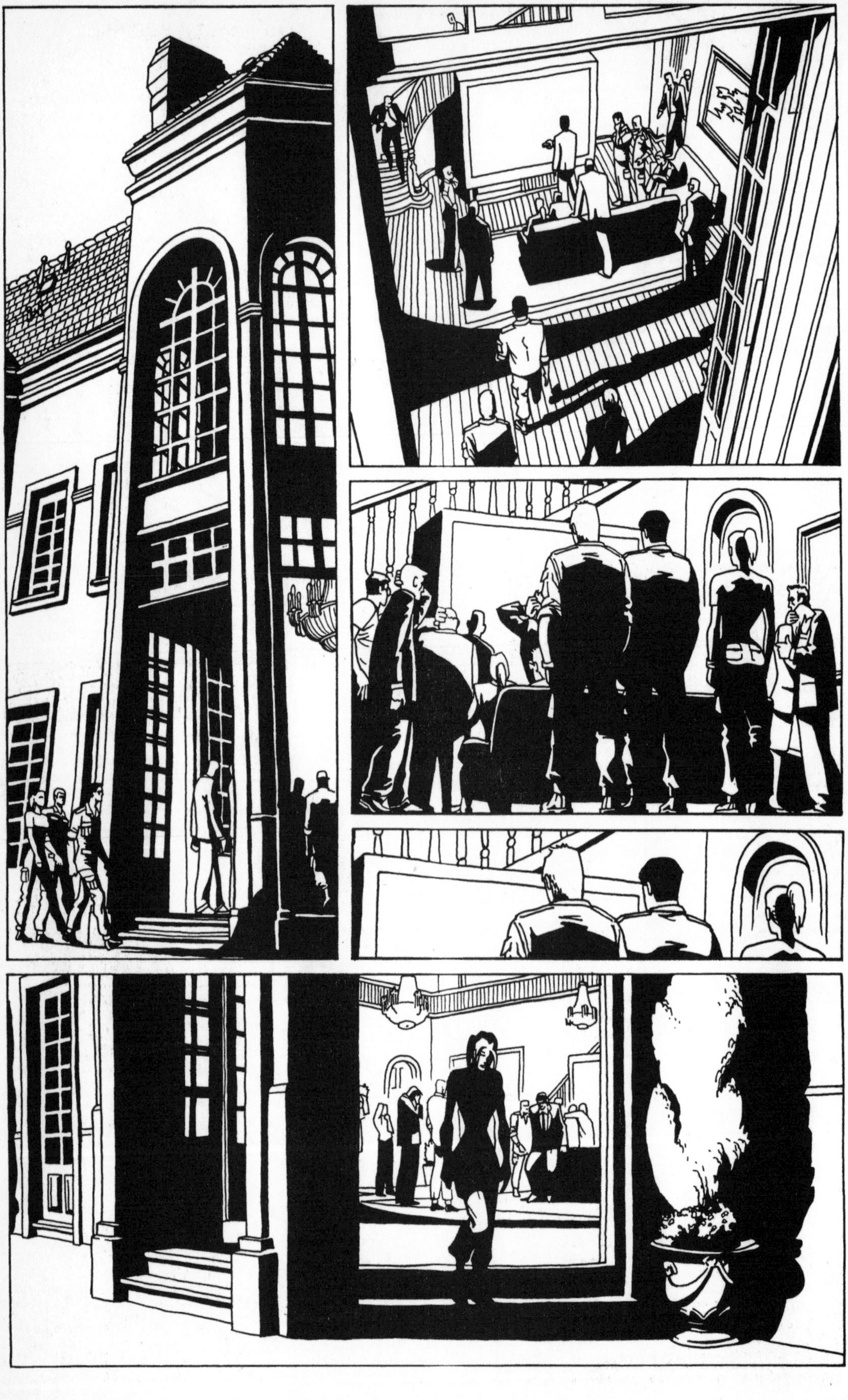

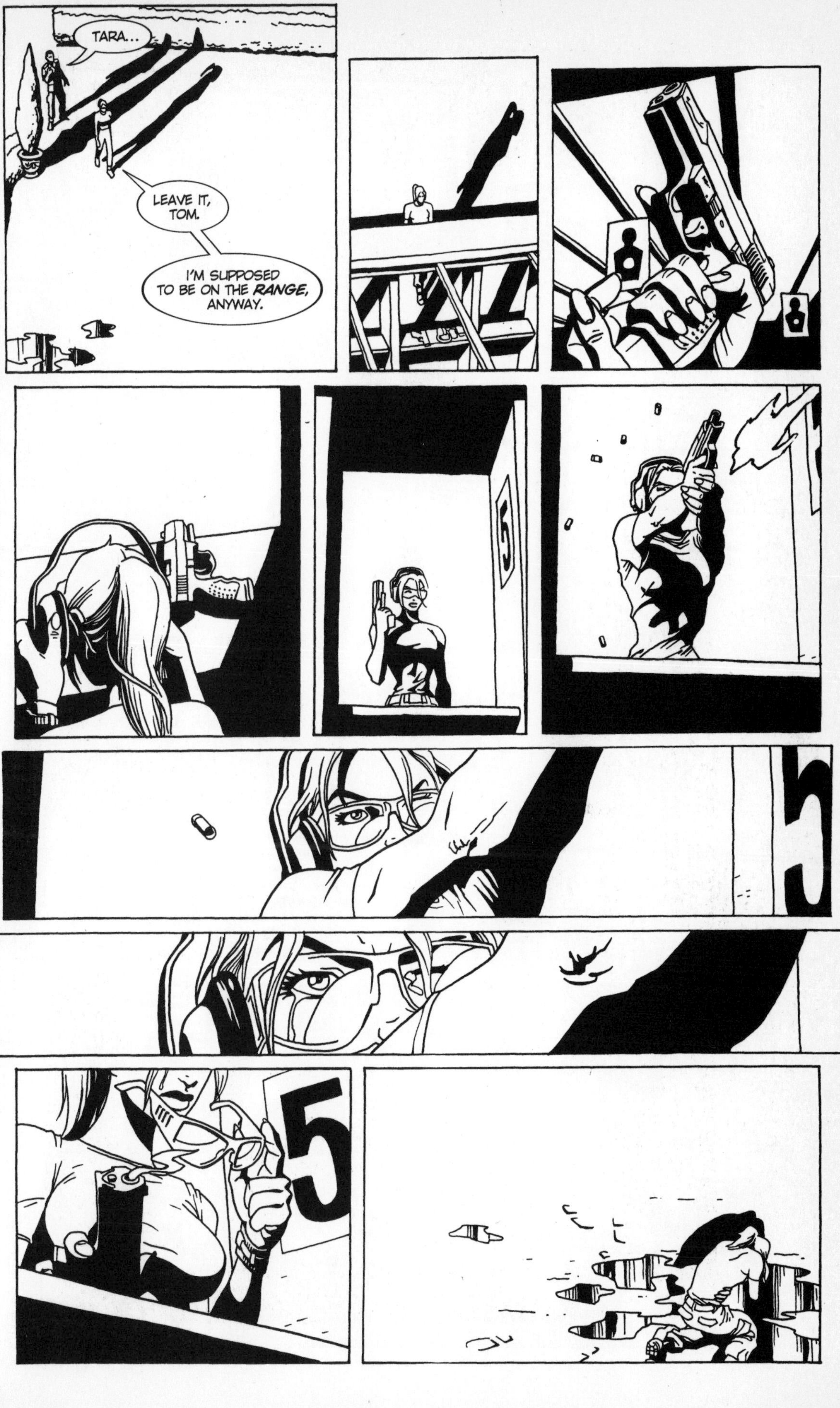
TARA...
LEAVE IT, TOM.
I'M SUPPOSED TO BE ON THE *RANGE*, ANYWAY.
5
5
5
5

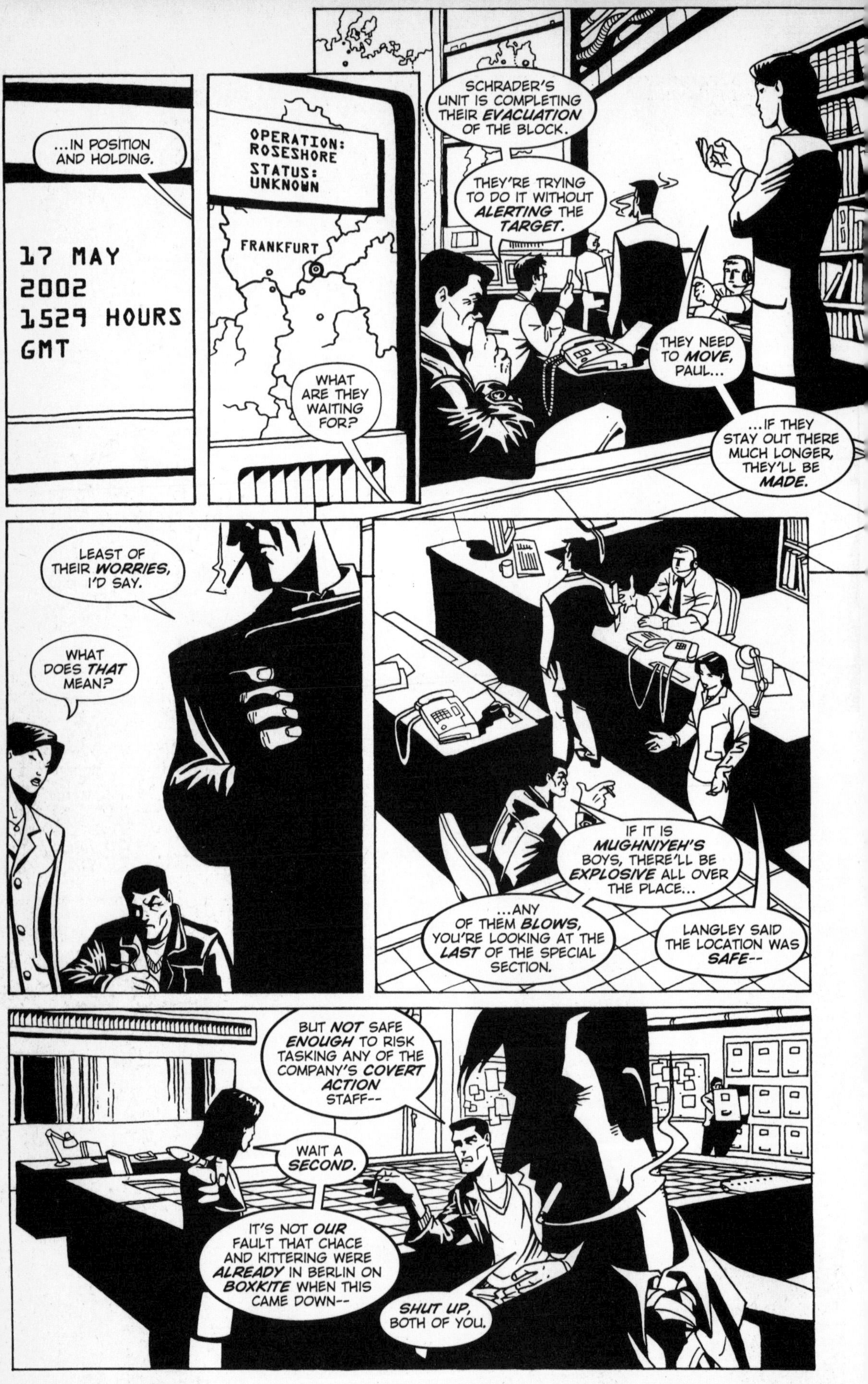
...IN POSITION AND HOLDING.
17 MAY 2002 1529 HOURS GMT
OPERATION: ROSESHORE STATUS: UNKNOWN
FRANKFURT
WHAT ARE THEY WAITING FOR?
SCHRADER'S UNIT IS COMPLETING THEIR EVACUATION OF THE BLOCK.
THEY'RE TRYING TO DO IT WITHOUT ALERTING THE TARGET.
THEY NEED TO MOVE, PAUL...
...IF THEY STAY OUT THERE MUCH LONGER, THEY'LL BE MADE.
LEAST OF THEIR WORRIES, I'D SAY.
WHAT DOES THAT MEAN?
IF IT IS MUGHNIYEH'S BOYS, THERE'LL BE EXPLOSIVE ALL OVER THE PLACE...
...ANY OF THEM BLOWS, YOU'RE LOOKING AT THE LAST OF THE SPECIAL SECTION.
LANGLEY SAID THE LOCATION WAS SAFE--
BUT NOT SAFE ENOUGH TO RISK TASKING ANY OF THE COMPANY'S COVERT ACTION STAFF--
WAIT A SECOND.
IT'S NOT OUR FAULT THAT CHACE AND KITTERING WERE ALREADY IN BERLIN ON BOXKITE WHEN THIS CAME DOWN--
SHUT UP, BOTH OF YOU.

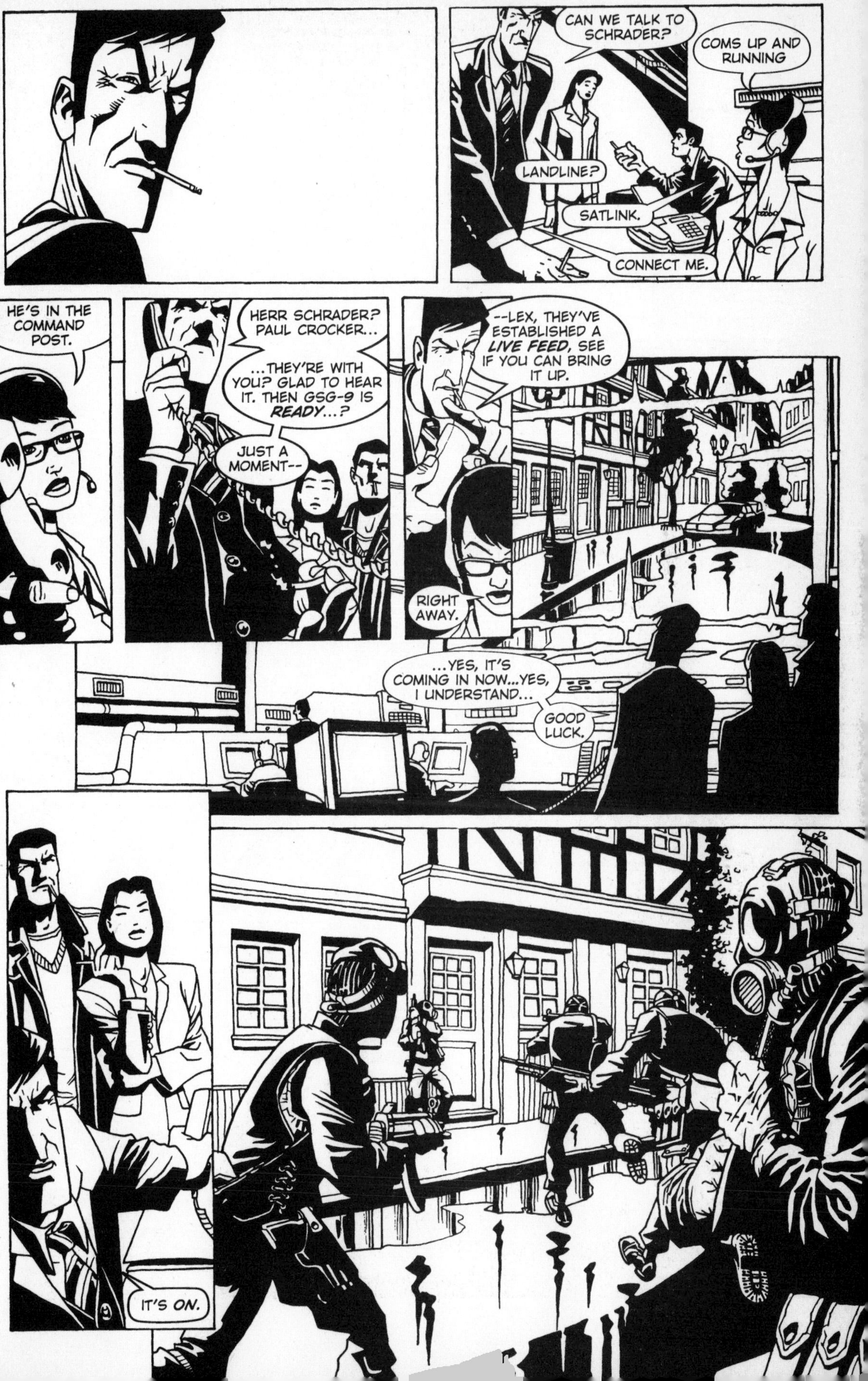
CAN WE TALK TO SCHRADER?
COMS UP AND RUNNING
LANDLINE?
SATLINK.
CONNECT ME.
HE'S IN THE COMMAND POST.
HERR SCHRADER? PAUL CROCKER...
...THEY'RE WITH YOU? GLAD TO HEAR IT. THEN GSG-9 IS *READY*...?
JUST A MOMENT--
--LEX, THEY'VE ESTABLISHED A *LIVE FEED*, SEE IF YOU CAN BRING IT UP.
RIGHT AWAY.
...YES, IT'S COMING IN NOW...YES, I UNDERSTAND...
GOOD LUCK.
IT'S *ON*.

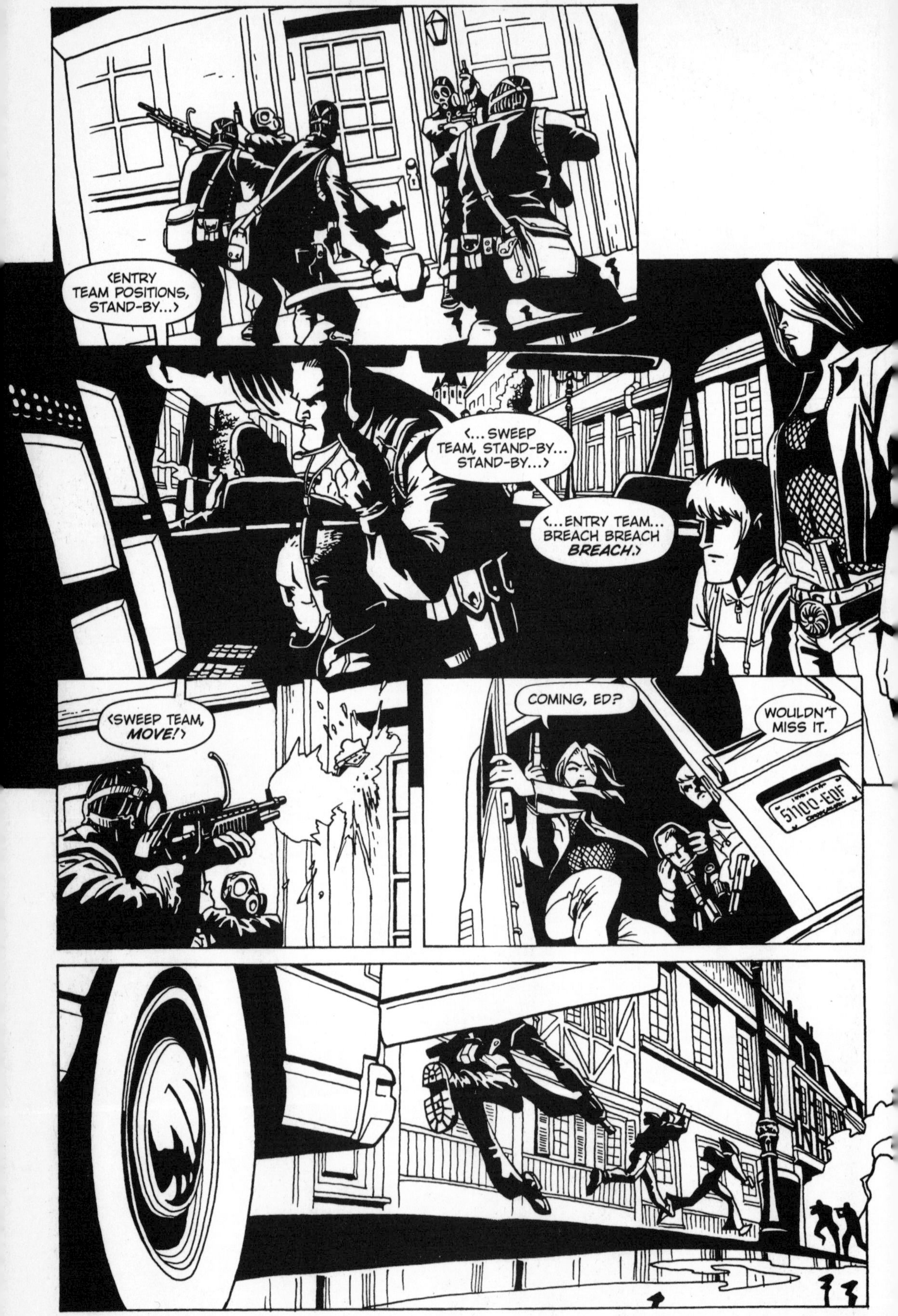
‹ENTRY TEAM POSITIONS, STAND-BY...›
‹... SWEEP TEAM, STAND-BY... STAND-BY...›
‹...ENTRY TEAM... BREACH BREACH *BREACH.*›
‹SWEEP TEAM, *MOVE!*›
COMING, ED?
WOULDN'T MISS IT.
51100-EOF

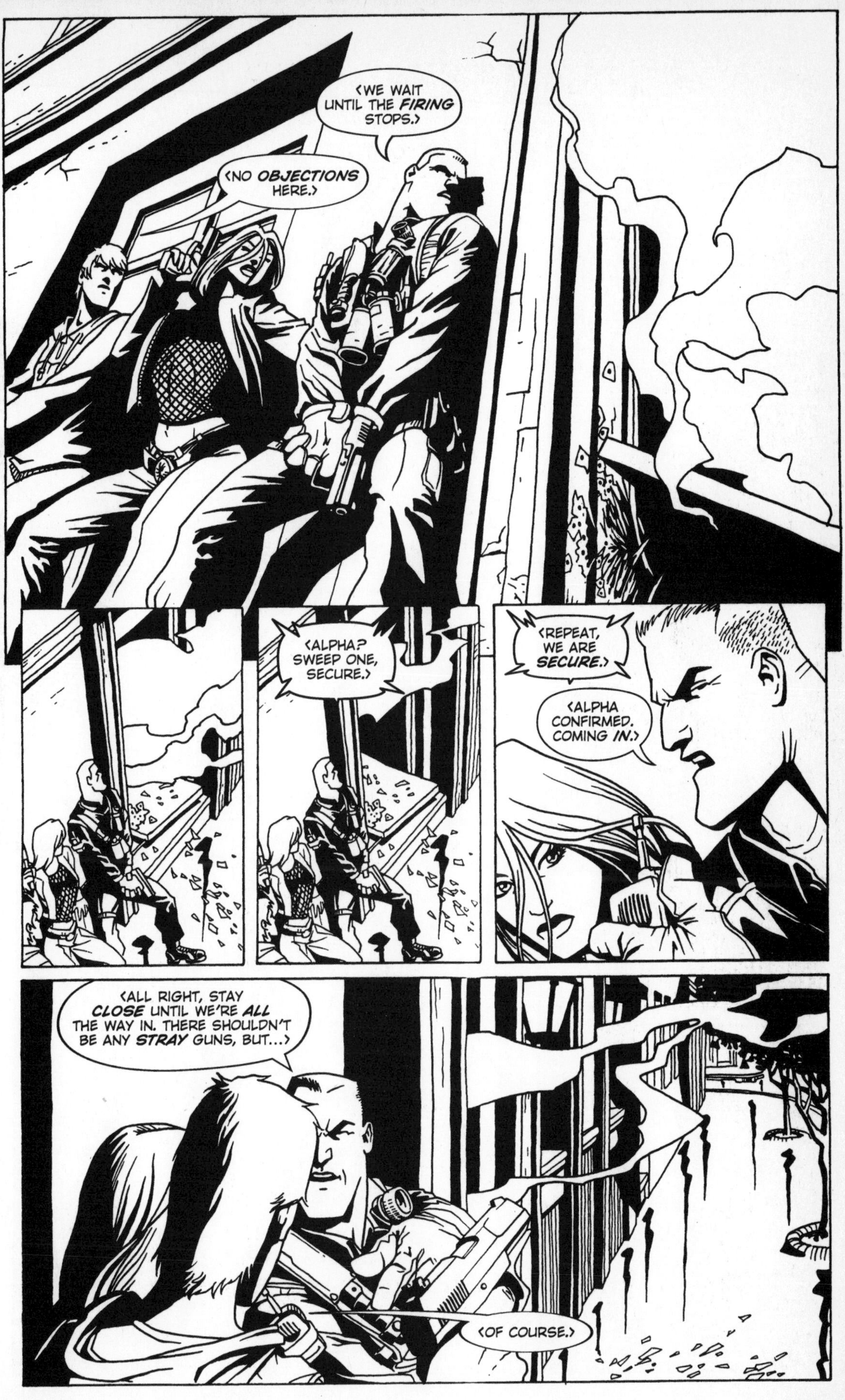

<WE WAIT UNTIL THE FIRING STOPS.>
<NO OBJECTIONS HERE.>
<ALPHA? SWEEP ONE, SECURE.>
<REPEAT, WE ARE SECURE.>
<ALPHA CONFIRMED. COMING IN.>
<ALL RIGHT, STAY CLOSE UNTIL WE'RE ALL THE WAY IN. THERE SHOULDN'T BE ANY STRAY GUNS, BUT...>
<OF COURSE.>

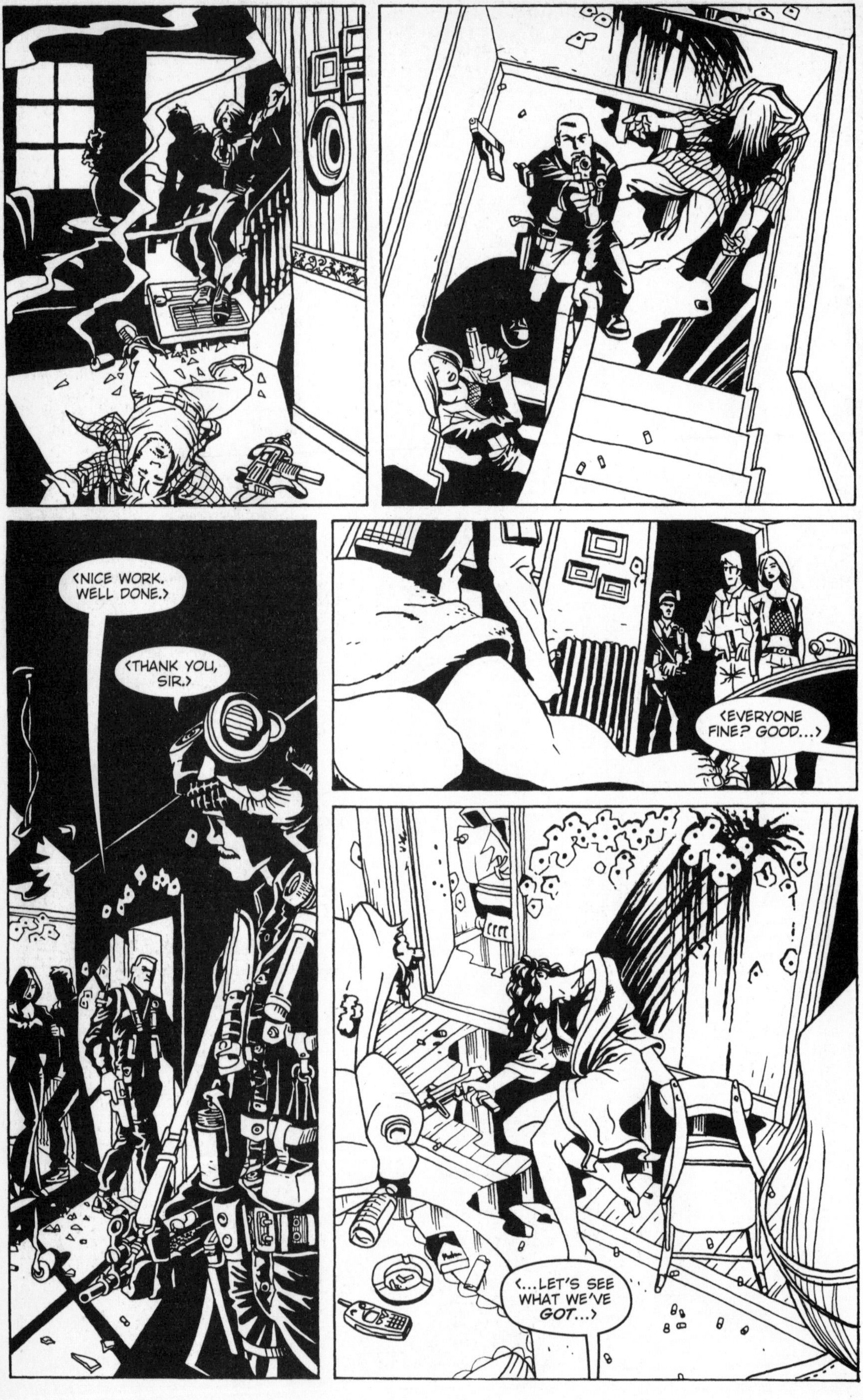
<NICE WORK. WELL DONE.>
<THANK YOU, SIR.>
<EVERYONE FINE? GOOD...>
<...LET'S SEE WHAT WE'VE GOT...>

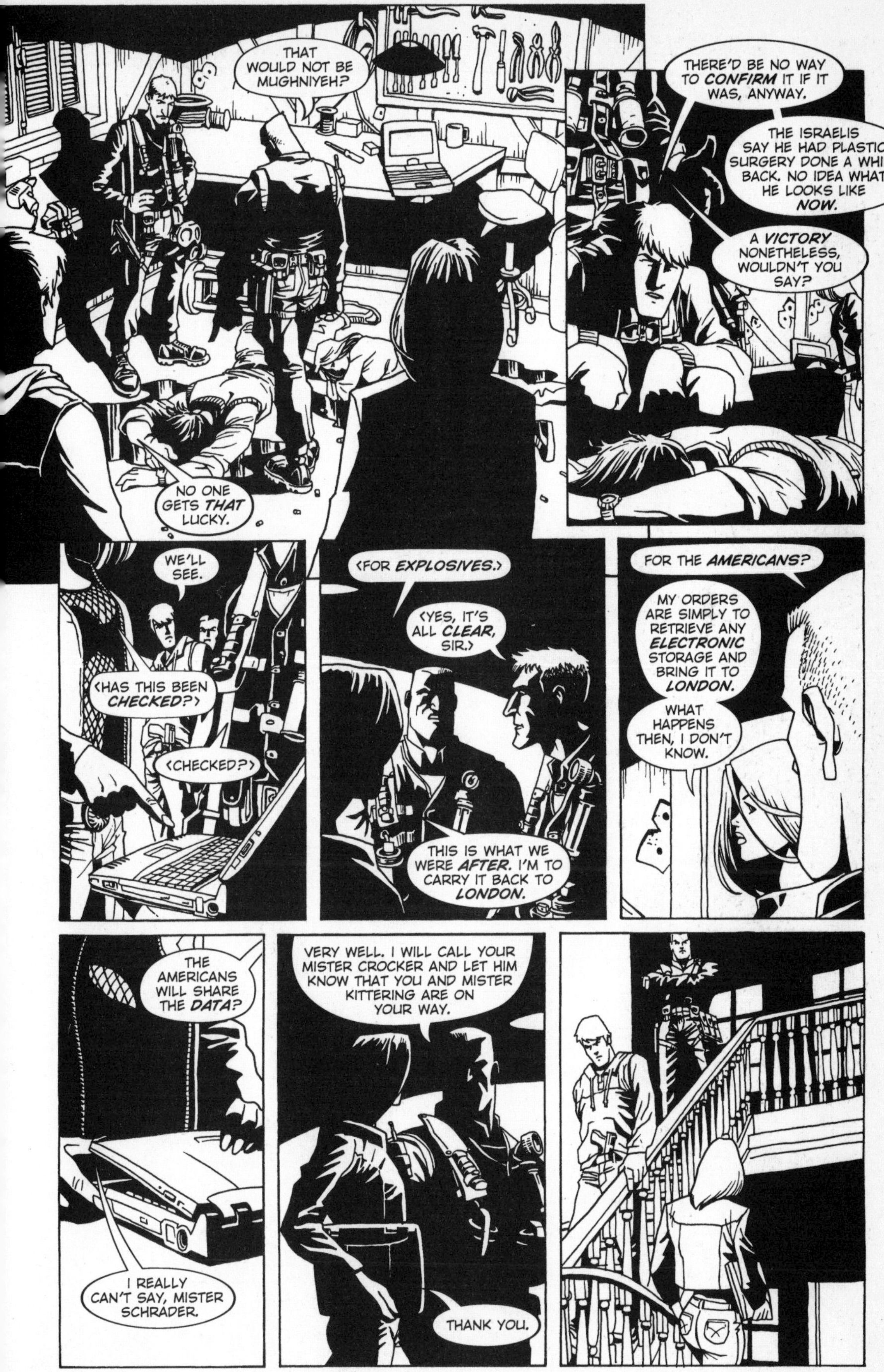
THAT WOULD NOT BE MUGHNIYEH?
NO ONE GETS THAT LUCKY.
THERE'D BE NO WAY TO CONFIRM IT IF IT WAS, ANYWAY.
THE ISRAELIS SAY HE HAD PLASTIC SURGERY DONE A WHILE BACK. NO IDEA WHAT HE LOOKS LIKE NOW.
A VICTORY NONETHELESS, WOULDN'T YOU SAY?
WE'LL SEE.
‹HAS THIS BEEN CHECKED?›
‹CHECKED?›
‹FOR EXPLOSIVES.›
‹YES, IT'S ALL CLEAR, SIR.›
THIS IS WHAT WE WERE AFTER. I'M TO CARRY IT BACK TO LONDON.
FOR THE AMERICANS?
MY ORDERS ARE SIMPLY TO RETRIEVE ANY ELECTRONIC STORAGE AND BRING IT TO LONDON.
WHAT HAPPENS THEN, I DON'T KNOW.
THE AMERICANS WILL SHARE THE DATA?
I REALLY CAN'T SAY, MISTER SCHRADER.
VERY WELL. I WILL CALL YOUR MISTER CROCKER AND LET HIM KNOW THAT YOU AND MISTER KITTERING ARE ON YOUR WAY.
THANK YOU.

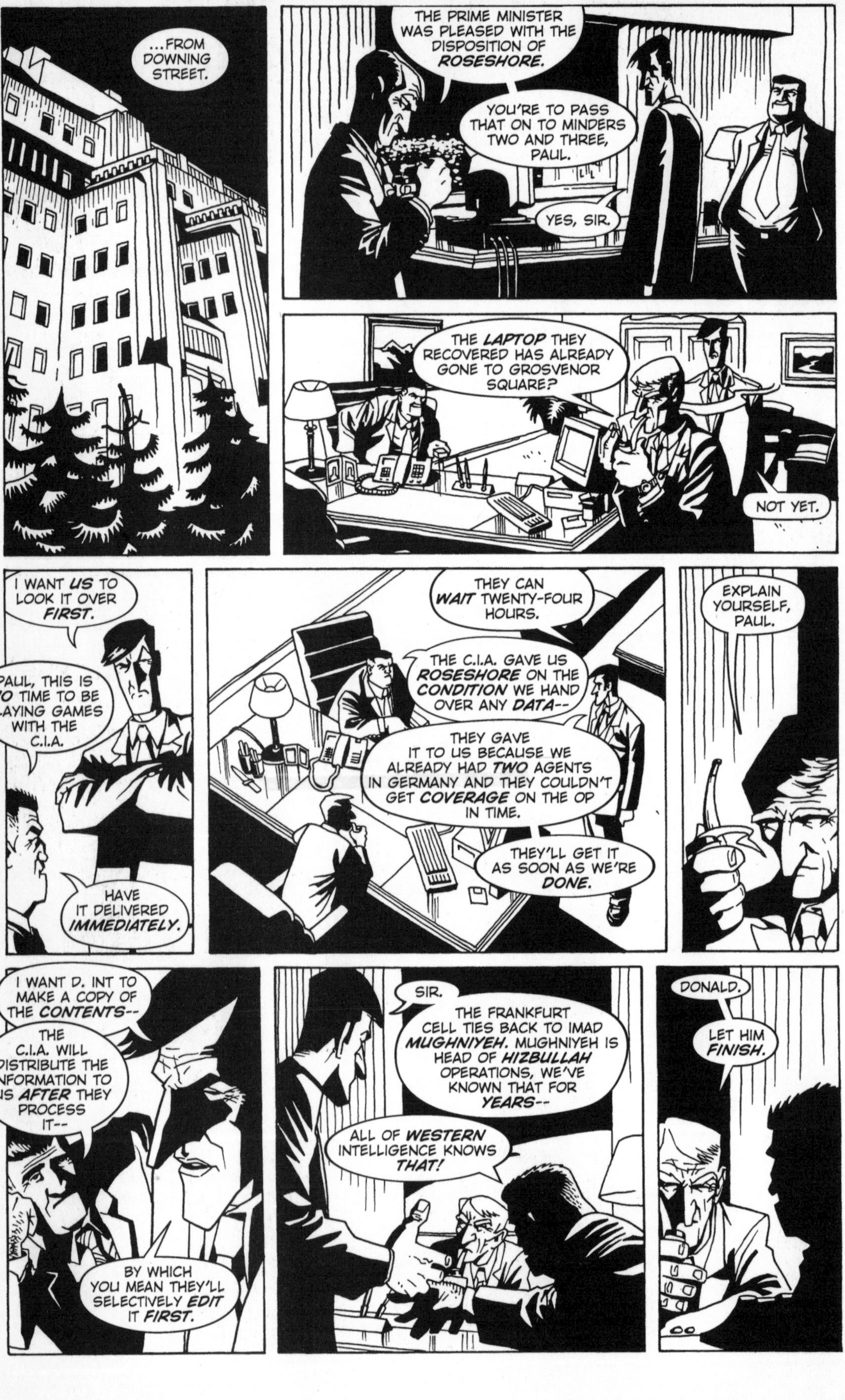

...FROM DOWNING STREET.
THE PRIME MINISTER WAS PLEASED WITH THE DISPOSITION OF ROSESHORE.
YOU'RE TO PASS THAT ON TO MINDERS TWO AND THREE, PAUL.
YES, SIR.
THE LAPTOP THEY RECOVERED HAS ALREADY GONE TO GROSVENOR SQUARE?
NOT YET.
I WANT US TO LOOK IT OVER FIRST.
PAUL, THIS IS NO TIME TO BE PLAYING GAMES WITH THE C.I.A.
HAVE IT DELIVERED IMMEDIATELY.
THEY CAN WAIT TWENTY-FOUR HOURS.
THE C.I.A. GAVE US ROSESHORE ON THE CONDITION WE HAND OVER ANY DATA--
THEY GAVE IT TO US BECAUSE WE ALREADY HAD TWO AGENTS IN GERMANY AND THEY COULDN'T GET COVERAGE ON THE OP IN TIME.
THEY'LL GET IT AS SOON AS WE'RE DONE.
EXPLAIN YOURSELF, PAUL.
I WANT D. INT TO MAKE A COPY OF THE CONTENTS--
THE C.I.A. WILL DISTRIBUTE THE INFORMATION TO US AFTER THEY PROCESS IT--
BY WHICH YOU MEAN THEY'LL SELECTIVELY EDIT IT FIRST.
SIR.
THE FRANKFURT CELL TIES BACK TO IMAD MUGHNIYEH. MUGHNIYEH IS HEAD OF HIZBULLAH OPERATIONS, WE'VE KNOWN THAT FOR YEARS--
ALL OF WESTERN INTELLIGENCE KNOWS THAT!
DONALD.
LET HIM FINISH.

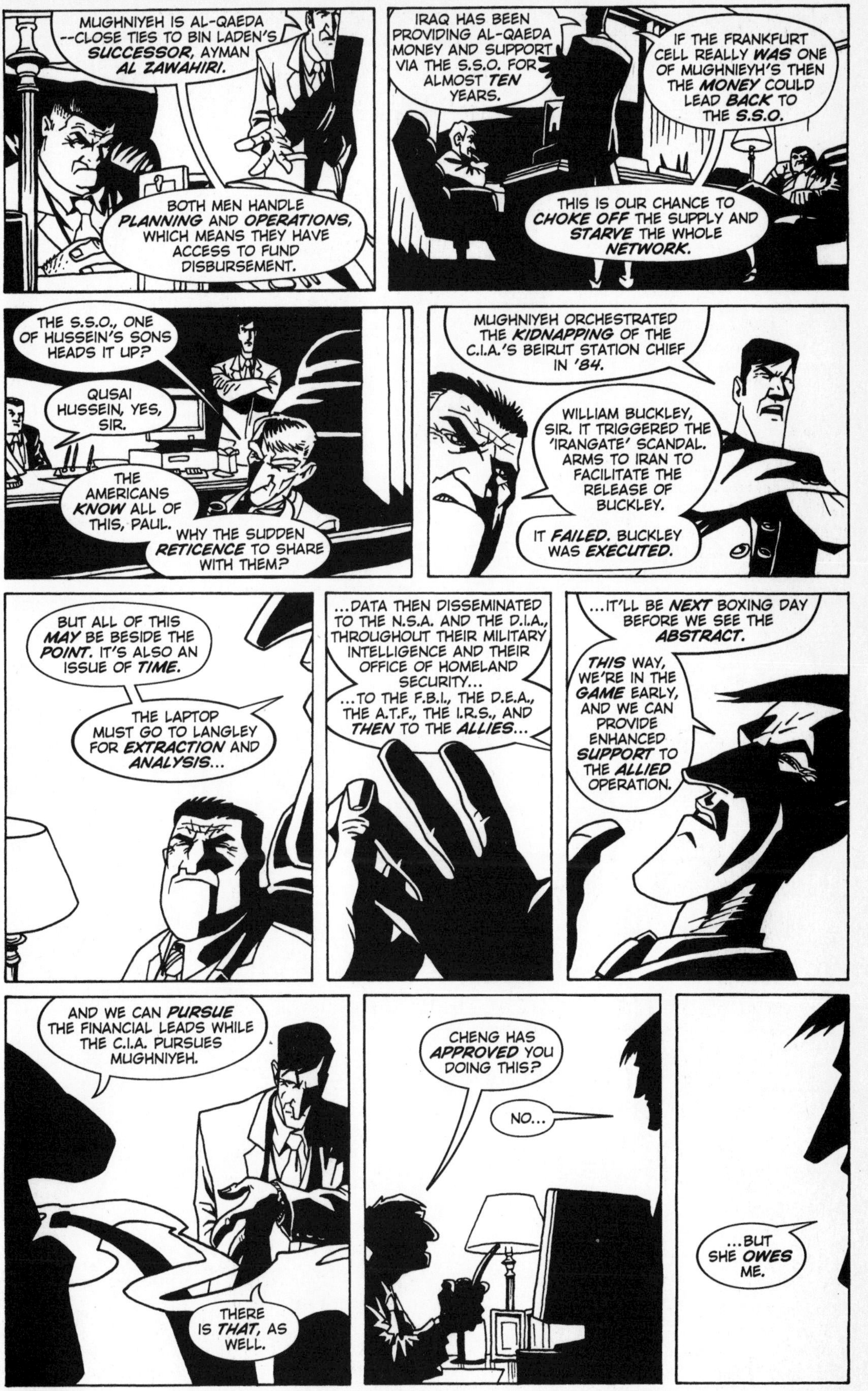
MUGHNIYEH IS AL-QAEDA --CLOSE TIES TO BIN LADEN'S SUCCESSOR, AYMAN AL ZAWAHIRI.
BOTH MEN HANDLE PLANNING AND OPERATIONS, WHICH MEANS THEY HAVE ACCESS TO FUND DISBURSEMENT.
IRAQ HAS BEEN PROVIDING AL-QAEDA MONEY AND SUPPORT VIA THE S.S.O. FOR ALMOST TEN YEARS.
IF THE FRANKFURT CELL REALLY WAS ONE OF MUGHNIEYH'S THEN THE MONEY COULD LEAD BACK TO THE S.S.O.
THIS IS OUR CHANCE TO CHOKE OFF THE SUPPLY AND STARVE THE WHOLE NETWORK.
THE S.S.O., ONE OF HUSSEIN'S SONS HEADS IT UP?
QUSAI HUSSEIN, YES, SIR.
THE AMERICANS KNOW ALL OF THIS, PAUL.
WHY THE SUDDEN RETICENCE TO SHARE WITH THEM?
MUGHNIYEH ORCHESTRATED THE KIDNAPPING OF THE C.I.A.'S BEIRUT STATION CHIEF IN '84.
WILLIAM BUCKLEY, SIR. IT TRIGGERED THE 'IRANGATE' SCANDAL. ARMS TO IRAN TO FACILITATE THE RELEASE OF BUCKLEY.
IT FAILED. BUCKLEY WAS EXECUTED.
BUT ALL OF THIS MAY BE BESIDE THE POINT. IT'S ALSO AN ISSUE OF TIME.
THE LAPTOP MUST GO TO LANGLEY FOR EXTRACTION AND ANALYSIS...
...DATA THEN DISSEMINATED TO THE N.S.A. AND THE D.I.A., THROUGHOUT THEIR MILITARY INTELLIGENCE AND THEIR OFFICE OF HOMELAND SECURITY...
...TO THE F.B.I., THE D.E.A., THE A.T.F., THE I.R.S., AND THEN TO THE ALLIES...
...IT'LL BE NEXT BOXING DAY BEFORE WE SEE THE ABSTRACT.
THIS WAY, WE'RE IN THE GAME EARLY, AND WE CAN PROVIDE ENHANCED SUPPORT TO THE ALLIED OPERATION.
AND WE CAN PURSUE THE FINANCIAL LEADS WHILE THE C.I.A. PURSUES MUGHNIYEH.
THERE IS THAT, AS WELL.
CHENG HAS APPROVED YOU DOING THIS?
NO...
...BUT SHE OWES ME.

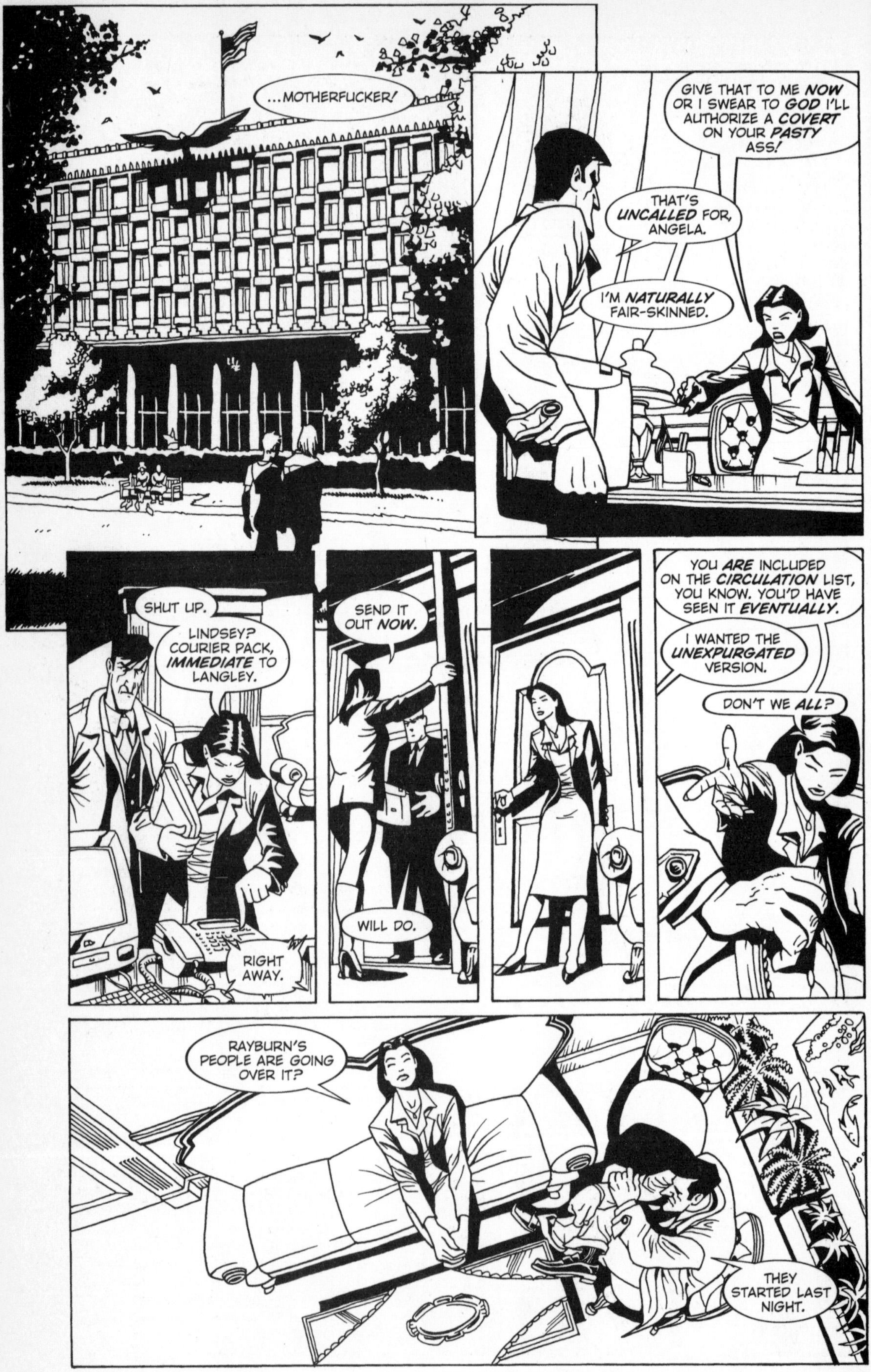

...MOTHERFUCKER!
GIVE THAT TO ME NOW OR I SWEAR TO GOD I'LL AUTHORIZE A COVERT ON YOUR PASTY ASS!
THAT'S UNCALLED FOR, ANGELA.
I'M NATURALLY FAIR-SKINNED.
SHUT UP.
LINDSEY? COURIER PACK, IMMEDIATE TO LANGLEY.
RIGHT AWAY.
SEND IT OUT NOW.
WILL DO.
YOU ARE INCLUDED ON THE CIRCULATION LIST, YOU KNOW. YOU'D HAVE SEEN IT EVENTUALLY.
I WANTED THE UNEXPURGATED VERSION.
DON'T WE ALL?
RAYBURN'S PEOPLE ARE GOING OVER IT?
THEY STARTED LAST NIGHT.

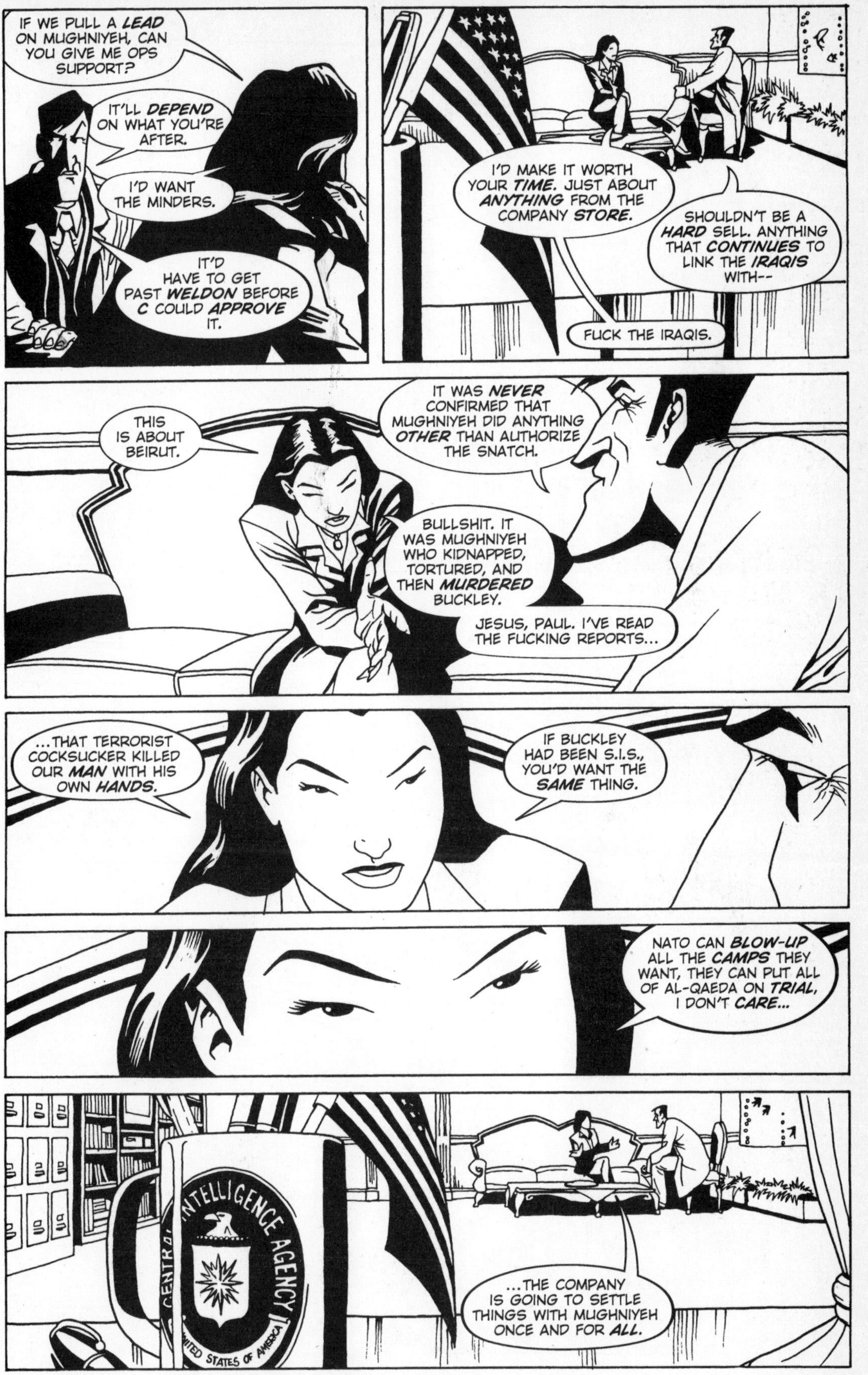
IF WE PULL A LEAD ON MUGHNIYEH, CAN YOU GIVE ME OPS SUPPORT?
IT'LL DEPEND ON WHAT YOU'RE AFTER.
I'D WANT THE MINDERS.
IT'D HAVE TO GET PAST WELDON BEFORE C COULD APPROVE IT.
I'D MAKE IT WORTH YOUR TIME. JUST ABOUT ANYTHING FROM THE COMPANY STORE.
SHOULDN'T BE A HARD SELL. ANYTHING THAT CONTINUES TO LINK THE IRAQIS WITH--
FUCK THE IRAQIS.
THIS IS ABOUT BEIRUT.
IT WAS NEVER CONFIRMED THAT MUGHNIYEH DID ANYTHING OTHER THAN AUTHORIZE THE SNATCH.
BULLSHIT. IT WAS MUGHNIYEH WHO KIDNAPPED, TORTURED, AND THEN MURDERED BUCKLEY.
JESUS, PAUL. I'VE READ THE FUCKING REPORTS...
...THAT TERRORIST COCKSUCKER KILLED OUR MAN WITH HIS OWN HANDS.
IF BUCKLEY HAD BEEN S.I.S., YOU'D WANT THE SAME THING.
NATO CAN BLOW-UP ALL THE CAMPS THEY WANT, THEY CAN PUT ALL OF AL-QAEDA ON TRIAL, I DON'T CARE...
CENTRAL INTELLIGENCE AGENCY
UNITED STATES OF AMERICA
...THE COMPANY IS GOING TO SETTLE THINGS WITH MUGHNIYEH ONCE AND FOR ALL.

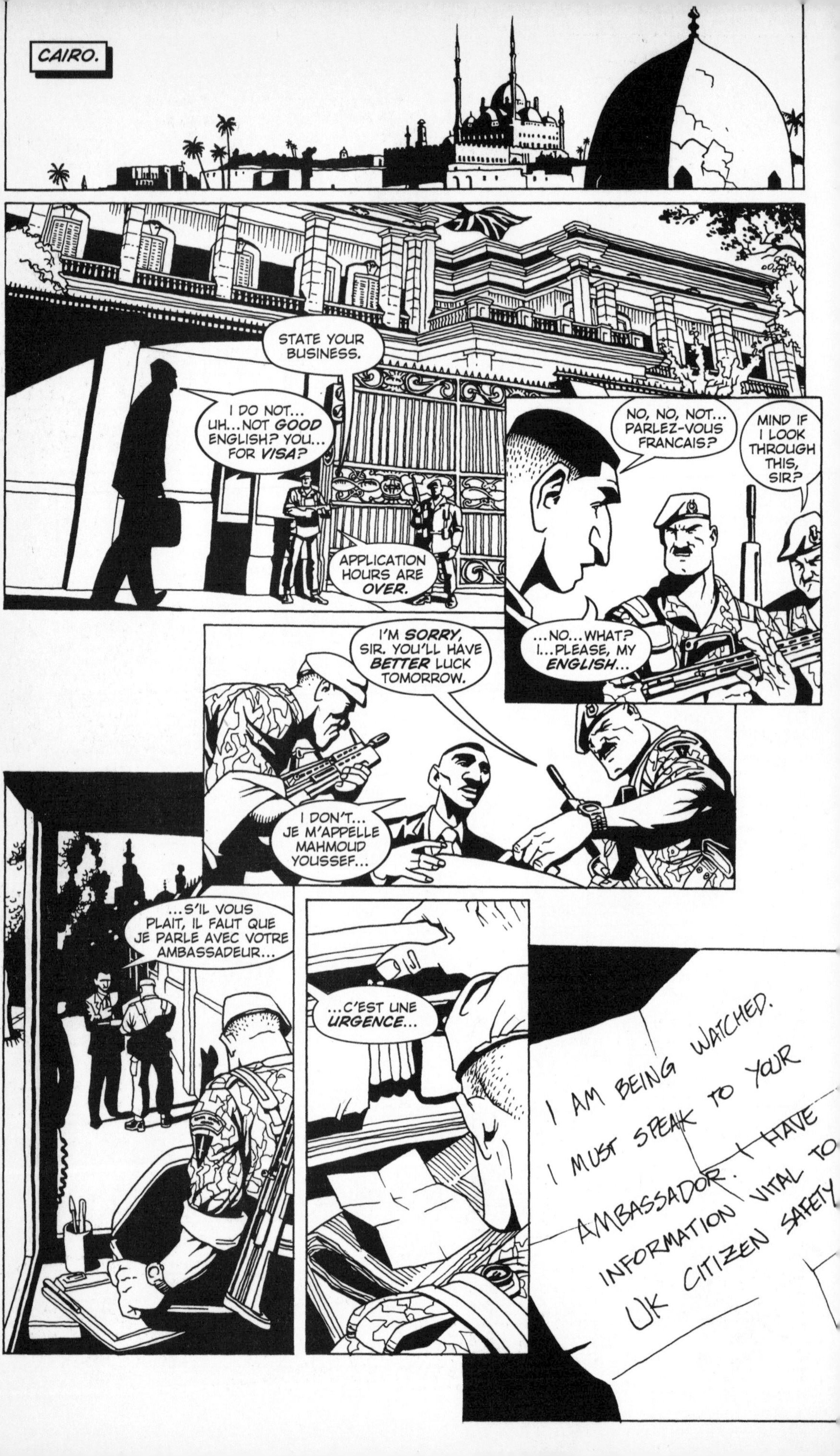

CAIRO.
STATE YOUR BUSINESS.
I DO NOT... UH...NOT GOOD ENGLISH? YOU... FOR VISA?
APPLICATION HOURS ARE OVER.
NO, NO, NOT... PARLEZ-VOUS FRANCAIS?
MIND IF I LOOK THROUGH THIS, SIR?
...NO...WHAT? I...PLEASE, MY ENGLISH...
I'M SORRY, SIR. YOU'LL HAVE BETTER LUCK TOMORROW.
I DON'T... JE M'APPELLE MAHMOUD YOUSSEF...
...S'IL VOUS PLAIT, IL FAUT QUE JE PARLE AVEC VOTRE AMBASSADEUR...
...C'EST UNE URGENCE...
I AM BEING WATCHED.
I MUST SPEAK TO YOUR
AMBASSADOR. I HAVE
INFORMATION VITAL TO
UK CITIZEN SAFETY

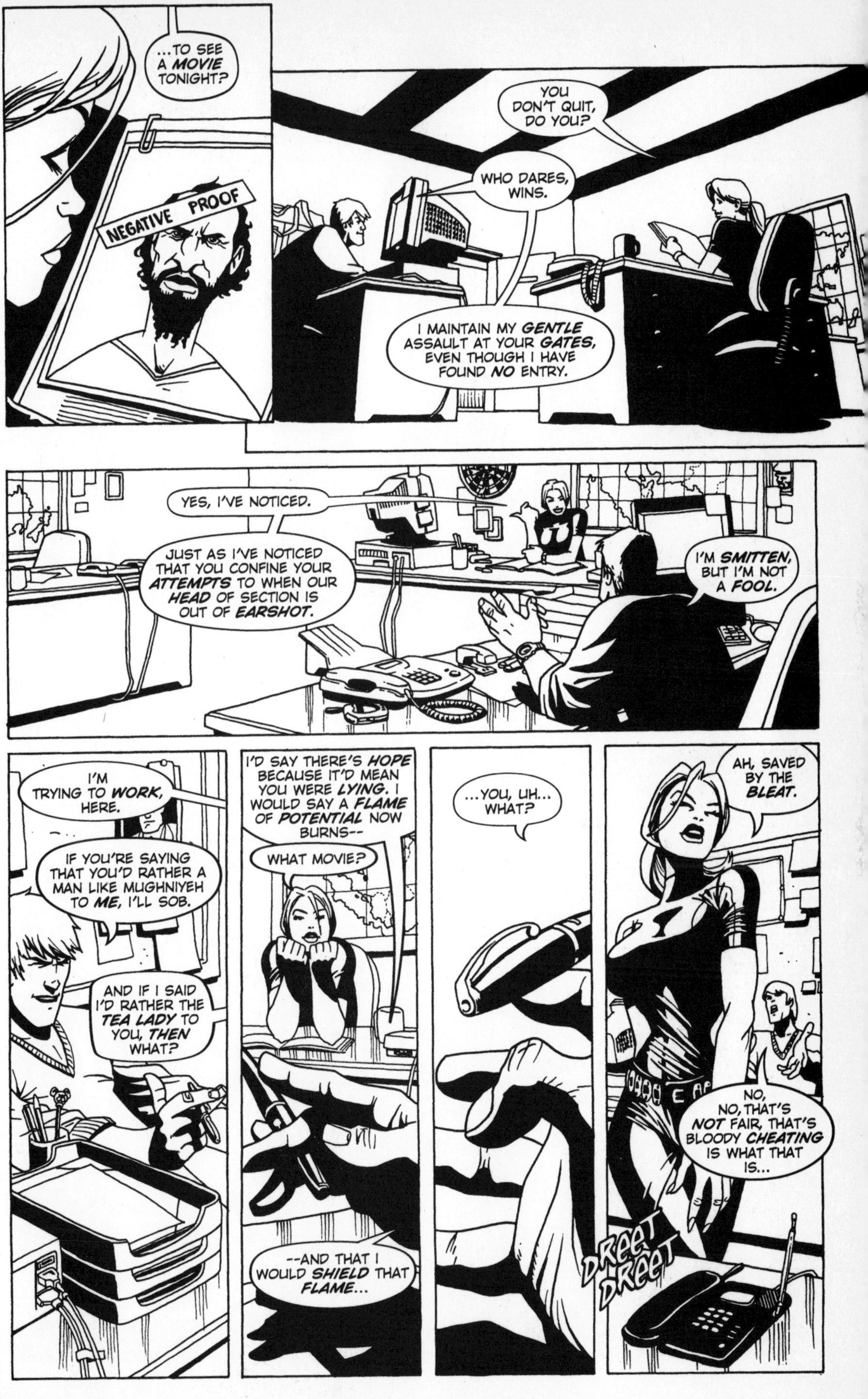
...TO SEE A MOVIE TONIGHT?
NEGATIVE PROOF
YOU DON'T QUIT, DO YOU?
WHO DARES, WINS.
I MAINTAIN MY GENTLE ASSAULT AT YOUR GATES, EVEN THOUGH I HAVE FOUND NO ENTRY.
YES, I'VE NOTICED.
JUST AS I'VE NOTICED THAT YOU CONFINE YOUR ATTEMPTS TO WHEN OUR HEAD OF SECTION IS OUT OF EARSHOT.
I'M SMITTEN, BUT I'M NOT A FOOL.
I'M TRYING TO WORK, HERE.
IF YOU'RE SAYING THAT YOU'D RATHER A MAN LIKE MUGHNIYEH TO ME, I'LL SOB.
AND IF I SAID I'D RATHER THE TEA LADY TO YOU, THEN WHAT?
I'D SAY THERE'S HOPE BECAUSE IT'D MEAN YOU WERE LYING. I WOULD SAY A FLAME OF POTENTIAL NOW BURNS--
WHAT MOVIE?
--AND THAT I WOULD SHIELD THAT FLAME...
...YOU, UH... WHAT?
AH, SAVED BY THE BLEAT.
NO, NO, THAT'S NOT FAIR, THAT'S BLOODY CHEATING IS WHAT THAT IS...
DREET DREET

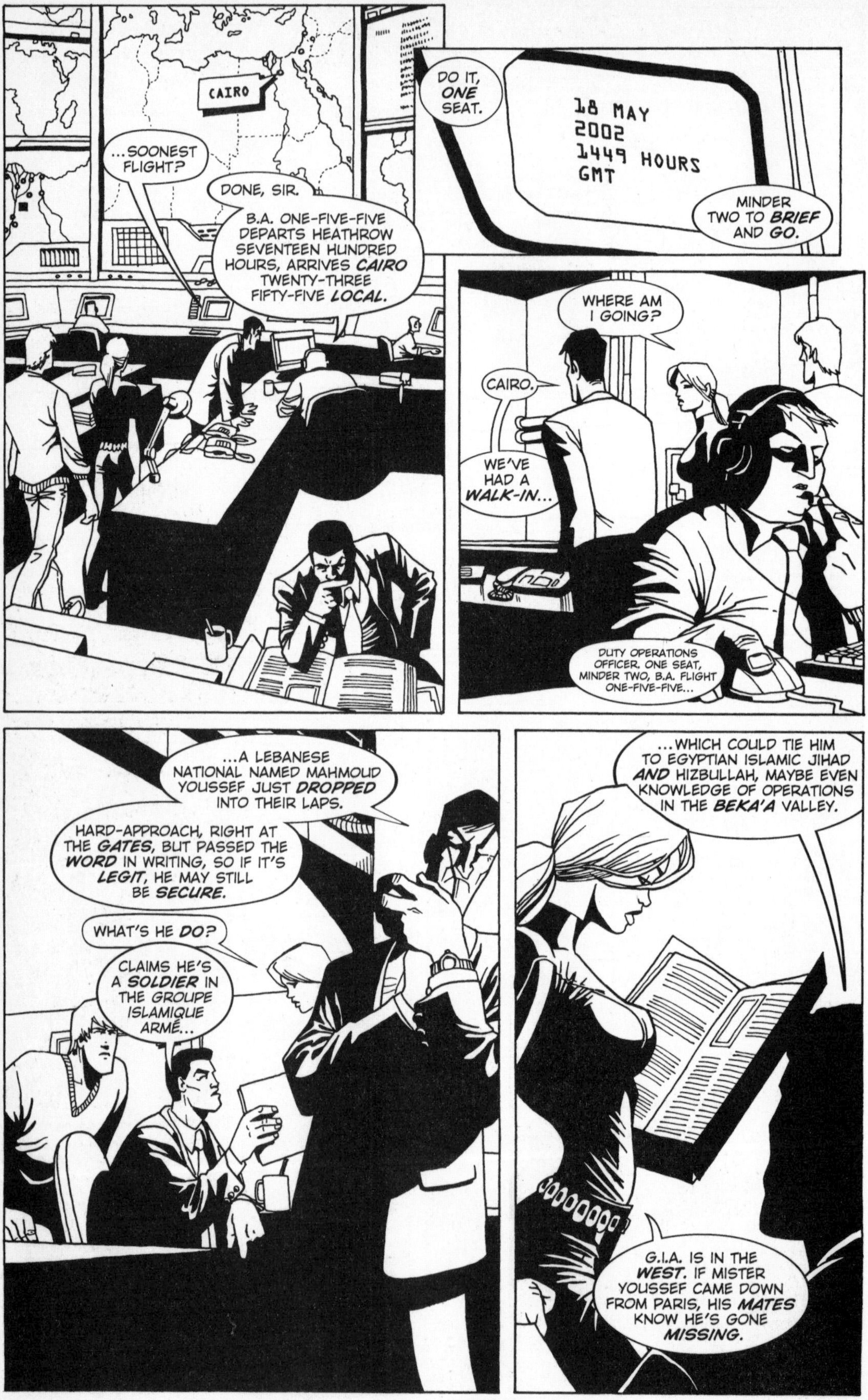
CAIRO
...SOONEST FLIGHT?
DONE, SIR.
B.A. ONE-FIVE-FIVE DEPARTS HEATHROW SEVENTEEN HUNDRED HOURS, ARRIVES CAIRO TWENTY-THREE FIFTY-FIVE LOCAL.
DO IT, ONE SEAT.
18 MAY 2002 1449 HOURS GMT
MINDER TWO TO BRIEF AND GO.
WHERE AM I GOING?
CAIRO.
WE'VE HAD A WALK-IN...
DUTY OPERATIONS OFFICER. ONE SEAT, MINDER TWO, B.A. FLIGHT ONE-FIVE-FIVE...
...A LEBANESE NATIONAL NAMED MAHMOUD YOUSSEF JUST DROPPED INTO THEIR LAPS.
HARD-APPROACH, RIGHT AT THE GATES, BUT PASSED THE WORD IN WRITING, SO IF IT'S LEGIT, HE MAY STILL BE SECURE.
WHAT'S HE DO?
CLAIMS HE'S A SOLDIER IN THE GROUPE ISLAMIQUE ARMÉ...
...WHICH COULD TIE HIM TO EGYPTIAN ISLAMIC JIHAD AND HIZBULLAH, MAYBE EVEN KNOWLEDGE OF OPERATIONS IN THE BEKA'A VALLEY.
G.I.A. IS IN THE WEST. IF MISTER YOUSSEF CAME DOWN FROM PARIS, HIS MATES KNOW HE'S GONE MISSING.

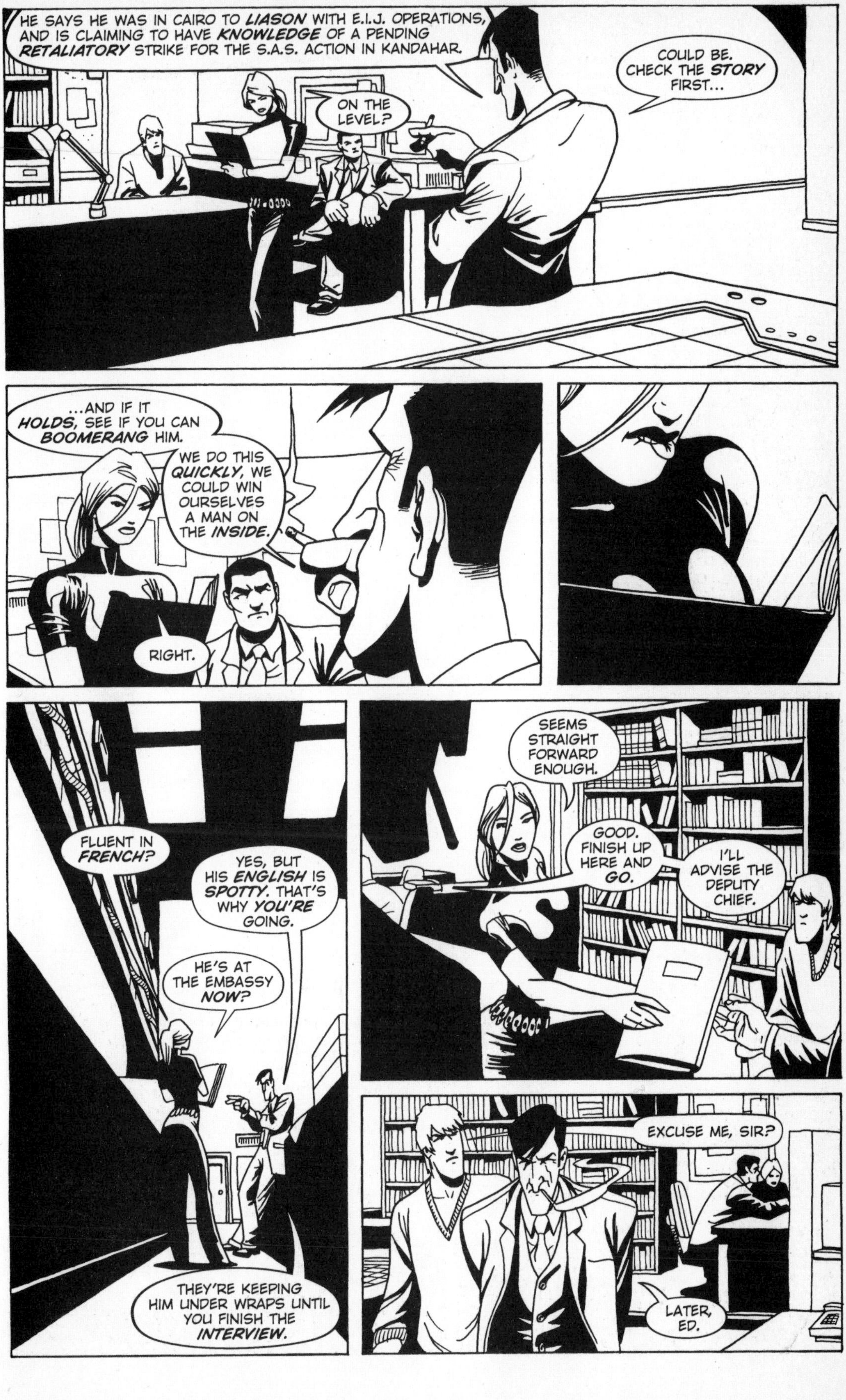
HE SAYS HE WAS IN CAIRO TO LIASON WITH E.I.J. OPERATIONS, AND IS CLAIMING TO HAVE KNOWLEDGE OF A PENDING RETALIATORY STRIKE FOR THE S.A.S. ACTION IN KANDAHAR.
ON THE LEVEL?
COULD BE. CHECK THE STORY FIRST...
...AND IF IT HOLDS, SEE IF YOU CAN BOOMERANG HIM.
WE DO THIS QUICKLY, WE COULD WIN OURSELVES A MAN ON THE INSIDE.
RIGHT.
FLUENT IN FRENCH?
YES, BUT HIS ENGLISH IS SPOTTY. THAT'S WHY YOU'RE GOING.
HE'S AT THE EMBASSY NOW?
THEY'RE KEEPING HIM UNDER WRAPS UNTIL YOU FINISH THE INTERVIEW.
SEEMS STRAIGHT FORWARD ENOUGH.
GOOD. FINISH UP HERE AND GO.
I'LL ADVISE THE DEPUTY CHIEF.
EXCUSE ME, SIR?
LATER, ED.

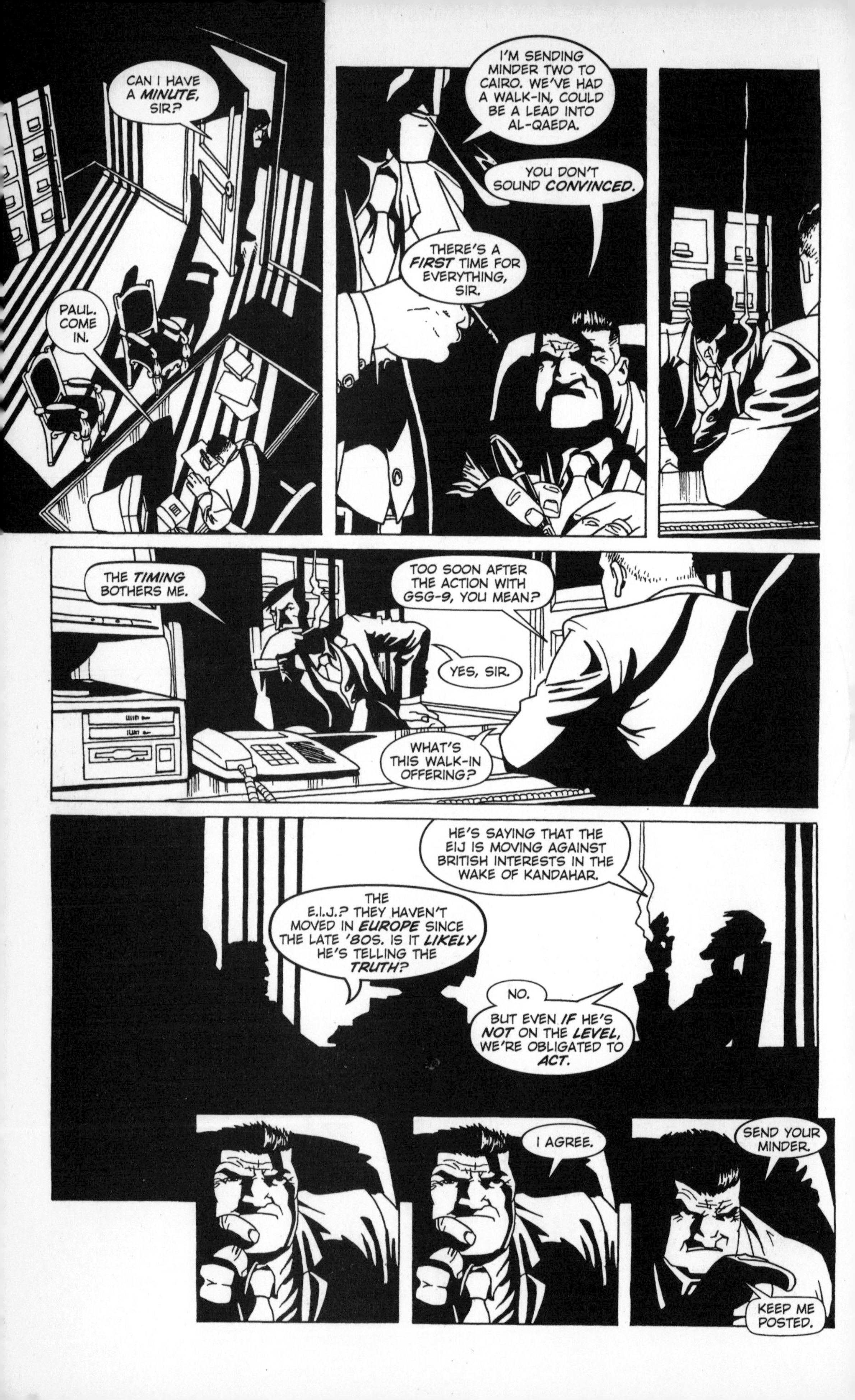

CAN I HAVE A *MINUTE*, SIR?
PAUL. COME IN.
I'M SENDING MINDER TWO TO CAIRO. WE'VE HAD A WALK-IN, COULD BE A LEAD INTO AL-QAEDA.
YOU DON'T SOUND *CONVINCED*.
THERE'S A *FIRST* TIME FOR EVERYTHING, SIR.
THE *TIMING* BOTHERS ME.
TOO SOON AFTER THE ACTION WITH *GSG-9*, YOU MEAN?
YES, SIR.
WHAT'S THIS WALK-IN OFFERING?
HE'S SAYING THAT THE EIJ IS MOVING AGAINST BRITISH INTERESTS IN THE WAKE OF KANDAHAR.
THE E.I.J.? THEY HAVEN'T MOVED IN *EUROPE* SINCE THE LATE '80S. IS IT *LIKELY* HE'S TELLING THE *TRUTH*?
NO.
BUT EVEN *IF* HE'S *NOT* ON THE *LEVEL*, WE'RE OBLIGATED TO *ACT*.
I AGREE.
SEND YOUR MINDER.
KEEP ME POSTED.

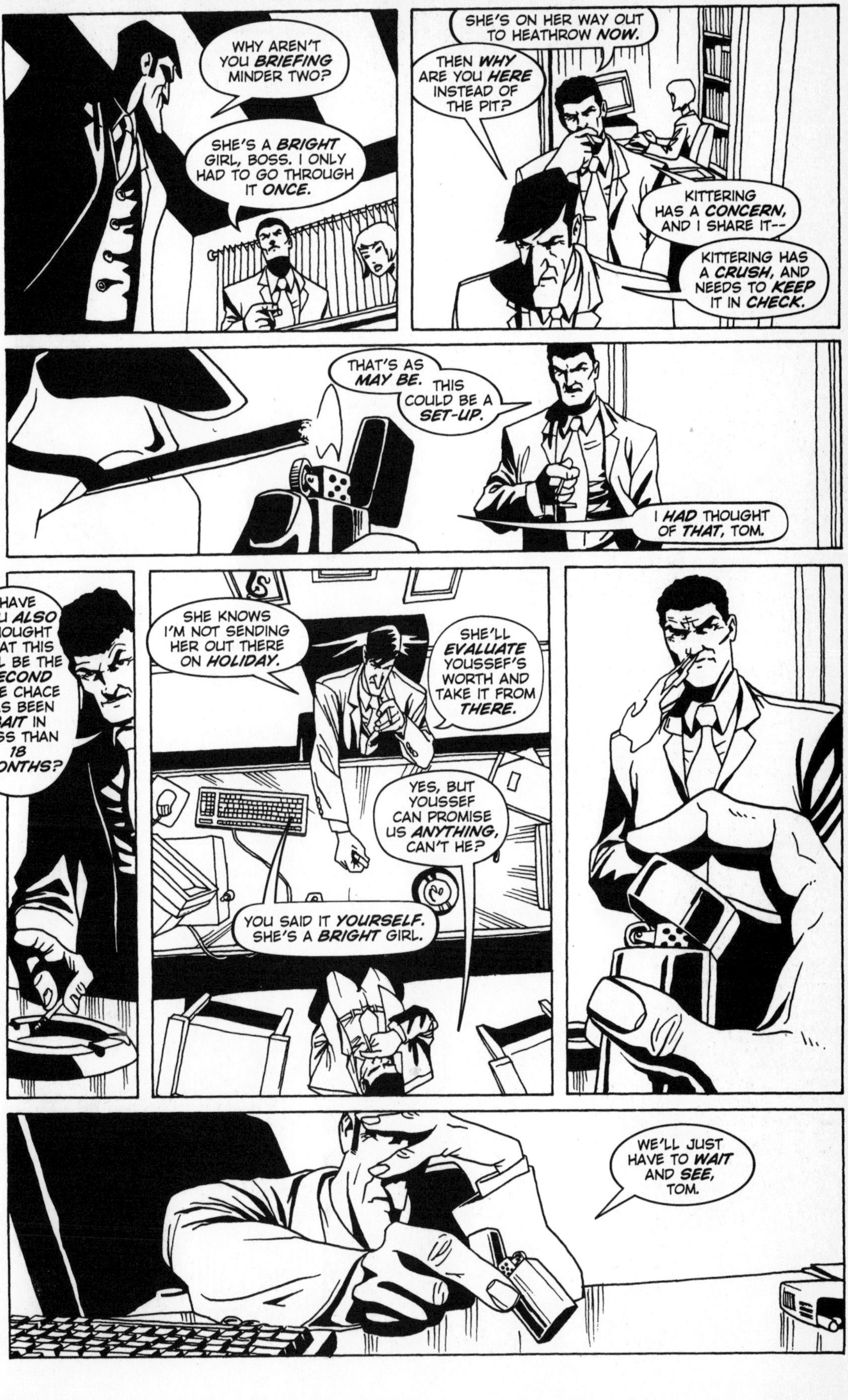
WHY AREN'T YOU BRIEFING MINDER TWO?
SHE'S A BRIGHT GIRL, BOSS. I ONLY HAD TO GO THROUGH IT ONCE.
SHE'S ON HER WAY OUT TO HEATHROW NOW.
THEN WHY ARE YOU HERE INSTEAD OF THE PIT?
KITTERING HAS A CONCERN, AND I SHARE IT--
KITTERING HAS A CRUSH, AND NEEDS TO KEEP IT IN CHECK.
THAT'S AS MAY BE. THIS COULD BE A SET-UP.
I HAD THOUGHT OF THAT, TOM.
HAVE YOU ALSO THOUGHT THAT THIS WILL BE THE SECOND TIME CHACE HAS BEEN BAIT IN LESS THAN 18 MONTHS?
SHE KNOWS I'M NOT SENDING HER OUT THERE ON HOLIDAY.
SHE'LL EVALUATE YOUSSEF'S WORTH AND TAKE IT FROM THERE.
YES, BUT YOUSSEF CAN PROMISE US ANYTHING, CAN'T HE?
YOU SAID IT YOURSELF. SHE'S A BRIGHT GIRL.
WE'LL JUST HAVE TO WAIT AND SEE, TOM.

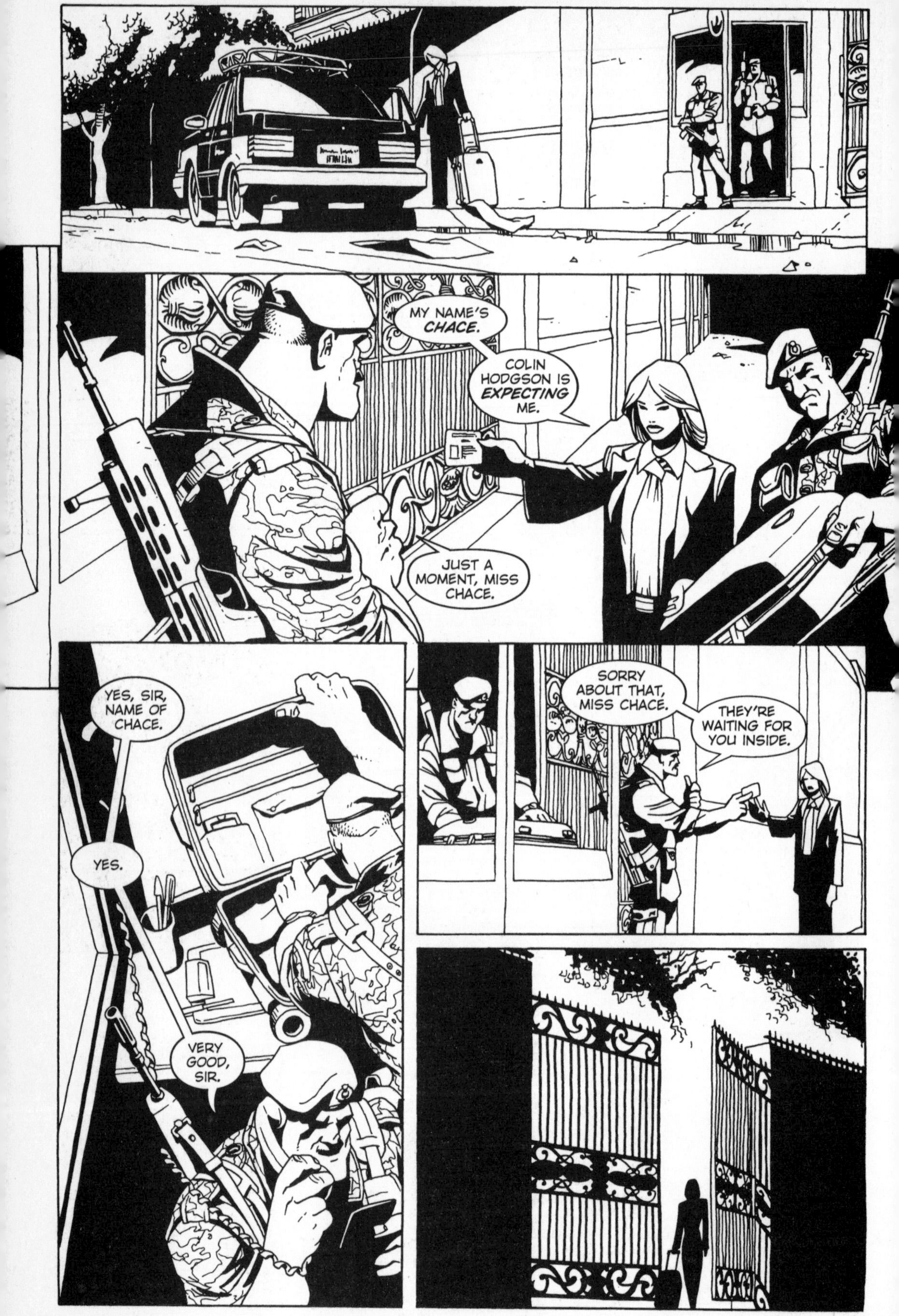
MY NAME'S *CHACE.*
COLIN HODGSON IS *EXPECTING* ME.
JUST A MOMENT, MISS CHACE.
YES, SIR, NAME OF CHACE.
YES.
VERY GOOD, SIR.
SORRY ABOUT THAT, MISS CHACE.
THEY'RE WAITING FOR YOU INSIDE.

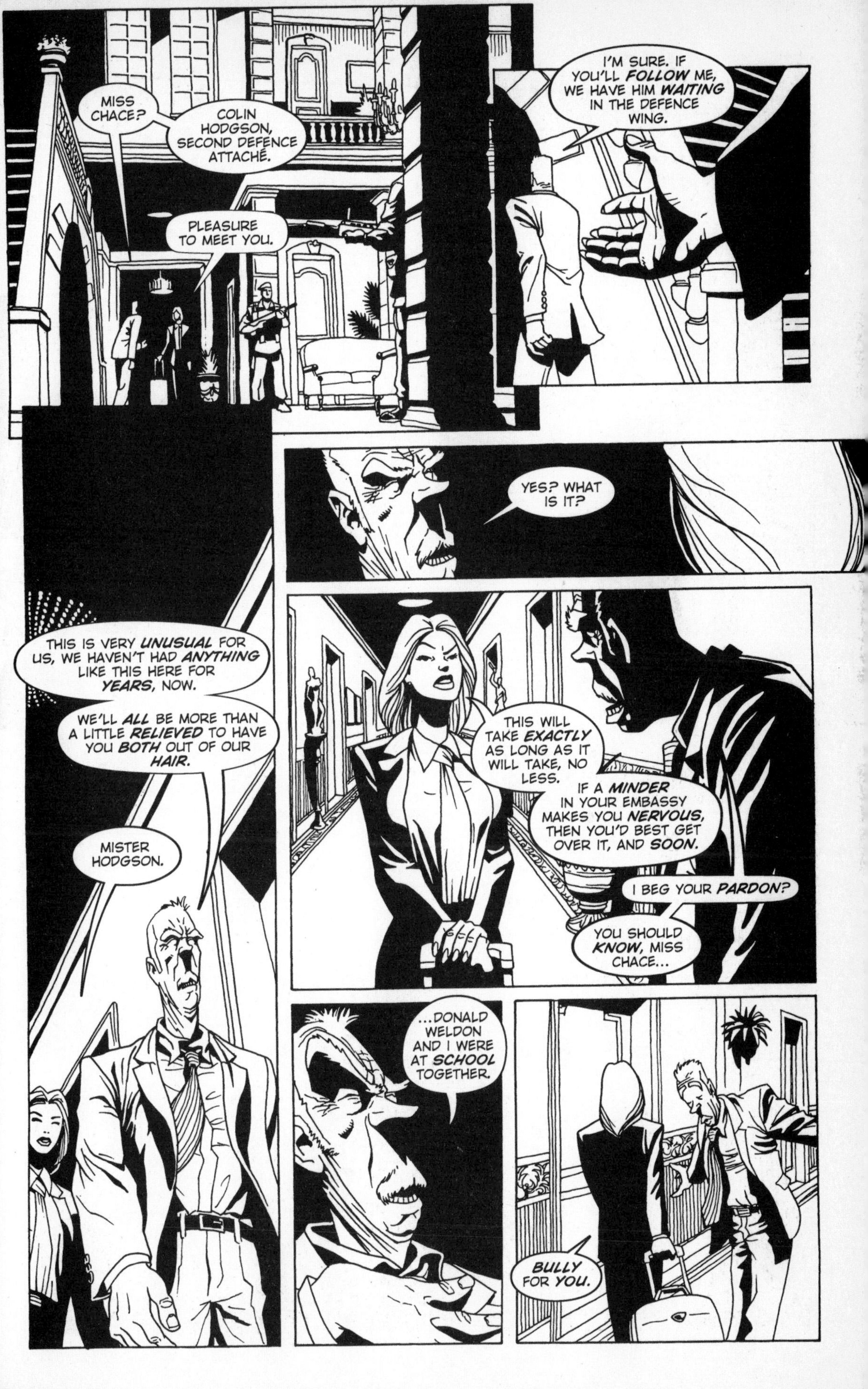
MISS CHACE?
COLIN HODGSON, SECOND DEFENCE ATTACHÉ.
PLEASURE TO MEET YOU.
I'M SURE. IF YOU'LL FOLLOW ME, WE HAVE HIM WAITING IN THE DEFENCE WING.
YES? WHAT IS IT?
THIS IS VERY UNUSUAL FOR US, WE HAVEN'T HAD ANYTHING LIKE THIS HERE FOR YEARS, NOW.
WE'LL ALL BE MORE THAN A LITTLE RELIEVED TO HAVE YOU BOTH OUT OF OUR HAIR.
MISTER HODGSON.
THIS WILL TAKE EXACTLY AS LONG AS IT WILL TAKE, NO LESS.
IF A MINDER IN YOUR EMBASSY MAKES YOU NERVOUS, THEN YOU'D BEST GET OVER IT, AND SOON.
I BEG YOUR PARDON?
YOU SHOULD KNOW, MISS CHACE...
...DONALD WELDON AND I WERE AT SCHOOL TOGETHER.
BULLY FOR YOU.

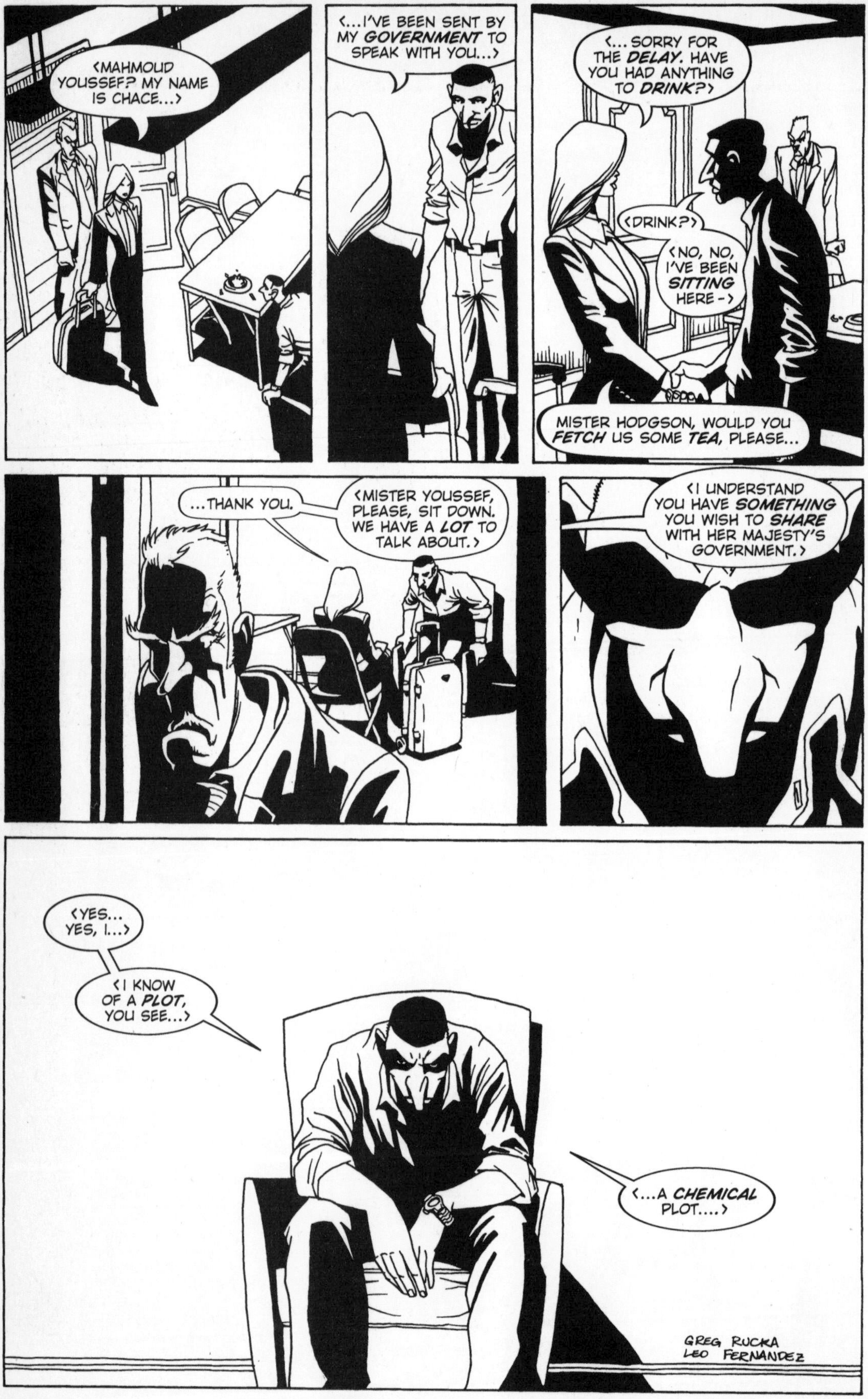

‹MAHMOUD YOUSSEF? MY NAME IS CHACE...›
‹...I'VE BEEN SENT BY MY GOVERNMENT TO SPEAK WITH YOU...›
‹... SORRY FOR THE DELAY. HAVE YOU HAD ANYTHING TO DRINK?›
‹DRINK?›
‹NO, NO, I'VE BEEN SITTING HERE -›
MISTER HODGSON, WOULD YOU FETCH US SOME TEA, PLEASE...
...THANK YOU.
‹MISTER YOUSSEF, PLEASE, SIT DOWN. WE HAVE A LOT TO TALK ABOUT.›
‹I UNDERSTAND YOU HAVE SOMETHING YOU WISH TO SHARE WITH HER MAJESTY'S GOVERNMENT.›
‹YES... YES, I...›
‹I KNOW OF A PLOT, YOU SEE...›
‹...A CHEMICAL PLOT....›
GREG RUCKA
LEO FERNANDEZ

CHAPTER 2

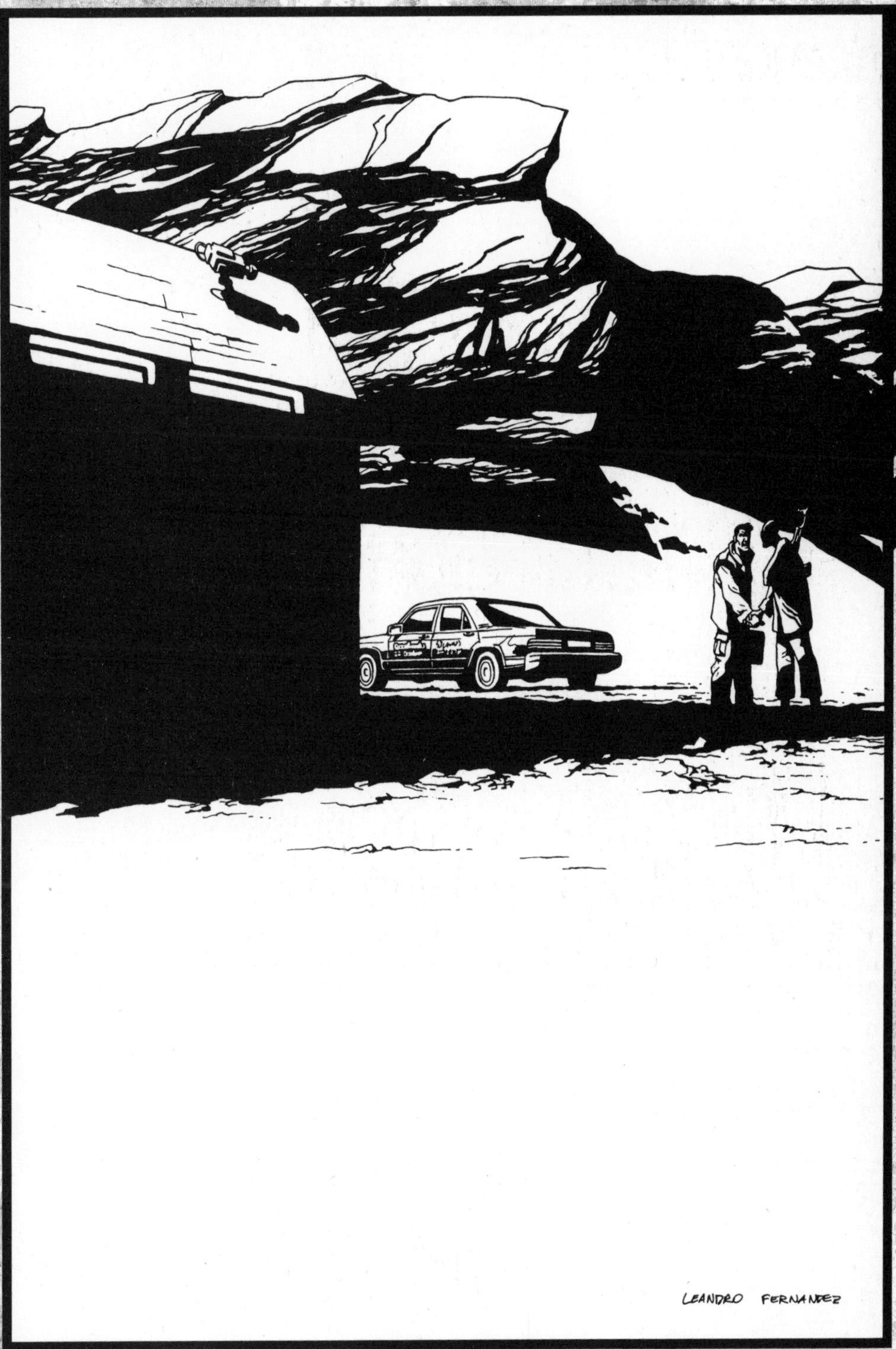
LEANDRO FERNANDEZ

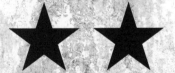

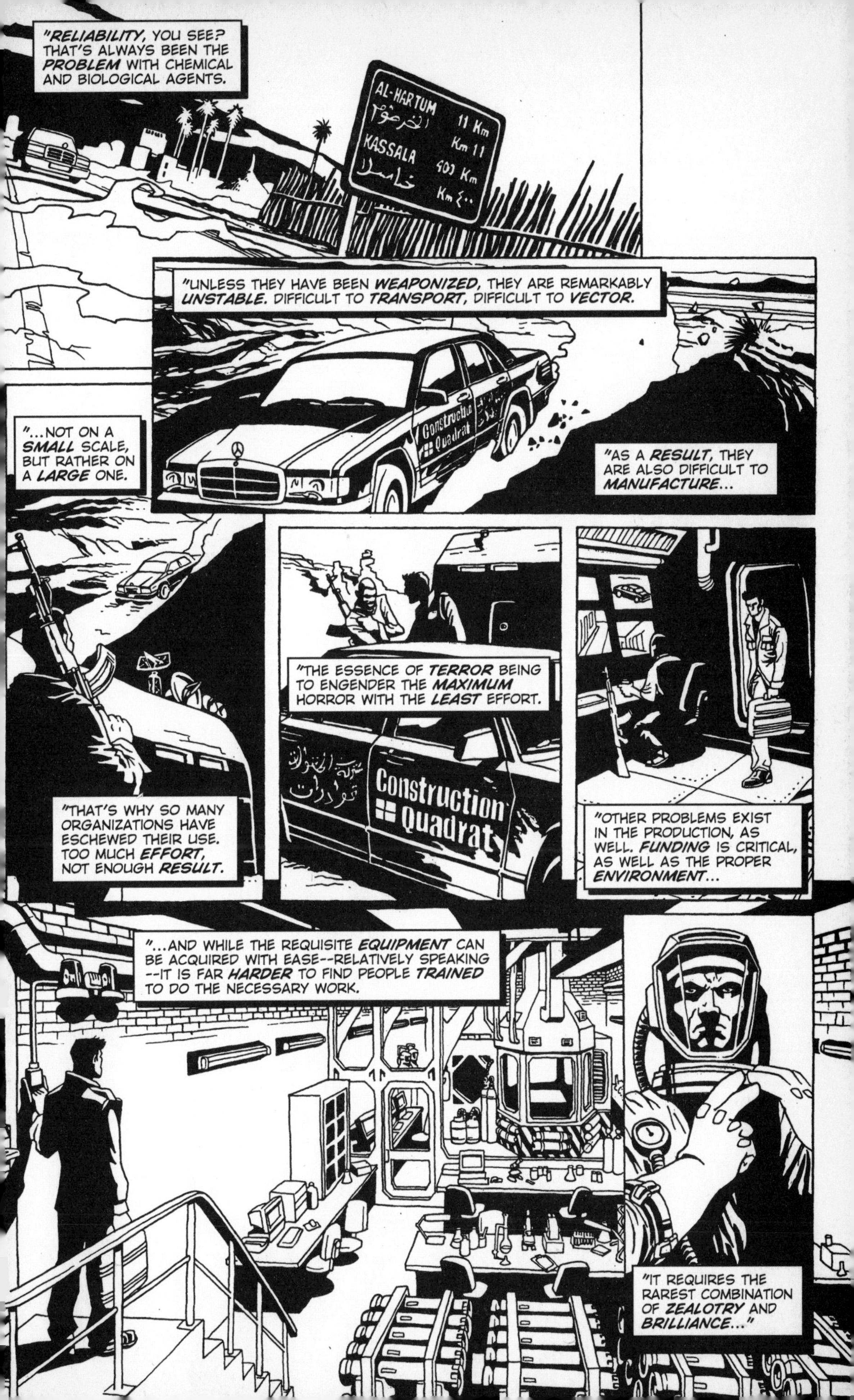
"RELIABILITY, YOU SEE? THAT'S ALWAYS BEEN THE PROBLEM WITH CHEMICAL AND BIOLOGICAL AGENTS.
AL-HARTUM 11 Km
Km 11
KASSALA 400 Km
"UNLESS THEY HAVE BEEN WEAPONIZED, THEY ARE REMARKABLY UNSTABLE. DIFFICULT TO TRANSPORT, DIFFICULT TO VECTOR.
Construction Quadrat
"AS A RESULT, THEY ARE ALSO DIFFICULT TO MANUFACTURE...
"...NOT ON A SMALL SCALE, BUT RATHER ON A LARGE ONE.
"THAT'S WHY SO MANY ORGANIZATIONS HAVE ESCHEWED THEIR USE. TOO MUCH EFFORT, NOT ENOUGH RESULT.
"THE ESSENCE OF TERROR BEING TO ENGENDER THE MAXIMUM HORROR WITH THE LEAST EFFORT.
Construction Quadrat
"OTHER PROBLEMS EXIST IN THE PRODUCTION, AS WELL. FUNDING IS CRITICAL, AS WELL AS THE PROPER ENVIRONMENT...
"...AND WHILE THE REQUISITE EQUIPMENT CAN BE ACQUIRED WITH EASE--RELATIVELY SPEAKING--IT IS FAR HARDER TO FIND PEOPLE TRAINED TO DO THE NECESSARY WORK.
"IT REQUIRES THE RAREST COMBINATION OF ZEALOTRY AND BRILLIANCE..."

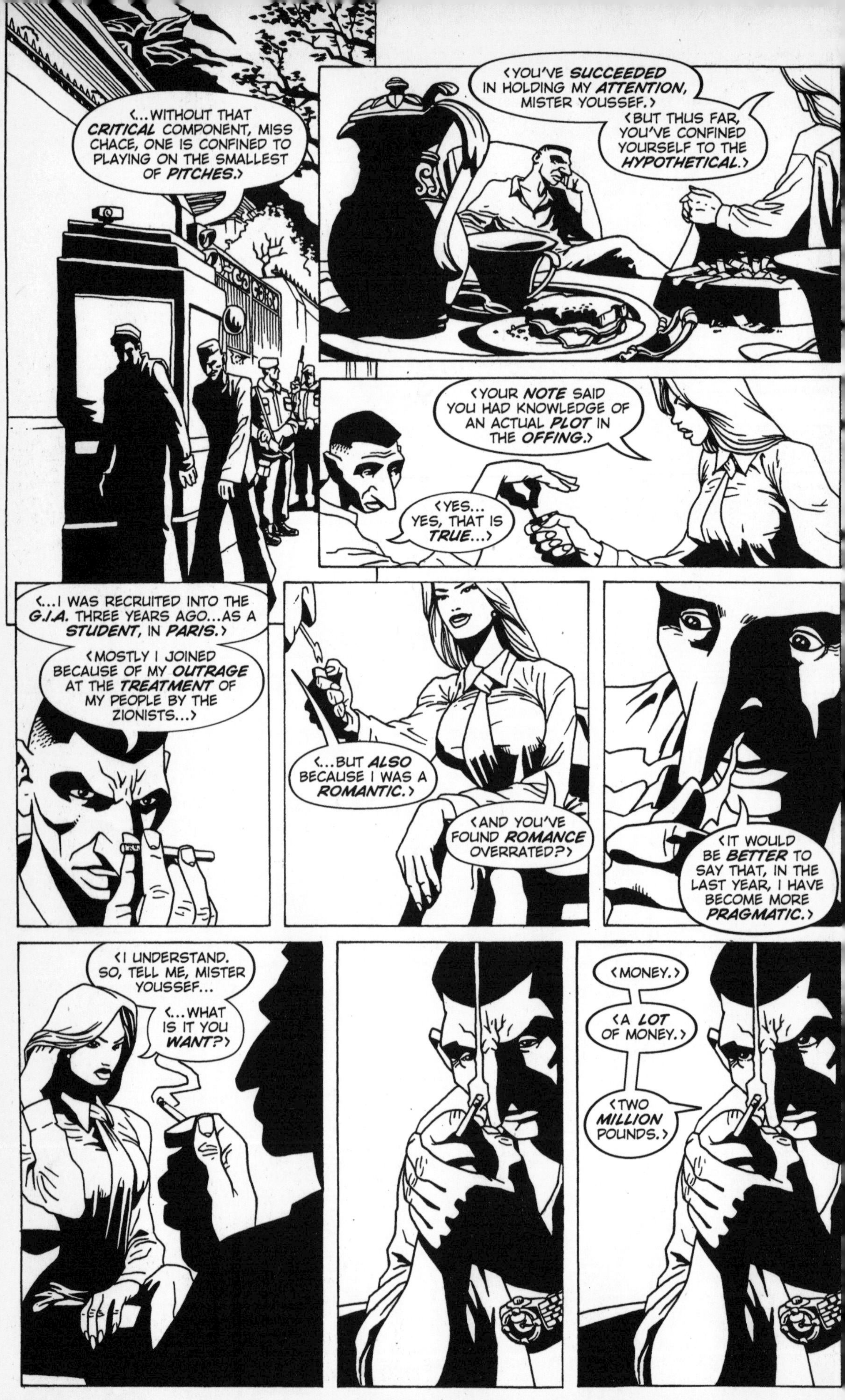

<...WITHOUT THAT CRITICAL COMPONENT, MISS CHACE, ONE IS CONFINED TO PLAYING ON THE SMALLEST OF PITCHES.>
<YOU'VE SUCCEEDED IN HOLDING MY ATTENTION, MISTER YOUSSEF.>
<BUT THUS FAR, YOU'VE CONFINED YOURSELF TO THE HYPOTHETICAL.>
<YOUR NOTE SAID YOU HAD KNOWLEDGE OF AN ACTUAL PLOT IN THE OFFING.>
<YES... YES, THAT IS TRUE...>
<...I WAS RECRUITED INTO THE G.I.A. THREE YEARS AGO...AS A STUDENT, IN PARIS.>
<MOSTLY I JOINED BECAUSE OF MY OUTRAGE AT THE TREATMENT OF MY PEOPLE BY THE ZIONISTS...>
<...BUT ALSO BECAUSE I WAS A ROMANTIC.>
<AND YOU'VE FOUND ROMANCE OVERRATED?>
<IT WOULD BE BETTER TO SAY THAT, IN THE LAST YEAR, I HAVE BECOME MORE PRAGMATIC.>
<I UNDERSTAND. SO, TELL ME, MISTER YOUSSEF...
<...WHAT IS IT YOU WANT?>
<MONEY.>
<A LOT OF MONEY.>
<TWO MILLION POUNDS.>

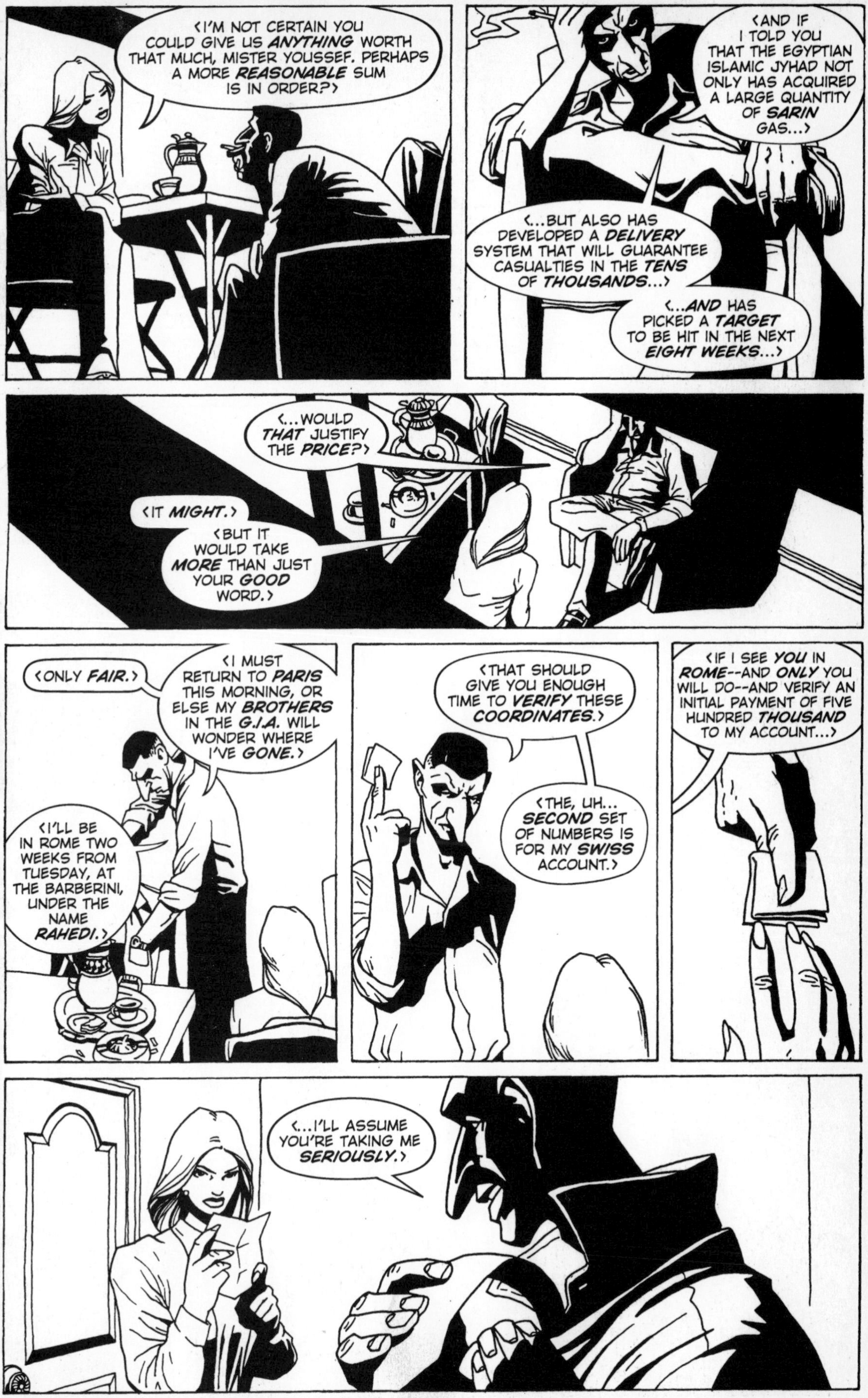
<I'M NOT CERTAIN YOU COULD GIVE US ANYTHING WORTH THAT MUCH, MISTER YOUSSEF. PERHAPS A MORE REASONABLE SUM IS IN ORDER?>
<AND IF I TOLD YOU THAT THE EGYPTIAN ISLAMIC JYHAD NOT ONLY HAS ACQUIRED A LARGE QUANTITY OF SARIN GAS...>
<...BUT ALSO HAS DEVELOPED A DELIVERY SYSTEM THAT WILL GUARANTEE CASUALTIES IN THE TENS OF THOUSANDS...>
<...AND HAS PICKED A TARGET TO BE HIT IN THE NEXT EIGHT WEEKS...>
<...WOULD THAT JUSTIFY THE PRICE?>
<IT MIGHT.>
<BUT IT WOULD TAKE MORE THAN JUST YOUR GOOD WORD.>
<ONLY FAIR.>
<I MUST RETURN TO PARIS THIS MORNING, OR ELSE MY BROTHERS IN THE G.I.A. WILL WONDER WHERE I'VE GONE.>
<I'LL BE IN ROME TWO WEEKS FROM TUESDAY, AT THE BARBERINI, UNDER THE NAME RAHEDI.>
<THAT SHOULD GIVE YOU ENOUGH TIME TO VERIFY THESE COORDINATES.>
<THE, UH... SECOND SET OF NUMBERS IS FOR MY SWISS ACCOUNT.>
<IF I SEE YOU IN ROME--AND ONLY YOU WILL DO--AND VERIFY AN INITIAL PAYMENT OF FIVE HUNDRED THOUSAND TO MY ACCOUNT...>
<...I'LL ASSUME YOU'RE TAKING ME SERIOUSLY.>

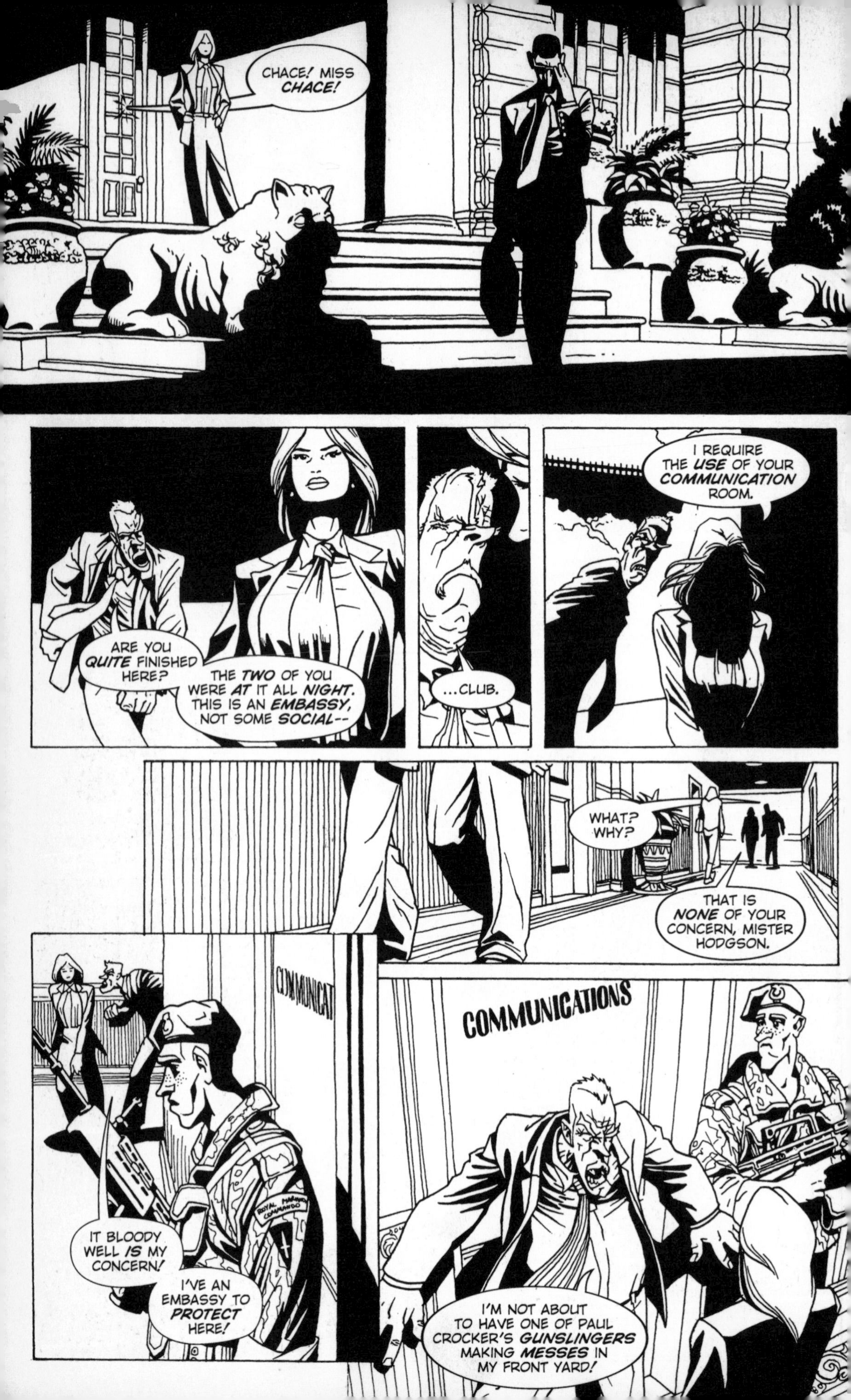

CHACE! MISS CHACE!
ARE YOU QUITE FINISHED HERE?
THE TWO OF YOU WERE AT IT ALL NIGHT. THIS IS AN EMBASSY, NOT SOME SOCIAL--
...CLUB.
I REQUIRE THE USE OF YOUR COMMUNICATION ROOM.
WHAT? WHY?
THAT IS NONE OF YOUR CONCERN, MISTER HODGSON.
COMMUNICAT
COMMUNICATIONS
IT BLOODY WELL IS MY CONCERN!
I'VE AN EMBASSY TO PROTECT HERE!
I'M NOT ABOUT TO HAVE ONE OF PAUL CROCKER'S GUNSLINGERS MAKING MESSES IN MY FRONT YARD!

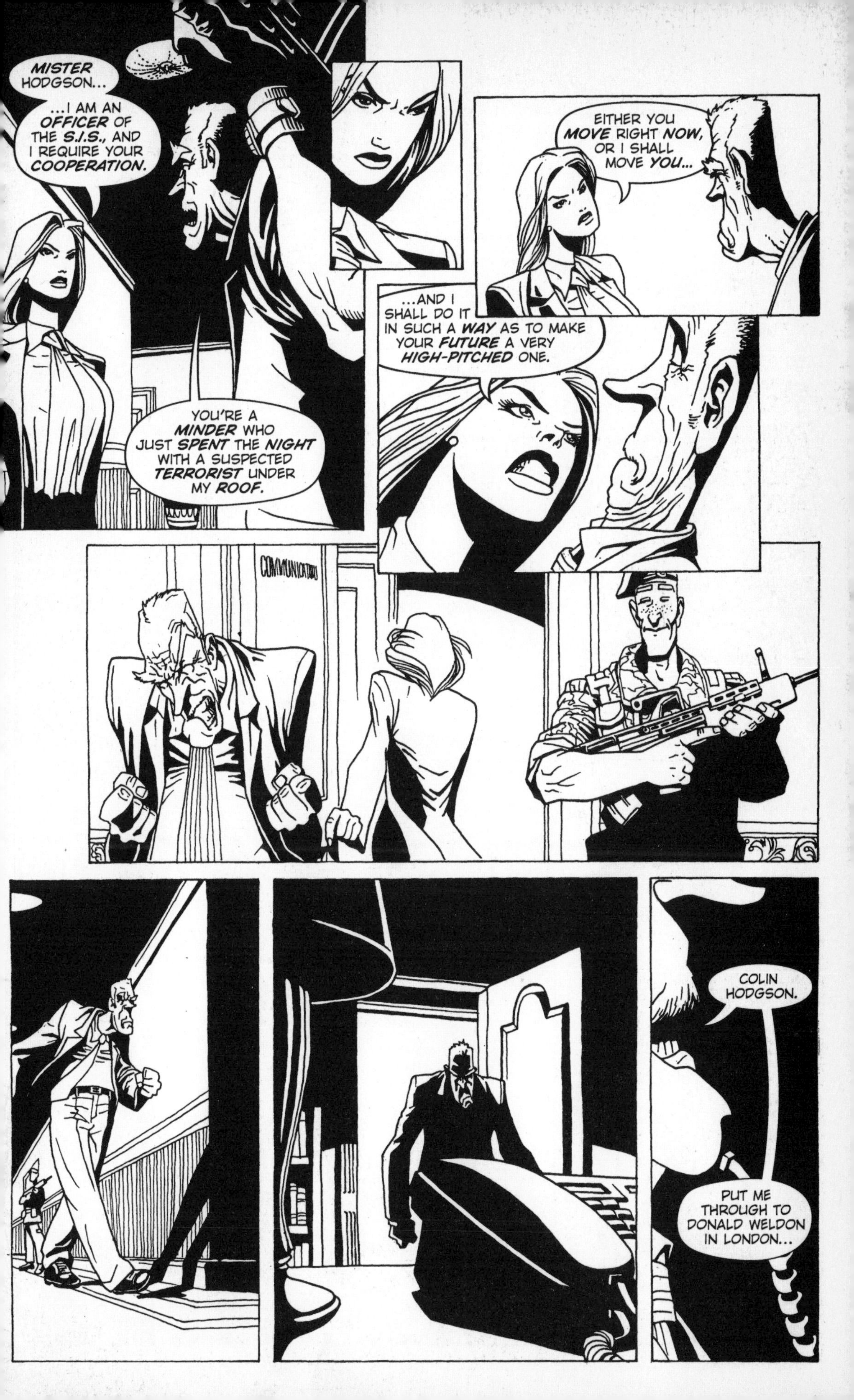
MISTER HODGSON...
...I AM AN OFFICER OF THE S.I.S., AND I REQUIRE YOUR COOPERATION.
YOU'RE A MINDER WHO JUST SPENT THE NIGHT WITH A SUSPECTED TERRORIST UNDER MY ROOF.
EITHER YOU MOVE RIGHT NOW, OR I SHALL MOVE YOU...
...AND I SHALL DO IT IN SUCH A WAY AS TO MAKE YOUR FUTURE A VERY HIGH-PITCHED ONE.
COMMUNICATIONS
COLIN HODGSON.
PUT ME THROUGH TO DONALD WELDON IN LONDON...

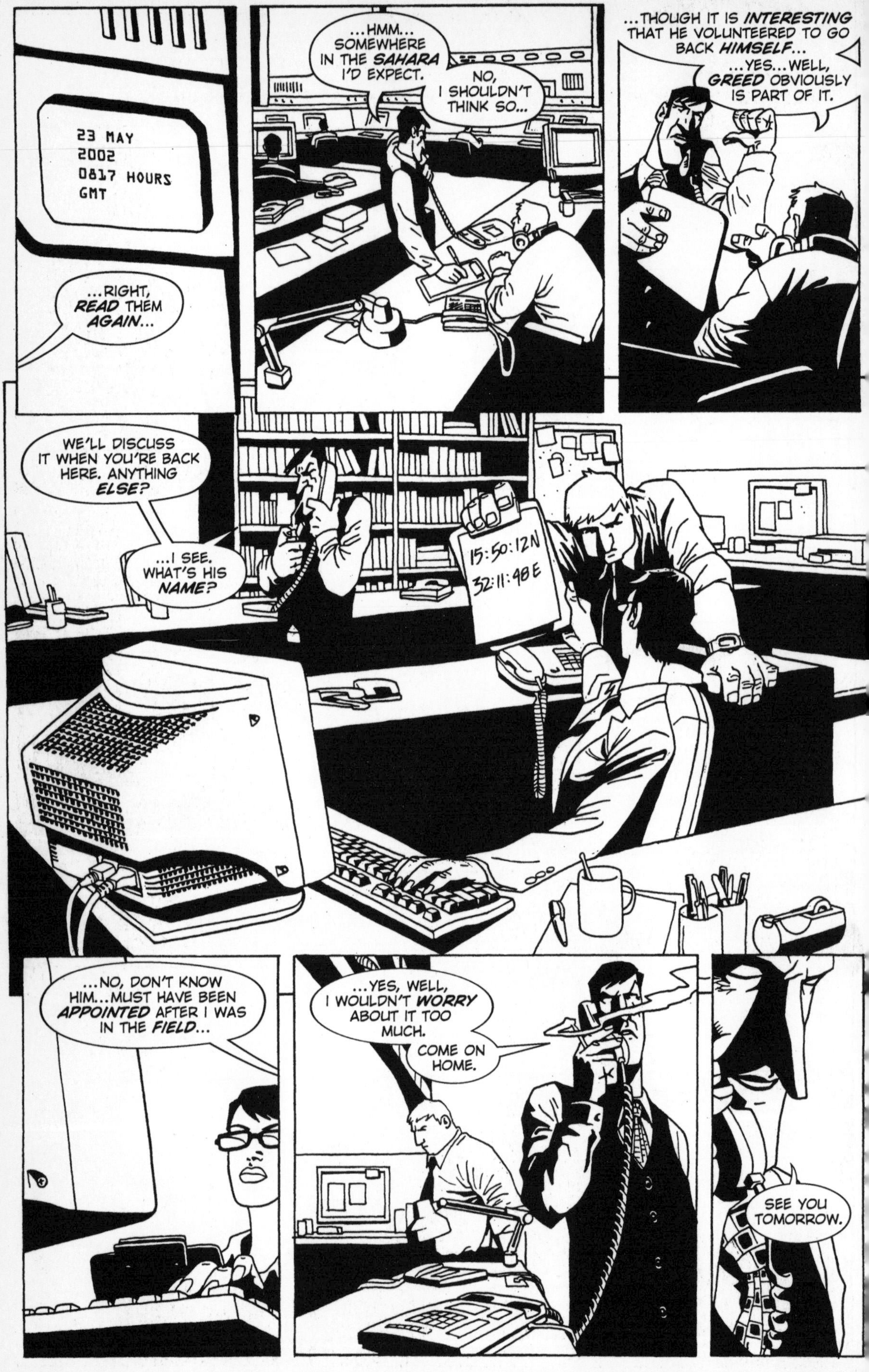

23 MAY
2002
0817 HOURS
GMT
...RIGHT, READ THEM AGAIN...
...HMM... SOMEWHERE IN THE SAHARA I'D EXPECT.
NO, I SHOULDN'T THINK SO...
...THOUGH IT IS INTERESTING THAT HE VOLUNTEERED TO GO BACK HIMSELF...
...YES...WELL, GREED OBVIOUSLY IS PART OF IT.
WE'LL DISCUSS IT WHEN YOU'RE BACK HERE. ANYTHING ELSE?
...I SEE. WHAT'S HIS NAME?
15:50:12N
32:11:48E
...NO, DON'T KNOW HIM...MUST HAVE BEEN APPOINTED AFTER I WAS IN THE FIELD...
...YES, WELL, I WOULDN'T WORRY ABOUT IT TOO MUCH.
COME ON HOME.
SEE YOU TOMORROW.

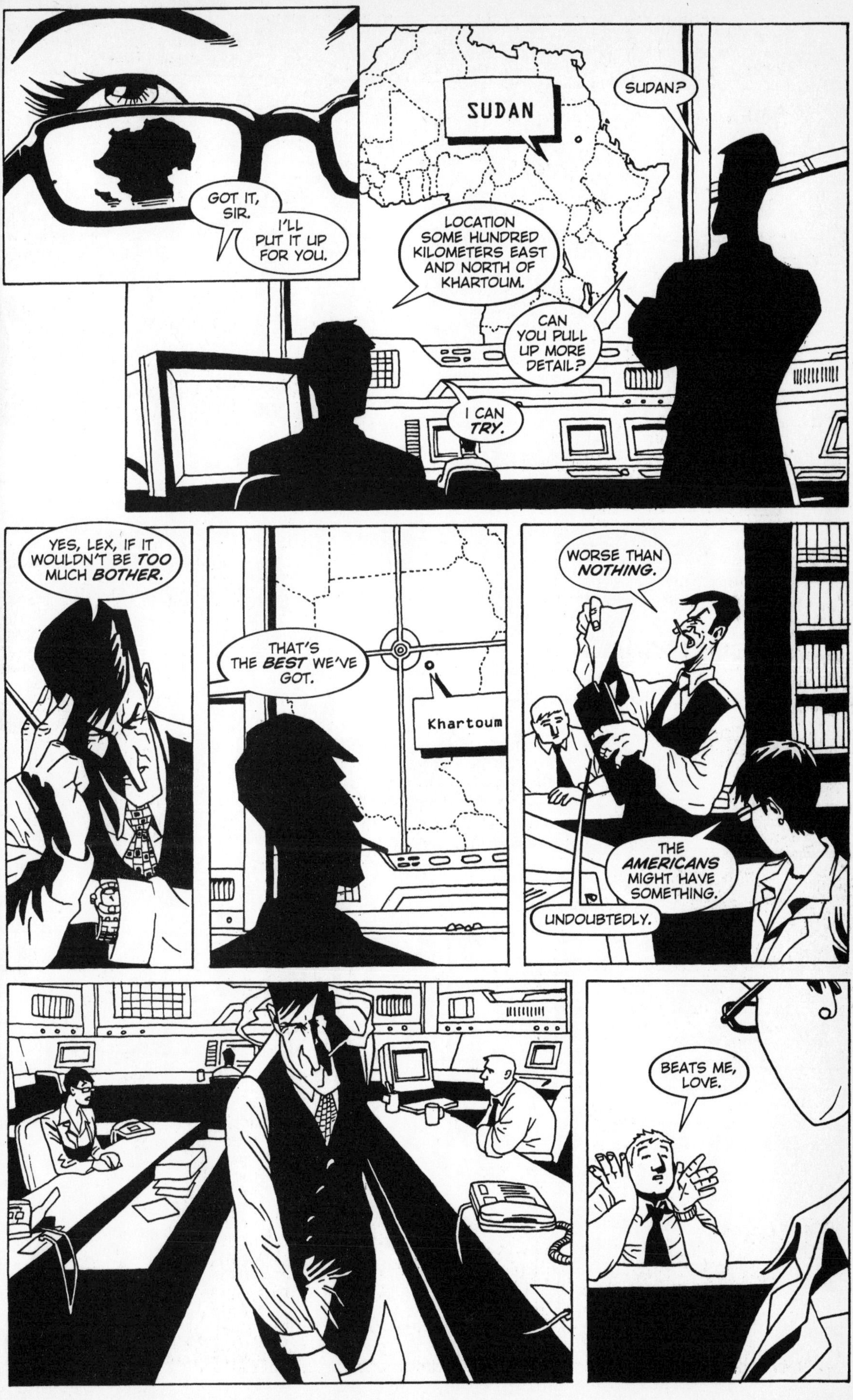
GOT IT, SIR.
I'LL PUT IT UP FOR YOU.
SUDAN
SUDAN?
LOCATION SOME HUNDRED KILOMETERS EAST AND NORTH OF KHARTOUM.
CAN YOU PULL UP MORE DETAIL?
I CAN *TRY*.
YES, LEX, IF IT WOULDN'T BE *TOO* MUCH *BOTHER*.
THAT'S THE *BEST* WE'VE GOT.
Khartoum
WORSE THAN *NOTHING*.
THE *AMERICANS* MIGHT HAVE SOMETHING.
UNDOUBTEDLY.
BEATS ME, LOVE.

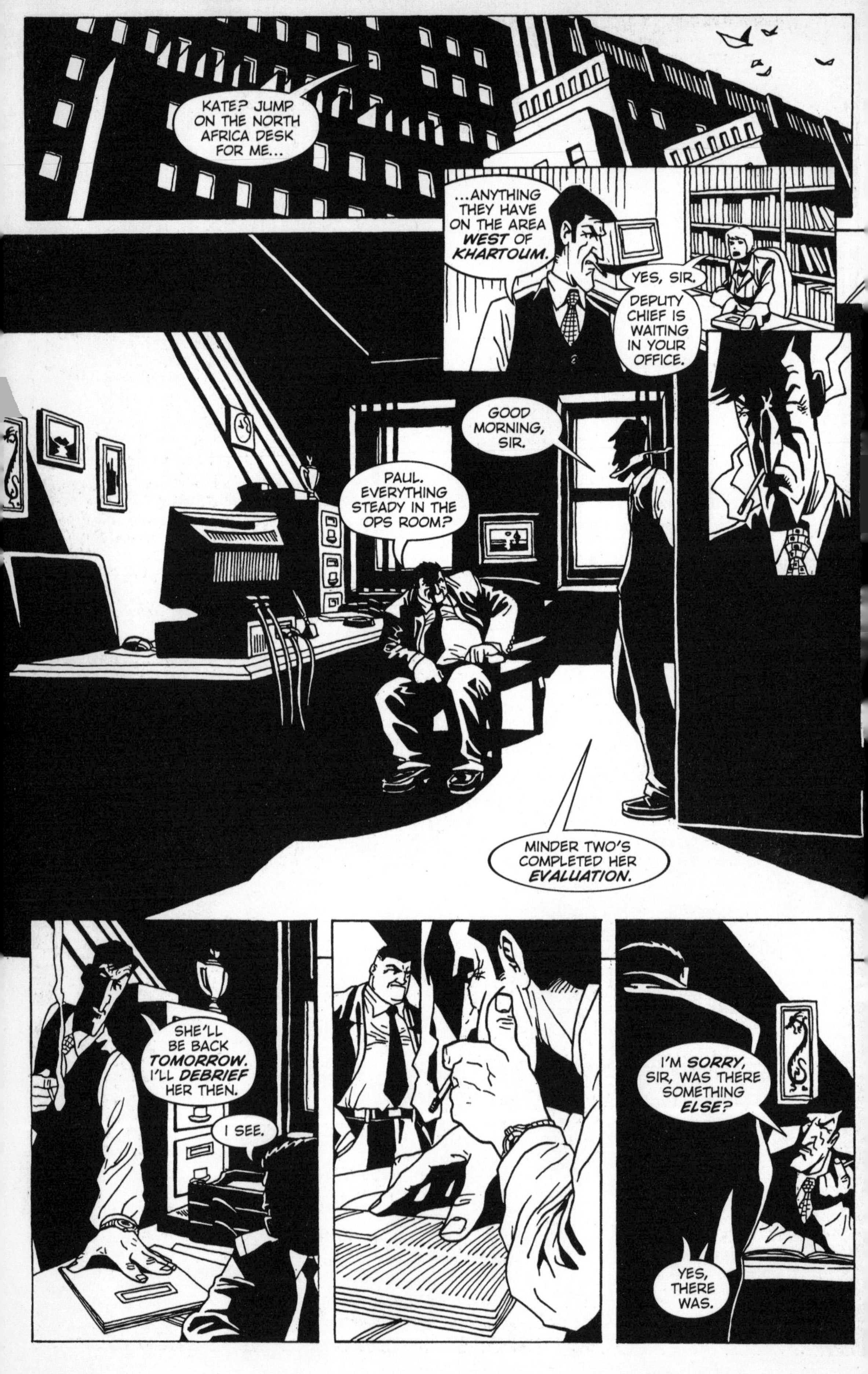
KATE? JUMP ON THE NORTH AFRICA DESK FOR ME...
...ANYTHING THEY HAVE ON THE AREA WEST OF KHARTOUM.
YES, SIR.
DEPUTY CHIEF IS WAITING IN YOUR OFFICE.
GOOD MORNING, SIR.
PAUL. EVERYTHING STEADY IN THE OPS ROOM?
MINDER TWO'S COMPLETED HER EVALUATION.
SHE'LL BE BACK TOMORROW. I'LL DEBRIEF HER THEN.
I SEE.
I'M SORRY, SIR, WAS THERE SOMETHING ELSE?
YES, THERE WAS.

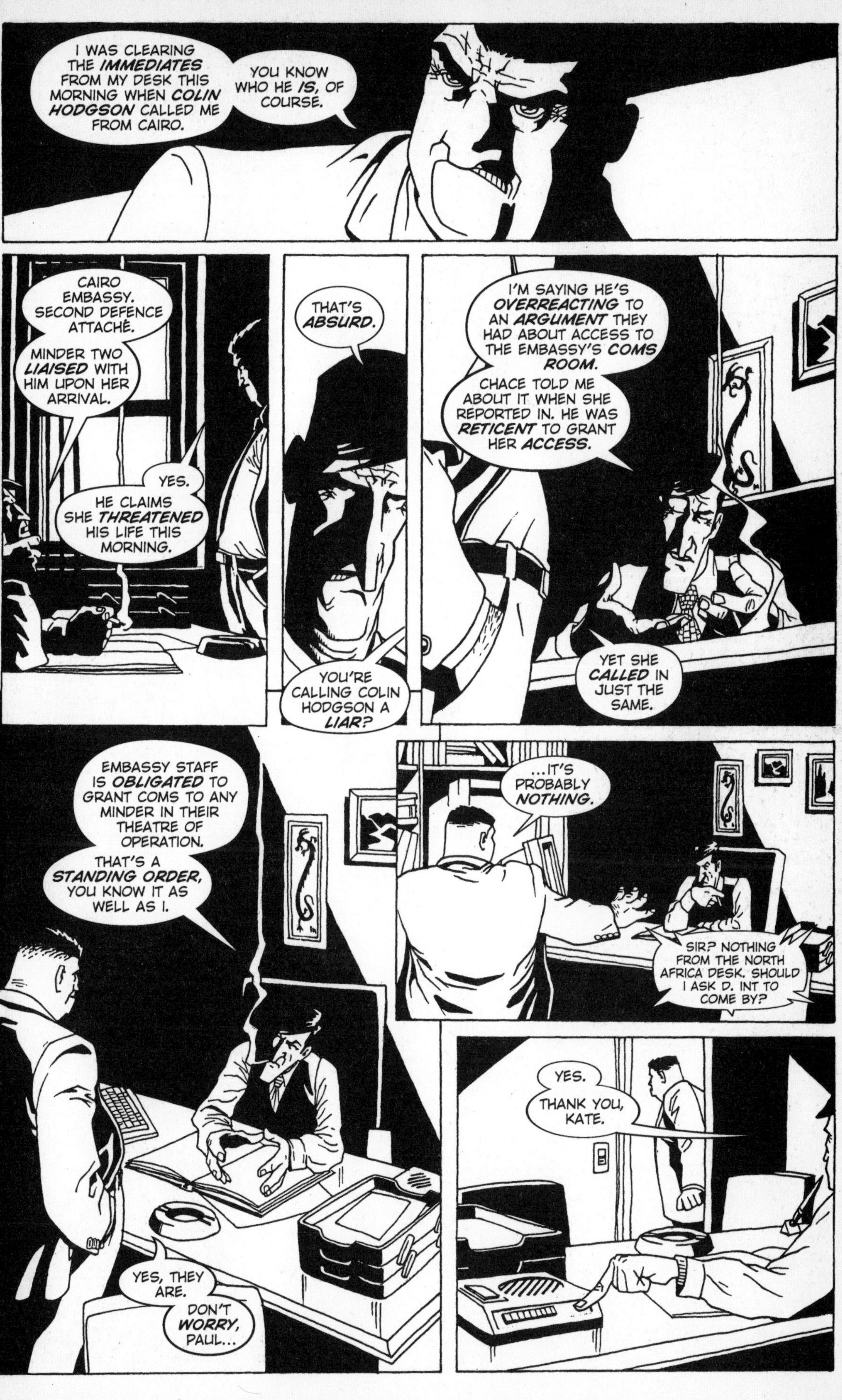

I WAS CLEARING THE *IMMEDIATES* FROM MY DESK THIS MORNING WHEN *COLIN HODGSON* CALLED ME FROM CAIRO.
YOU KNOW WHO HE *IS,* OF COURSE.
CAIRO EMBASSY. SECOND DEFENCE ATTACHÉ.
MINDER TWO *LIAISED* WITH HIM UPON HER ARRIVAL.
YES.
HE CLAIMS SHE *THREATENED* HIS LIFE THIS MORNING.
THAT'S *ABSURD.*
YOU'RE CALLING COLIN HODGSON A *LIAR?*
I'M SAYING HE'S *OVERREACTING* TO AN *ARGUMENT* THEY HAD ABOUT ACCESS TO THE EMBASSY'S *COMS ROOM.*
CHACE TOLD ME ABOUT IT WHEN SHE REPORTED IN. HE WAS *RETICENT* TO GRANT HER *ACCESS.*
YET SHE *CALLED* IN JUST THE SAME.
EMBASSY STAFF IS *OBLIGATED* TO GRANT COMS TO ANY MINDER IN THEIR THEATRE OF OPERATION.
THAT'S A *STANDING ORDER,* YOU KNOW IT AS WELL AS I.
YES, THEY ARE.
DON'T *WORRY,* PAUL...
...IT'S PROBABLY *NOTHING.*
SIR? NOTHING FROM THE NORTH AFRICA DESK. SHOULD I ASK D. INT TO COME BY?
YES.
THANK YOU, KATE.

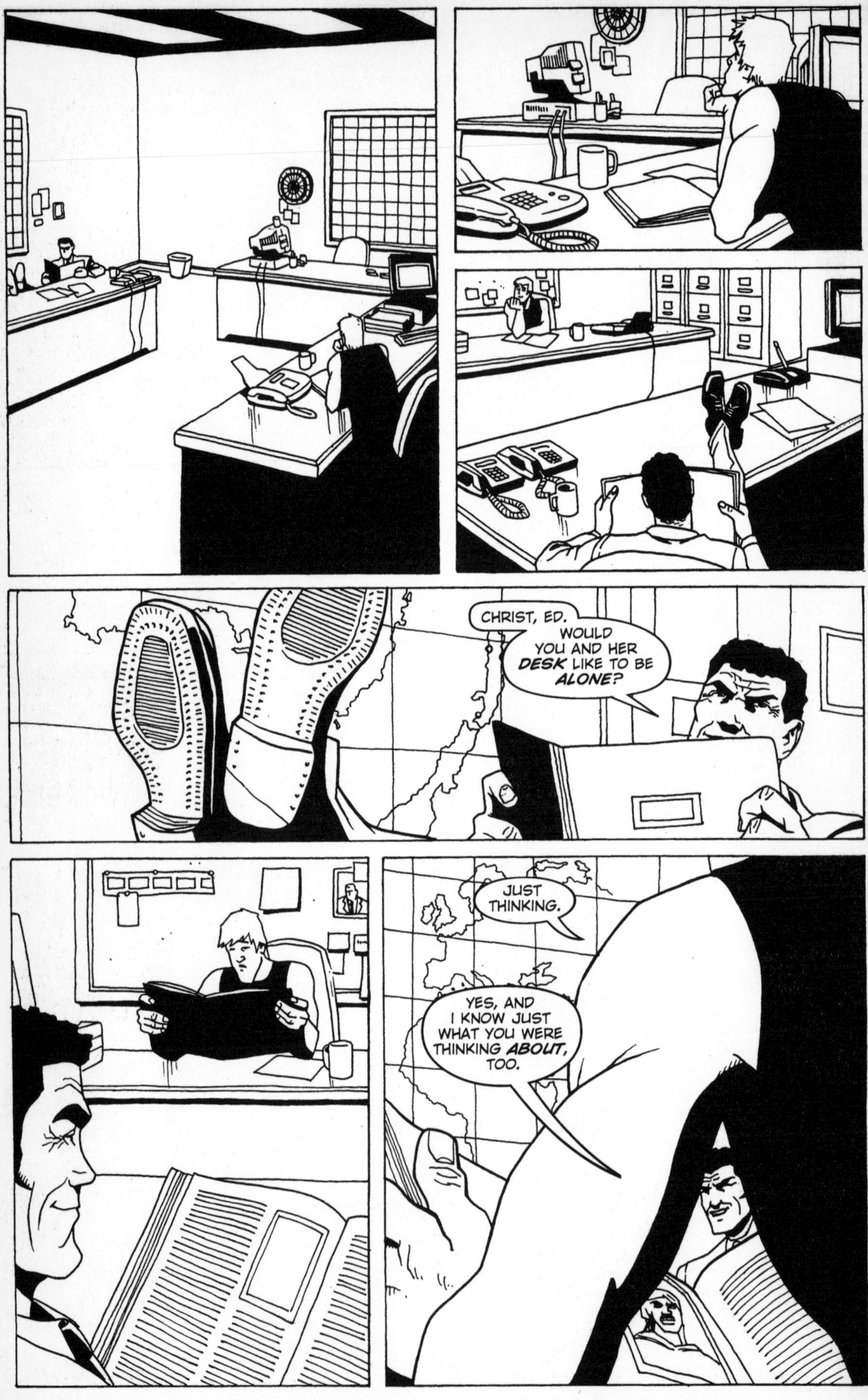
CHRIST, ED. WOULD YOU AND HER *DESK* LIKE TO BE *ALONE*?
JUST THINKING.
YES, AND I KNOW JUST WHAT YOU WERE THINKING *ABOUT*, TOO.

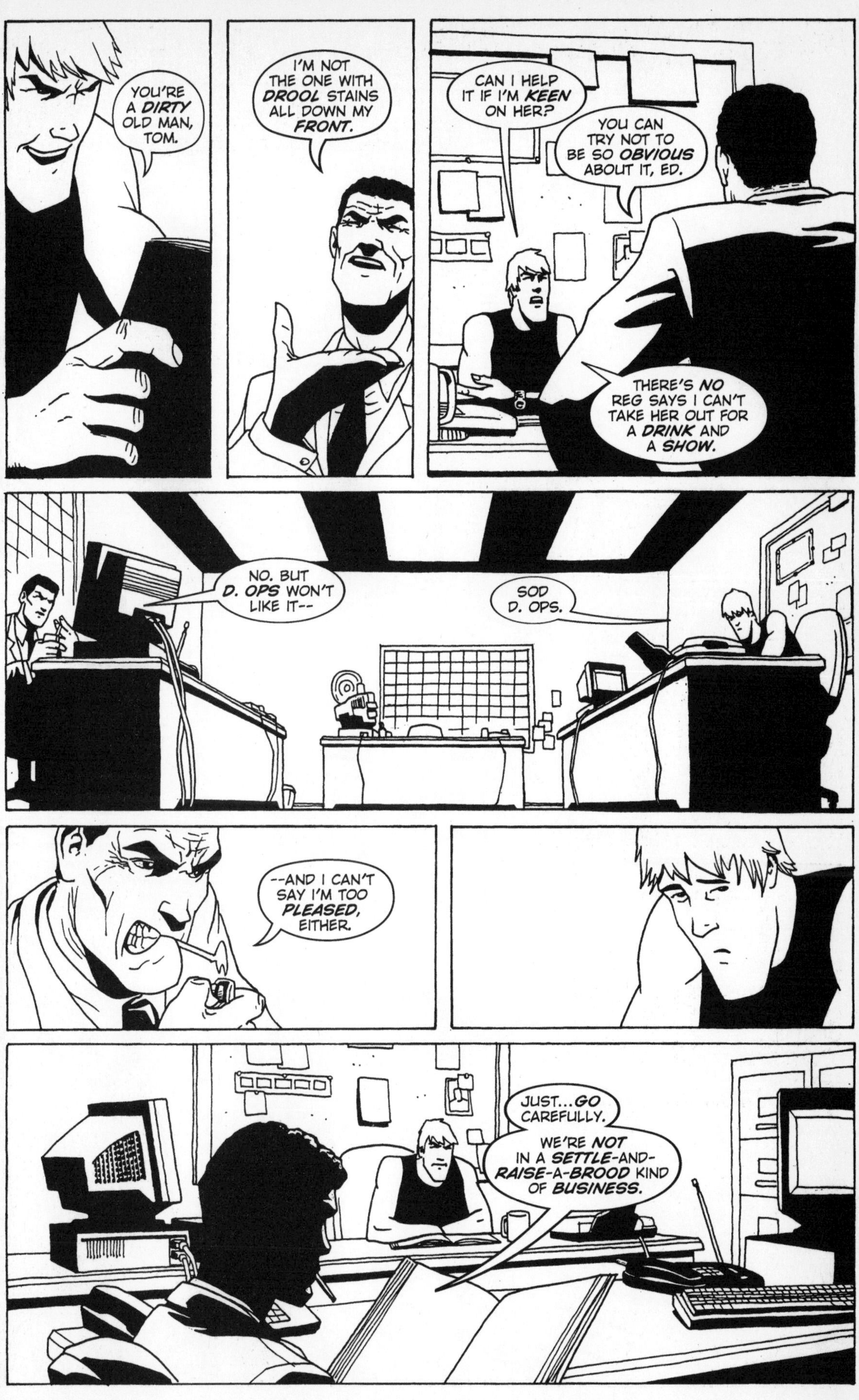
YOU'RE A DIRTY OLD MAN, TOM.
I'M NOT THE ONE WITH DROOL STAINS ALL DOWN MY FRONT.
CAN I HELP IT IF I'M KEEN ON HER?
YOU CAN TRY NOT TO BE SO OBVIOUS ABOUT IT, ED.
THERE'S NO REG SAYS I CAN'T TAKE HER OUT FOR A DRINK AND A SHOW.
NO. BUT D. OPS WON'T LIKE IT--
SOD D. OPS.
--AND I CAN'T SAY I'M TOO PLEASED, EITHER.
JUST...GO CAREFULLY.
WE'RE NOT IN A SETTLE-AND-RAISE-A-BROOD KIND OF BUSINESS.

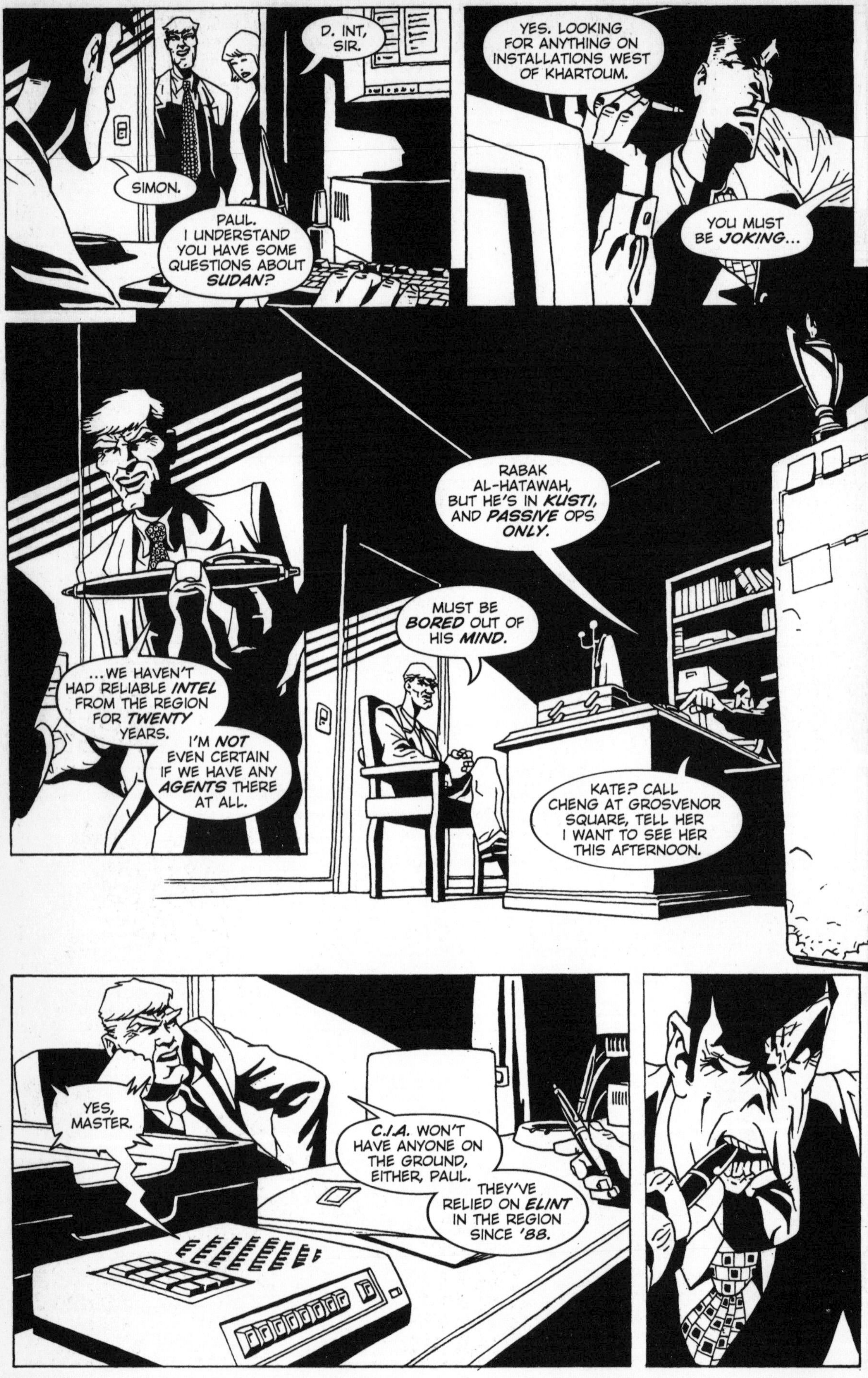
SIMON.
D. INT, SIR.
PAUL. I UNDERSTAND YOU HAVE SOME QUESTIONS ABOUT SUDAN?
YES. LOOKING FOR ANYTHING ON INSTALLATIONS WEST OF KHARTOUM.
YOU MUST BE JOKING...
...WE HAVEN'T HAD RELIABLE INTEL FROM THE REGION FOR TWENTY YEARS.
I'M NOT EVEN CERTAIN IF WE HAVE ANY AGENTS THERE AT ALL.
RABAK AL-HATAWAH, BUT HE'S IN KUSTI, AND PASSIVE OPS ONLY.
MUST BE BORED OUT OF HIS MIND.
KATE? CALL CHENG AT GROSVENOR SQUARE, TELL HER I WANT TO SEE HER THIS AFTERNOON.
YES, MASTER.
C.I.A. WON'T HAVE ANYONE ON THE GROUND, EITHER, PAUL.
THEY'VE RELIED ON ELINT IN THE REGION SINCE '88.

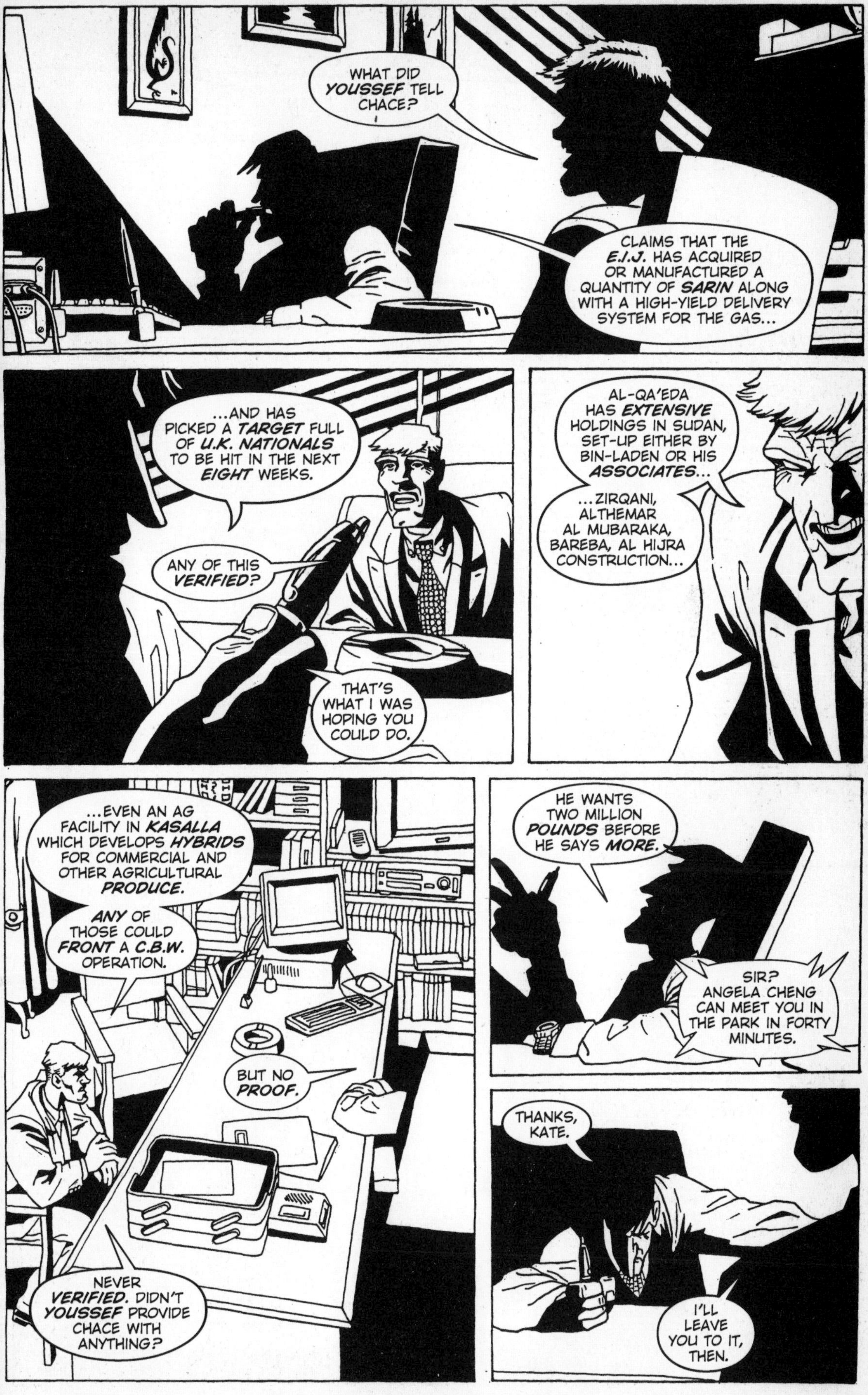
WHAT DID YOUSSEF TELL CHACE?
CLAIMS THAT THE E.I.J. HAS ACQUIRED OR MANUFACTURED A QUANTITY OF SARIN ALONG WITH A HIGH-YIELD DELIVERY SYSTEM FOR THE GAS...
...AND HAS PICKED A TARGET FULL OF U.K. NATIONALS TO BE HIT IN THE NEXT EIGHT WEEKS.
ANY OF THIS VERIFIED?
THAT'S WHAT I WAS HOPING YOU COULD DO.
AL-QA'EDA HAS EXTENSIVE HOLDINGS IN SUDAN, SET-UP EITHER BY BIN-LADEN OR HIS ASSOCIATES...
...ZIRQANI, ALTHEMAR AL MUBARAKA, BAREBA, AL HIJRA CONSTRUCTION...
...EVEN AN AG FACILITY IN KASALLA WHICH DEVELOPS HYBRIDS FOR COMMERCIAL AND OTHER AGRICULTURAL PRODUCE.
ANY OF THOSE COULD FRONT A C.B.W. OPERATION.
BUT NO PROOF.
NEVER VERIFIED. DIDN'T YOUSSEF PROVIDE CHACE WITH ANYTHING?
HE WANTS TWO MILLION POUNDS BEFORE HE SAYS MORE.
SIR? ANGELA CHENG CAN MEET YOU IN THE PARK IN FORTY MINUTES.
THANKS, KATE.
I'LL LEAVE YOU TO IT, THEN.

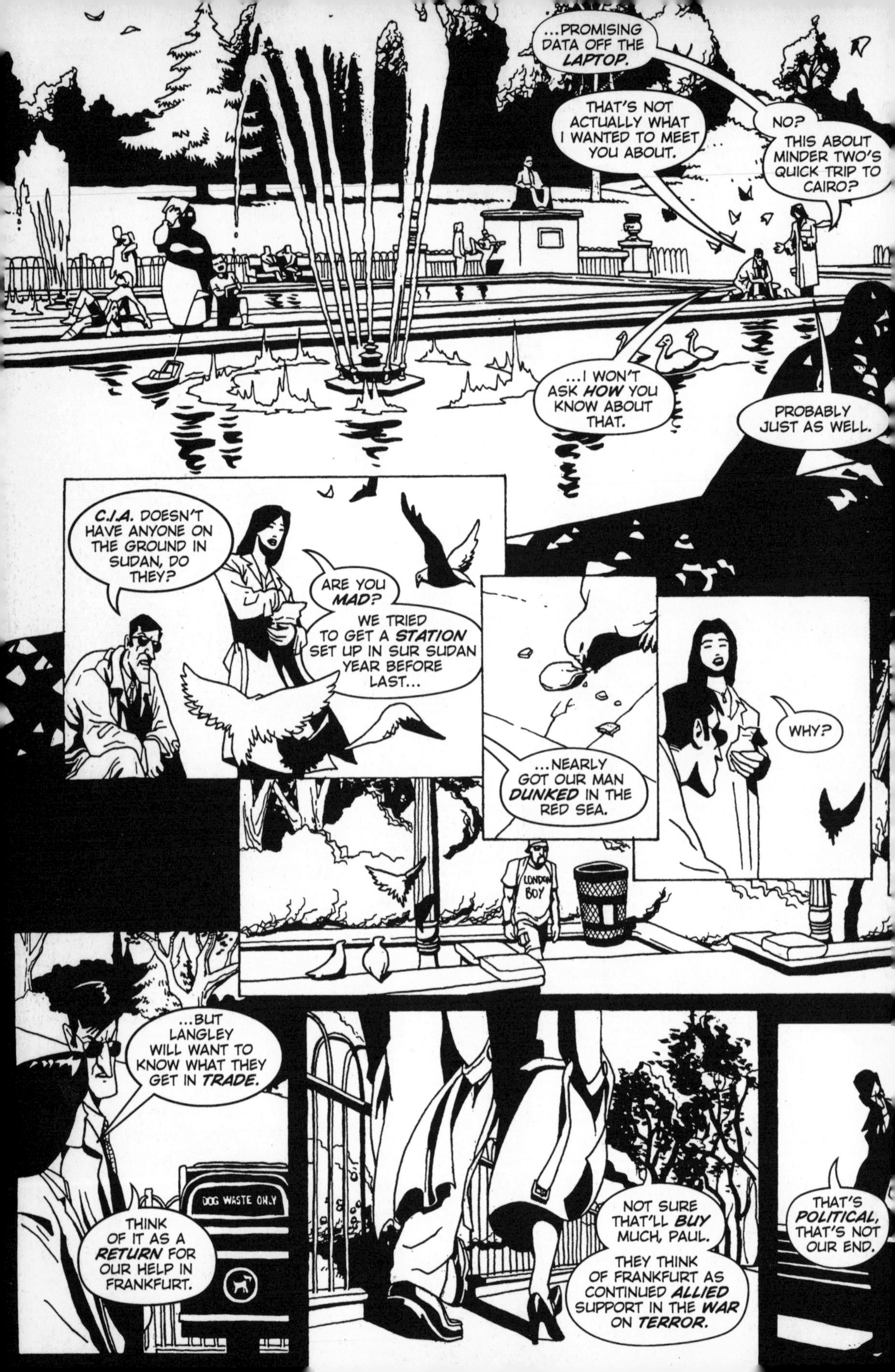
...PROMISING DATA OFF THE LAPTOP.
THAT'S NOT ACTUALLY WHAT I WANTED TO MEET YOU ABOUT.
NO? THIS ABOUT MINDER TWO'S QUICK TRIP TO CAIRO?
...I WON'T ASK HOW YOU KNOW ABOUT THAT.
PROBABLY JUST AS WELL.
C.I.A. DOESN'T HAVE ANYONE ON THE GROUND IN SUDAN, DO THEY?
ARE YOU MAD?
WE TRIED TO GET A STATION SET UP IN SUR SUDAN YEAR BEFORE LAST...
...NEARLY GOT OUR MAN DUNKED IN THE RED SEA.
WHY?
LONDON BOY
...BUT LANGLEY WILL WANT TO KNOW WHAT THEY GET IN TRADE.
DOG WASTE ONLY
THINK OF IT AS A RETURN FOR OUR HELP IN FRANKFURT.
NOT SURE THAT'LL BUY MUCH, PAUL.
THEY THINK OF FRANKFURT AS CONTINUED ALLIED SUPPORT IN THE WAR ON TERROR.
THAT'S POLITICAL, THAT'S NOT OUR END.

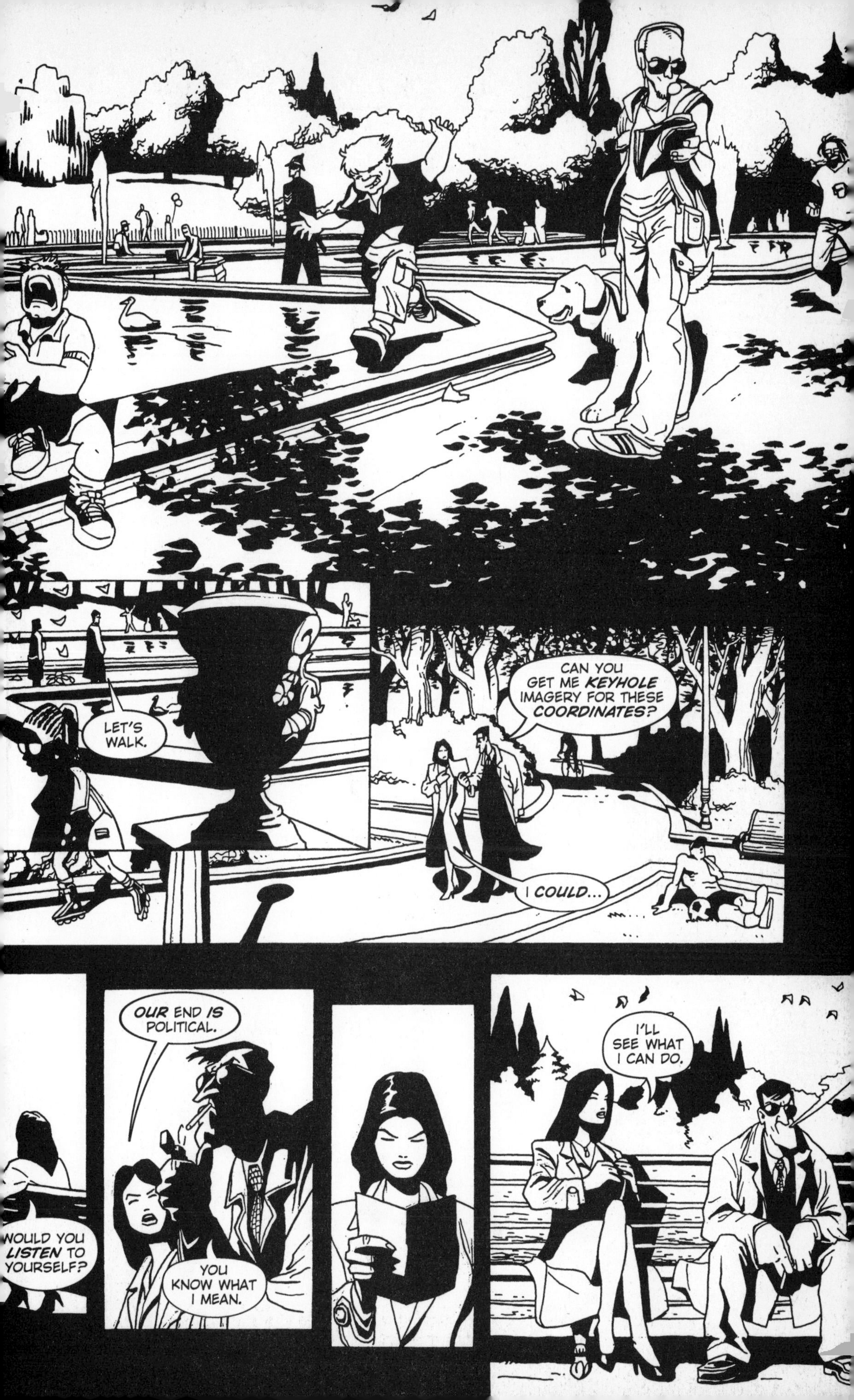
LET'S WALK.
CAN YOU GET ME KEYHOLE IMAGERY FOR THESE COORDINATES?
I COULD...
WOULD YOU LISTEN TO YOURSELF?
OUR END IS POLITICAL.
YOU KNOW WHAT I MEAN.
I'LL SEE WHAT I CAN DO.

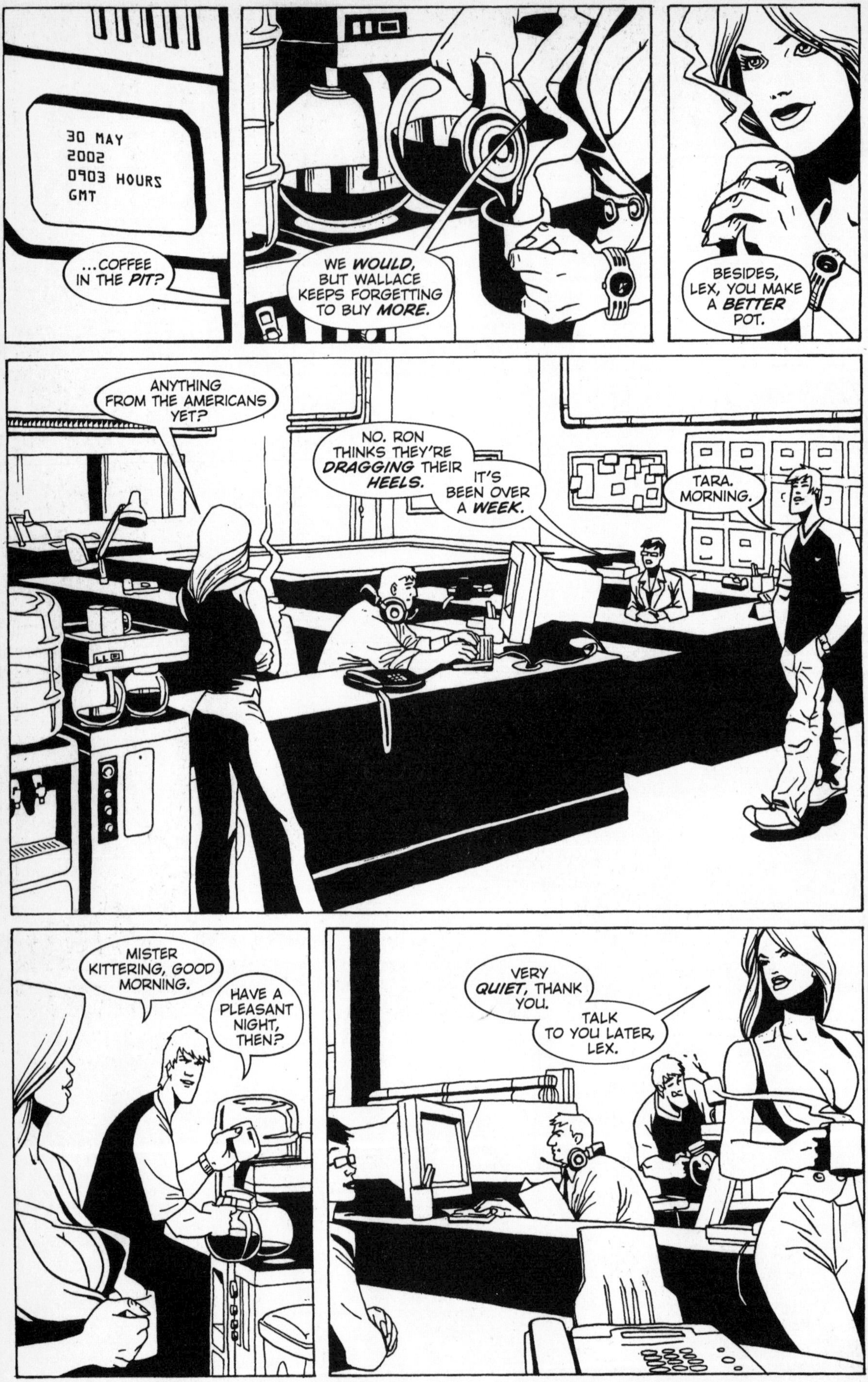
30 MAY
2002
0903 HOURS
GMT
...COFFEE IN THE PIT?
WE WOULD, BUT WALLACE KEEPS FORGETTING TO BUY MORE.
BESIDES, LEX, YOU MAKE A BETTER POT.
ANYTHING FROM THE AMERICANS YET?
NO. RON THINKS THEY'RE DRAGGING THEIR HEELS.
IT'S BEEN OVER A WEEK.
TARA. MORNING.
MISTER KITTERING, GOOD MORNING.
HAVE A PLEASANT NIGHT, THEN?
VERY QUIET, THANK YOU.
TALK TO YOU LATER, LEX.

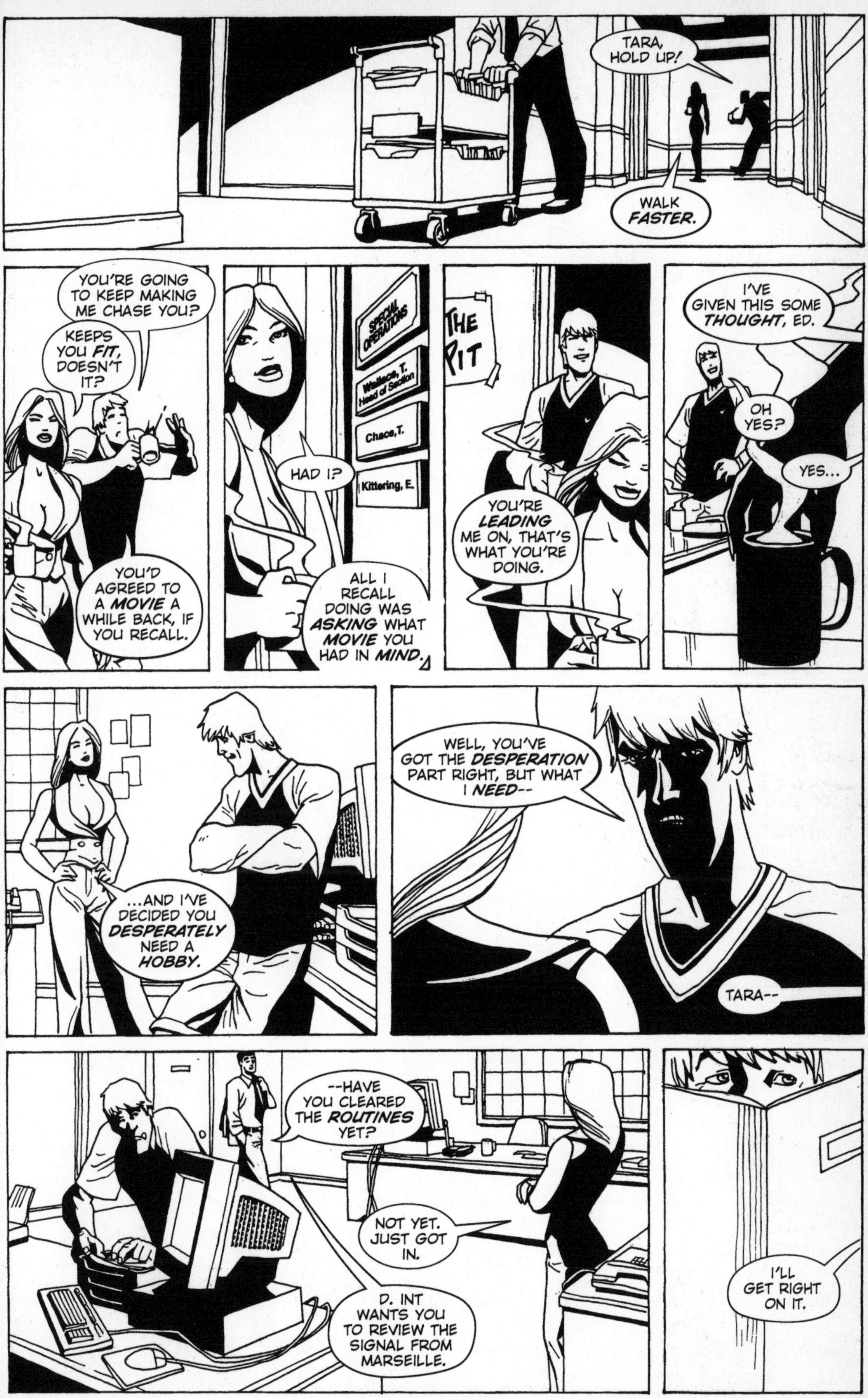
TARA, HOLD UP!
WALK FASTER.
YOU'RE GOING TO KEEP MAKING ME CHASE YOU?
KEEPS YOU FIT, DOESN'T IT?
YOU'D AGREED TO A MOVIE A WHILE BACK, IF YOU RECALL.
SPECIAL OPERATIONS
Wallace, T. Head of Section
Chace, T.
Kittering, E.
HAD I?
ALL I RECALL DOING WAS ASKING WHAT MOVIE YOU HAD IN MIND.
THE PIT
YOU'RE LEADING ME ON, THAT'S WHAT YOU'RE DOING.
I'VE GIVEN THIS SOME THOUGHT, ED.
OH YES?
YES...
...AND I'VE DECIDED YOU DESPERATELY NEED A HOBBY.
WELL, YOU'VE GOT THE DESPERATION PART RIGHT, BUT WHAT I NEED--
TARA--
--HAVE YOU CLEARED THE ROUTINES YET?
NOT YET. JUST GOT IN.
D. INT WANTS YOU TO REVIEW THE SIGNAL FROM MARSEILLE.
I'LL GET RIGHT ON IT.

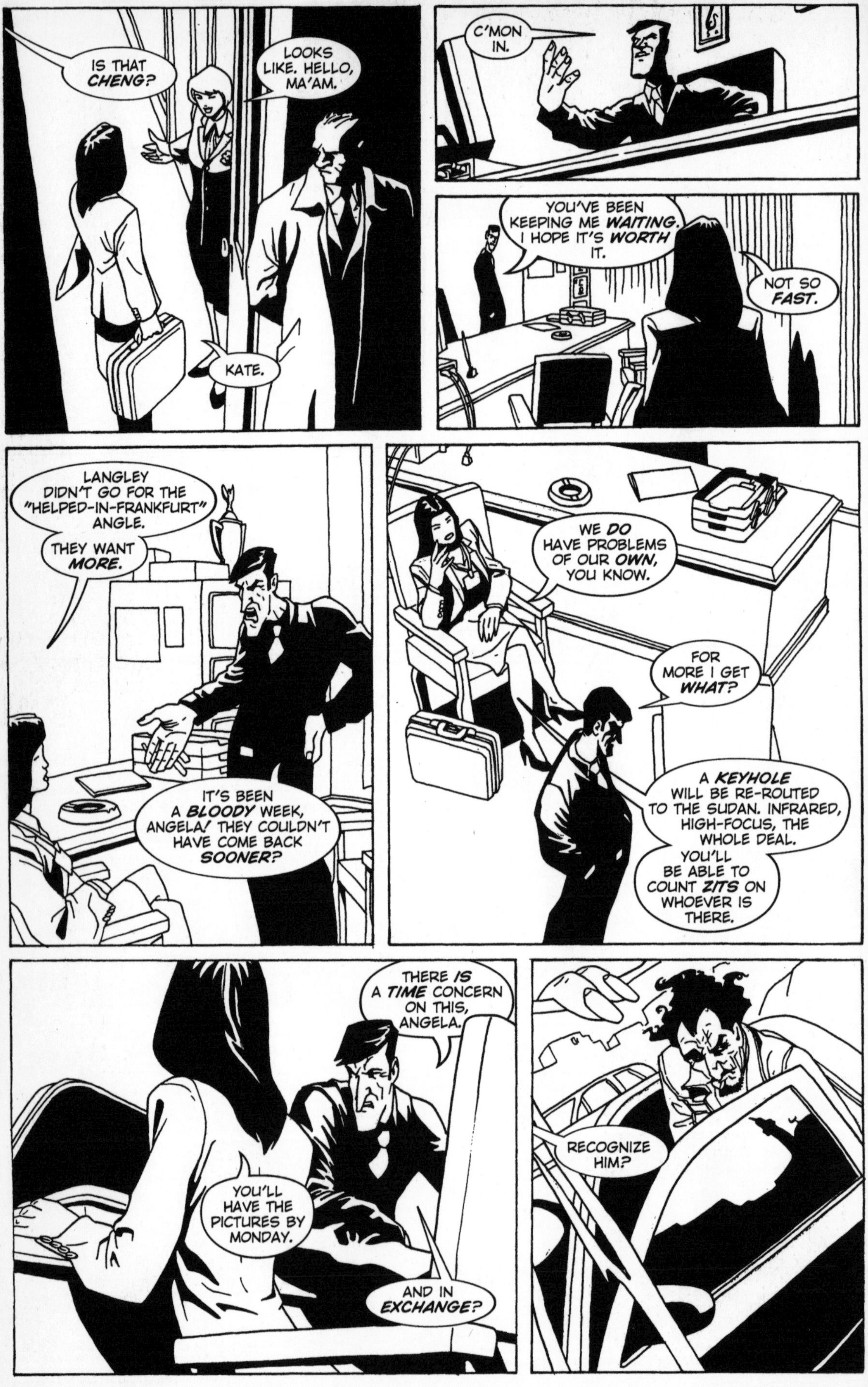
IS THAT CHENG?
LOOKS LIKE. HELLO, MA'AM.
KATE.
C'MON IN.
YOU'VE BEEN KEEPING ME WAITING. I HOPE IT'S WORTH IT.
NOT SO FAST.
LANGLEY DIDN'T GO FOR THE "HELPED-IN-FRANKFURT" ANGLE.
THEY WANT MORE.
IT'S BEEN A BLOODY WEEK, ANGELA! THEY COULDN'T HAVE COME BACK SOONER?
WE DO HAVE PROBLEMS OF OUR OWN, YOU KNOW.
FOR MORE I GET WHAT?
A KEYHOLE WILL BE RE-ROUTED TO THE SUDAN. INFRARED, HIGH-FOCUS, THE WHOLE DEAL.
YOU'LL BE ABLE TO COUNT ZITS ON WHOEVER IS THERE.
THERE IS A TIME CONCERN ON THIS, ANGELA.
YOU'LL HAVE THE PICTURES BY MONDAY.
AND IN EXCHANGE?
RECOGNIZE HIM?

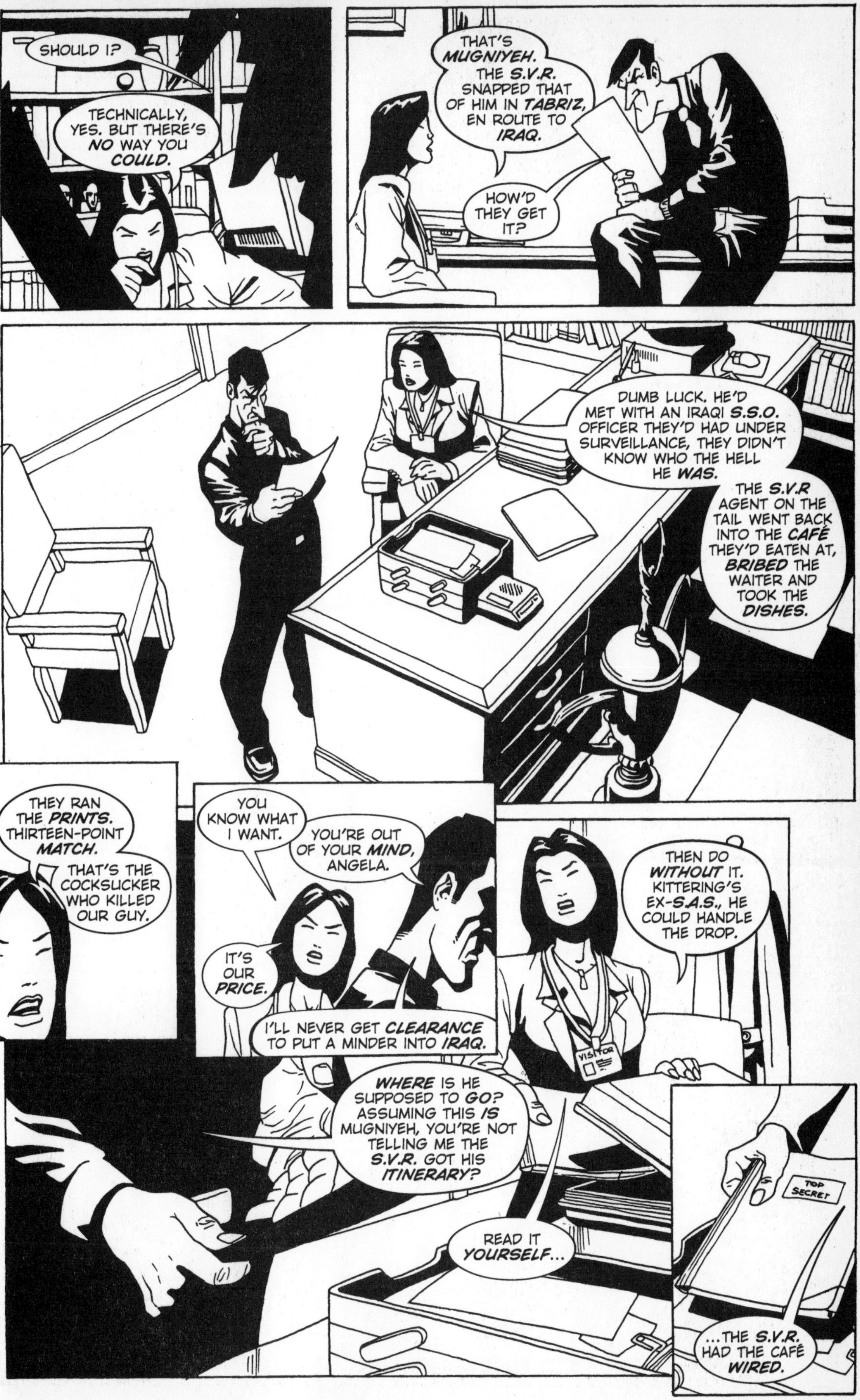

SHOULD I?
TECHNICALLY, YES. BUT THERE'S NO WAY YOU COULD.
THAT'S MUGNIYEH. THE S.V.R. SNAPPED THAT OF HIM IN TABRIZ, EN ROUTE TO IRAQ.
HOW'D THEY GET IT?
DUMB LUCK. HE'D MET WITH AN IRAQI S.S.O. OFFICER THEY'D HAD UNDER SURVEILLANCE, THEY DIDN'T KNOW WHO THE HELL HE WAS.
THE S.V.R AGENT ON THE TAIL WENT BACK INTO THE CAFÉ THEY'D EATEN AT, BRIBED THE WAITER AND TOOK THE DISHES.
THEY RAN THE PRINTS. THIRTEEN-POINT MATCH.
THAT'S THE COCKSUCKER WHO KILLED OUR GUY.
YOU KNOW WHAT I WANT.
YOU'RE OUT OF YOUR MIND, ANGELA.
IT'S OUR PRICE.
I'LL NEVER GET CLEARANCE TO PUT A MINDER INTO IRAQ.
THEN DO WITHOUT IT. KITTERING'S EX-S.A.S., HE COULD HANDLE THE DROP.
VISITOR
WHERE IS HE SUPPOSED TO GO? ASSUMING THIS IS MUGNIYEH, YOU'RE NOT TELLING ME THE S.V.R. GOT HIS ITINERARY?
READ IT YOURSELF...
TOP SECRET
...THE S.V.R. HAD THE CAFÉ WIRED.

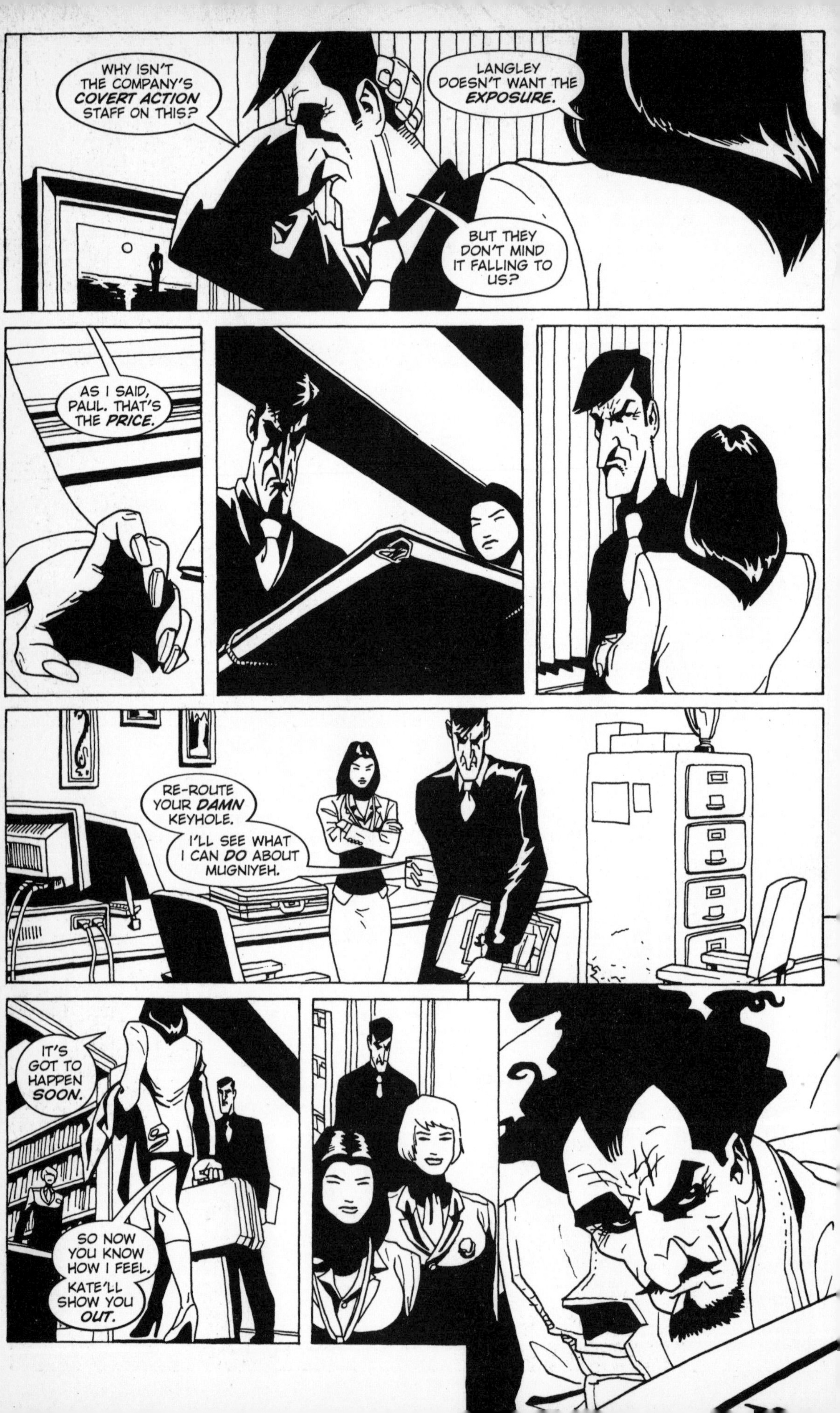

WHY ISN'T THE COMPANY'S *COVERT ACTION* STAFF ON THIS?
LANGLEY DOESN'T WANT THE *EXPOSURE*.
BUT THEY DON'T MIND IT FALLING TO US?
AS I SAID, PAUL. THAT'S THE *PRICE*.
RE-ROUTE YOUR *DAMN* KEYHOLE.
I'LL SEE WHAT I CAN *DO* ABOUT MUGNIYEH.
IT'S GOT TO HAPPEN *SOON*.
SO NOW YOU KNOW HOW I FEEL. KATE'LL SHOW YOU *OUT*.

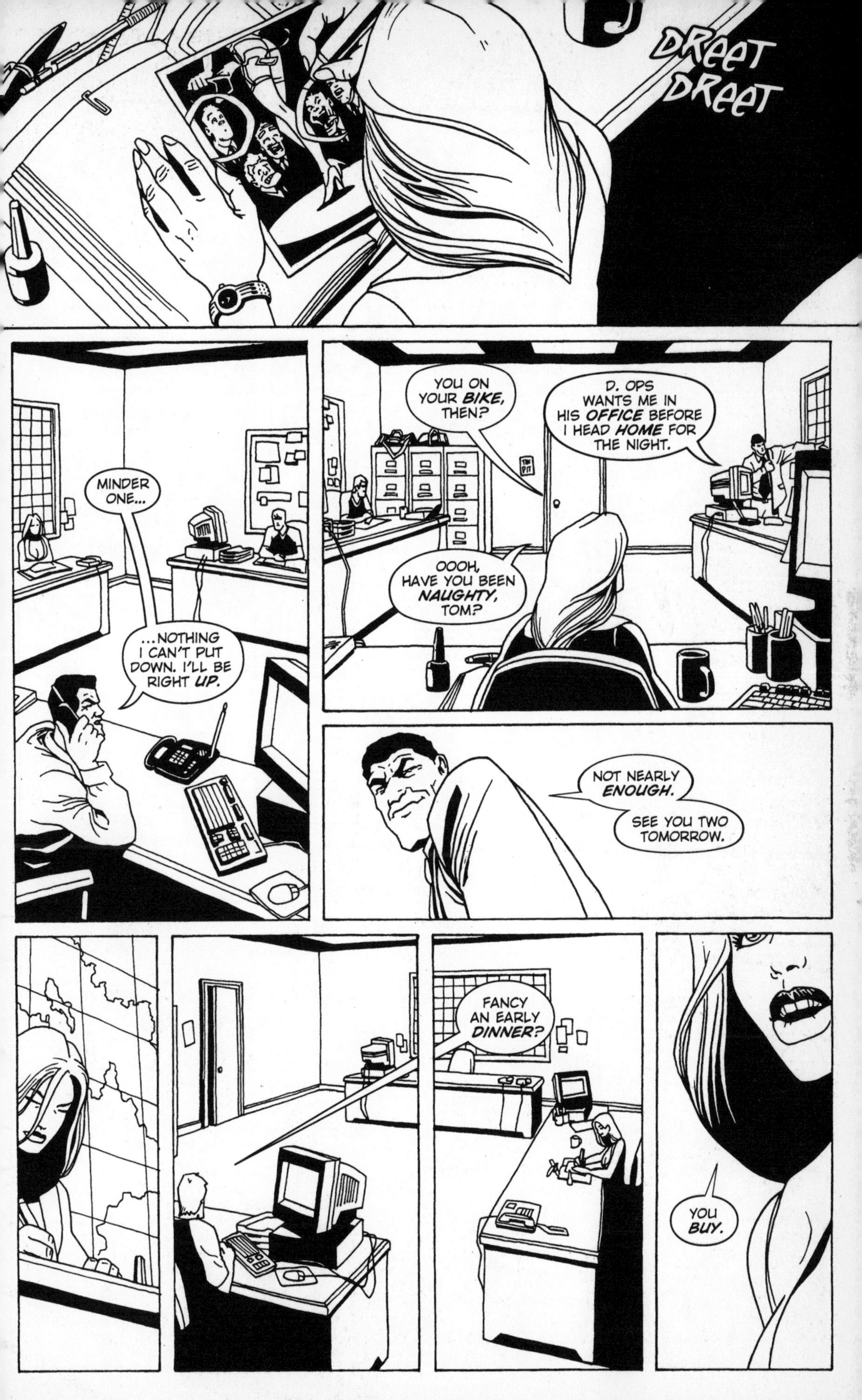
DREET
DREET
MINDER ONE...
...NOTHING I CAN'T PUT DOWN. I'LL BE RIGHT *UP.*
YOU ON YOUR *BIKE,* THEN?
D. OPS WANTS ME IN HIS *OFFICE* BEFORE I HEAD *HOME* FOR THE NIGHT.
OOOH, HAVE YOU BEEN *NAUGHTY,* TOM?
NOT NEARLY *ENOUGH.*
SEE YOU TWO TOMORROW.
FANCY AN EARLY *DINNER?*
YOU *BUY.*

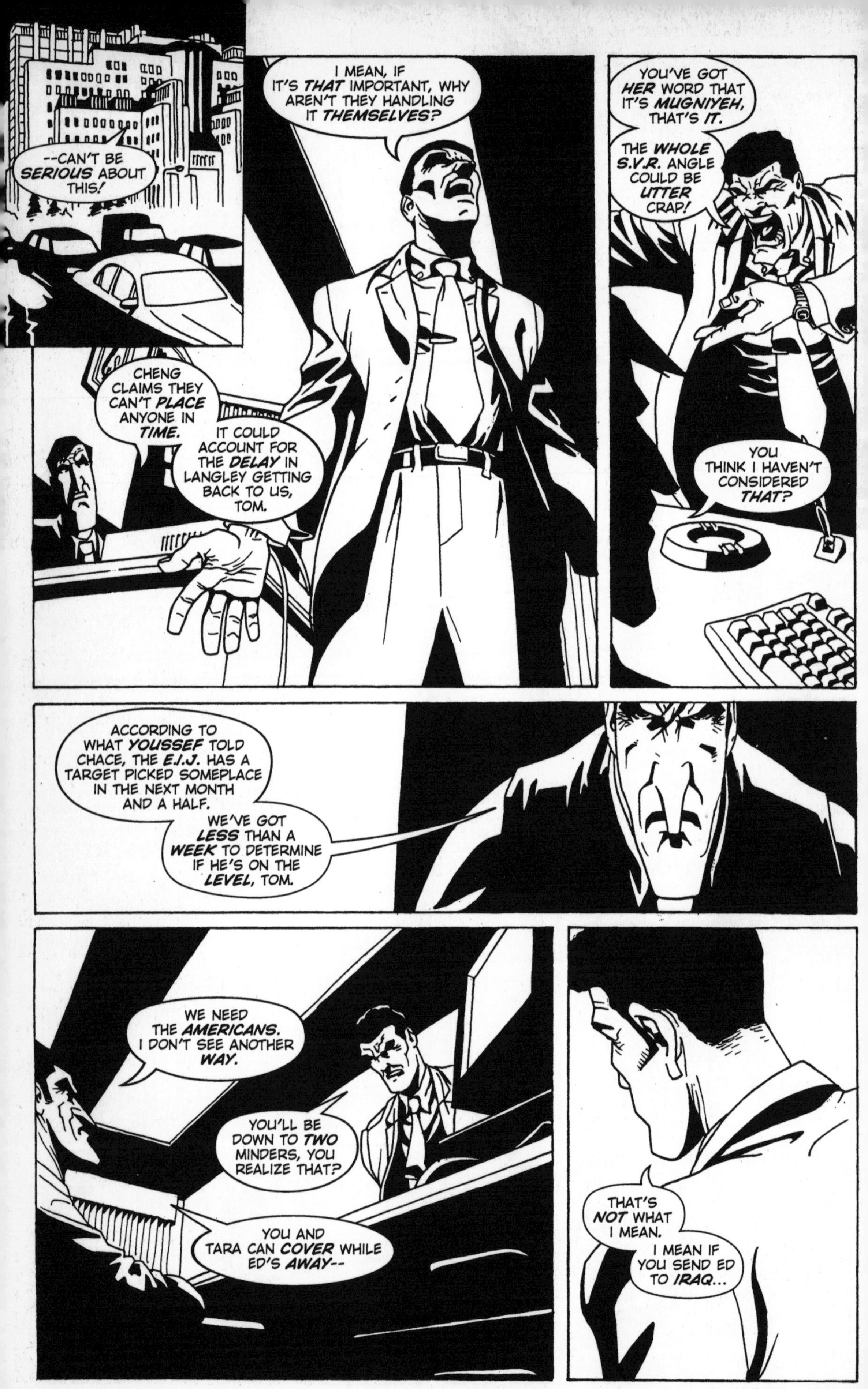
--CAN'T BE SERIOUS ABOUT THIS!
I MEAN, IF IT'S THAT IMPORTANT, WHY AREN'T THEY HANDLING IT THEMSELVES?
CHENG CLAIMS THEY CAN'T PLACE ANYONE IN TIME.
IT COULD ACCOUNT FOR THE DELAY IN LANGLEY GETTING BACK TO US, TOM.
YOU'VE GOT HER WORD THAT IT'S MUGNIYEH, THAT'S IT.
THE WHOLE S.V.R. ANGLE COULD BE UTTER CRAP!
YOU THINK I HAVEN'T CONSIDERED THAT?
ACCORDING TO WHAT YOUSSEF TOLD CHACE, THE E.I.J. HAS A TARGET PICKED SOMEPLACE IN THE NEXT MONTH AND A HALF.
WE'VE GOT LESS THAN A WEEK TO DETERMINE IF HE'S ON THE LEVEL, TOM.
WE NEED THE AMERICANS. I DON'T SEE ANOTHER WAY.
YOU'LL BE DOWN TO TWO MINDERS, YOU REALIZE THAT?
YOU AND TARA CAN COVER WHILE ED'S AWAY--
THAT'S NOT WHAT I MEAN.
I MEAN IF YOU SEND ED TO IRAQ...

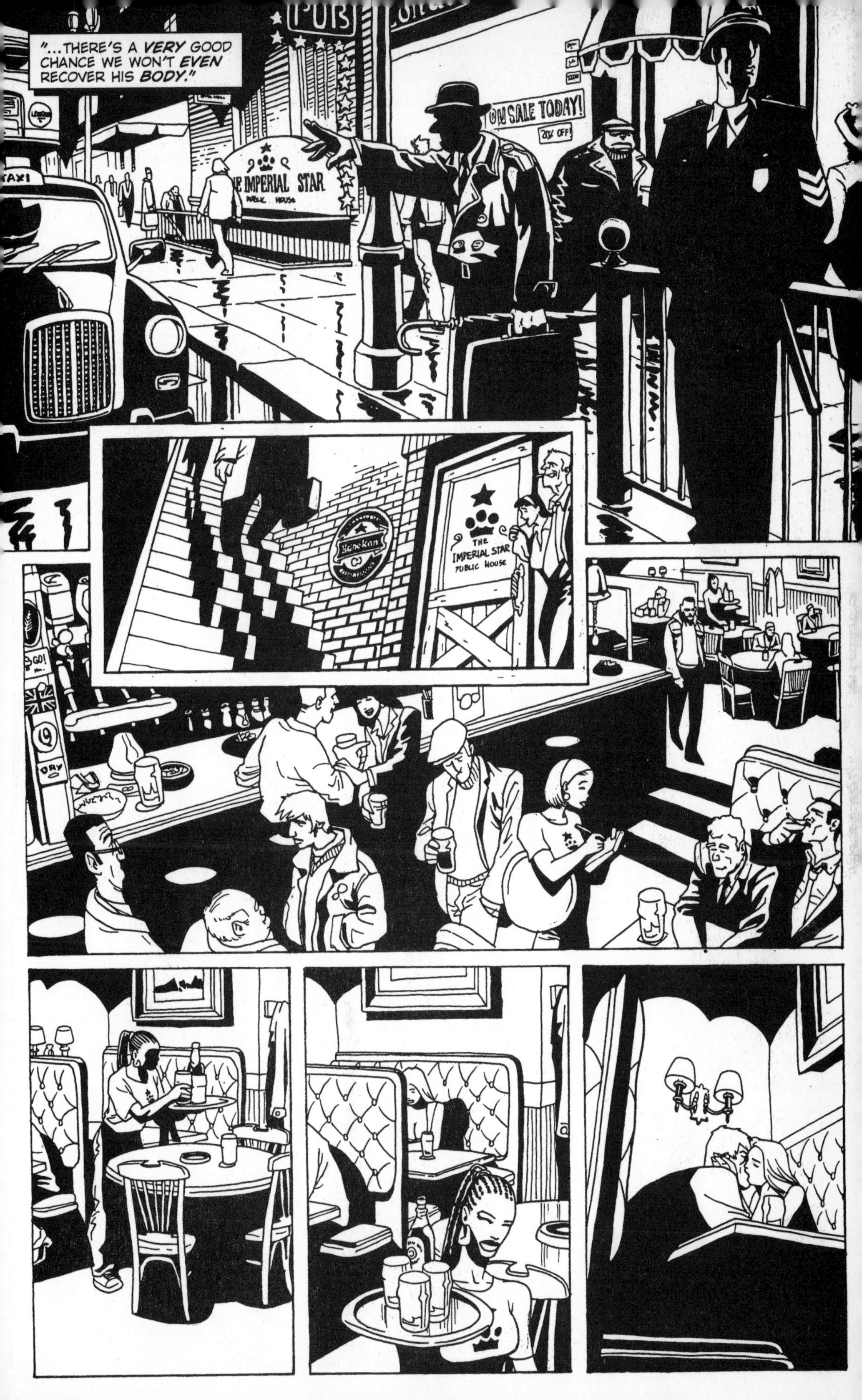
"...THERE'S A VERY GOOD CHANCE WE WON'T EVEN RECOVER HIS BODY."
PUB
ON SALE TODAY!
20% OFF!
TAXI
THE IMPERIAL STAR
PUBLIC HOUSE
THE IMPERIAL STAR
PUBLIC HOUSE

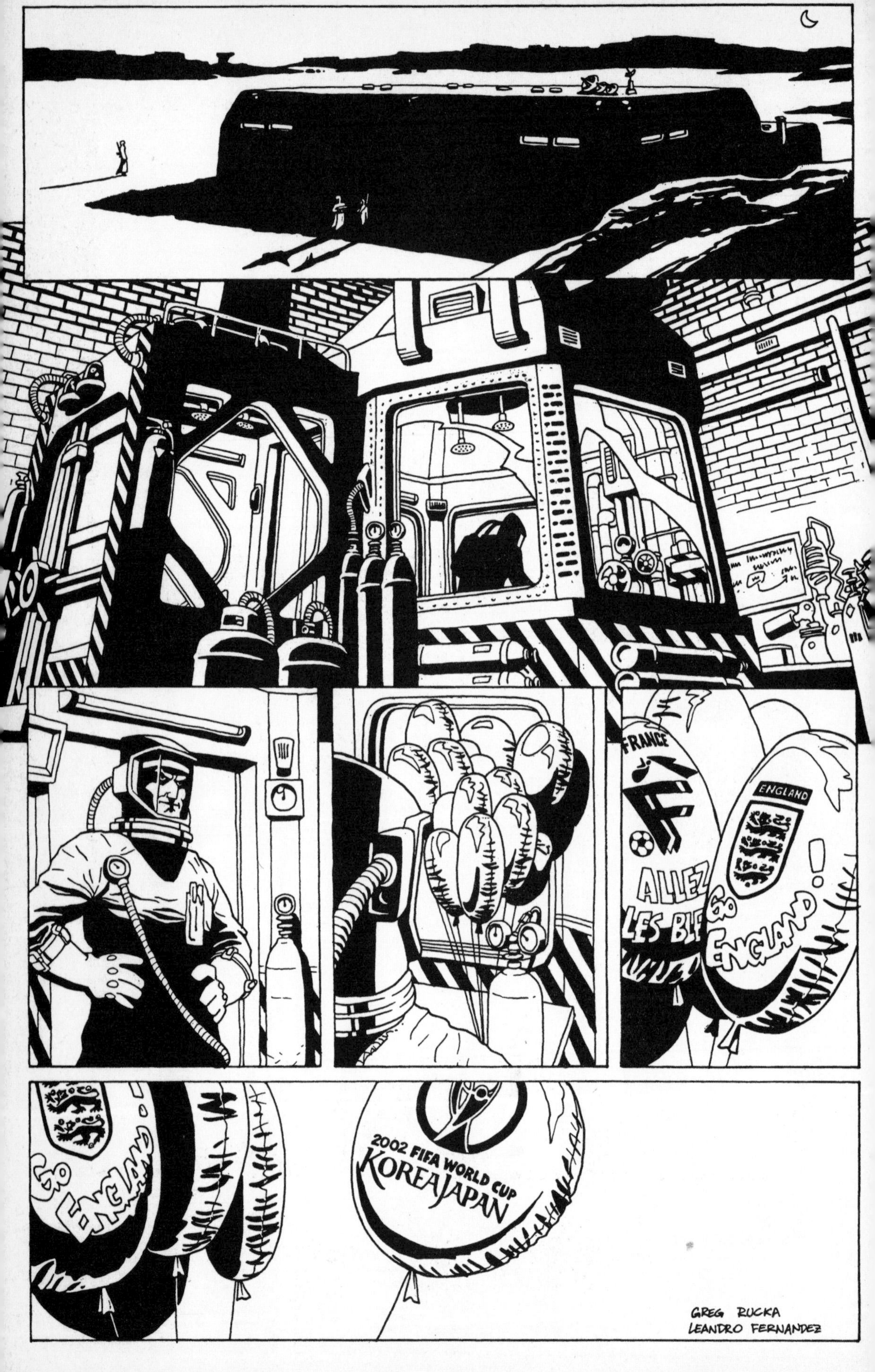
FRANCE
ALLEZ
LES BL
ENGLAND
GO ENGLAND!
GO ENGLAND!
2002 FIFA WORLD CUP
KOREA JAPAN
GREG RUCKA
LEANDRO FERNANDEZ

CHAPTER 3

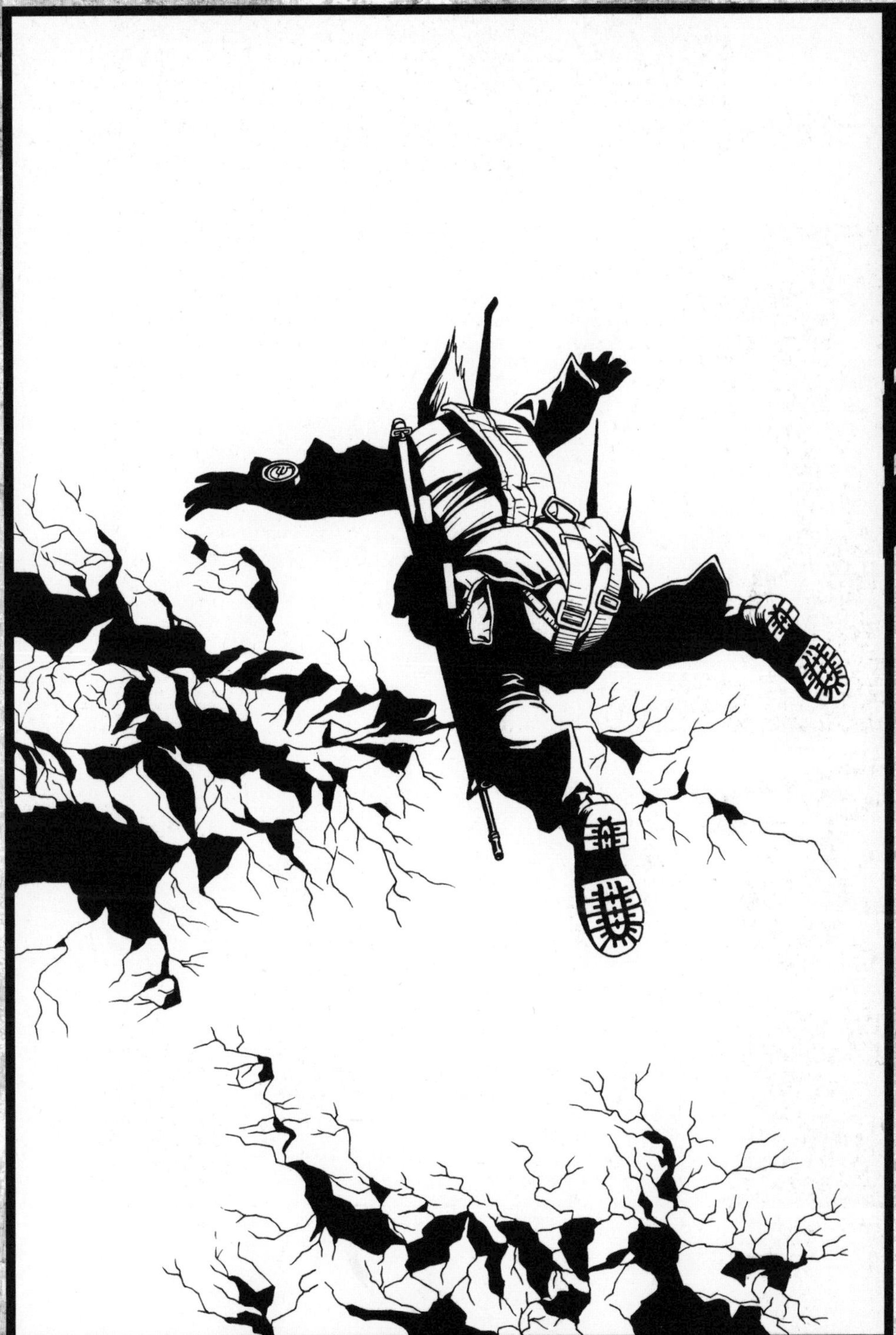

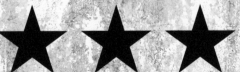

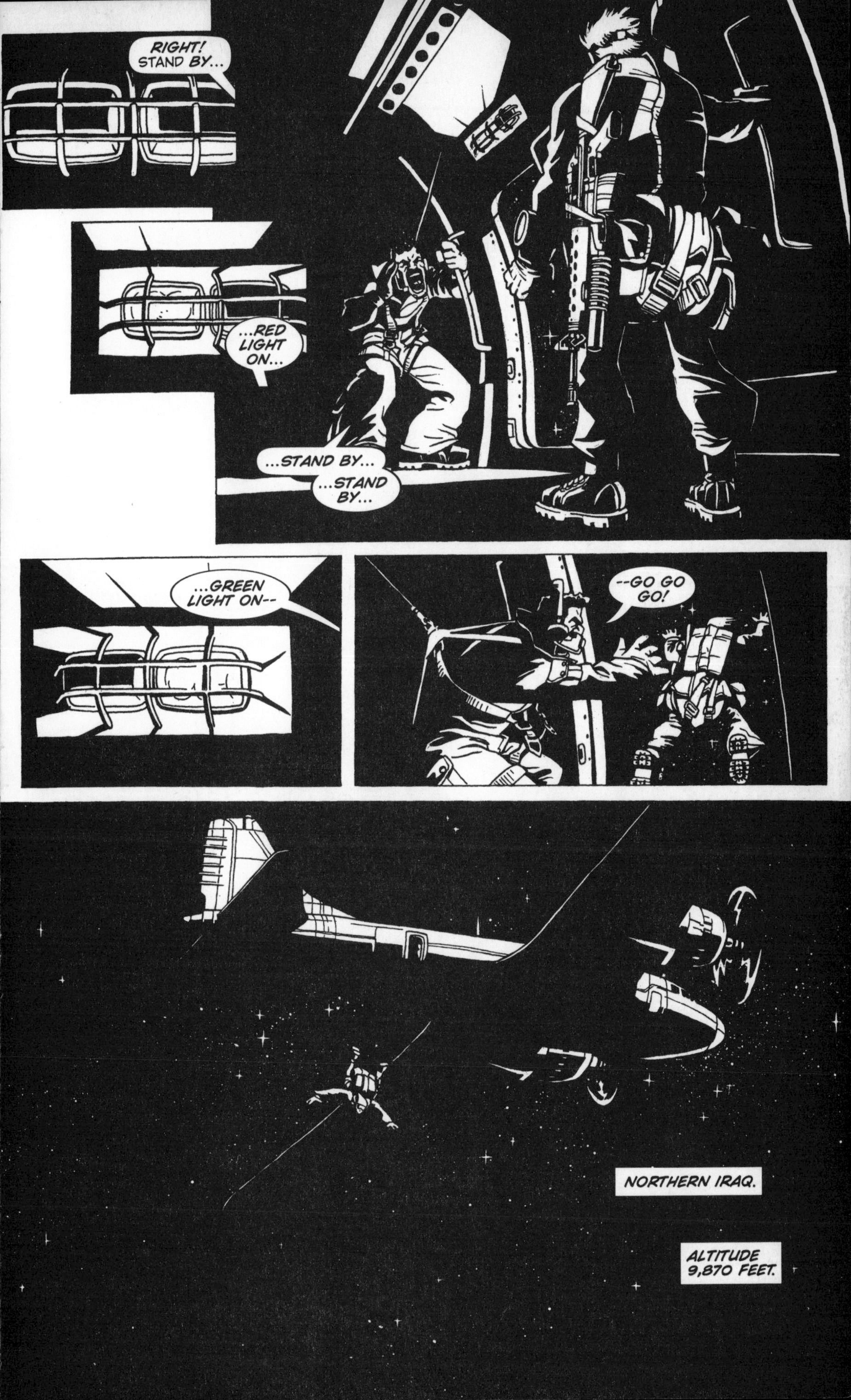
RIGHT! STAND BY...
...RED LIGHT ON...
...STAND BY...
...STAND BY...
...GREEN LIGHT ON--
--GO GO GO!
NORTHERN IRAQ.
ALTITUDE 9,870 FEET.

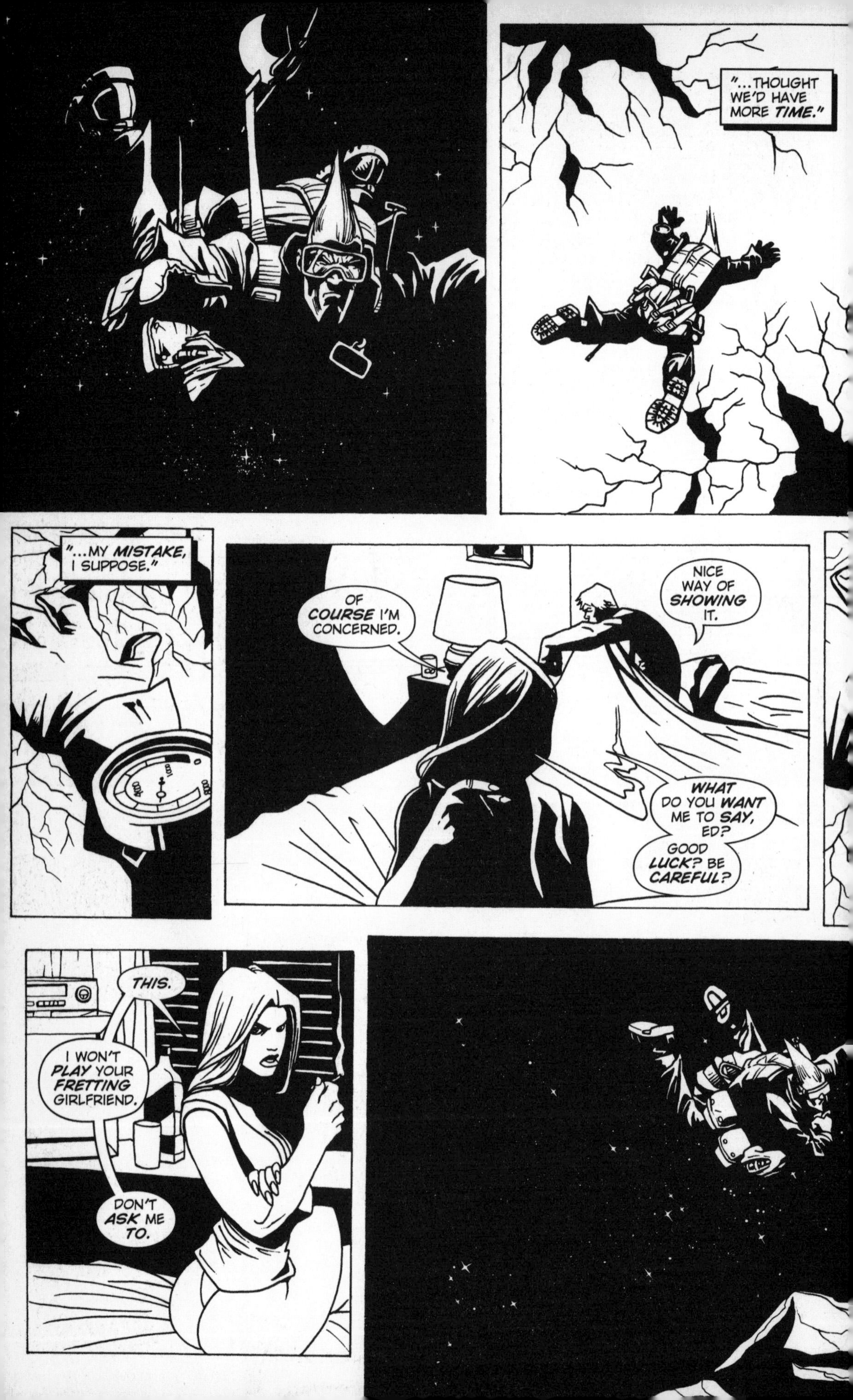
"...THOUGHT WE'D HAVE MORE *TIME.*"
"...MY *MISTAKE,* I SUPPOSE."
OF *COURSE* I'M CONCERNED.
NICE WAY OF *SHOWING* IT.
WHAT DO YOU *WANT* ME TO *SAY,* ED?
GOOD *LUCK?* BE *CAREFUL?*
THIS.
I WON'T *PLAY* YOUR *FRETTING* GIRLFRIEND.
DON'T *ASK* ME *TO.*

IT DOESN'T *MATTER.*

ARE YOU *ANGRY* AT ME?

DON'T BE *DAFT,* ED...

"...IT'S NOT AS IF WE DIDN'T *KNOW* THIS WOULD *HAPPEN.*"

NO... JUST THAT IT CAME UP SO *SUDDENLY.*

AND IT *IS* IRAQ...

WHAT DO YOU *WANT* ME TO *SAY?*

I DON'T *WANT* YOU TO *SAY* ANYTHING. I JUST THOUGHT IT MIGHT *CONCERN* YOU...

"THOSE ARE A *START.*"

BUT THAT'S *NOT* WHAT YOU *WANT,* IS IT?

I *WON'T* DO THIS, ED. I *WON'T.*

DO *WHAT?*

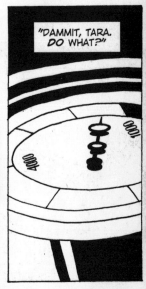

"DAMMIT, TARA. *DO* WHAT?"

"I *WON'T* DO IT..."

...I *CAN'T.*

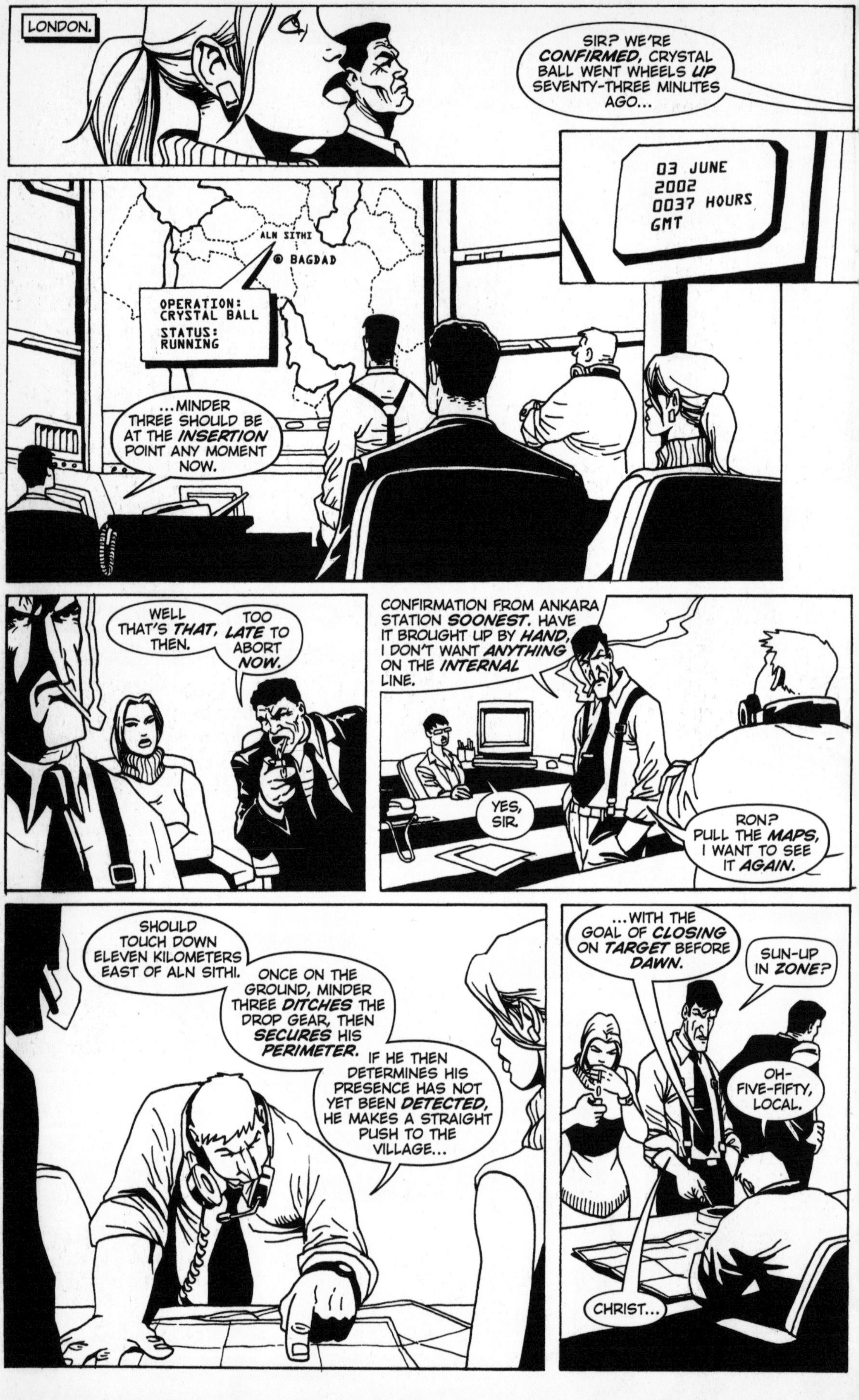

LONDON.
SIR? WE'RE CONFIRMED, CRYSTAL BALL WENT WHEELS UP SEVENTY-THREE MINUTES AGO...
03 JUNE 2002 0037 HOURS GMT
ALN SITHI
BAGDAD
OPERATION: CRYSTAL BALL
STATUS: RUNNING
...MINDER THREE SHOULD BE AT THE INSERTION POINT ANY MOMENT NOW.
WELL THAT'S THAT, THEN.
TOO LATE TO ABORT NOW.
CONFIRMATION FROM ANKARA STATION SOONEST. HAVE IT BROUGHT UP BY HAND, I DON'T WANT ANYTHING ON THE INTERNAL LINE.
YES, SIR.
RON? PULL THE MAPS, I WANT TO SEE IT AGAIN.
SHOULD TOUCH DOWN ELEVEN KILOMETERS EAST OF ALN SITHI.
ONCE ON THE GROUND, MINDER THREE DITCHES THE DROP GEAR, THEN SECURES HIS PERIMETER.
IF HE THEN DETERMINES HIS PRESENCE HAS NOT YET BEEN DETECTED, HE MAKES A STRAIGHT PUSH TO THE VILLAGE...
...WITH THE GOAL OF CLOSING ON TARGET BEFORE DAWN.
SUN-UP IN ZONE?
OH-FIVE-FIFTY, LOCAL.
CHRIST...

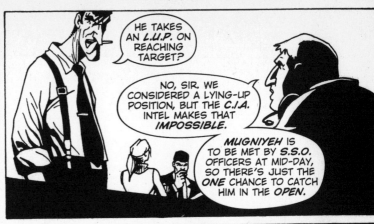

HE TAKES AN *L.U.P.* ON REACHING TARGET?

NO, SIR. WE CONSIDERED A LYING-UP POSITION, BUT THE *C.I.A.* INTEL MAKES THAT *IMPOSSIBLE.*

MUGNIYEH IS TO BE MET BY *S.S.O.* OFFICERS AT MID-DAY, SO THERE'S JUST THE *ONE* CHANCE TO CATCH HIM IN THE *OPEN.*

SO NOW IT'S *BROAD* DAYLIGHT, AND ED'S OPENING FIRE.

MINDER THREE IS AT HIS *DISCRETION* TO DETERMINE *MEANS* AND *METHOD.*

...THAT GIVES HIM *LESS* THAN *TWO* HOURS, ASSUMING HE DIDN'T *SNAP* HIS LEGS ON *LANDING.*

IF HE'S BEEN *BLOWN,* THEN WHAT?

IF *ABLE,* HE *CONTINUES* TO TARGET IN THE HOPES OF *COMPLETING* THE MISSION. IF THE TARGET IS *LOCKED,* BUT HE'S STILL AT *LIBERTY*...

...HE'LL ENTER STANDARD *E&E* WITH THE HOPE OF MAKING ONE OF THE *R.V.*S ON THE BORDER WITH *TURKEY.*

AND IF HE'S *NOT* AT LIBERTY, HE'S *DEAD,* SO IT'S NOT REALLY AN *ISSUE,* IS IT?

RIGHT, THAT'LL DO, RON. THANKS.

MINDER ONE, MY OFFICE.

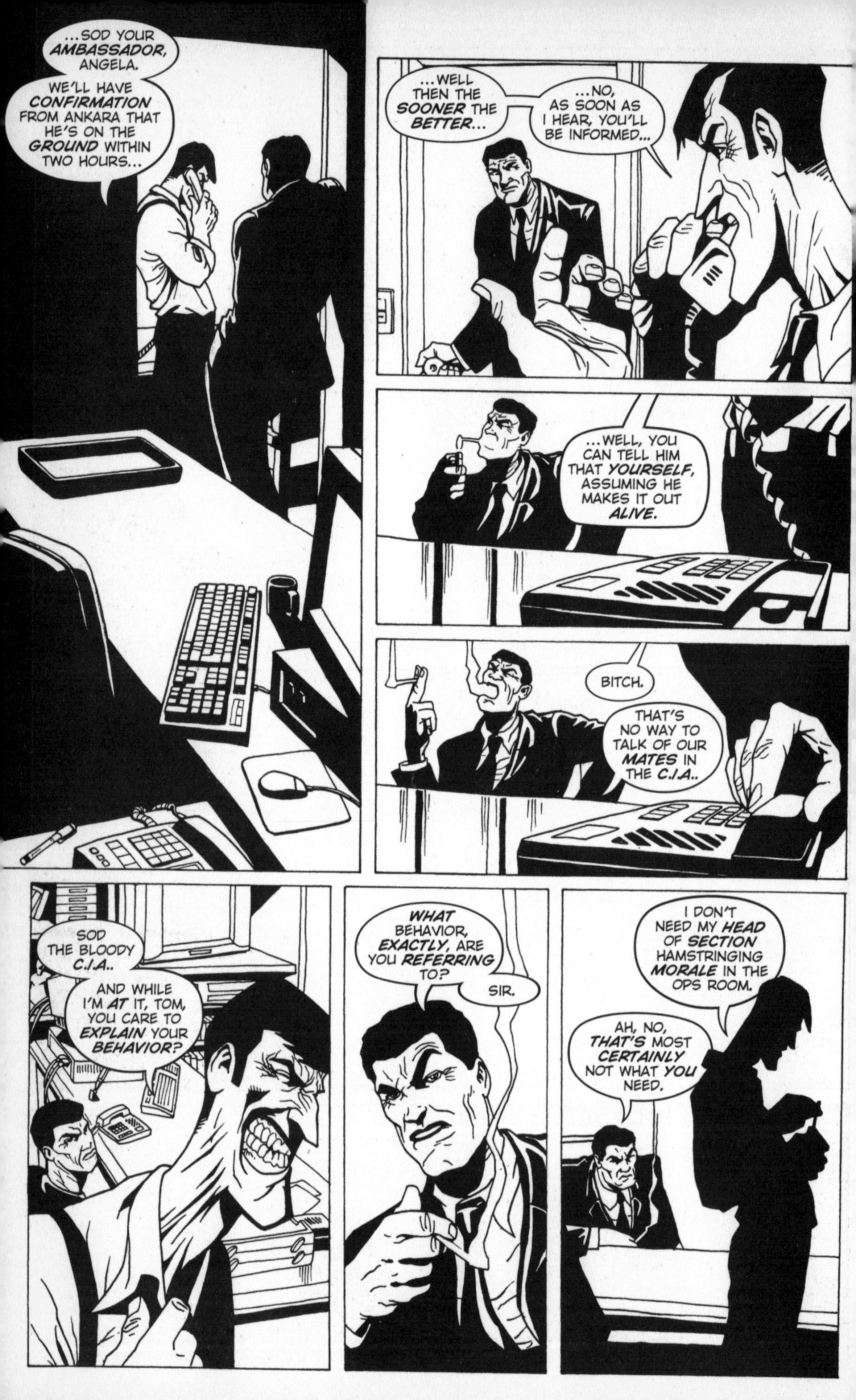
...SOD YOUR AMBASSADOR, ANGELA.
WE'LL HAVE CONFIRMATION FROM ANKARA THAT HE'S ON THE GROUND WITHIN TWO HOURS...
...WELL THEN THE SOONER THE BETTER...
...NO, AS SOON AS I HEAR, YOU'LL BE INFORMED...
...WELL, YOU CAN TELL HIM THAT YOURSELF, ASSUMING HE MAKES IT OUT ALIVE.
BITCH.
THAT'S NO WAY TO TALK OF OUR MATES IN THE C.I.A..
SOD THE BLOODY C.I.A..
AND WHILE I'M AT IT, TOM, YOU CARE TO EXPLAIN YOUR BEHAVIOR?
WHAT BEHAVIOR, EXACTLY, ARE YOU REFERRING TO?
SIR.
I DON'T NEED MY HEAD OF SECTION HAMSTRINGING MORALE IN THE OPS ROOM.
AH, NO, THAT'S MOST CERTAINLY NOT WHAT YOU NEED.

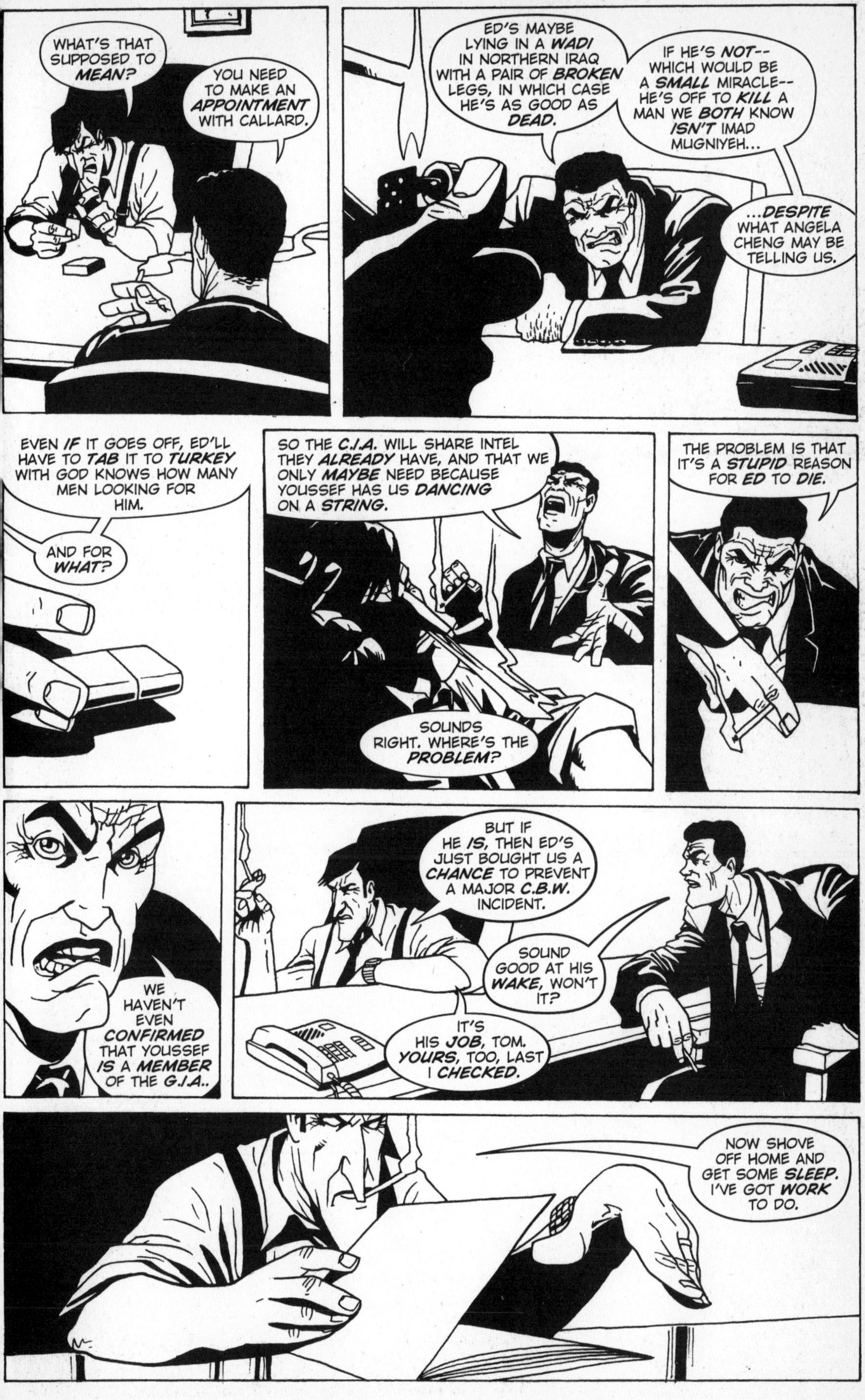
WHAT'S THAT SUPPOSED TO MEAN?
YOU NEED TO MAKE AN APPOINTMENT WITH CALLARD.
ED'S MAYBE LYING IN A WADI IN NORTHERN IRAQ WITH A PAIR OF BROKEN LEGS, IN WHICH CASE HE'S AS GOOD AS DEAD.
IF HE'S NOT-- WHICH WOULD BE A SMALL MIRACLE-- HE'S OFF TO KILL A MAN WE BOTH KNOW ISN'T IMAD MUGNIYEH...
...DESPITE WHAT ANGELA CHENG MAY BE TELLING US.
EVEN IF IT GOES OFF, ED'LL HAVE TO TAB IT TO TURKEY WITH GOD KNOWS HOW MANY MEN LOOKING FOR HIM.
AND FOR WHAT?
SO THE C.I.A. WILL SHARE INTEL THEY ALREADY HAVE, AND THAT WE ONLY MAYBE NEED BECAUSE YOUSSEF HAS US DANCING ON A STRING.
SOUNDS RIGHT. WHERE'S THE PROBLEM?
THE PROBLEM IS THAT IT'S A STUPID REASON FOR ED TO DIE.
WE HAVEN'T EVEN CONFIRMED THAT YOUSSEF IS A MEMBER OF THE G.I.A..
BUT IF HE IS, THEN ED'S JUST BOUGHT US A CHANCE TO PREVENT A MAJOR C.B.W. INCIDENT.
SOUND GOOD AT HIS WAKE, WON'T IT?
IT'S HIS JOB, TOM. YOURS, TOO, LAST I CHECKED.
NOW SHOVE OFF HOME AND GET SOME SLEEP. I'VE GOT WORK TO DO.

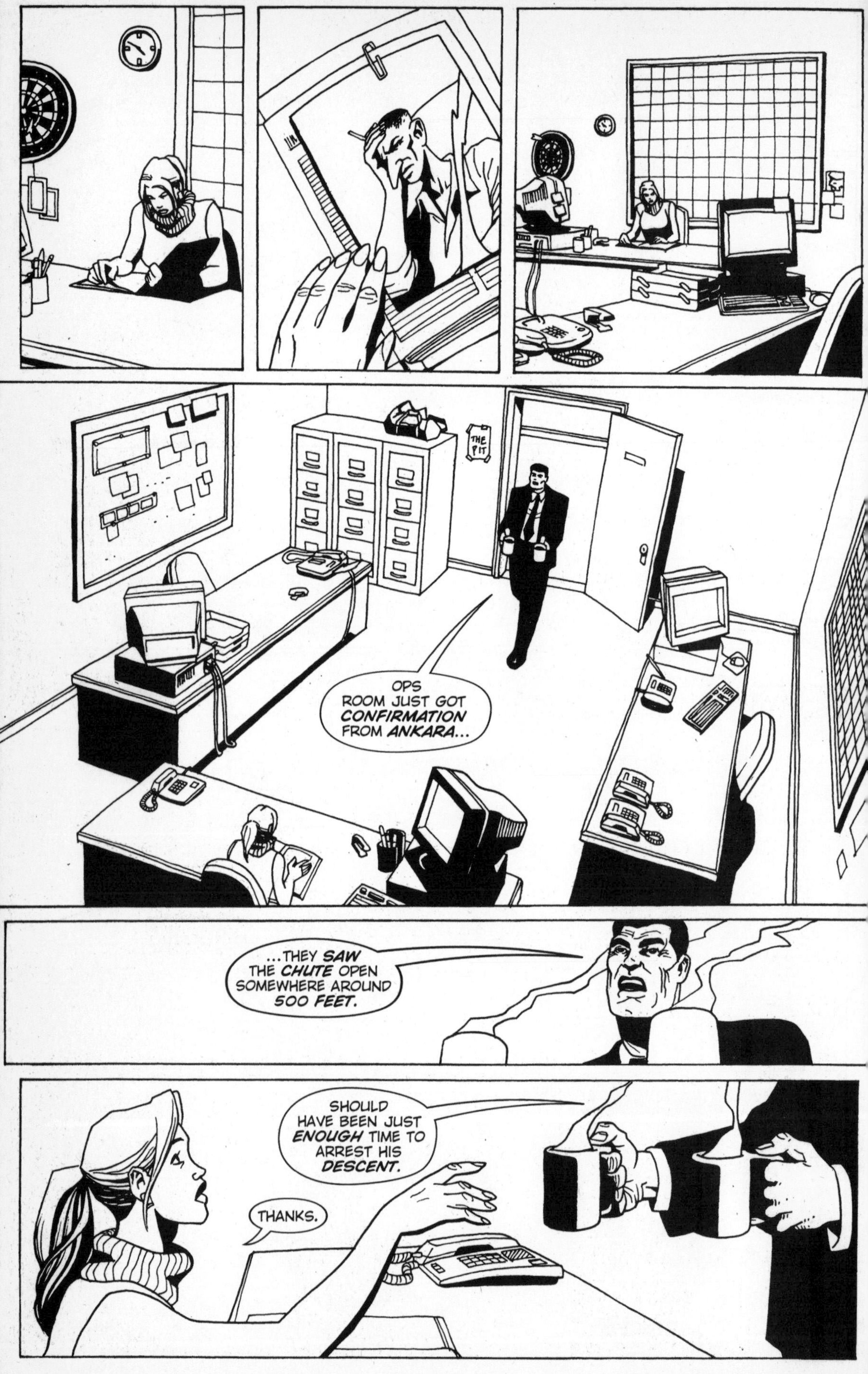
OPS ROOM JUST GOT CONFIRMATION FROM ANKARA...
...THEY SAW THE CHUTE OPEN SOMEWHERE AROUND 500 FEET.
SHOULD HAVE BEEN JUST ENOUGH TIME TO ARREST HIS DESCENT.
THANKS.

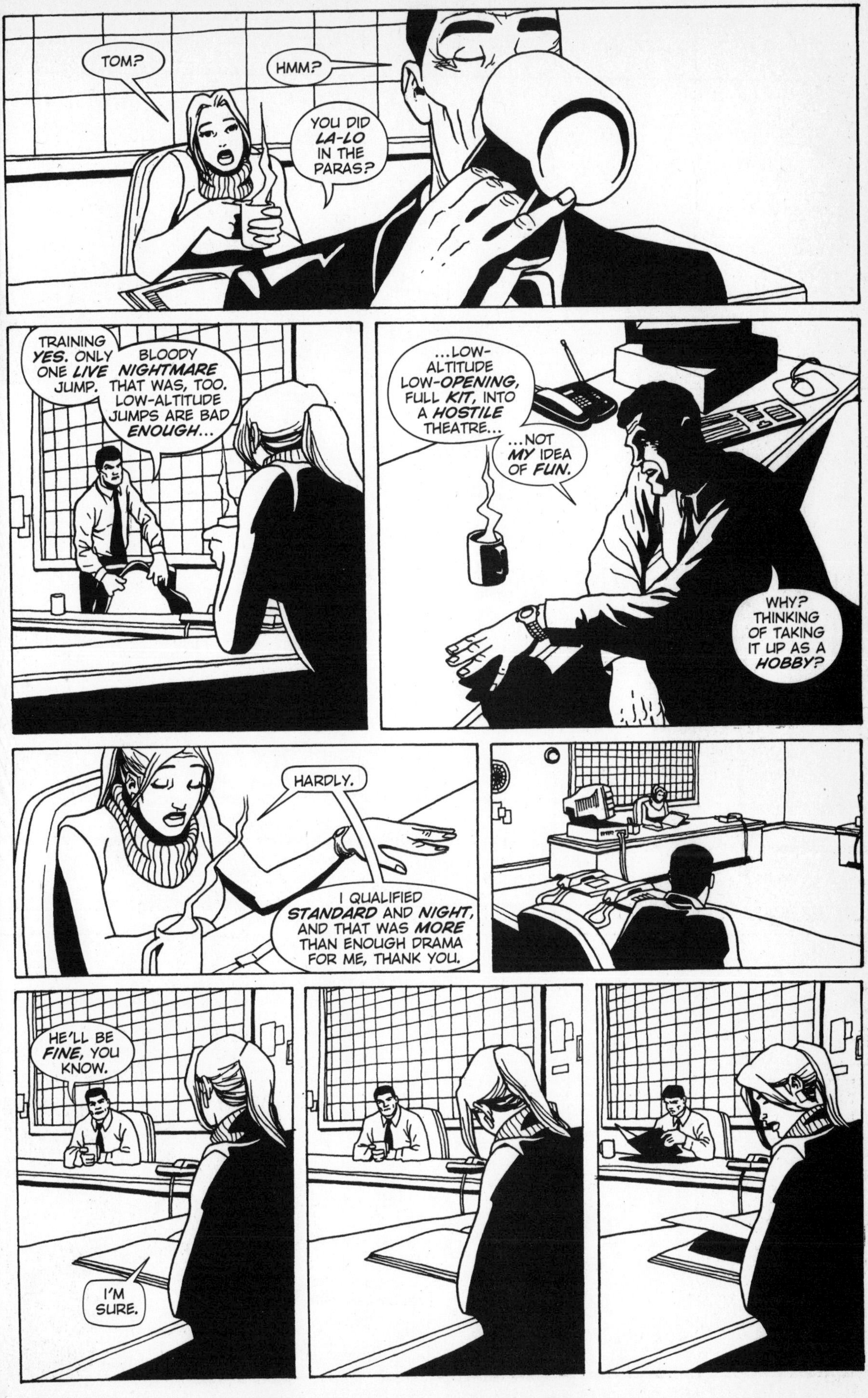
TOM?
HMM?
YOU DID LA-LO IN THE PARAS?
TRAINING YES. ONLY ONE LIVE JUMP.
BLOODY NIGHTMARE THAT WAS, TOO. LOW-ALTITUDE JUMPS ARE BAD ENOUGH...
...LOW-ALTITUDE LOW-OPENING, FULL KIT, INTO A HOSTILE THEATRE...
...NOT MY IDEA OF FUN.
WHY? THINKING OF TAKING IT UP AS A HOBBY?
HARDLY.
I QUALIFIED STANDARD AND NIGHT, AND THAT WAS MORE THAN ENOUGH DRAMA FOR ME, THANK YOU.
HE'LL BE FINE, YOU KNOW.
I'M SURE.

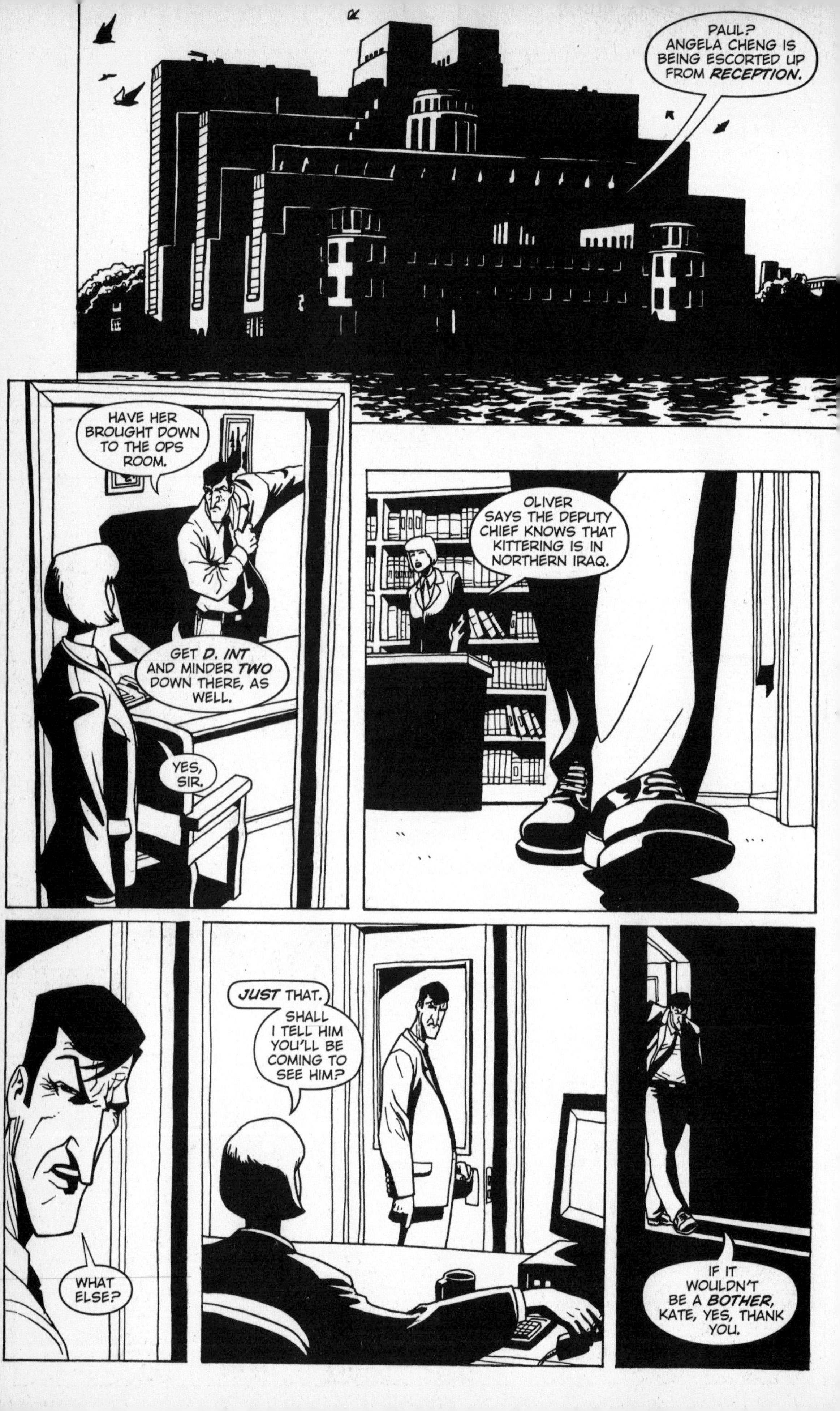
PAUL? ANGELA CHENG IS BEING ESCORTED UP FROM *RECEPTION*.
HAVE HER BROUGHT DOWN TO THE OPS ROOM.
GET *D. INT* AND MINDER *TWO* DOWN THERE, AS WELL.
YES, SIR.
OLIVER SAYS THE DEPUTY CHIEF KNOWS THAT KITTERING IS IN NORTHERN IRAQ.
WHAT ELSE?
JUST THAT. SHALL I TELL HIM YOU'LL BE COMING TO SEE HIM?
IF IT WOULDN'T BE A *BOTHER*, KATE, YES, THANK YOU.

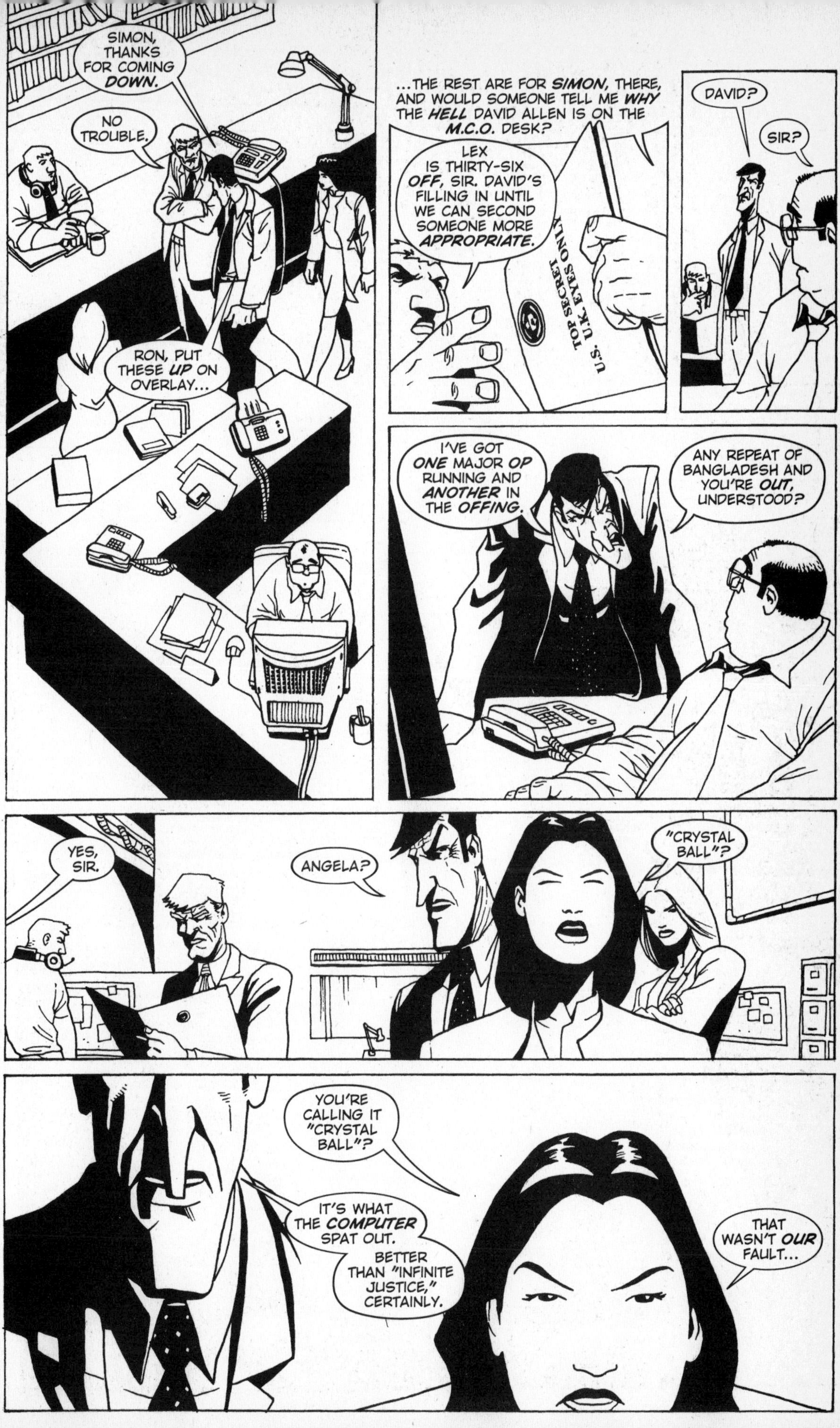
SIMON, THANKS FOR COMING DOWN.
NO TROUBLE.
RON, PUT THESE UP ON OVERLAY...
...THE REST ARE FOR SIMON, THERE, AND WOULD SOMEONE TELL ME WHY THE HELL DAVID ALLEN IS ON THE M.C.O. DESK?
LEX IS THIRTY-SIX OFF, SIR. DAVID'S FILLING IN UNTIL WE CAN SECOND SOMEONE MORE APPROPRIATE.
TOP SECRET
U.S. U.K. EYES ONLY
DAVID?
SIR?
I'VE GOT ONE MAJOR OP RUNNING AND ANOTHER IN THE OFFING.
ANY REPEAT OF BANGLADESH AND YOU'RE OUT, UNDERSTOOD?
YES, SIR.
ANGELA?
"CRYSTAL BALL"?
YOU'RE CALLING IT "CRYSTAL BALL"?
IT'S WHAT THE COMPUTER SPAT OUT.
BETTER THAN "INFINITE JUSTICE," CERTAINLY.
THAT WASN'T OUR FAULT...

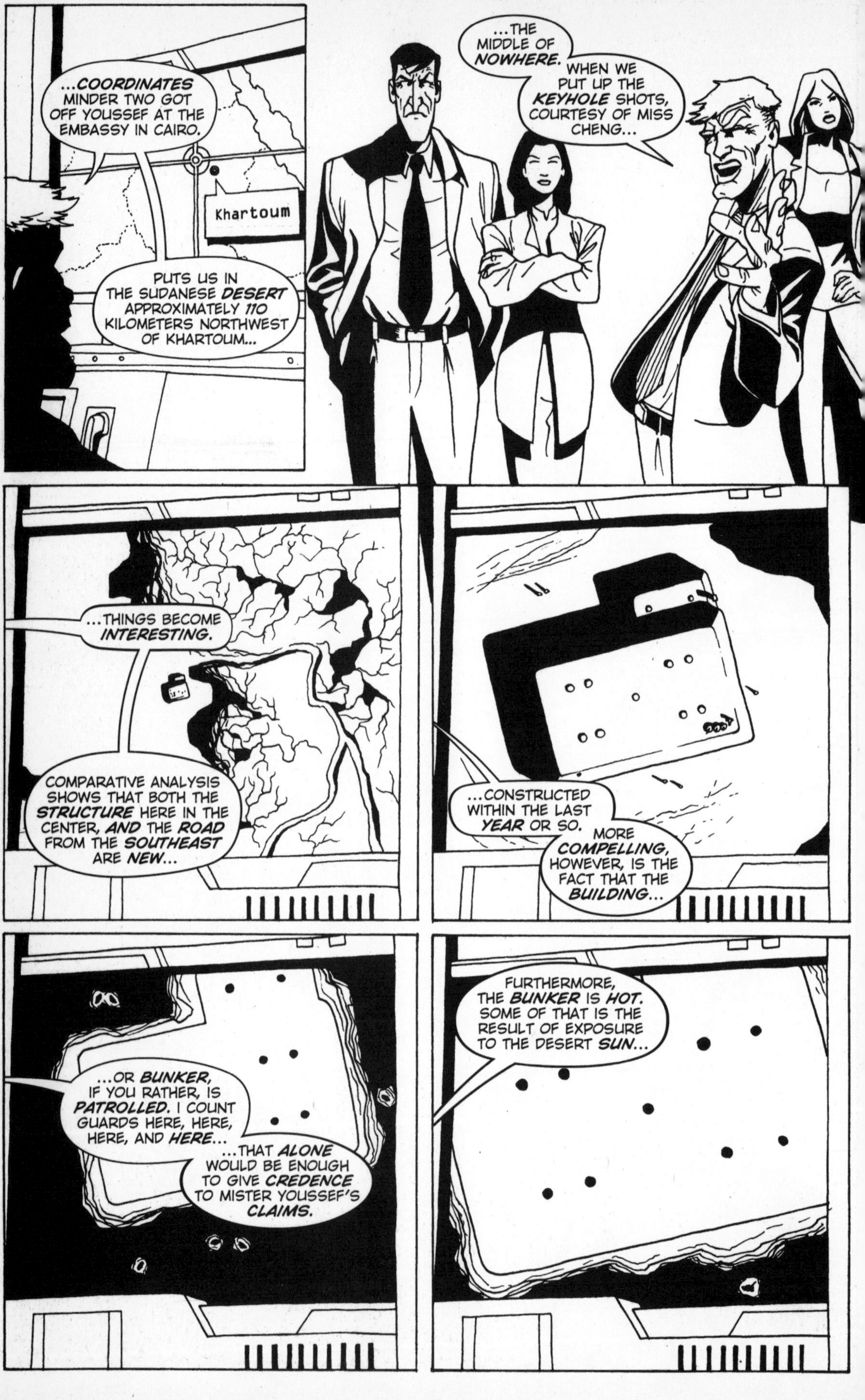
...COORDINATES MINDER TWO GOT OFF YOUSSEF AT THE EMBASSY IN CAIRO.
Khartoum
PUTS US IN THE SUDANESE DESERT APPROXIMATELY 110 KILOMETERS NORTHWEST OF KHARTOUM...
...THE MIDDLE OF NOWHERE.
WHEN WE PUT UP THE KEYHOLE SHOTS, COURTESY OF MISS CHENG...
...THINGS BECOME INTERESTING.
COMPARATIVE ANALYSIS SHOWS THAT BOTH THE STRUCTURE HERE IN THE CENTER, AND THE ROAD FROM THE SOUTHEAST ARE NEW...
...CONSTRUCTED WITHIN THE LAST YEAR OR SO.
MORE COMPELLING, HOWEVER, IS THE FACT THAT THE BUILDING...
...OR BUNKER, IF YOU RATHER, IS PATROLLED. I COUNT GUARDS HERE, HERE, HERE, AND HERE...
...THAT ALONE WOULD BE ENOUGH TO GIVE CREDENCE TO MISTER YOUSSEF'S CLAIMS.
FURTHERMORE, THE BUNKER IS HOT. SOME OF THAT IS THE RESULT OF EXPOSURE TO THE DESERT SUN...

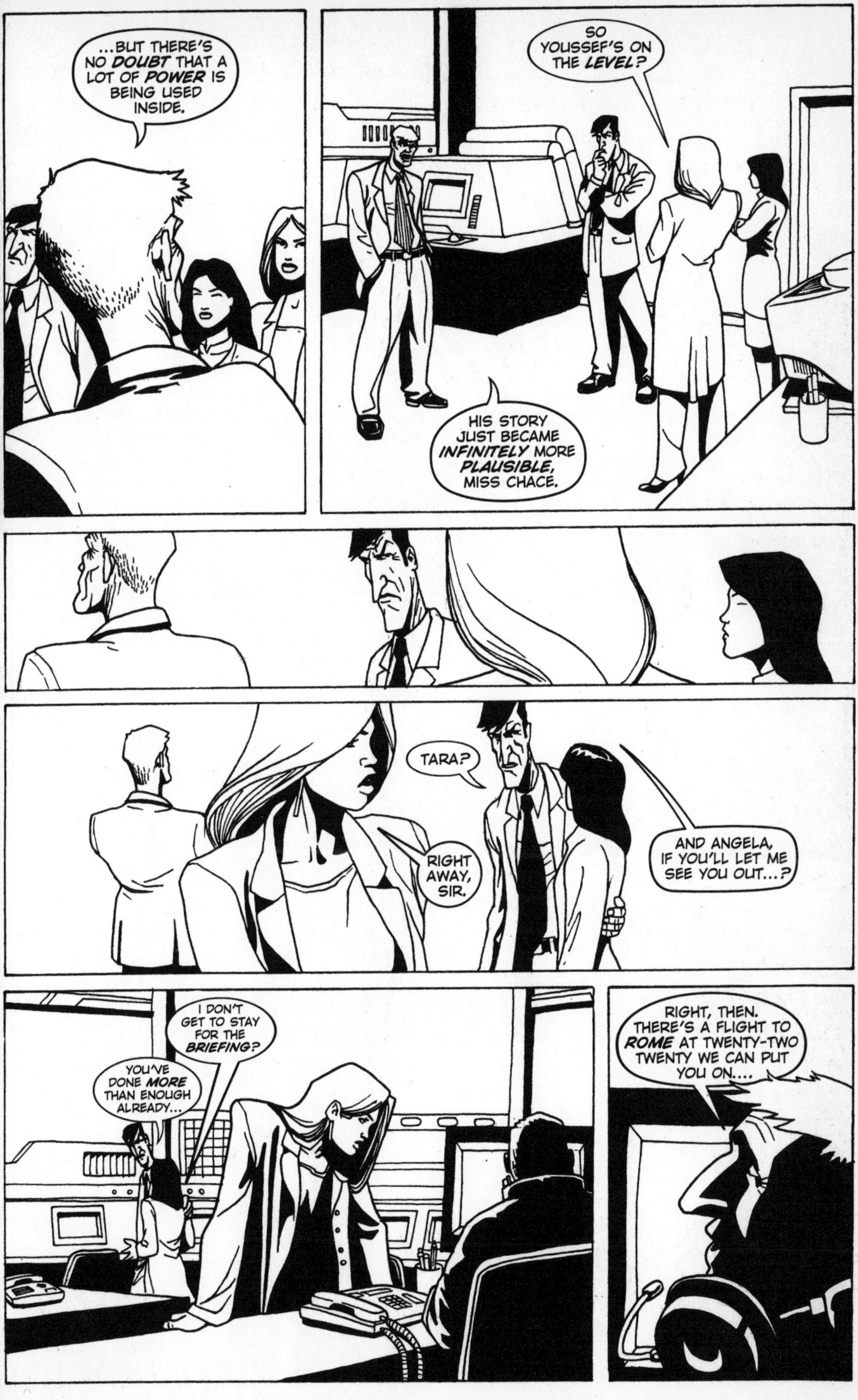
...BUT THERE'S NO DOUBT THAT A LOT OF POWER IS BEING USED INSIDE.
SO YOUSSEF'S ON THE LEVEL?
HIS STORY JUST BECAME INFINITELY MORE PLAUSIBLE, MISS CHACE.
TARA?
RIGHT AWAY, SIR.
AND ANGELA, IF YOU'LL LET ME SEE YOU OUT...?
I DON'T GET TO STAY FOR THE BRIEFING?
YOU'VE DONE MORE THAN ENOUGH ALREADY...
RIGHT, THEN. THERE'S A FLIGHT TO ROME AT TWENTY-TWO TWENTY WE CAN PUT YOU ON....

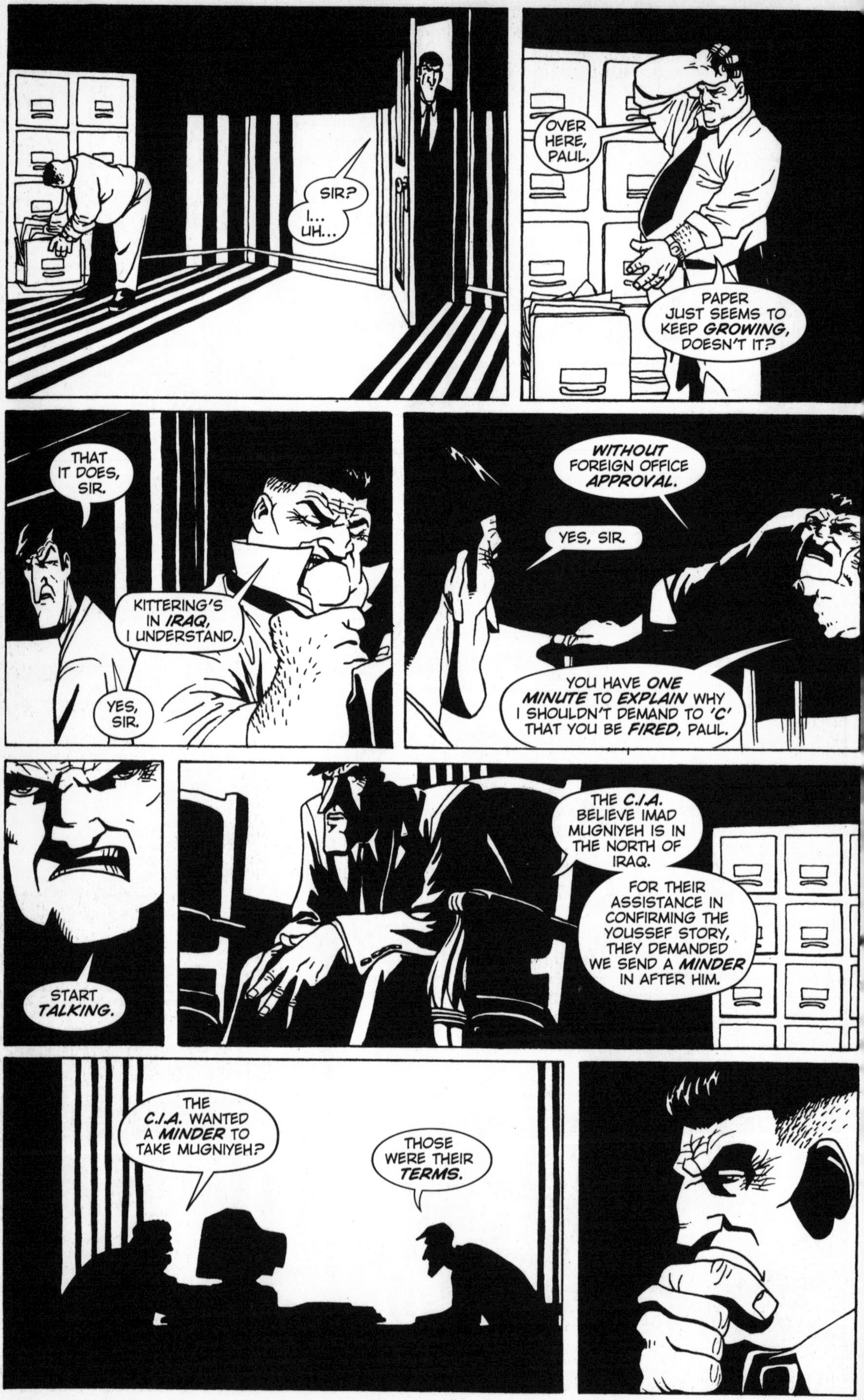
SIR?
I... UH...
OVER HERE, PAUL.
PAPER JUST SEEMS TO KEEP GROWING, DOESN'T IT?
THAT IT DOES, SIR.
KITTERING'S IN IRAQ, I UNDERSTAND.
YES, SIR.
WITHOUT FOREIGN OFFICE APPROVAL.
YES, SIR.
YOU HAVE ONE MINUTE TO EXPLAIN WHY I SHOULDN'T DEMAND TO 'C' THAT YOU BE FIRED, PAUL.
START TALKING.
THE C.I.A. BELIEVE IMAD MUGNIYEH IS IN THE NORTH OF IRAQ.
FOR THEIR ASSISTANCE IN CONFIRMING THE YOUSSEF STORY, THEY DEMANDED WE SEND A MINDER IN AFTER HIM.
THE C.I.A. WANTED A MINDER TO TAKE MUGNIYEH?
THOSE WERE THEIR TERMS.

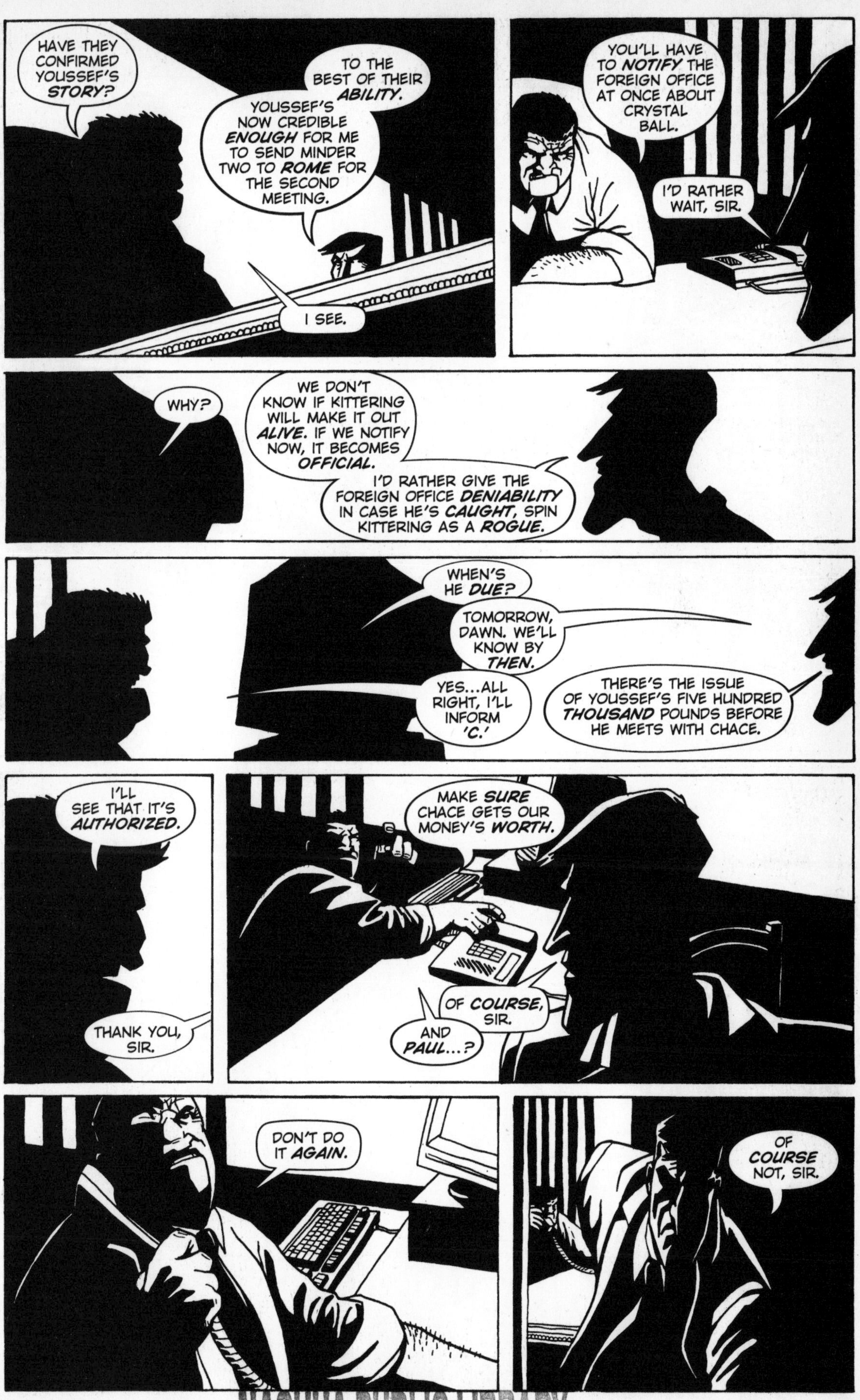
HAVE THEY CONFIRMED YOUSSEF'S STORY?
TO THE BEST OF THEIR ABILITY.
YOUSSEF'S NOW CREDIBLE ENOUGH FOR ME TO SEND MINDER TWO TO ROME FOR THE SECOND MEETING.
I SEE.
YOU'LL HAVE TO NOTIFY THE FOREIGN OFFICE AT ONCE ABOUT CRYSTAL BALL.
I'D RATHER WAIT, SIR.
WHY?
WE DON'T KNOW IF KITTERING WILL MAKE IT OUT ALIVE. IF WE NOTIFY NOW, IT BECOMES OFFICIAL.
I'D RATHER GIVE THE FOREIGN OFFICE DENIABILITY IN CASE HE'S CAUGHT, SPIN KITTERING AS A ROGUE.
WHEN'S HE DUE?
TOMORROW, DAWN. WE'LL KNOW BY THEN.
YES...ALL RIGHT, I'LL INFORM 'C.'
THERE'S THE ISSUE OF YOUSSEF'S FIVE HUNDRED THOUSAND POUNDS BEFORE HE MEETS WITH CHACE.
I'LL SEE THAT IT'S AUTHORIZED.
THANK YOU, SIR.
MAKE SURE CHACE GETS OUR MONEY'S WORTH.
OF COURSE, SIR.
AND PAUL...?
DON'T DO IT AGAIN.
OF COURSE NOT, SIR.

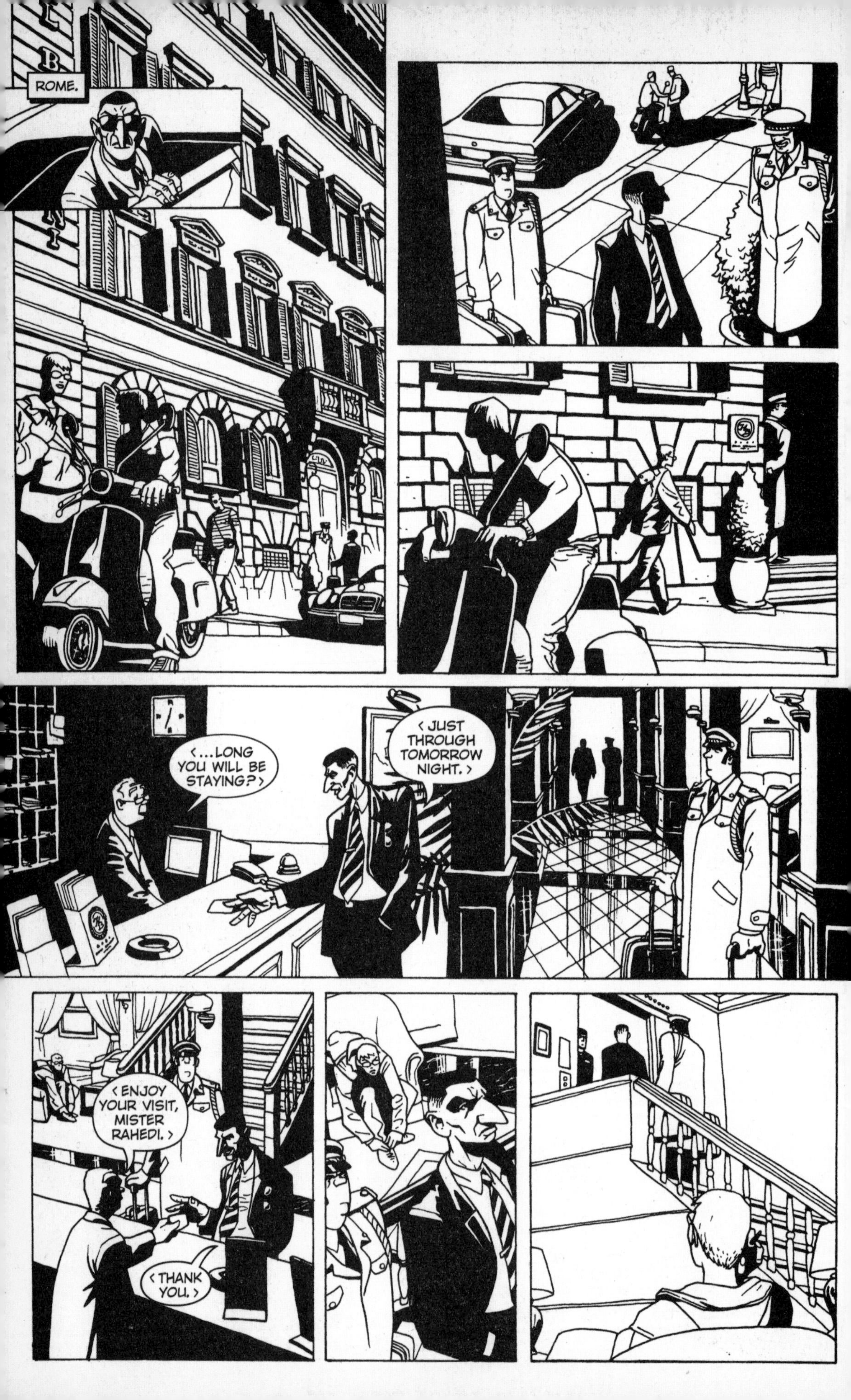
ROME.
< ...LONG YOU WILL BE STAYING? >
< JUST THROUGH TOMORROW NIGHT. >
< ENJOY YOUR VISIT, MISTER RAHEDI. >
< THANK YOU. >

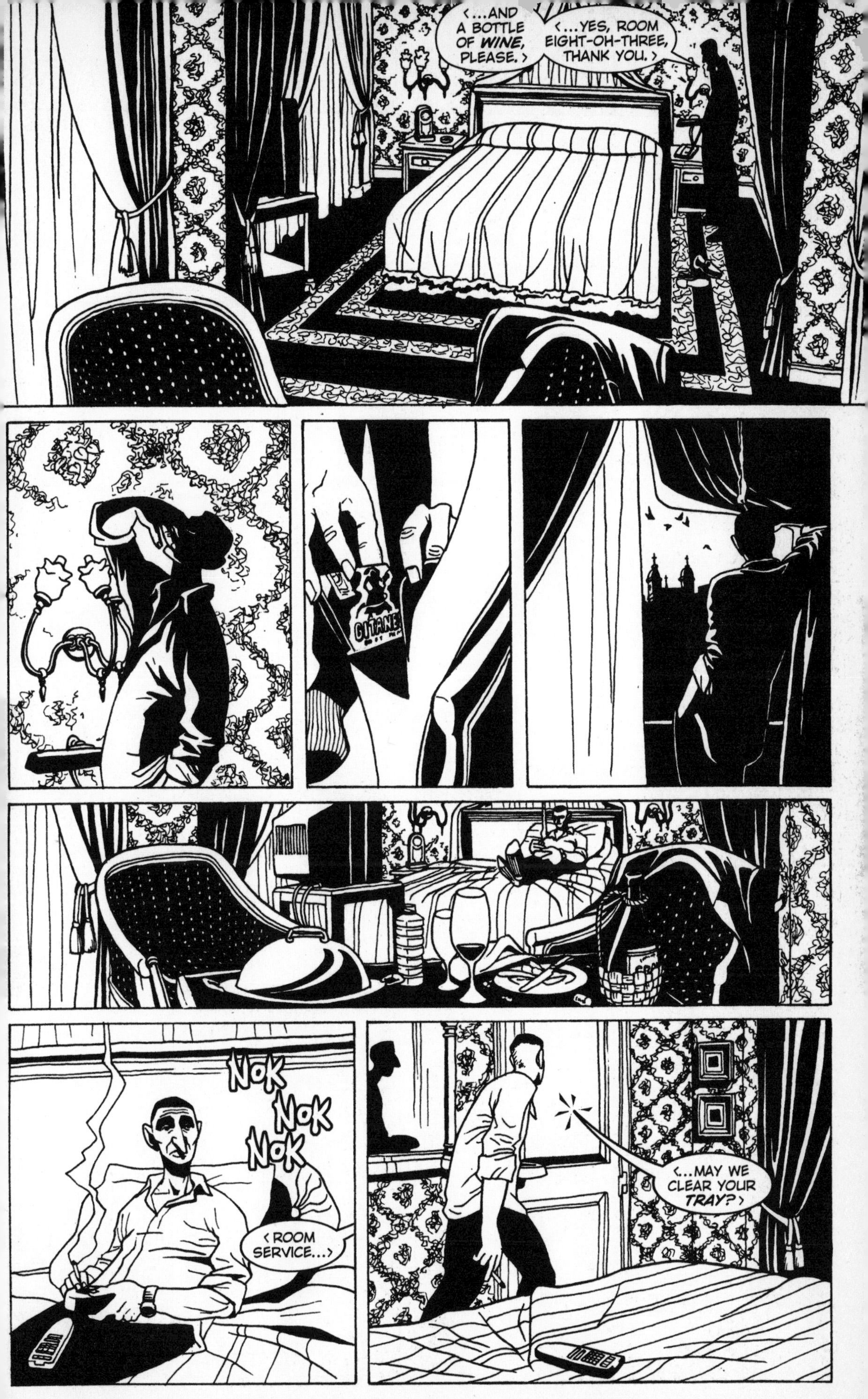
‹...AND A BOTTLE OF WINE, PLEASE.›
‹...YES, ROOM EIGHT-OH-THREE, THANK YOU.›
GITANES
NOK NOK NOK
‹ROOM SERVICE...›
‹...MAY WE CLEAR YOUR TRAY?›

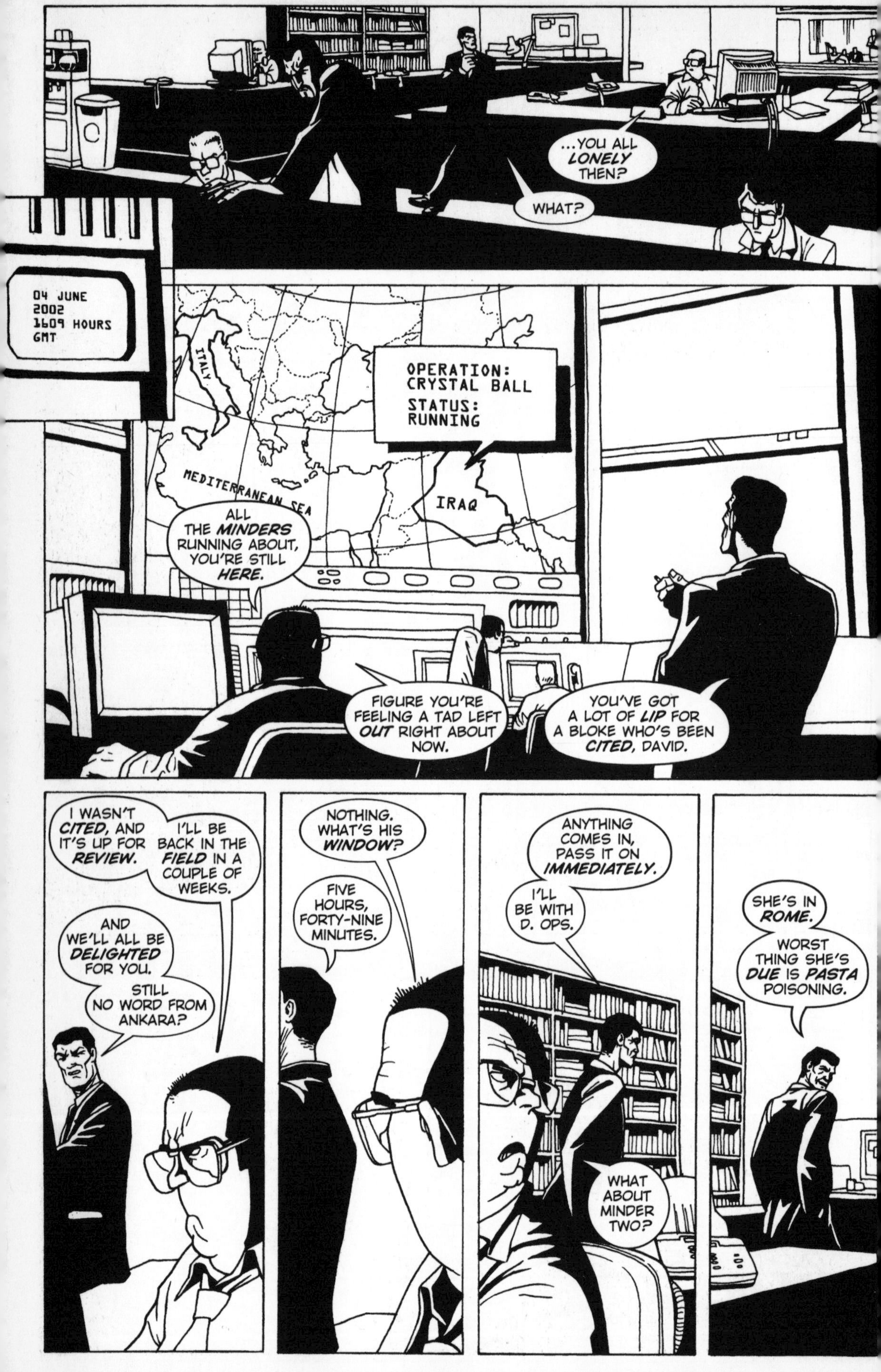

...YOU ALL LONELY THEN?
WHAT?
04 JUNE 2002 1609 HOURS GMT
ITALY
OPERATION: CRYSTAL BALL
STATUS: RUNNING
MEDITERRANEAN SEA
IRAQ
ALL THE MINDERS RUNNING ABOUT, YOU'RE STILL HERE.
FIGURE YOU'RE FEELING A TAD LEFT OUT RIGHT ABOUT NOW.
YOU'VE GOT A LOT OF LIP FOR A BLOKE WHO'S BEEN CITED, DAVID.
I WASN'T CITED, AND IT'S UP FOR REVIEW.
I'LL BE BACK IN THE FIELD IN A COUPLE OF WEEKS.
AND WE'LL ALL BE DELIGHTED FOR YOU.
STILL NO WORD FROM ANKARA?
NOTHING. WHAT'S HIS WINDOW?
FIVE HOURS, FORTY-NINE MINUTES.
ANYTHING COMES IN, PASS IT ON IMMEDIATELY.
I'LL BE WITH D. OPS.
WHAT ABOUT MINDER TWO?
SHE'S IN ROME.
WORST THING SHE'S DUE IS PASTA POISONING.

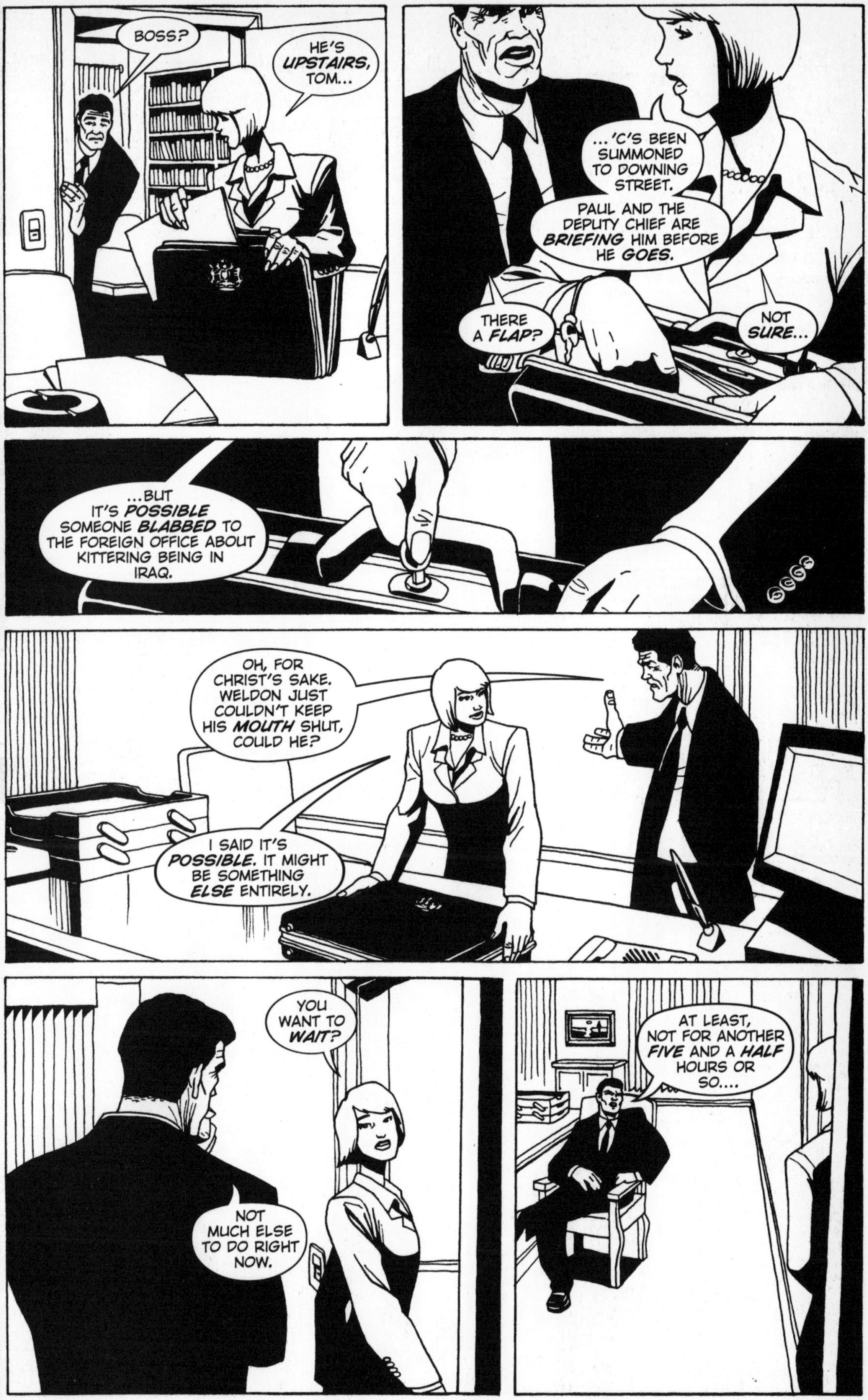
BOSS?
HE'S *UPSTAIRS,* TOM...
...'C'S BEEN SUMMONED TO DOWNING STREET.
PAUL AND THE DEPUTY CHIEF ARE *BRIEFING* HIM BEFORE HE *GOES.*
THERE A *FLAP?*
NOT *SURE...*
...BUT IT'S *POSSIBLE* SOMEONE *BLABBED* TO THE FOREIGN OFFICE ABOUT KITTERING BEING IN IRAQ.
OH, FOR CHRIST'S SAKE. WELDON JUST COULDN'T KEEP HIS *MOUTH* SHUT, COULD HE?
I SAID IT'S *POSSIBLE.* IT MIGHT BE SOMETHING *ELSE* ENTIRELY.
YOU WANT TO *WAIT?*
NOT MUCH ELSE TO DO RIGHT NOW.
AT LEAST, NOT FOR ANOTHER *FIVE* AND A *HALF* HOURS OR SO....

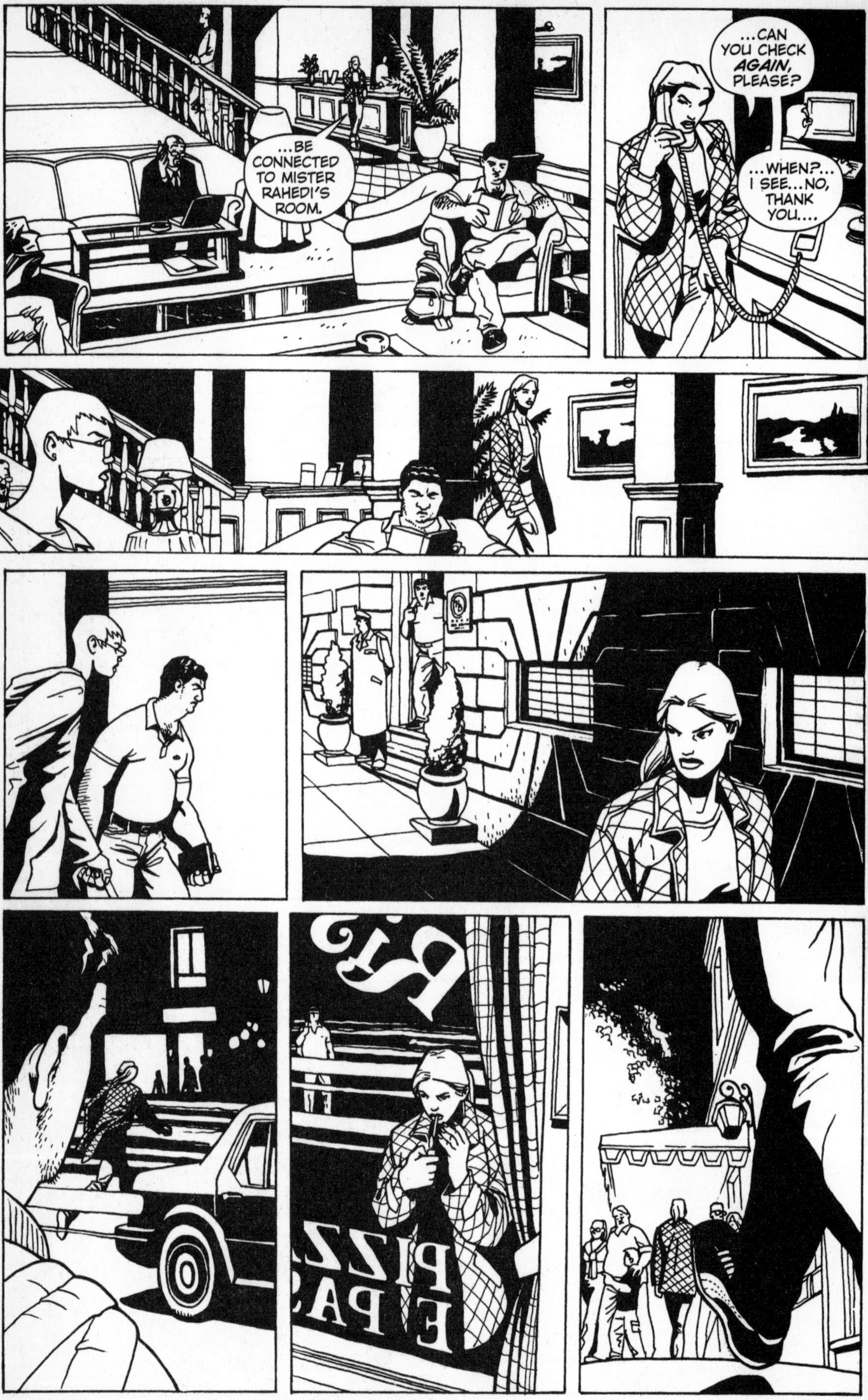
...BE CONNECTED TO MISTER RAHEDI'S ROOM.
...CAN YOU CHECK AGAIN, PLEASE?
...WHEN?... I SEE...NO, THANK YOU....
PIZZ
E PAS

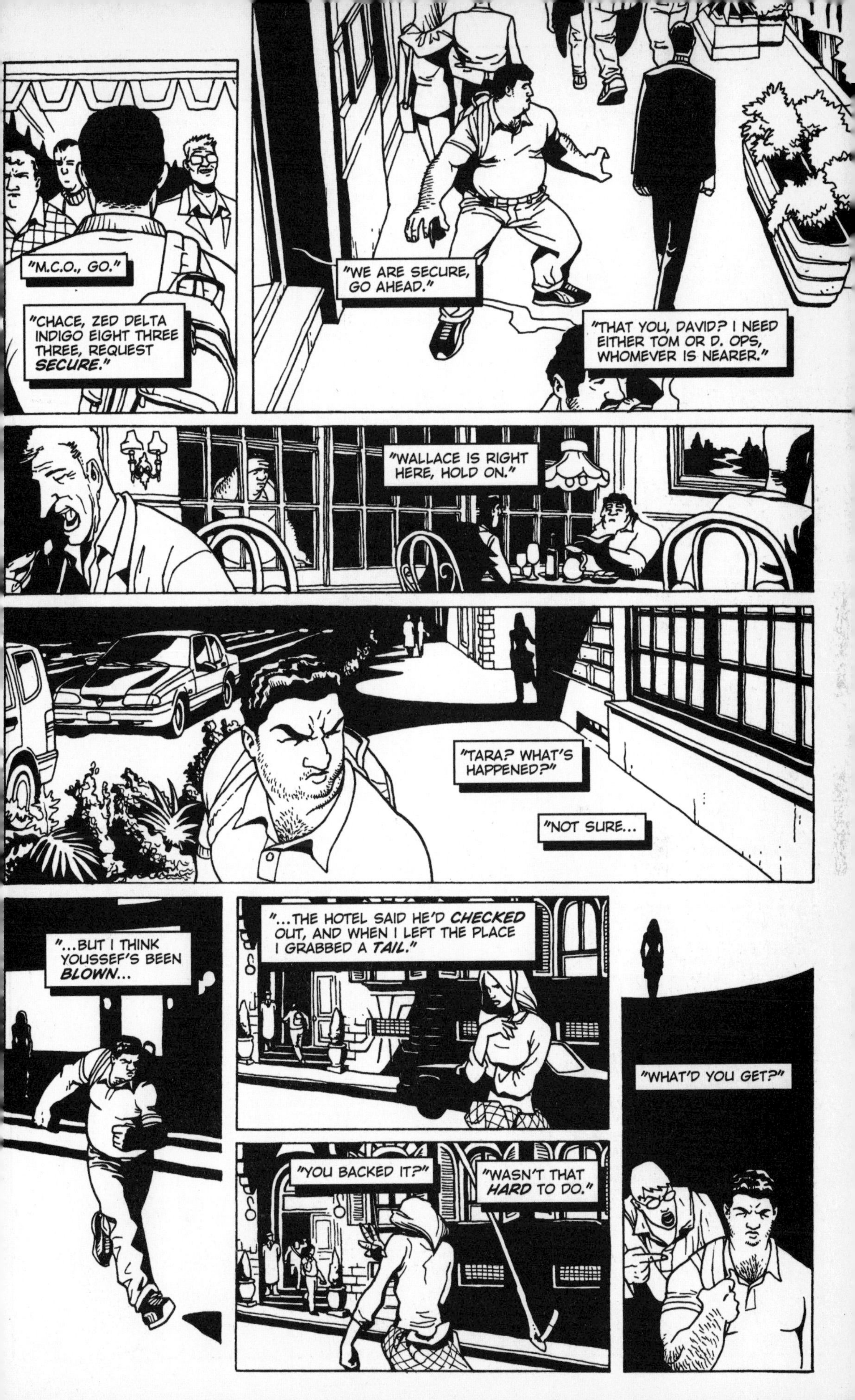
"M.C.O., GO."
"CHACE, ZED DELTA INDIGO EIGHT THREE THREE, REQUEST **SECURE.**"
"WE ARE SECURE, GO AHEAD."
"THAT YOU, DAVID? I NEED EITHER TOM OR D. OPS, WHOMEVER IS NEARER."
"WALLACE IS RIGHT HERE, HOLD ON."
"TARA? WHAT'S HAPPENED?"
"NOT SURE...
"...BUT I THINK YOUSSEF'S BEEN **BLOWN**...
"...THE HOTEL SAID HE'D **CHECKED** OUT, AND WHEN I LEFT THE PLACE I GRABBED A **TAIL.**"
"WHAT'D YOU GET?"
"YOU BACKED IT?"
"WASN'T THAT **HARD** TO DO."

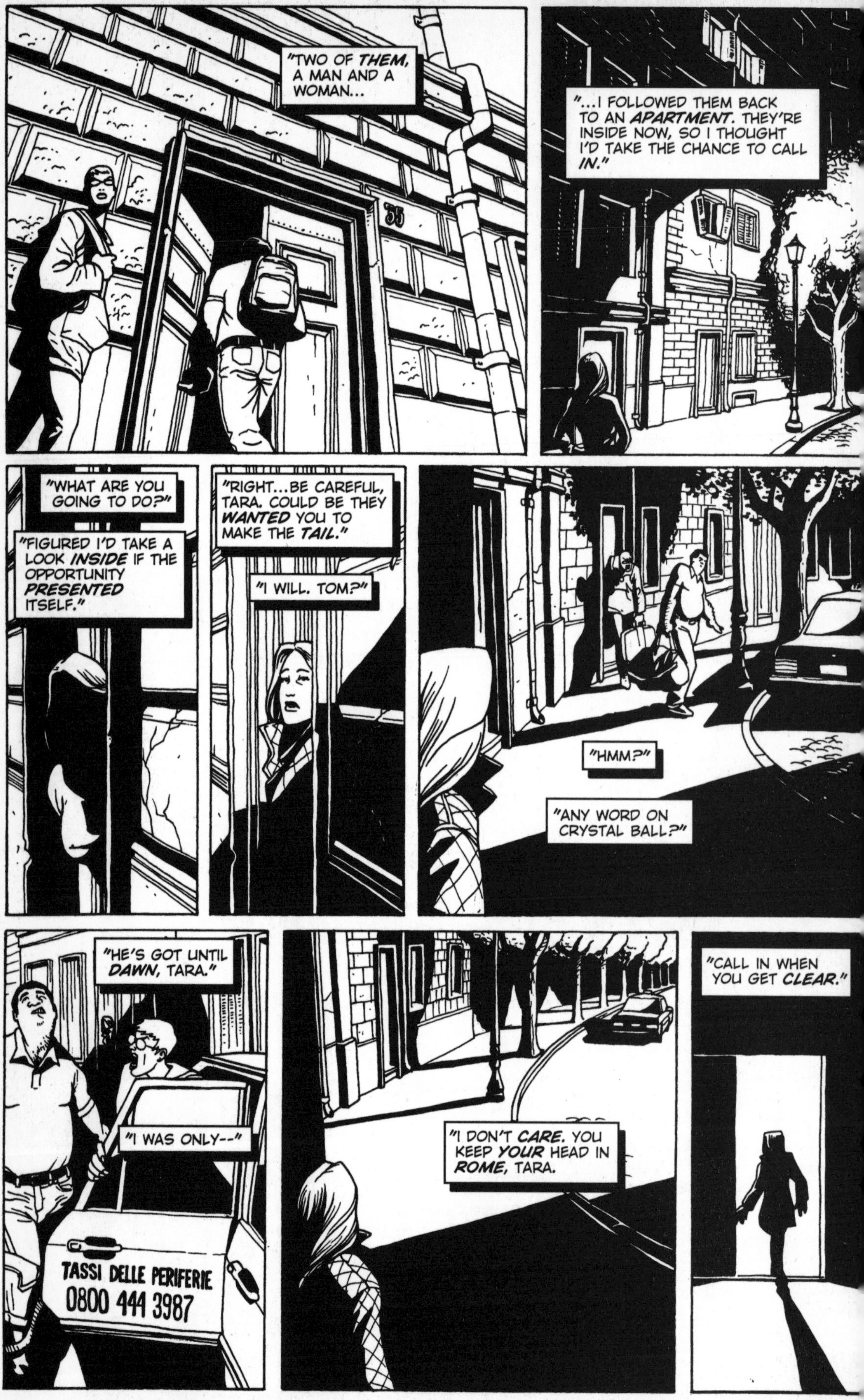
"TWO OF THEM, A MAN AND A WOMAN...
"...I FOLLOWED THEM BACK TO AN APARTMENT. THEY'RE INSIDE NOW, SO I THOUGHT I'D TAKE THE CHANCE TO CALL IN."
"WHAT ARE YOU GOING TO DO?"
"FIGURED I'D TAKE A LOOK INSIDE IF THE OPPORTUNITY PRESENTED ITSELF."
"RIGHT...BE CAREFUL, TARA. COULD BE THEY WANTED YOU TO MAKE THE TAIL."
"I WILL. TOM?"
"HMM?"
"ANY WORD ON CRYSTAL BALL?"
"HE'S GOT UNTIL DAWN, TARA."
"I WAS ONLY--"
TASSI DELLE PERIFERIE
0800 444 3987
"I DON'T CARE. YOU KEEP YOUR HEAD IN ROME, TARA.
"CALL IN WHEN YOU GET CLEAR."

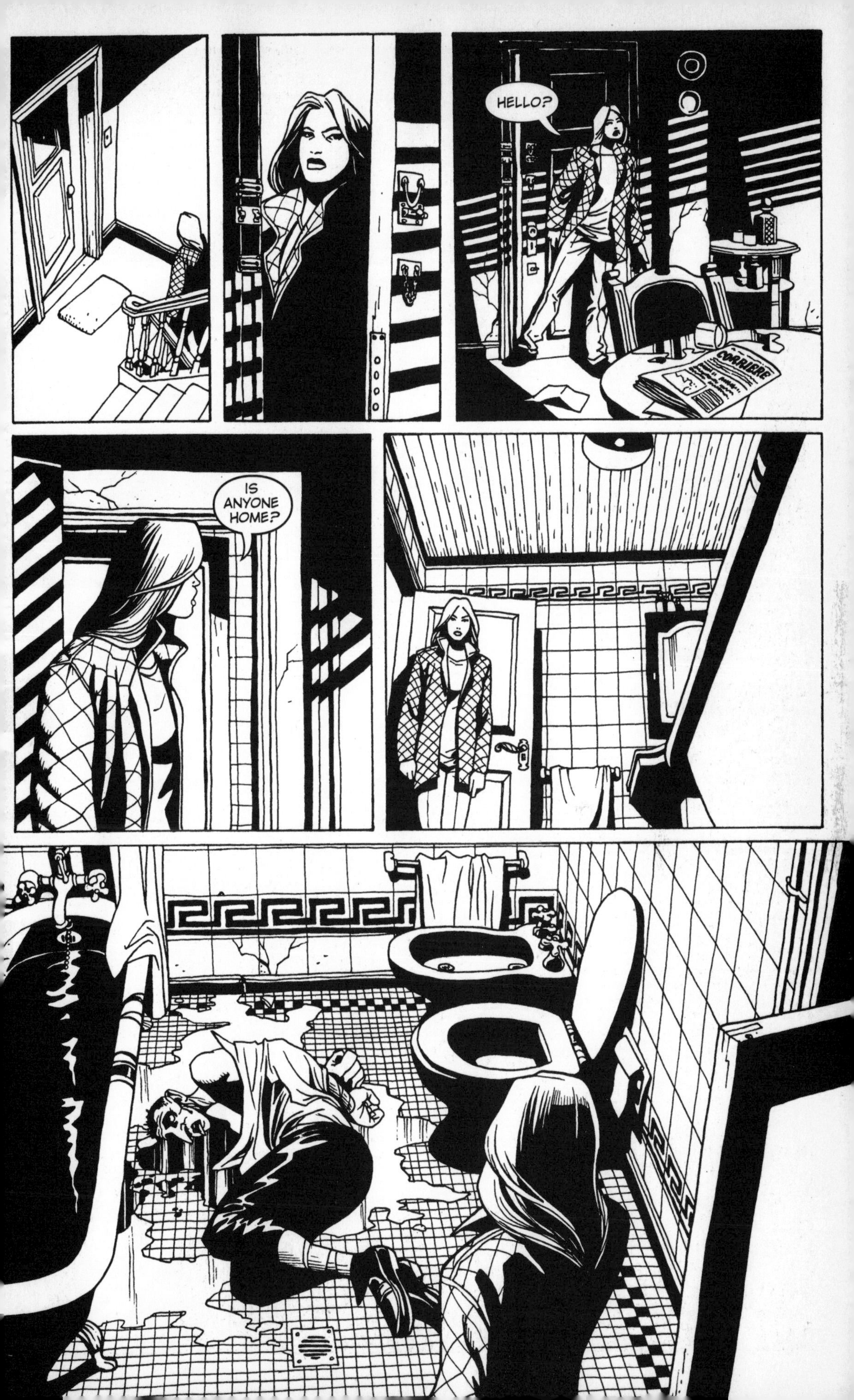
HELLO?
CORRIERE
IS ANYONE HOME?

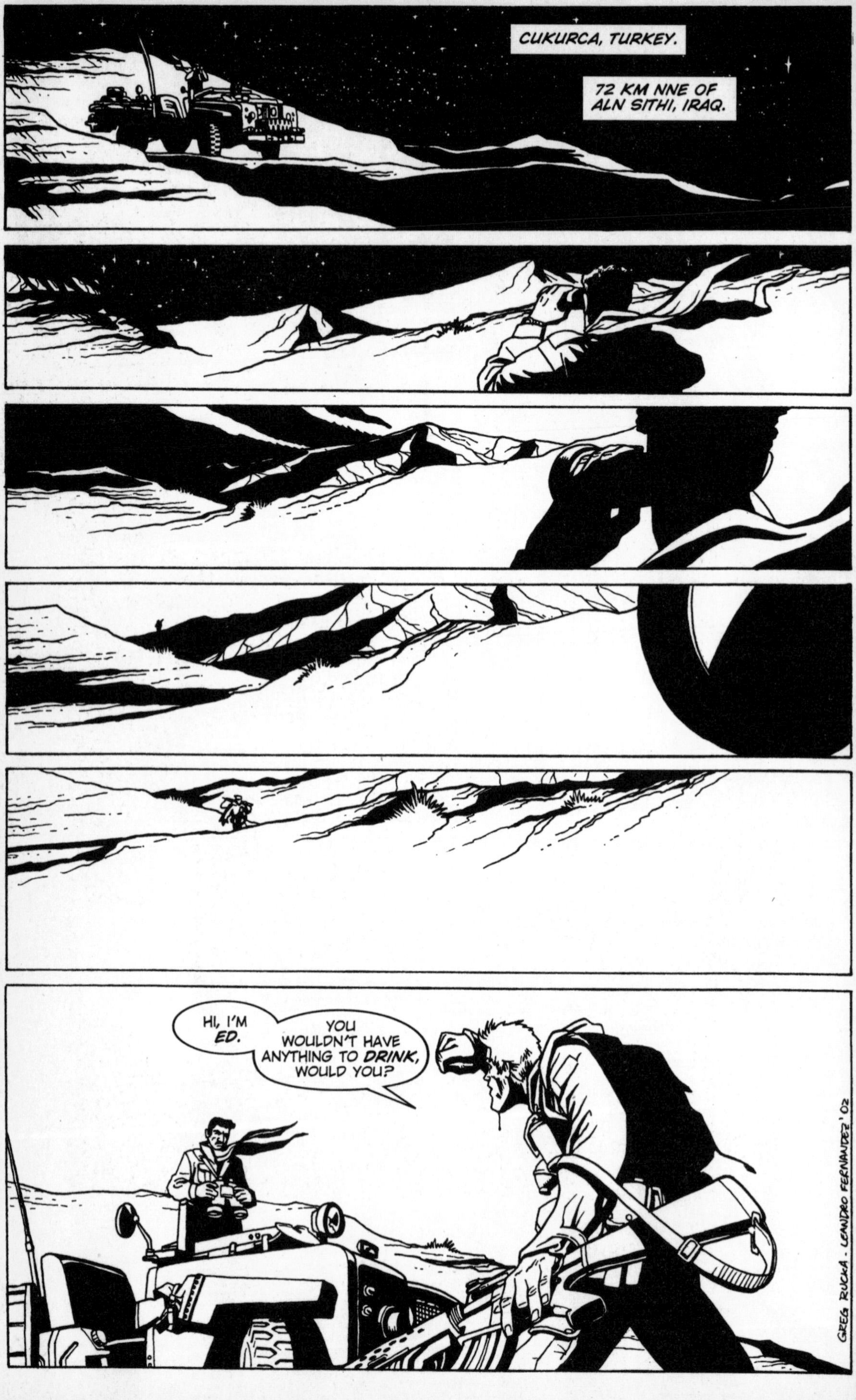
CUKURCA, TURKEY.
72 KM NNE OF ALN SITHI, IRAQ.
HI, I'M ED.
YOU WOULDN'T HAVE ANYTHING TO DRINK, WOULD YOU?
GREG RUCKA · LEANDRO FERNANDEZ '02

CHAPTER 4

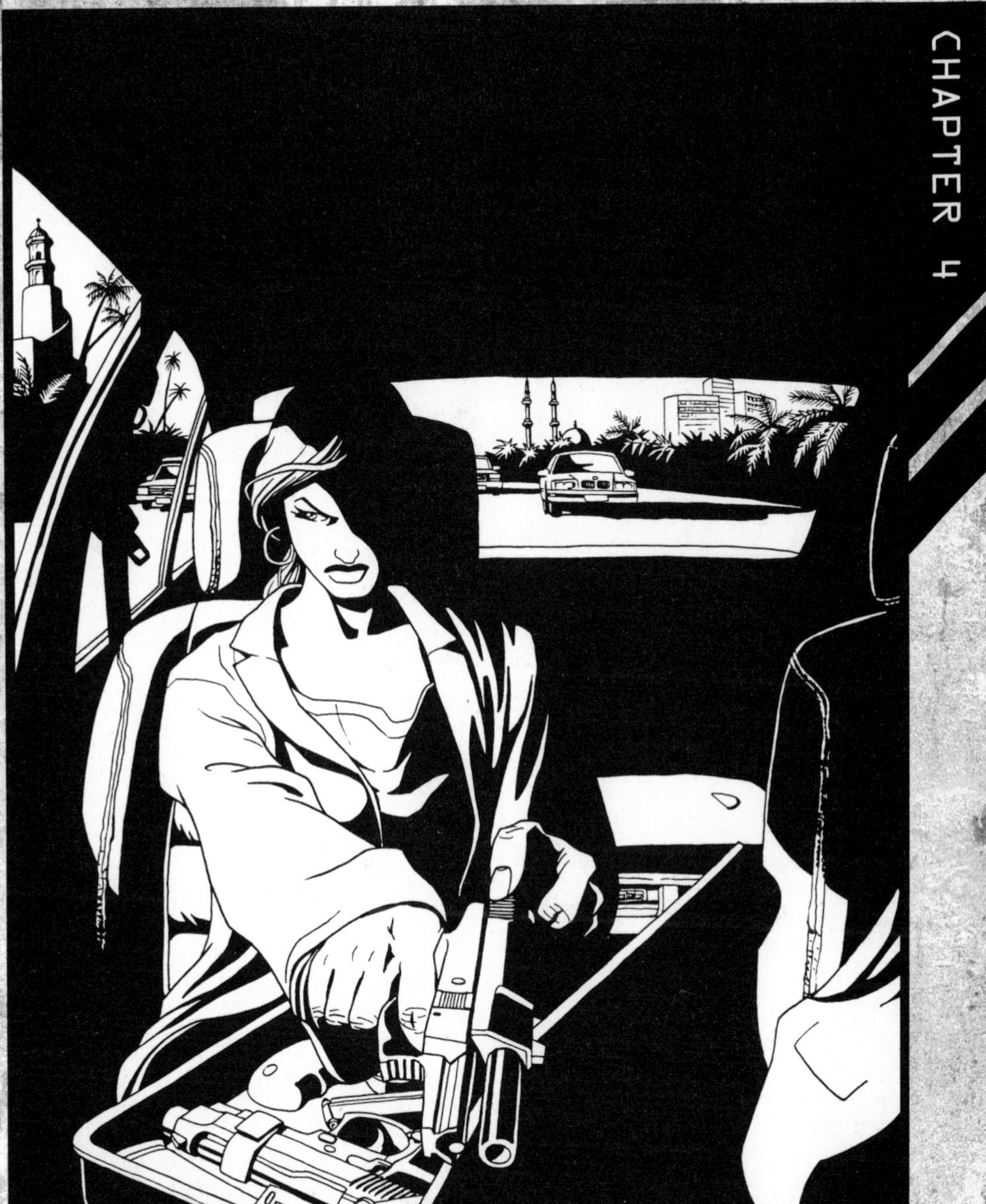
LEANDRO FERNANDEZ '02

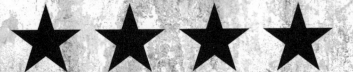

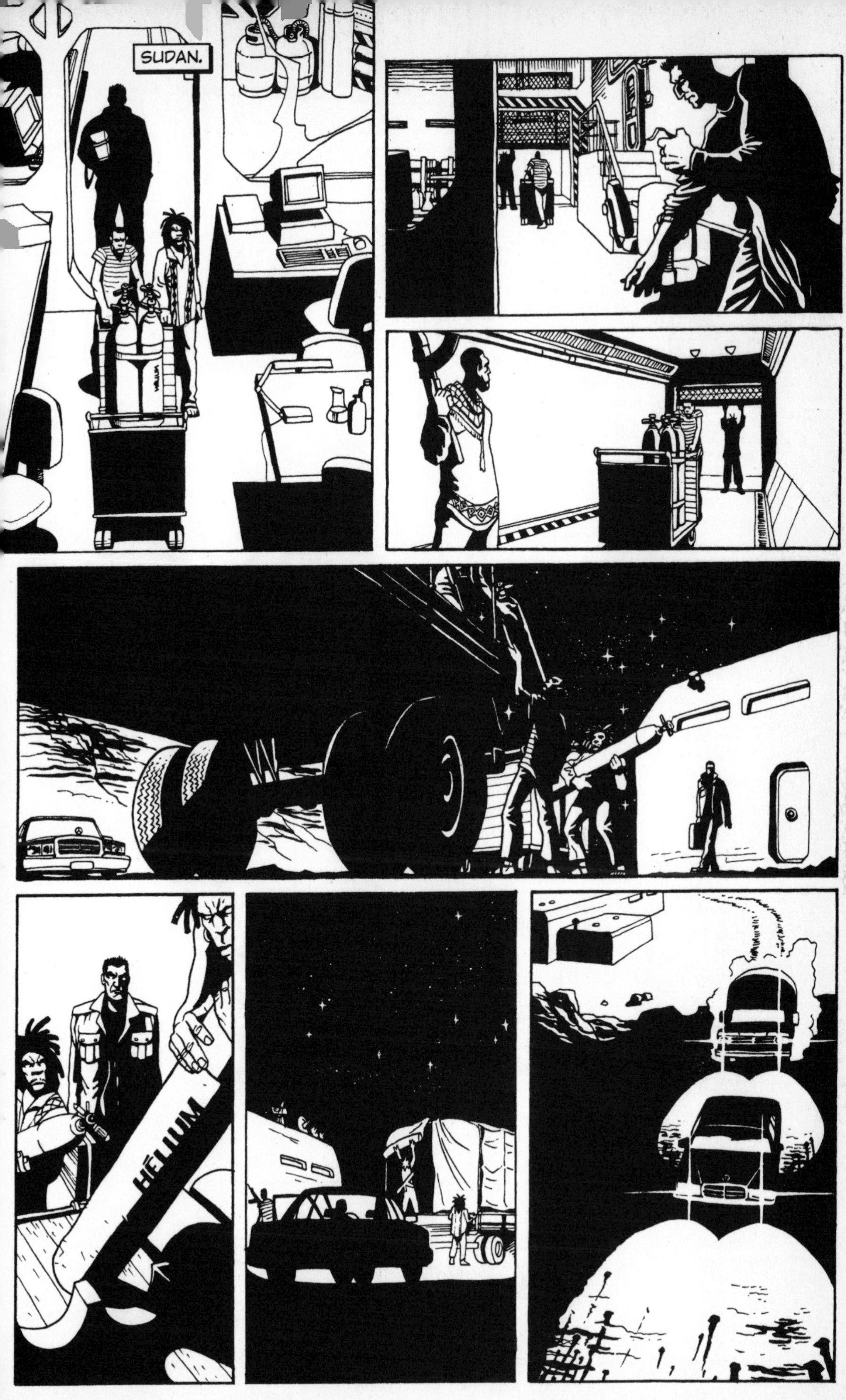
SUDAN.
HELIUM

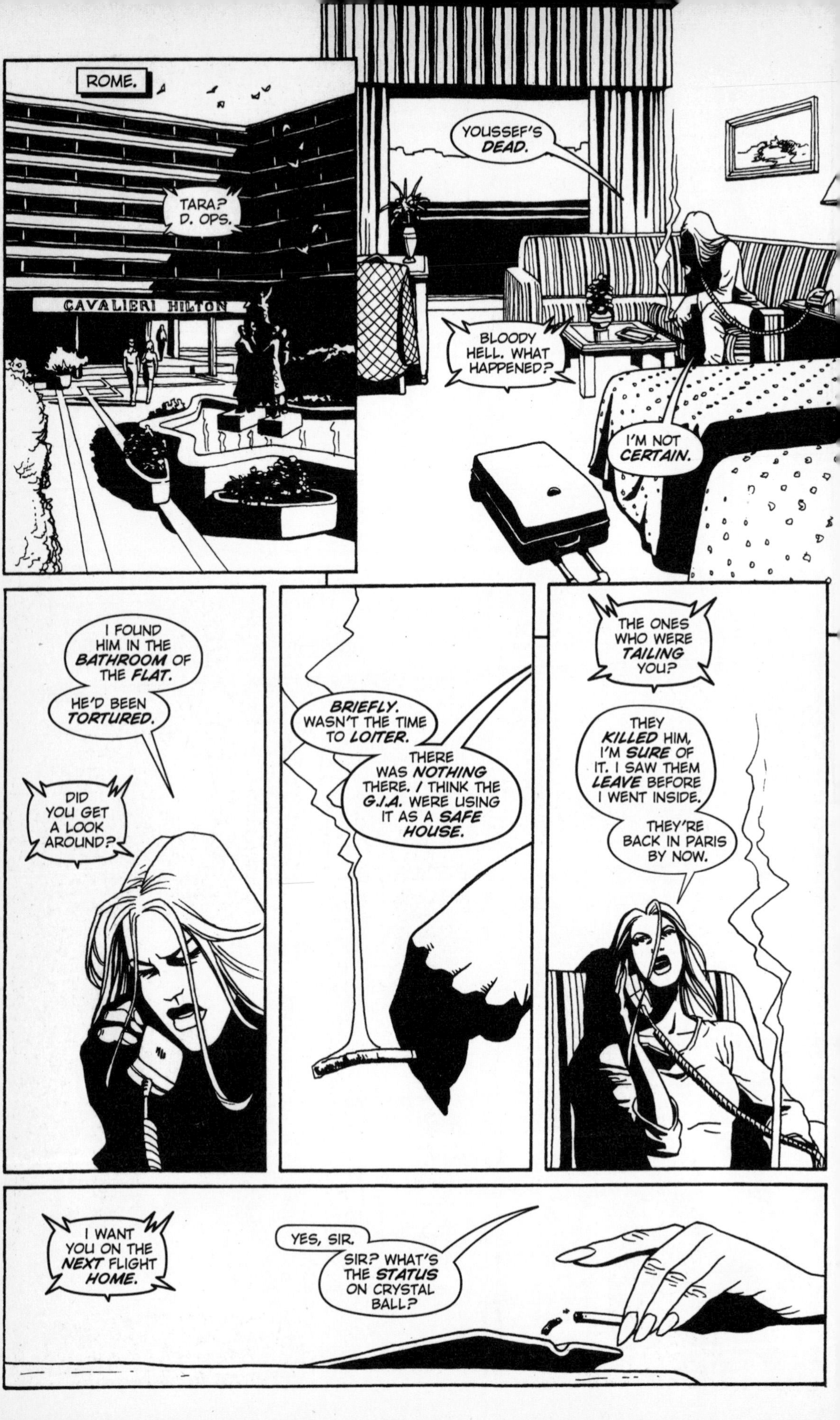
ROME.
TARA? D. OPS.
YOUSSEF'S DEAD.
BLOODY HELL. WHAT HAPPENED?
I'M NOT CERTAIN.
I FOUND HIM IN THE BATHROOM OF THE FLAT.
HE'D BEEN TORTURED.
DID YOU GET A LOOK AROUND?
BRIEFLY. WASN'T THE TIME TO LOITER.
THERE WAS NOTHING THERE. I THINK THE G.I.A. WERE USING IT AS A SAFE HOUSE.
THE ONES WHO WERE TAILING YOU?
THEY KILLED HIM, I'M SURE OF IT. I SAW THEM LEAVE BEFORE I WENT INSIDE.
THEY'RE BACK IN PARIS BY NOW.
I WANT YOU ON THE NEXT FLIGHT HOME.
YES, SIR.
SIR? WHAT'S THE STATUS ON CRYSTAL BALL?

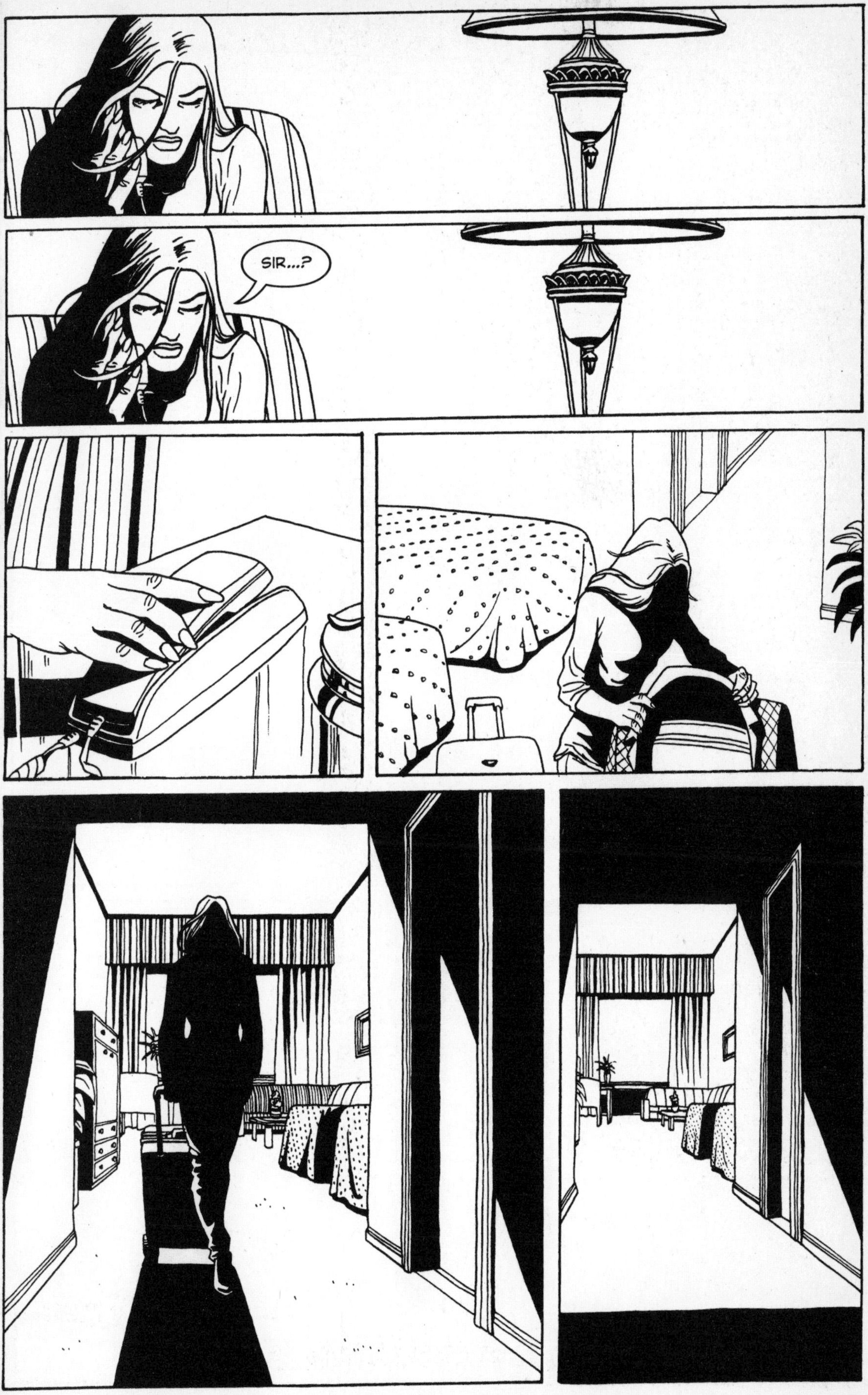
SIR...?

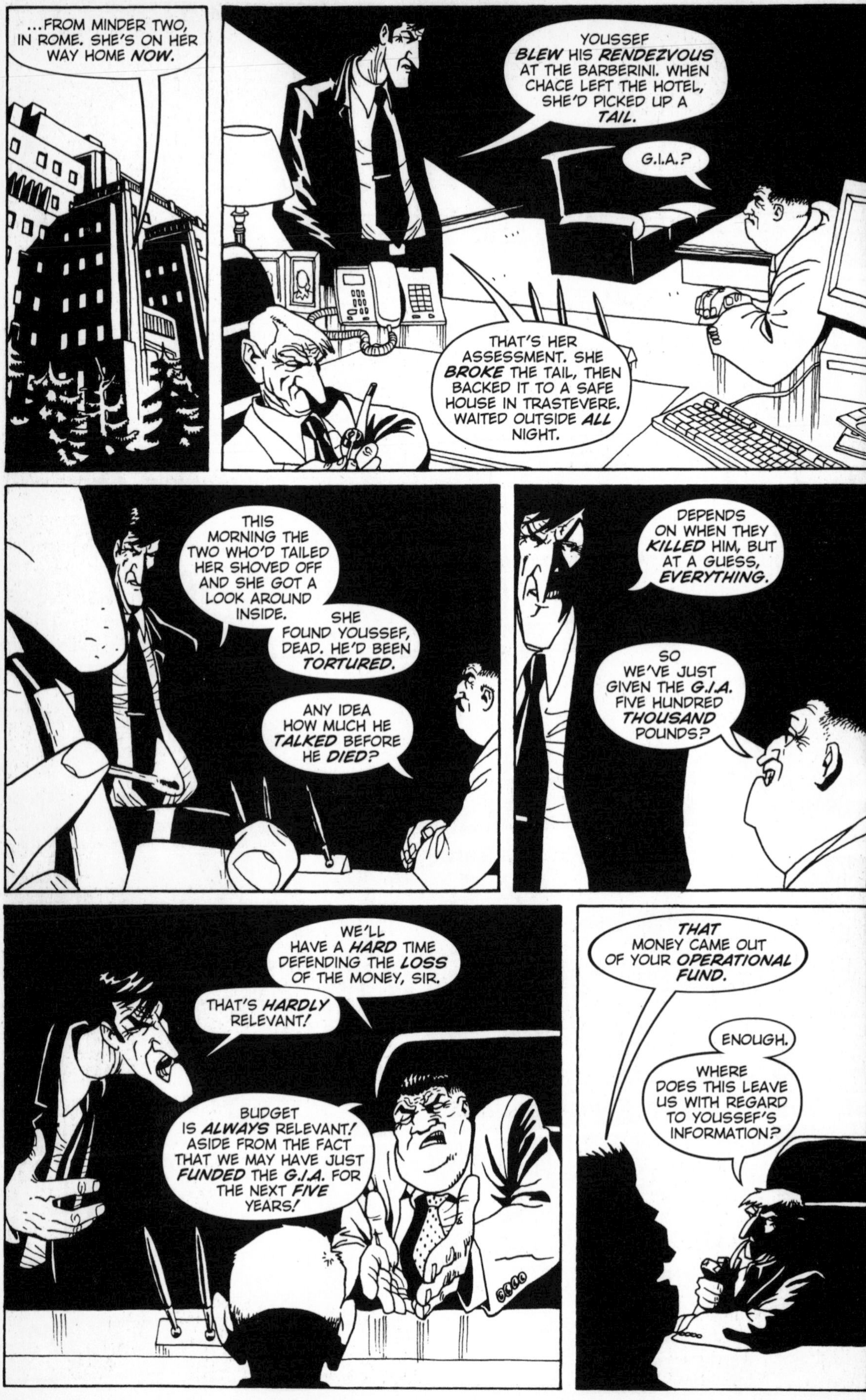
...FROM MINDER TWO, IN ROME. SHE'S ON HER WAY HOME *NOW.*
YOUSSEF *BLEW* HIS *RENDEZVOUS* AT THE BARBERINI. WHEN CHACE LEFT THE HOTEL, SHE'D PICKED UP A *TAIL.*
G.I.A.?
THAT'S HER ASSESSMENT. SHE *BROKE* THE TAIL, THEN BACKED IT TO A SAFE HOUSE IN TRASTEVERE. WAITED OUTSIDE *ALL* NIGHT.
THIS MORNING THE TWO WHO'D TAILED HER SHOVED OFF AND SHE GOT A LOOK AROUND INSIDE.
SHE FOUND YOUSSEF, DEAD. HE'D BEEN *TORTURED.*
ANY IDEA HOW MUCH HE *TALKED* BEFORE HE *DIED?*
DEPENDS ON WHEN THEY *KILLED* HIM, BUT AT A GUESS, *EVERYTHING.*
SO WE'VE JUST GIVEN THE *G.I.A.* FIVE HUNDRED *THOUSAND* POUNDS?
WE'LL HAVE A *HARD* TIME DEFENDING THE *LOSS* OF THE MONEY, SIR.
THAT'S *HARDLY* RELEVANT!
BUDGET IS *ALWAYS* RELEVANT! ASIDE FROM THE FACT THAT WE MAY HAVE JUST *FUNDED* THE *G.I.A.* FOR THE NEXT *FIVE* YEARS!
THAT MONEY CAME OUT OF YOUR *OPERATIONAL FUND.*
ENOUGH.
WHERE DOES THIS LEAVE US WITH REGARD TO YOUSSEF'S INFORMATION?

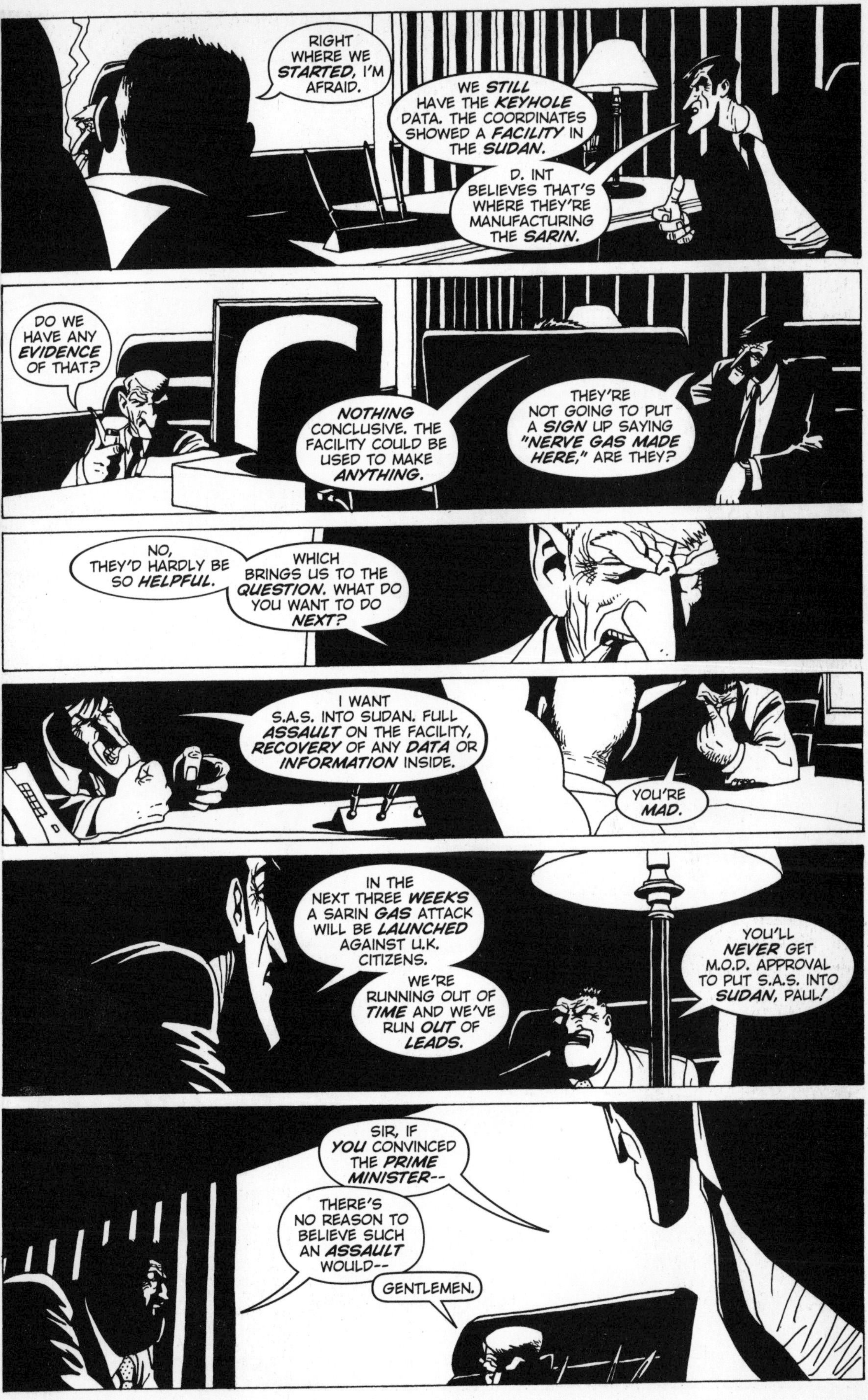
RIGHT WHERE WE STARTED, I'M AFRAID.
WE STILL HAVE THE KEYHOLE DATA. THE COORDINATES SHOWED A FACILITY IN THE SUDAN.
D. INT BELIEVES THAT'S WHERE THEY'RE MANUFACTURING THE SARIN.
DO WE HAVE ANY EVIDENCE OF THAT?
NOTHING CONCLUSIVE. THE FACILITY COULD BE USED TO MAKE ANYTHING.
THEY'RE NOT GOING TO PUT A SIGN UP SAYING "NERVE GAS MADE HERE," ARE THEY?
NO, THEY'D HARDLY BE SO HELPFUL.
WHICH BRINGS US TO THE QUESTION. WHAT DO YOU WANT TO DO NEXT?
I WANT S.A.S. INTO SUDAN. FULL ASSAULT ON THE FACILITY, RECOVERY OF ANY DATA OR INFORMATION INSIDE.
YOU'RE MAD.
IN THE NEXT THREE WEEKS A SARIN GAS ATTACK WILL BE LAUNCHED AGAINST U.K. CITIZENS.
WE'RE RUNNING OUT OF TIME AND WE'VE RUN OUT OF LEADS.
YOU'LL NEVER GET M.O.D. APPROVAL TO PUT S.A.S. INTO SUDAN, PAUL!
SIR, IF YOU CONVINCED THE PRIME MINISTER--
THERE'S NO REASON TO BELIEVE SUCH AN ASSAULT WOULD--
GENTLEMEN.

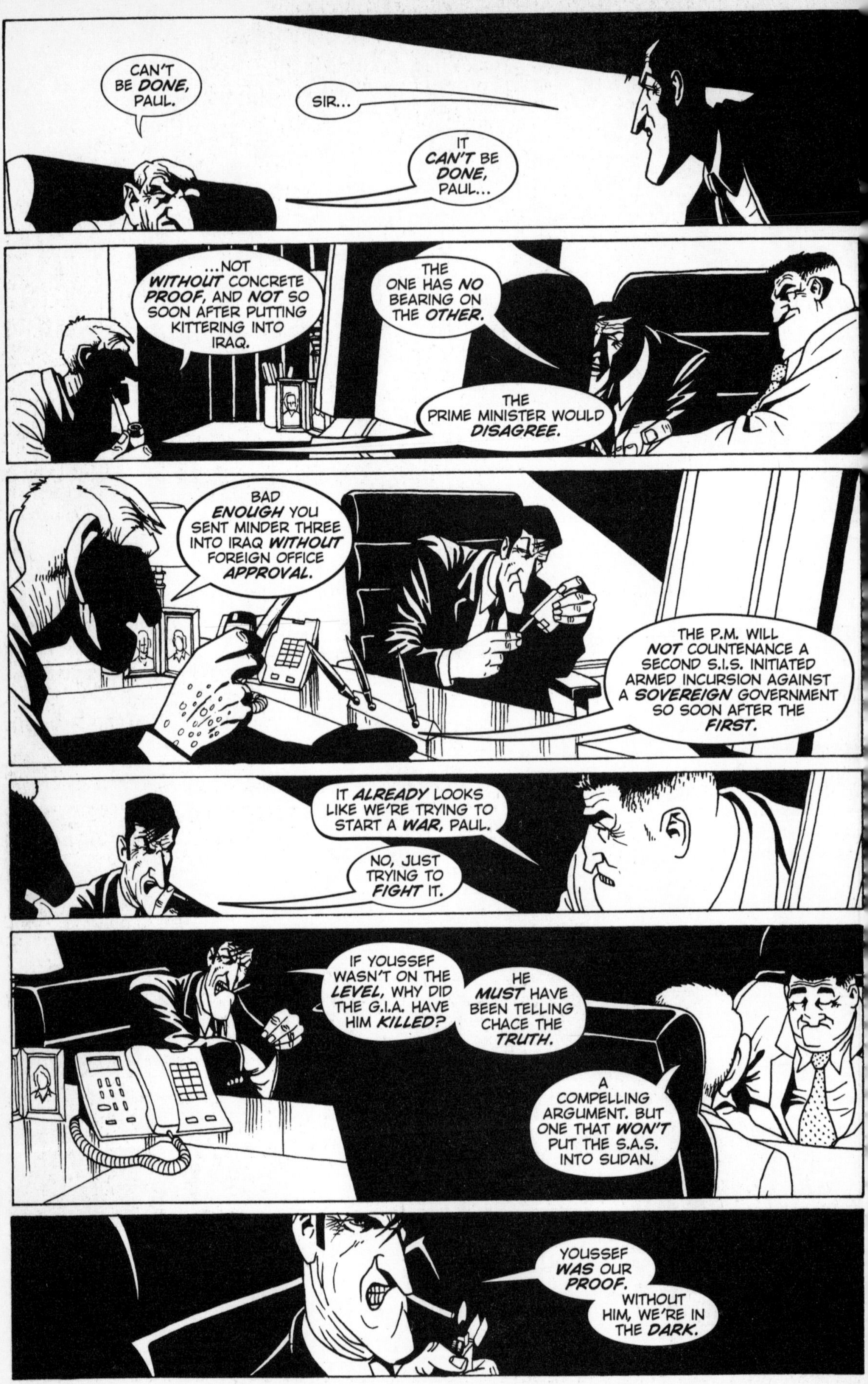
CAN'T BE DONE, PAUL.
SIR...
IT CAN'T BE DONE, PAUL...
...NOT WITHOUT CONCRETE PROOF, AND NOT SO SOON AFTER PUTTING KITTERING INTO IRAQ.
THE ONE HAS NO BEARING ON THE OTHER.
THE PRIME MINISTER WOULD DISAGREE.
BAD ENOUGH YOU SENT MINDER THREE INTO IRAQ WITHOUT FOREIGN OFFICE APPROVAL.
THE P.M. WILL NOT COUNTENANCE A SECOND S.I.S. INITIATED ARMED INCURSION AGAINST A SOVEREIGN GOVERNMENT SO SOON AFTER THE FIRST.
IT ALREADY LOOKS LIKE WE'RE TRYING TO START A WAR, PAUL.
NO, JUST TRYING TO FIGHT IT.
IF YOUSSEF WASN'T ON THE LEVEL, WHY DID THE G.I.A. HAVE HIM KILLED?
HE MUST HAVE BEEN TELLING CHACE THE TRUTH.
A COMPELLING ARGUMENT. BUT ONE THAT WON'T PUT THE S.A.S. INTO SUDAN.
YOUSSEF WAS OUR PROOF.
WITHOUT HIM, WE'RE IN THE DARK.

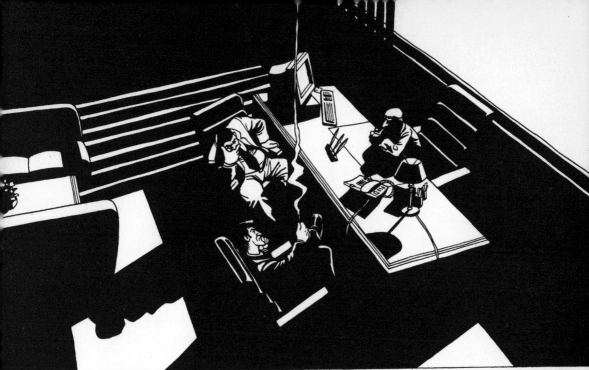

FIND **SOMETHING**, PAUL.

I'LL HAPPILY GO TO DOWNING STREET AND **FIGHT** FOR YOU...

...BUT I'LL NEED **AMMUNITION**.

BRING IT TO ME, I'LL GET YOU THE S.A.S.

THANK YOU, SIR.

...AND *HAIL* THE *CONQUERING* HERO.

BACK FROM IRAQ WITH NOT A *SCRATCH* TO SHOW FOR IT.

OH, I'VE GOT *SCRATCHES*...

...JUST *NONE* THAT I'M WILLING TO SHOW *YOU*.

WHERE'S MINDER TWO?

OOOH, MINDER *TWO*, IS IT?

NOT TARA? NOT THE *LOVELY* MISS CHACE?

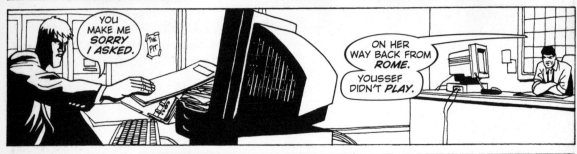

YOU MAKE ME *SORRY* I ASKED.

ON HER WAY BACK FROM *ROME*. YOUSSEF DIDN'T *PLAY*.

HE GOT *MADE* FOR A *LIAR?*

HE GOT *MADE* FOR *DEAD*.

6' JUNE 2002

TARA'S *FINE*.

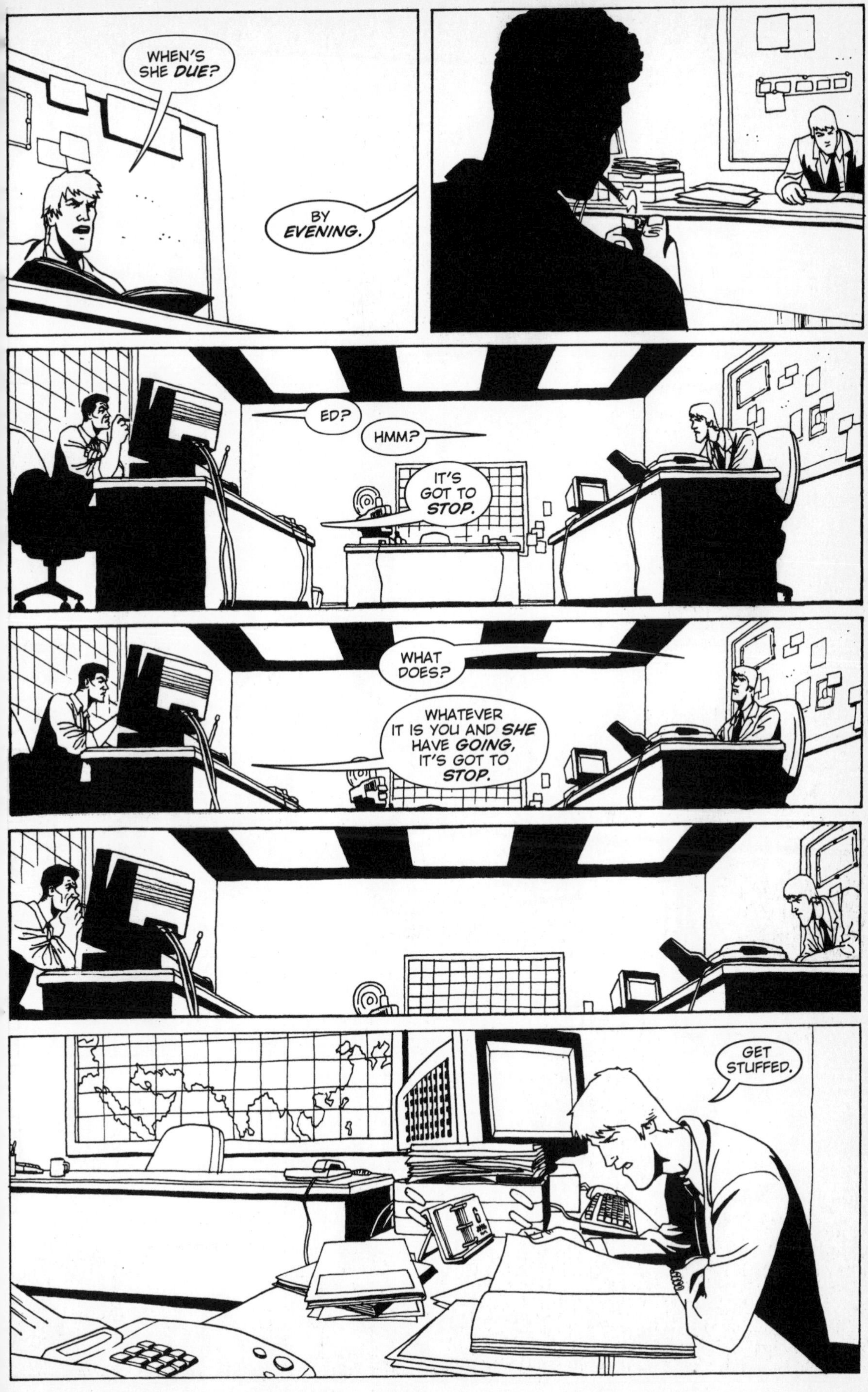
WHEN'S SHE *DUE?*
BY *EVENING.*
ED?
HMM?
IT'S GOT TO *STOP.*
WHAT DOES?
WHATEVER IT IS YOU AND *SHE* HAVE *GOING,* IT'S GOT TO *STOP.*
GET STUFFED.

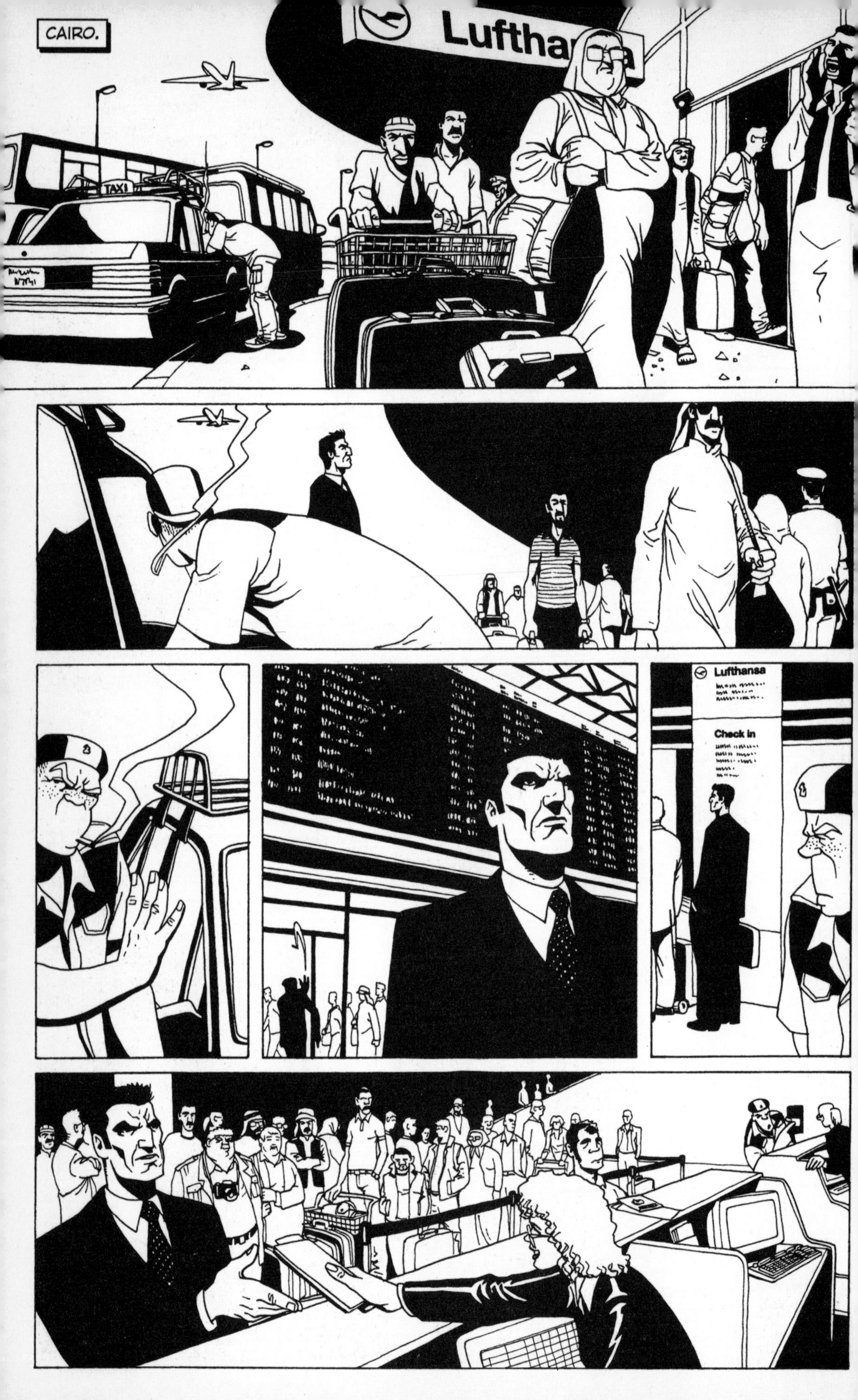
CAIRO.
Lufthansa
TAXI
Lufthansa
Check in

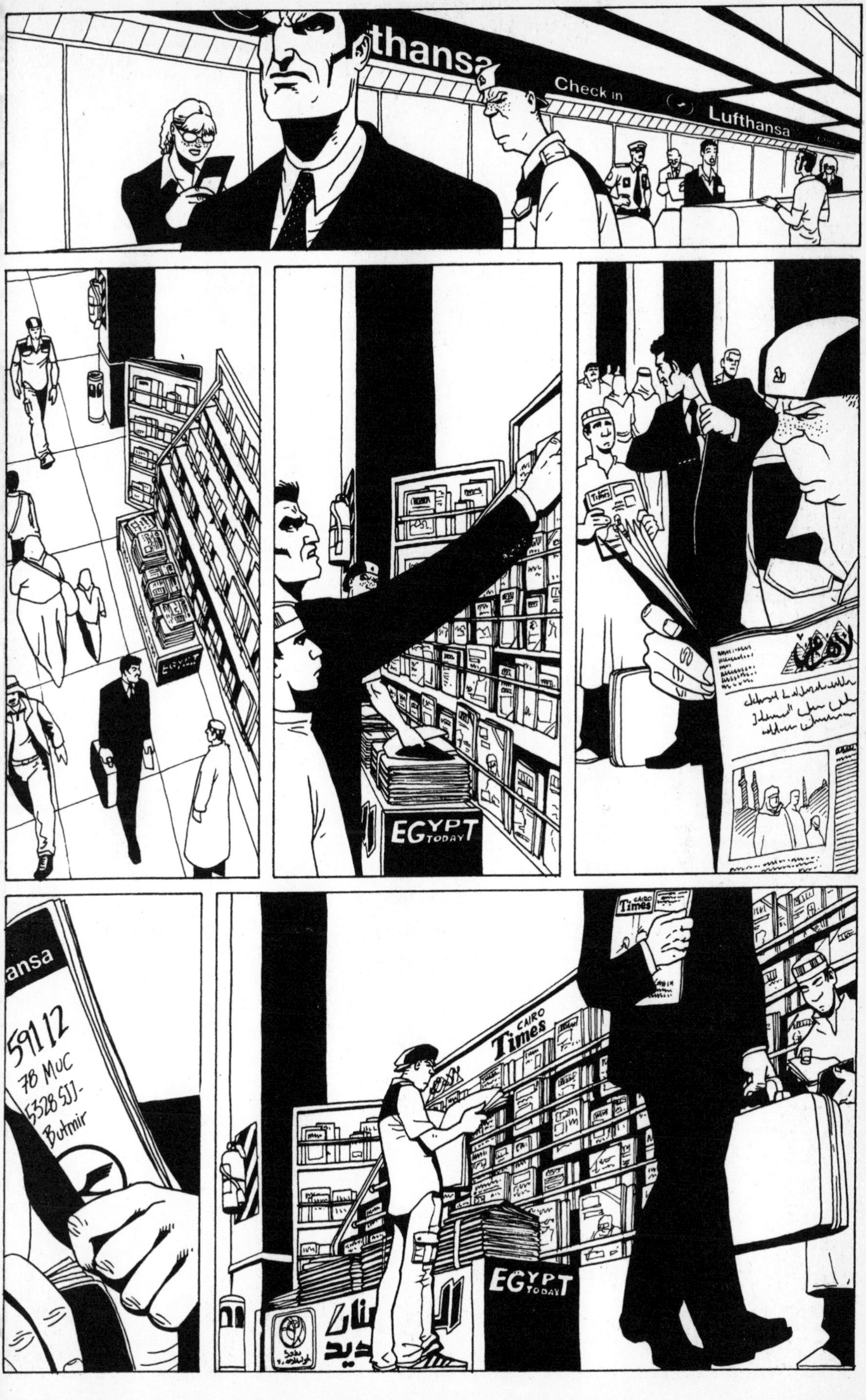

thansa
Check in
Lufthansa
EGYPT
EGYPT TODAY
CAIRO Times
ansa
591 12
78 MUC
5328 SJJ-
Butmir

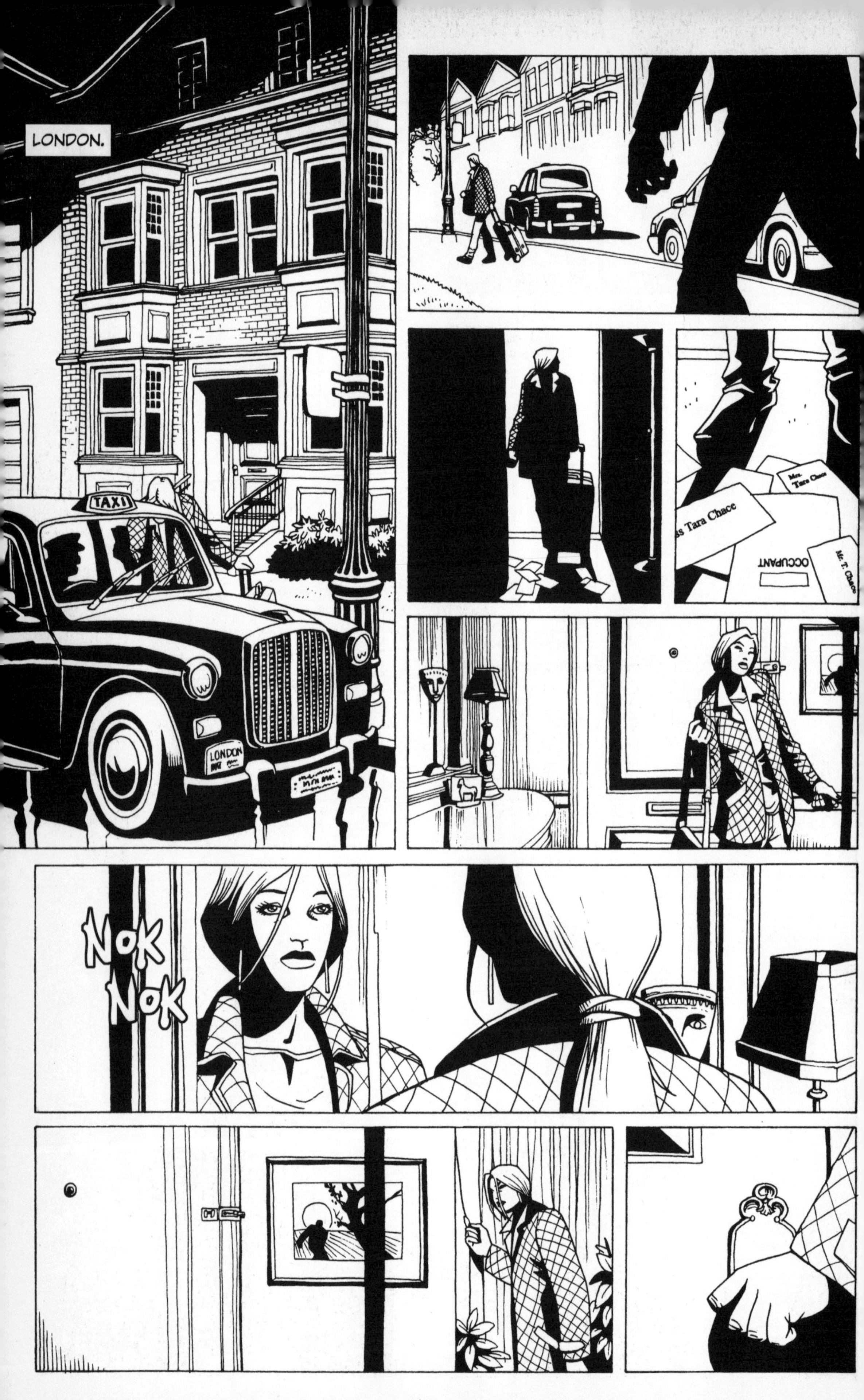

LONDON.
TAXI
LONDON
Mrs. Tara Chace
ss Tara Chace
OCCUPANT
Mr. T. Chace
NOK NOK

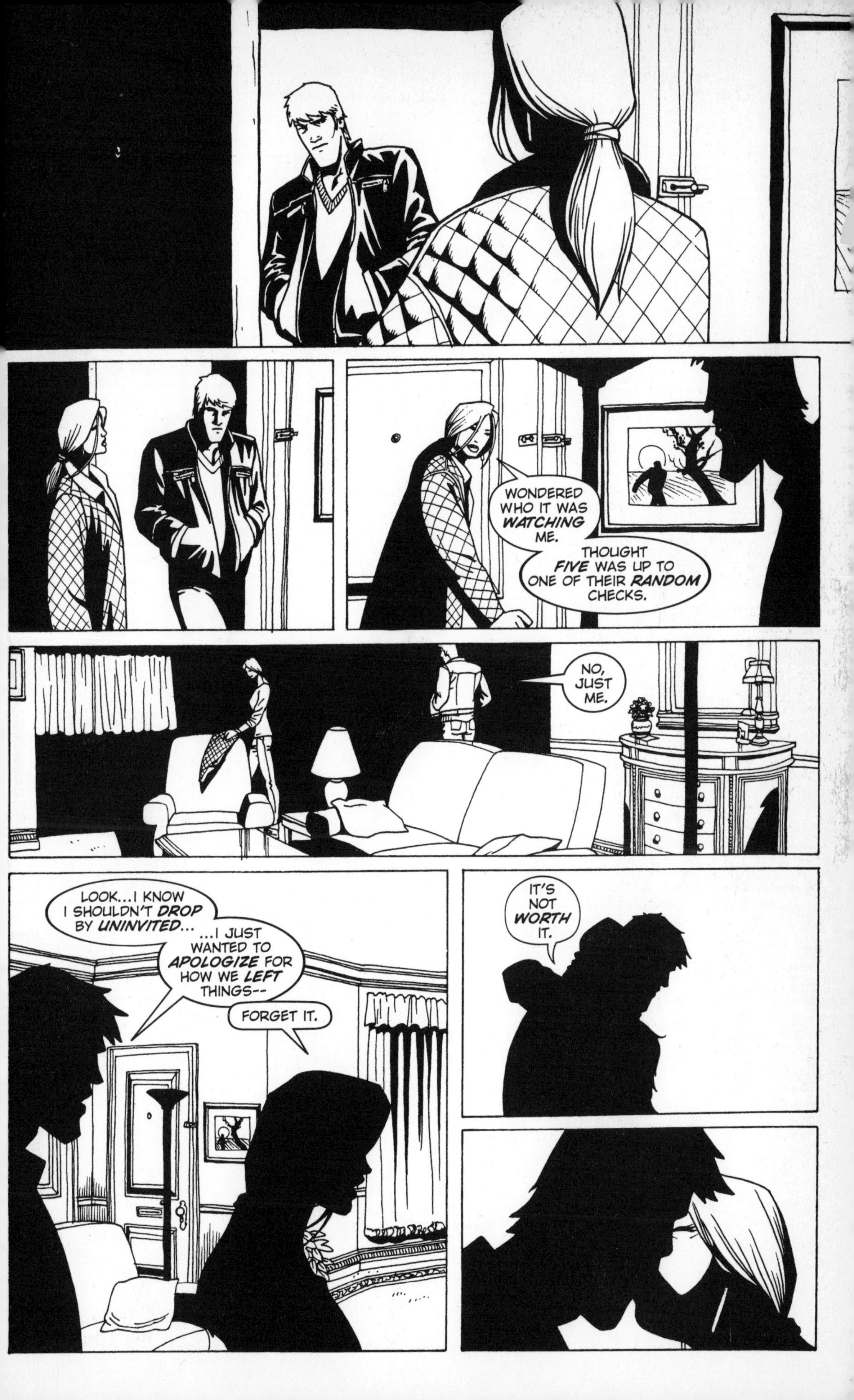
WONDERED WHO IT WAS WATCHING ME.
THOUGHT FIVE WAS UP TO ONE OF THEIR RANDOM CHECKS.
NO, JUST ME.
LOOK...I KNOW I SHOULDN'T DROP BY UNINVITED...
...I JUST WANTED TO APOLOGIZE FOR HOW WE LEFT THINGS--
FORGET IT.
IT'S NOT WORTH IT.

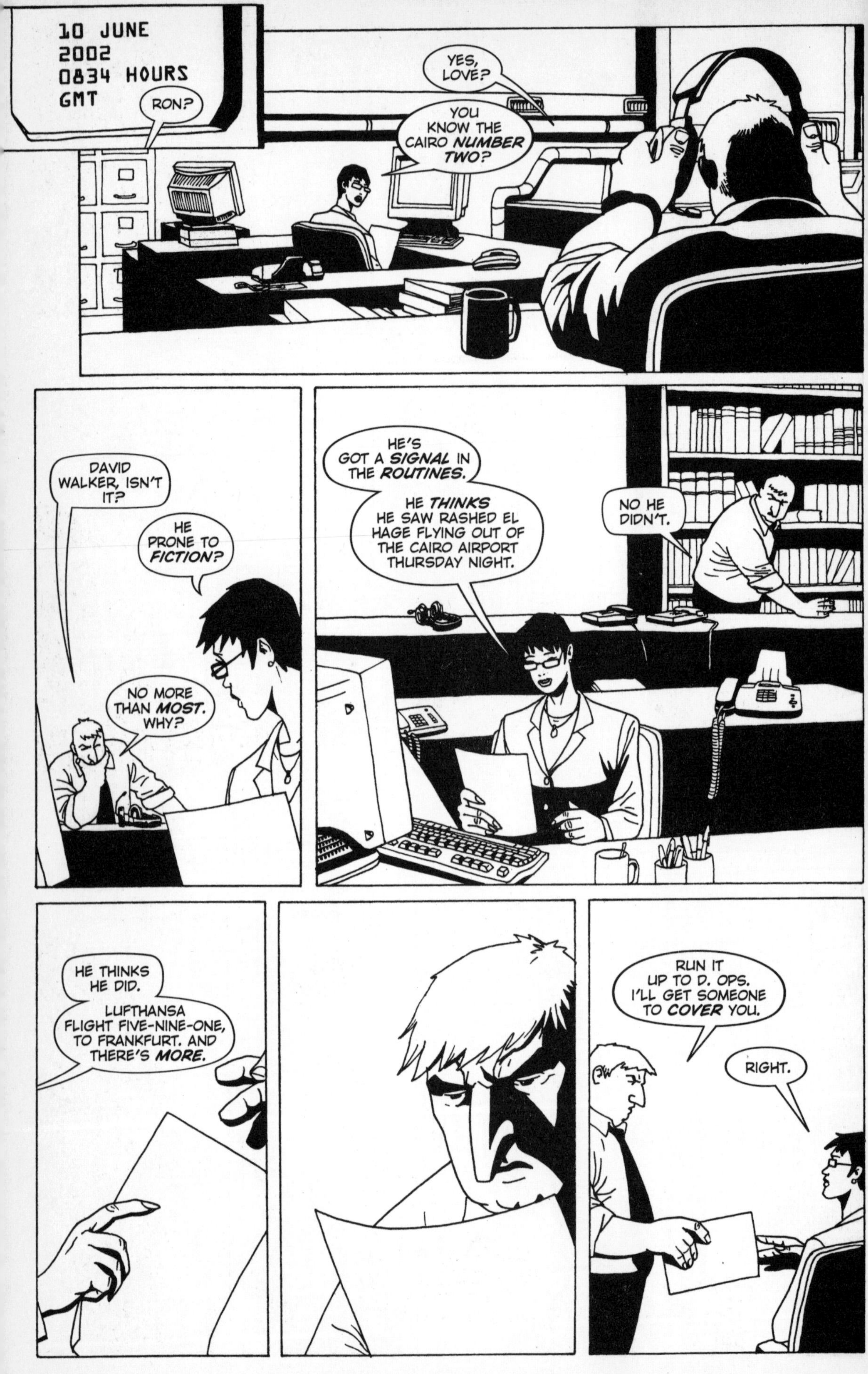
10 JUNE 2002 0834 HOURS GMT
RON?
YES, LOVE?
YOU KNOW THE CAIRO NUMBER TWO?
DAVID WALKER, ISN'T IT?
HE PRONE TO FICTION?
NO MORE THAN MOST. WHY?
HE'S GOT A SIGNAL IN THE ROUTINES.
HE THINKS HE SAW RASHED EL HAGE FLYING OUT OF THE CAIRO AIRPORT THURSDAY NIGHT.
NO HE DIDN'T.
HE THINKS HE DID.
LUFTHANSA FLIGHT FIVE-NINE-ONE, TO FRANKFURT. AND THERE'S MORE.
RUN IT UP TO D. OPS. I'LL GET SOMEONE TO COVER YOU.
RIGHT.

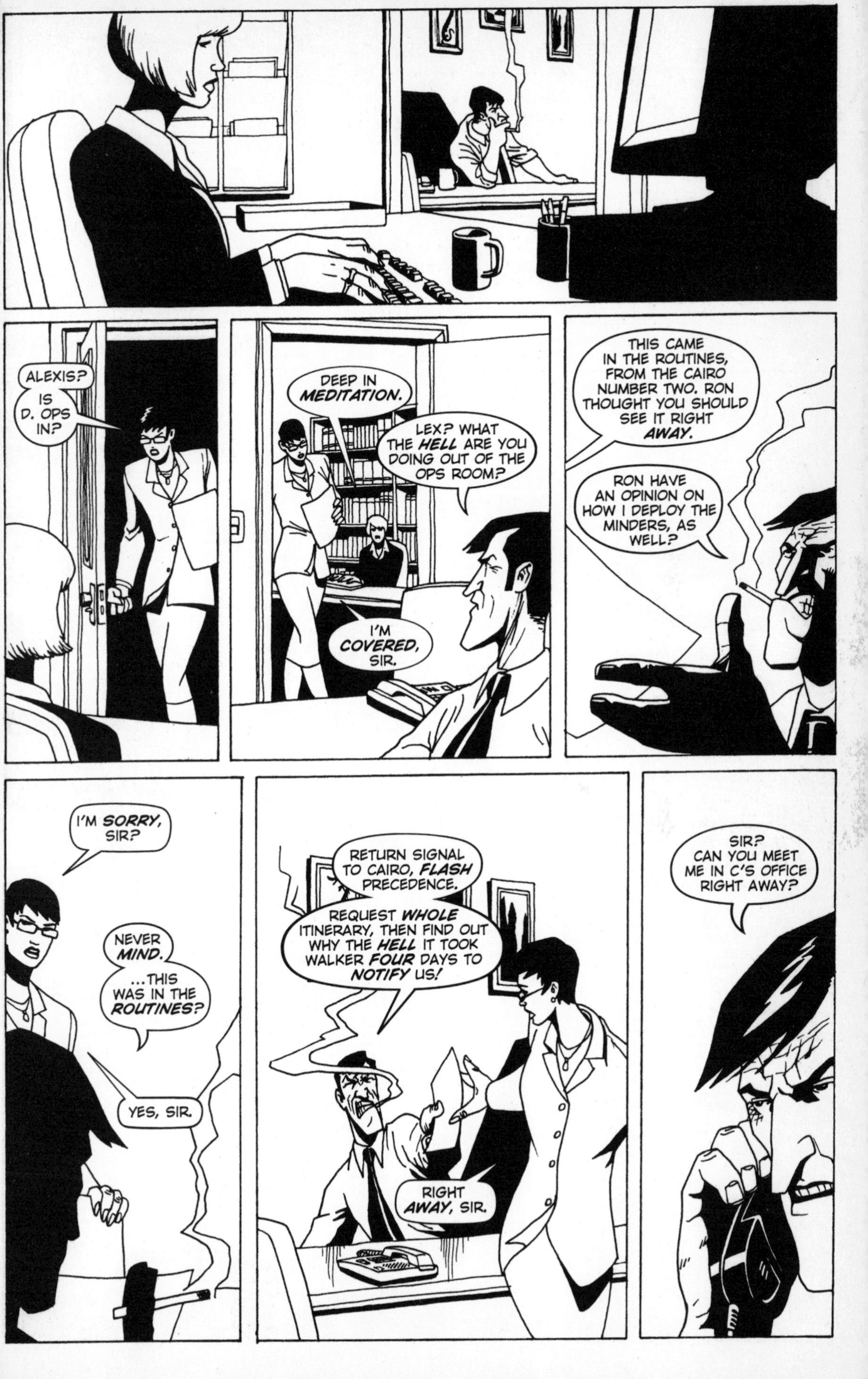
ALEXIS?
IS D. OPS IN?
DEEP IN MEDITATION.
LEX? WHAT THE HELL ARE YOU DOING OUT OF THE OPS ROOM?
I'M COVERED, SIR.
THIS CAME IN THE ROUTINES, FROM THE CAIRO NUMBER TWO. RON THOUGHT YOU SHOULD SEE IT RIGHT AWAY.
RON HAVE AN OPINION ON HOW I DEPLOY THE MINDERS, AS WELL?
I'M SORRY, SIR?
NEVER MIND.
...THIS WAS IN THE ROUTINES?
YES, SIR.
RETURN SIGNAL TO CAIRO, FLASH PRECEDENCE.
REQUEST WHOLE ITINERARY, THEN FIND OUT WHY THE HELL IT TOOK WALKER FOUR DAYS TO NOTIFY US!
RIGHT AWAY, SIR.
SIR? CAN YOU MEET ME IN C'S OFFICE RIGHT AWAY?

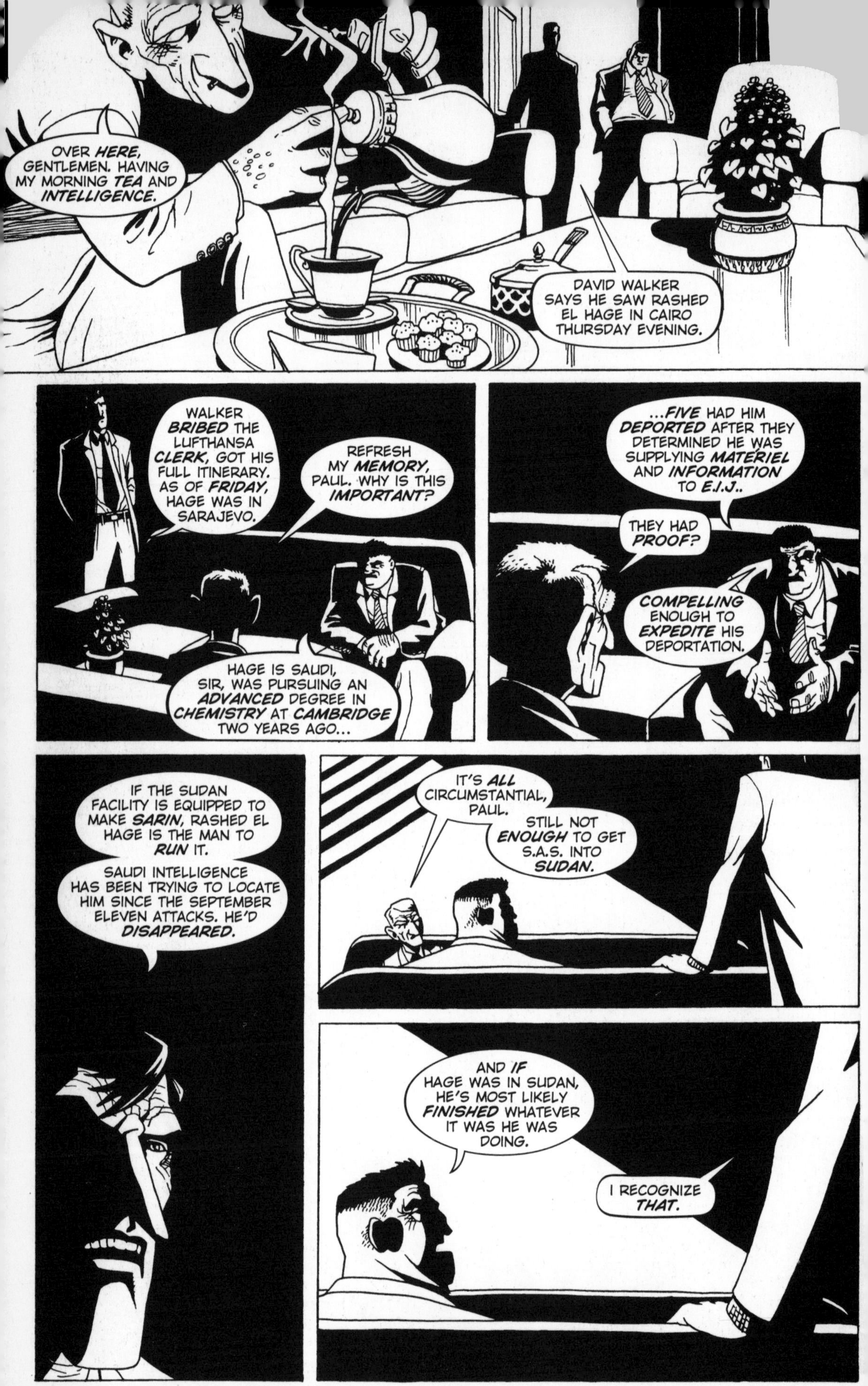
OVER HERE, GENTLEMEN. HAVING MY MORNING TEA AND INTELLIGENCE.
DAVID WALKER SAYS HE SAW RASHED EL HAGE IN CAIRO THURSDAY EVENING.
WALKER BRIBED THE LUFTHANSA CLERK, GOT HIS FULL ITINERARY. AS OF FRIDAY, HAGE WAS IN SARAJEVO.
REFRESH MY MEMORY, PAUL. WHY IS THIS IMPORTANT?
HAGE IS SAUDI, SIR, WAS PURSUING AN ADVANCED DEGREE IN CHEMISTRY AT CAMBRIDGE TWO YEARS AGO...
...FIVE HAD HIM DEPORTED AFTER THEY DETERMINED HE WAS SUPPLYING MATÉRIEL AND INFORMATION TO E.I.J..
THEY HAD PROOF?
COMPELLING ENOUGH TO EXPEDITE HIS DEPORTATION.
IF THE SUDAN FACILITY IS EQUIPPED TO MAKE SARIN, RASHED EL HAGE IS THE MAN TO RUN IT.
SAUDI INTELLIGENCE HAS BEEN TRYING TO LOCATE HIM SINCE THE SEPTEMBER ELEVEN ATTACKS. HE'D DISAPPEARED.
IT'S ALL CIRCUMSTANTIAL, PAUL.
STILL NOT ENOUGH TO GET S.A.S. INTO SUDAN.
AND IF HAGE WAS IN SUDAN, HE'S MOST LIKELY FINISHED WHATEVER IT WAS HE WAS DOING.
I RECOGNIZE THAT.

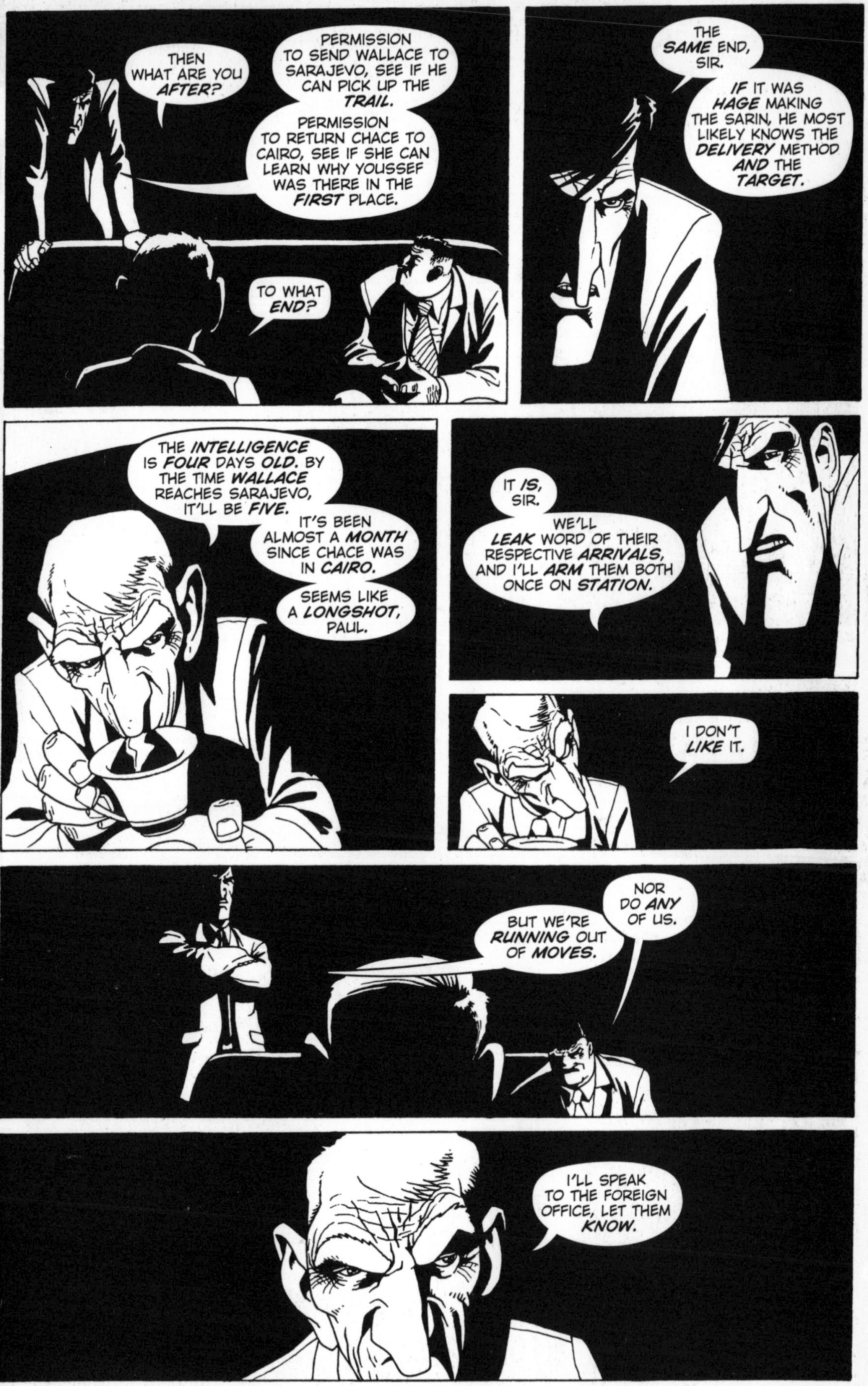
THEN WHAT ARE YOU AFTER?
PERMISSION TO SEND WALLACE TO SARAJEVO, SEE IF HE CAN PICK UP THE TRAIL.
PERMISSION TO RETURN CHACE TO CAIRO, SEE IF SHE CAN LEARN WHY YOUSSEF WAS THERE IN THE FIRST PLACE.
TO WHAT END?
THE SAME END, SIR.
IF IT WAS HAGE MAKING THE SARIN, HE MOST LIKELY KNOWS THE DELIVERY METHOD AND THE TARGET.
THE INTELLIGENCE IS FOUR DAYS OLD. BY THE TIME WALLACE REACHES SARAJEVO, IT'LL BE FIVE.
IT'S BEEN ALMOST A MONTH SINCE CHACE WAS IN CAIRO.
SEEMS LIKE A LONGSHOT, PAUL.
IT IS, SIR.
WE'LL LEAK WORD OF THEIR RESPECTIVE ARRIVALS, AND I'LL ARM THEM BOTH ONCE ON STATION.
I DON'T LIKE IT.
BUT WE'RE RUNNING OUT OF MOVES.
NOR DO ANY OF US.
I'LL SPEAK TO THE FOREIGN OFFICE, LET THEM KNOW.

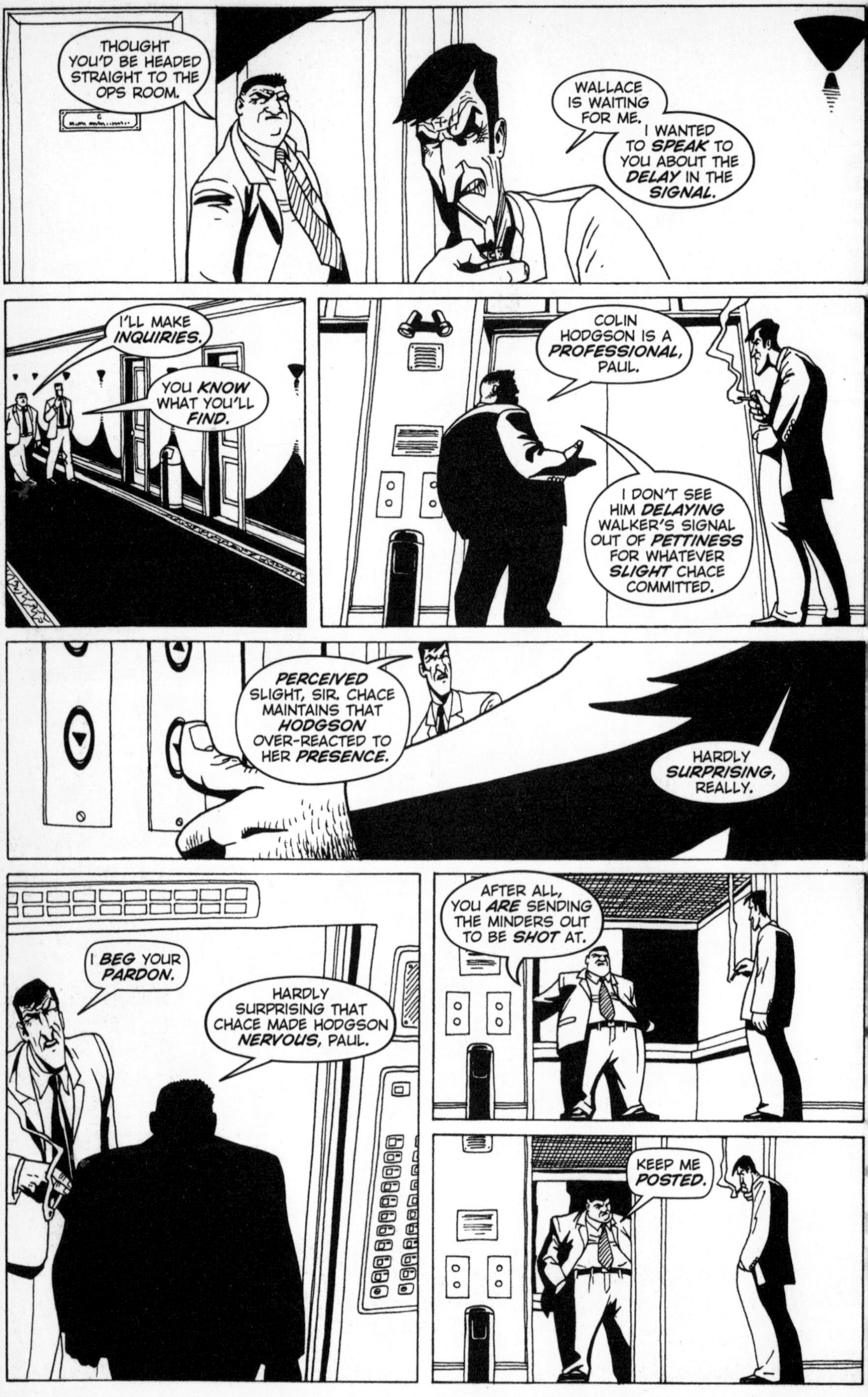
THOUGHT YOU'D BE HEADED STRAIGHT TO THE OPS ROOM.
WALLACE IS WAITING FOR ME.
I WANTED TO SPEAK TO YOU ABOUT THE DELAY IN THE SIGNAL.
I'LL MAKE INQUIRIES.
YOU KNOW WHAT YOU'LL FIND.
COLIN HODGSON IS A PROFESSIONAL, PAUL.
I DON'T SEE HIM DELAYING WALKER'S SIGNAL OUT OF PETTINESS FOR WHATEVER SLIGHT CHACE COMMITTED.
PERCEIVED SLIGHT, SIR. CHACE MAINTAINS THAT HODGSON OVER-REACTED TO HER PRESENCE.
HARDLY SURPRISING, REALLY.
I BEG YOUR PARDON.
HARDLY SURPRISING THAT CHACE MADE HODGSON NERVOUS, PAUL.
AFTER ALL, YOU ARE SENDING THE MINDERS OUT TO BE SHOT AT.
KEEP ME POSTED.

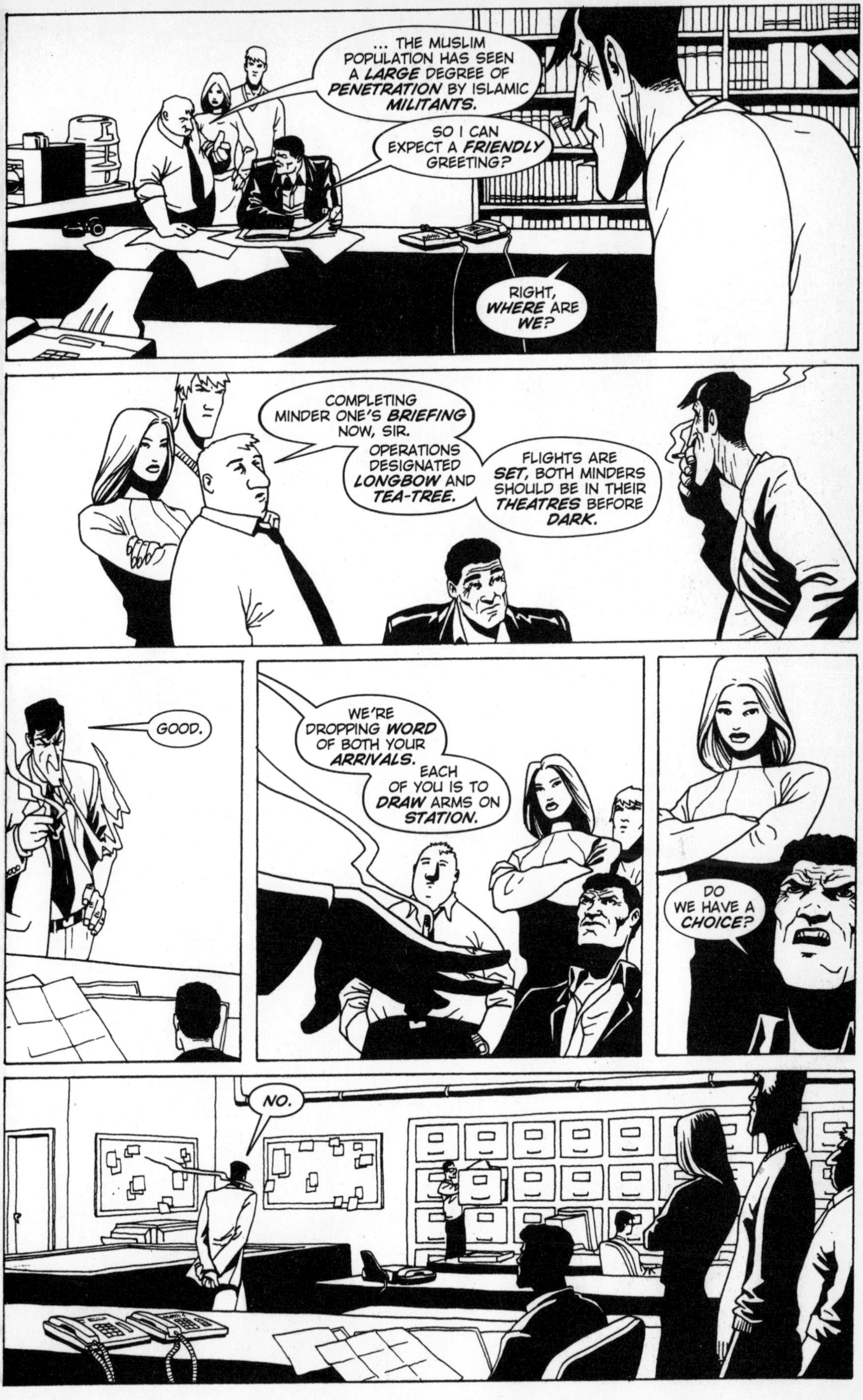
... THE MUSLIM POPULATION HAS SEEN A LARGE DEGREE OF PENETRATION BY ISLAMIC MILITANTS.
SO I CAN EXPECT A FRIENDLY GREETING?
RIGHT, WHERE ARE WE?
COMPLETING MINDER ONE'S BRIEFING NOW, SIR.
OPERATIONS DESIGNATED LONGBOW AND TEA-TREE.
FLIGHTS ARE SET, BOTH MINDERS SHOULD BE IN THEIR THEATRES BEFORE DARK.
GOOD.
WE'RE DROPPING WORD OF BOTH YOUR ARRIVALS.
EACH OF YOU IS TO DRAW ARMS ON STATION.
DO WE HAVE A CHOICE?
NO.

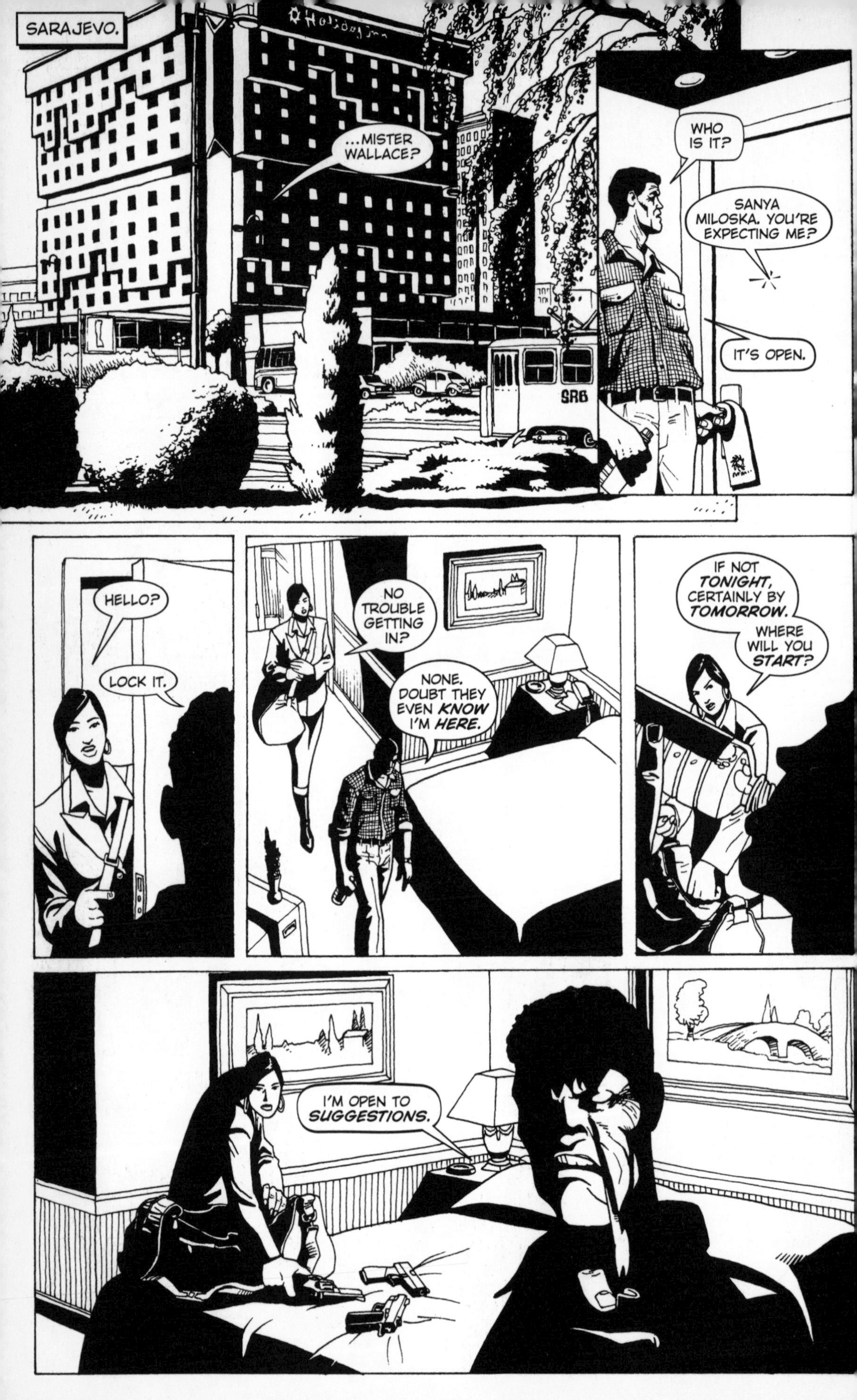
SARAJEVO.
...MISTER WALLACE?
WHO IS IT?
SANYA MILOSKA. YOU'RE EXPECTING ME?
IT'S OPEN.
HELLO?
LOCK IT.
NO TROUBLE GETTING IN?
NONE. DOUBT THEY EVEN *KNOW* I'M *HERE.*
IF NOT *TONIGHT,* CERTAINLY BY *TOMORROW.*
WHERE WILL YOU *START?*
I'M OPEN TO *SUGGESTIONS.*

NONE OF MY *INFORMANTS* HAVE SEEN HAGE.

OR IF THEY *HAVE*, THEY'RE NOT *TELLING*.

WHERE WOULD HE *GO?*

THERE ARE A *FEW* PLACES, *CAFES* AND THE *LIKE*, THAT THE *MILITANTS* ARE *RUMORED* TO *FREQUENT*.

INFORMATION HAS BEEN *DIFFICULT* TO GET SINCE THE END OF THE *WAR*.

I CAN GIVE YOU A LIST OF *NAMES* AND *ADDRESSES*.

THAT'D BE VERY *HELPFUL*, THANK YOU.

WILL YOU *USE* IT?

THIS *THING*, YOU MEAN?

YES.

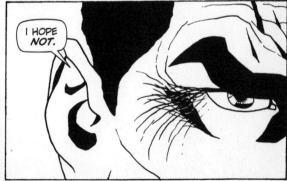

I HOPE *NOT*.

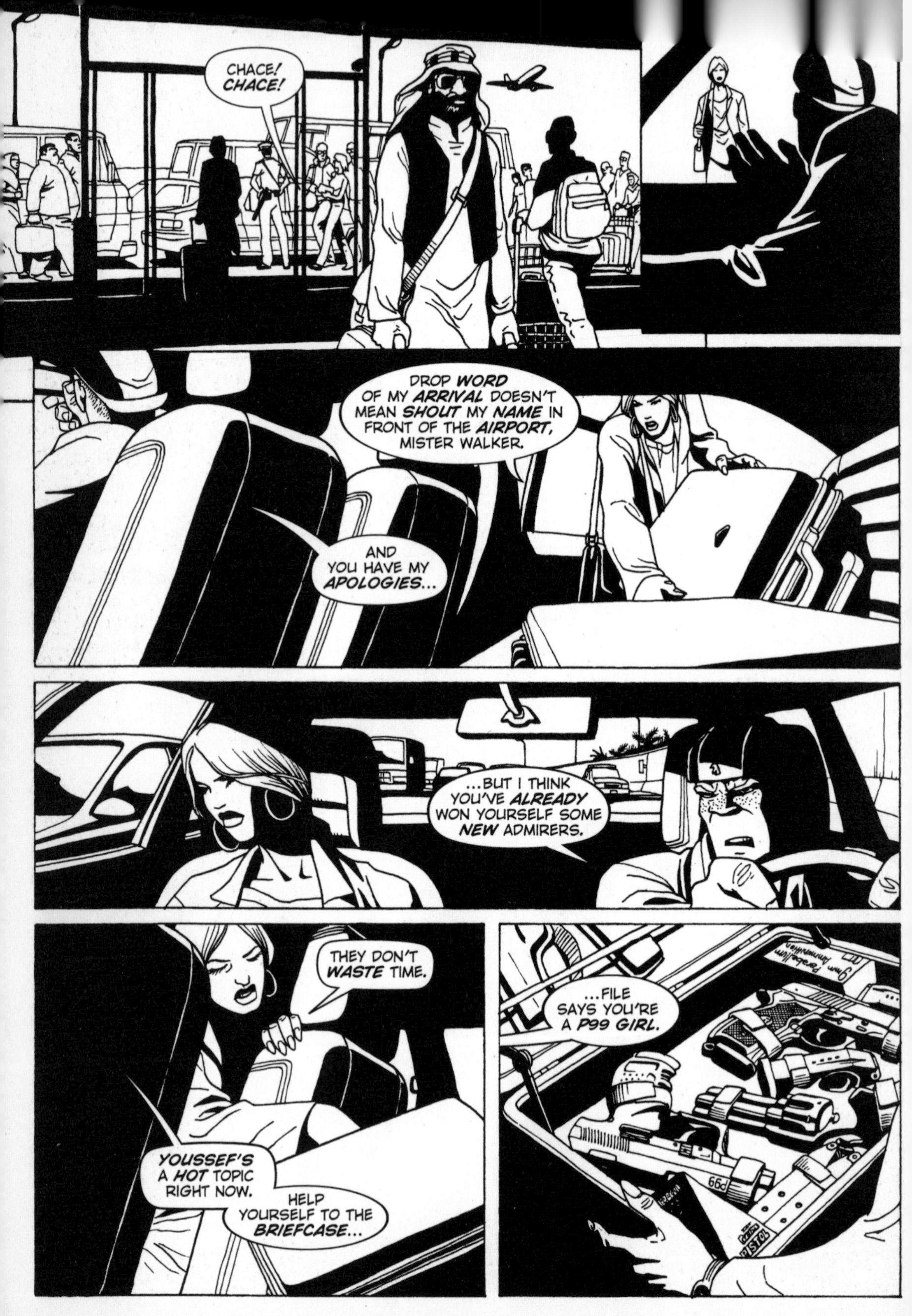
CHACE! CHACE!
DROP WORD OF MY ARRIVAL DOESN'T MEAN SHOUT MY NAME IN FRONT OF THE AIRPORT, MISTER WALKER.
AND YOU HAVE MY APOLOGIES...
...BUT I THINK YOU'VE ALREADY WON YOURSELF SOME NEW ADMIRERS.
THEY DON'T WASTE TIME.
YOUSSEF'S A HOT TOPIC RIGHT NOW.
HELP YOURSELF TO THE BRIEFCASE...
...FILE SAYS YOU'RE A P99 GIRL.

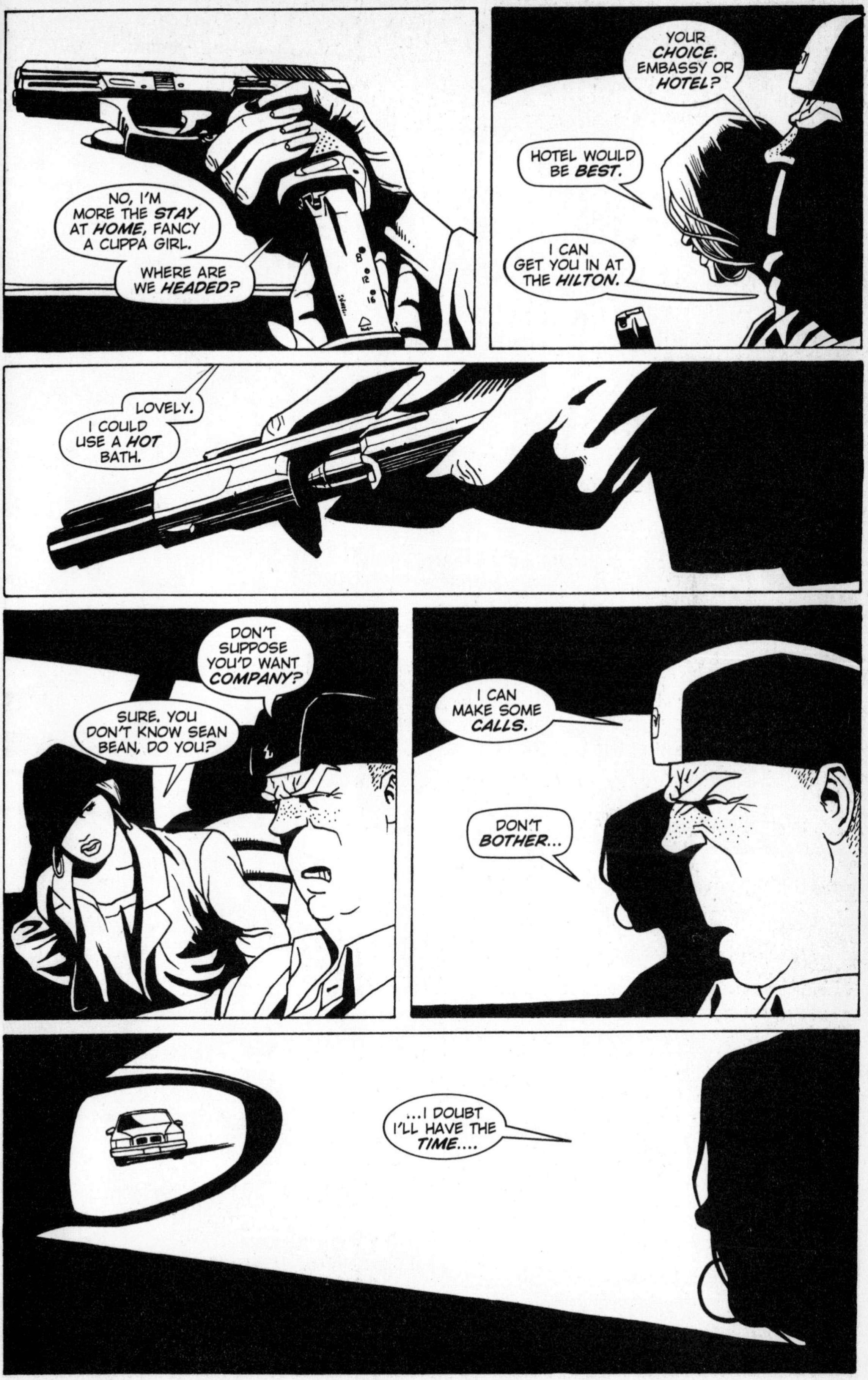

NO, I'M MORE THE STAY AT HOME, FANCY A CUPPA GIRL.
WHERE ARE WE HEADED?
YOUR CHOICE. EMBASSY OR HOTEL?
HOTEL WOULD BE BEST.
I CAN GET YOU IN AT THE HILTON.
LOVELY. I COULD USE A HOT BATH.
DON'T SUPPOSE YOU'D WANT COMPANY?
SURE. YOU DON'T KNOW SEAN BEAN, DO YOU?
I CAN MAKE SOME CALLS.
DON'T BOTHER...
...I DOUBT I'LL HAVE THE TIME....

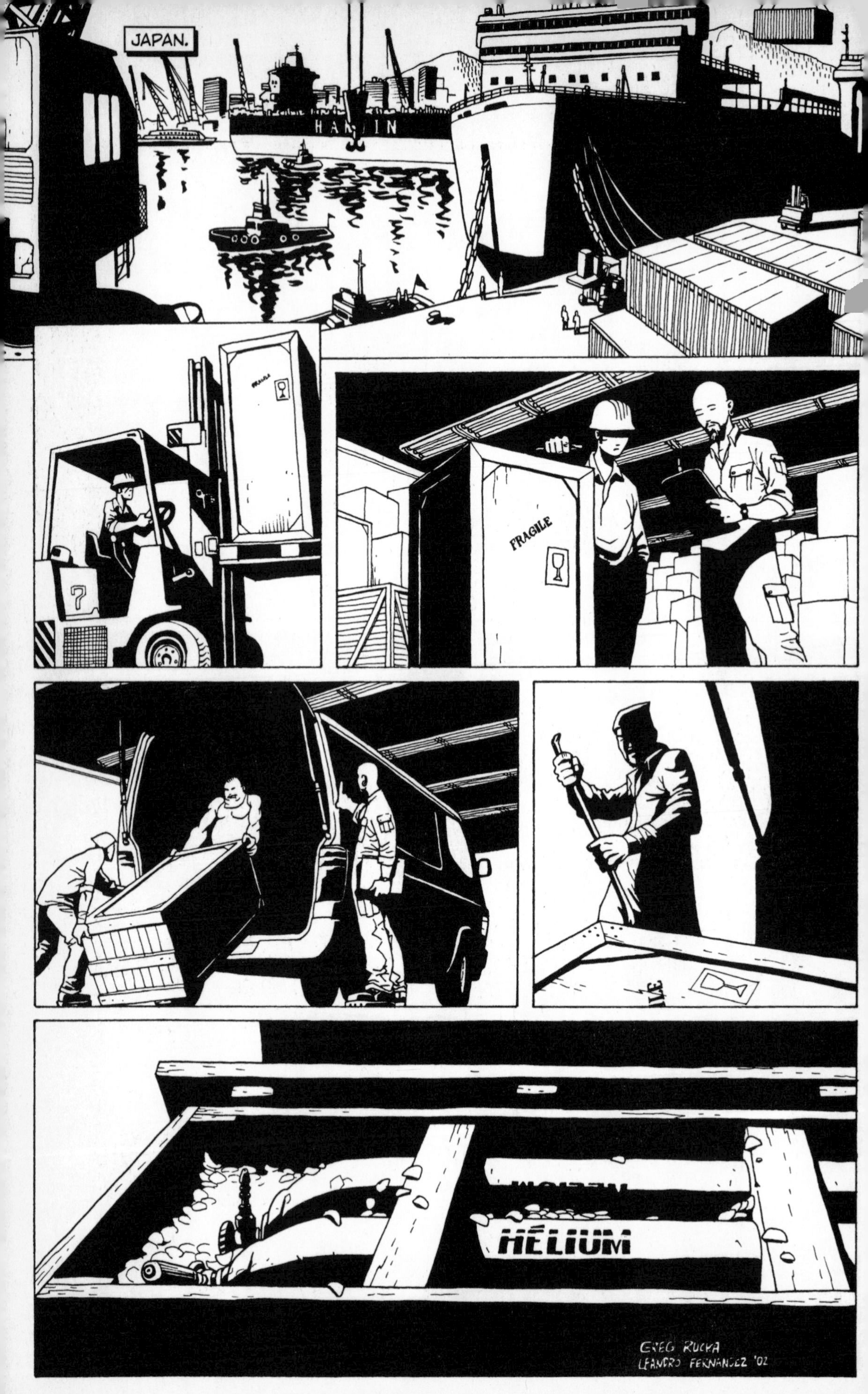
JAPAN.
FRAGILE
HÉLIUM
GREG RUCKA
LEANDRO FERNANDEZ '02

CHAPTER 5

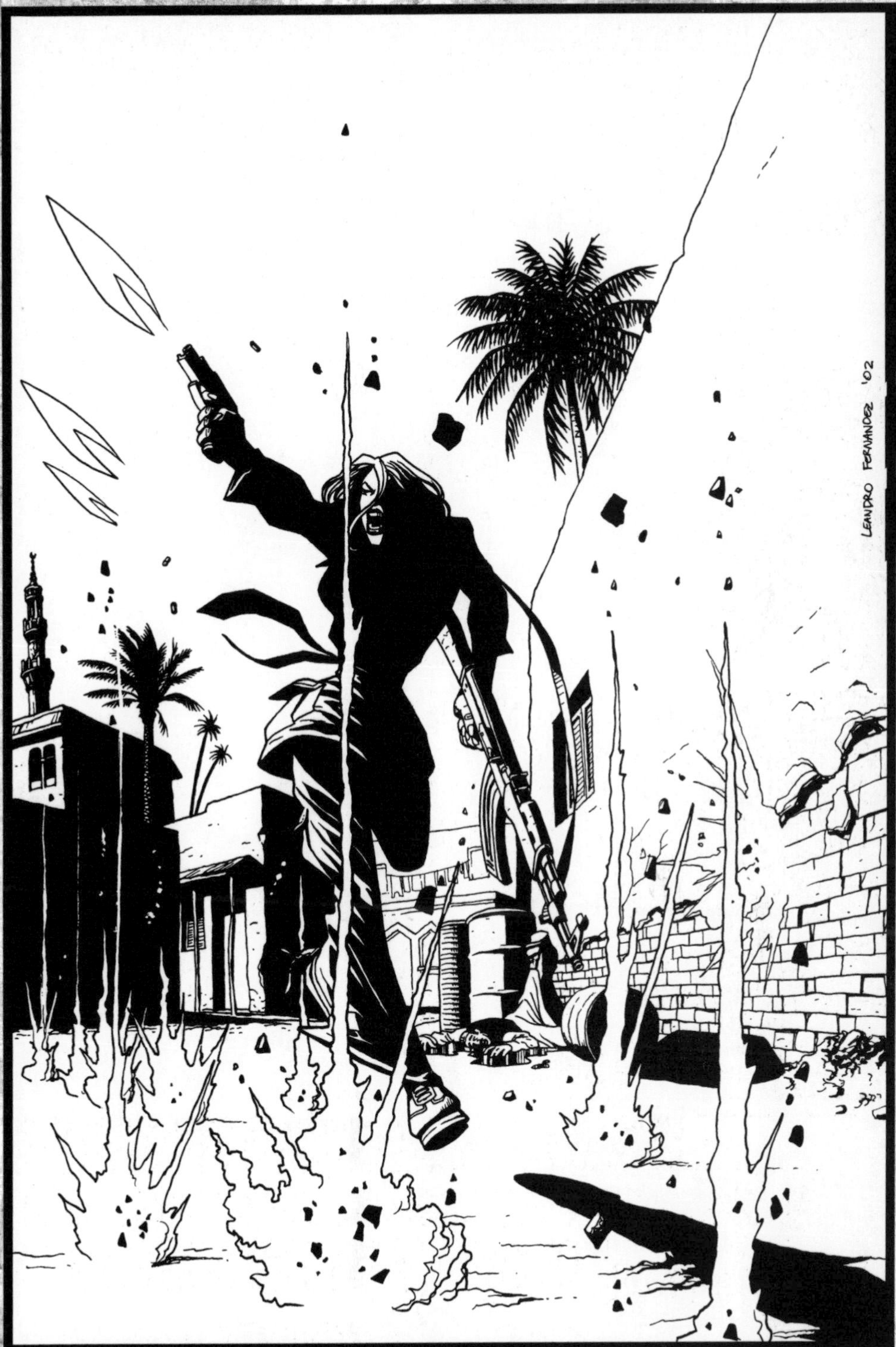
LEANDRO FERNANDEZ '02

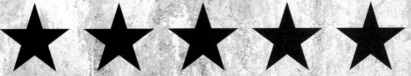

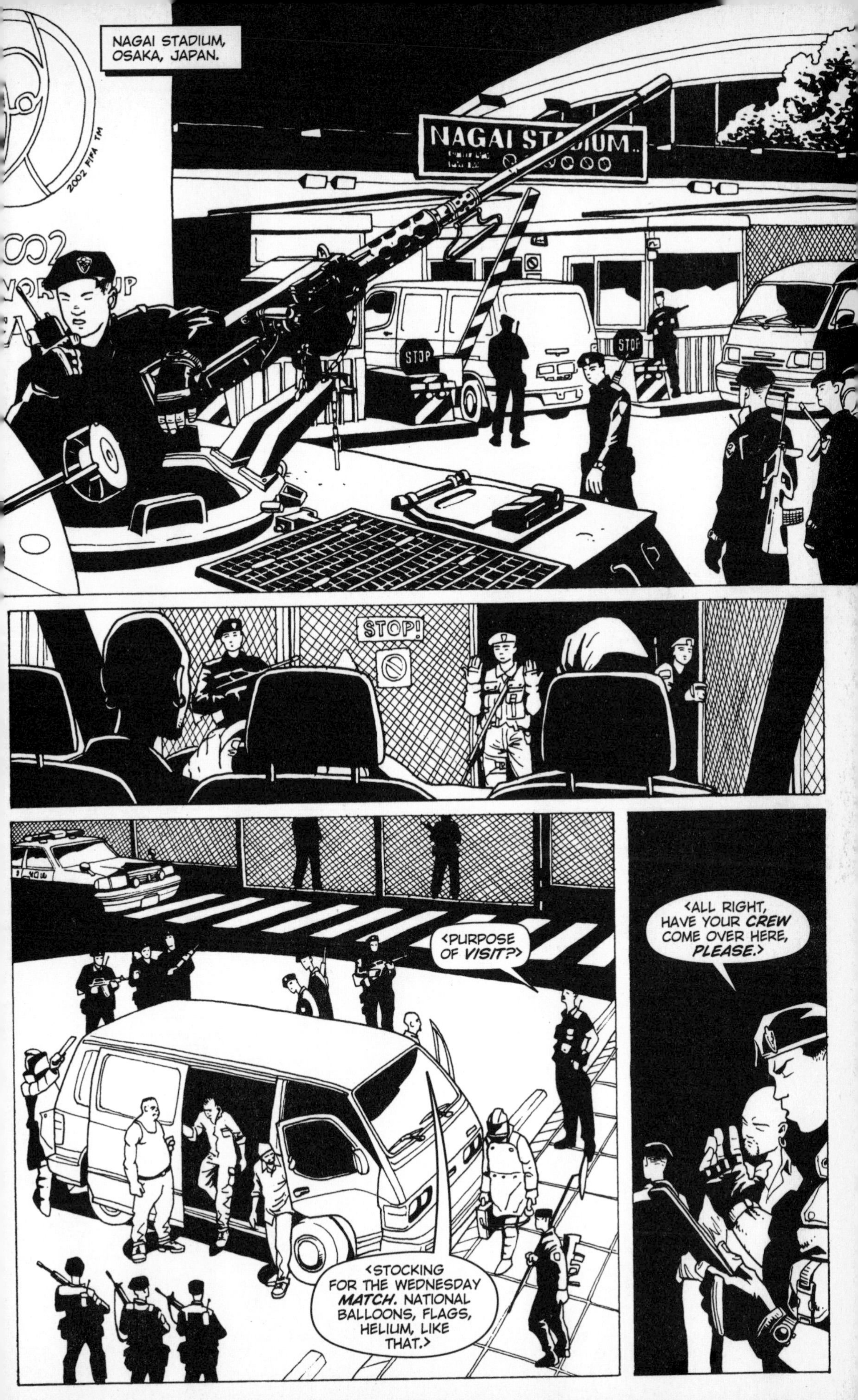
NAGAI STADIUM,
OSAKA, JAPAN.
2002 FIFA TM
NAGAI STADIUM
STOP
STOP
STOP!
<PURPOSE OF VISIT?>
<STOCKING FOR THE WEDNESDAY MATCH. NATIONAL BALLOONS, FLAGS, HELIUM, LIKE THAT.>
<ALL RIGHT, HAVE YOUR CREW COME OVER HERE, PLEASE.>

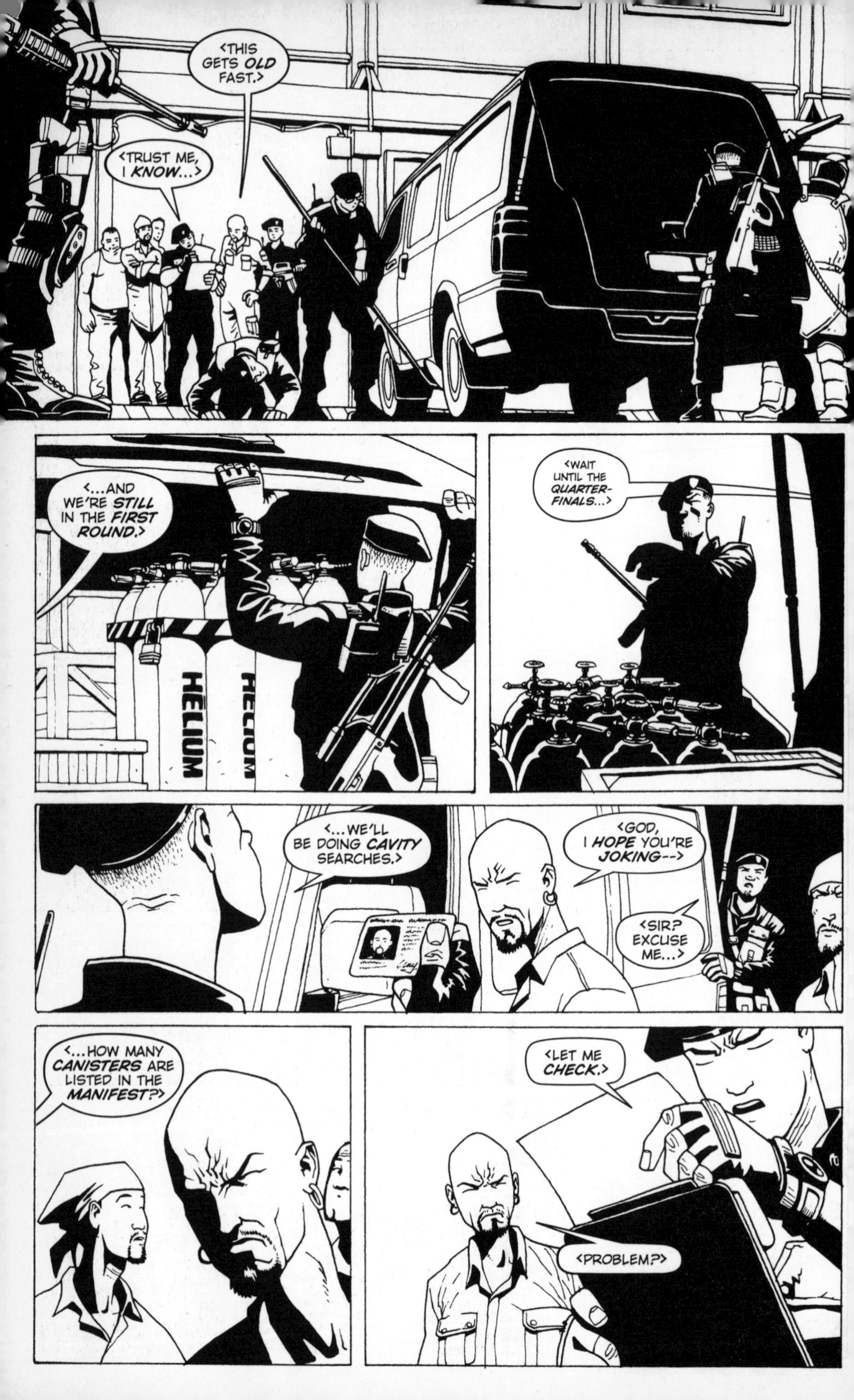
<TRUST ME, I KNOW...>
<THIS GETS OLD FAST.>
<...AND WE'RE STILL IN THE FIRST ROUND.>
<WAIT UNTIL THE QUARTER-FINALS...>
HELIUM
HELIUM
<...WE'LL BE DOING CAVITY SEARCHES.>
<GOD, I HOPE YOU'RE JOKING-->
<SIR? EXCUSE ME...>
<...HOW MANY CANISTERS ARE LISTED IN THE MANIFEST?>
<LET ME CHECK.>
<PROBLEM?>

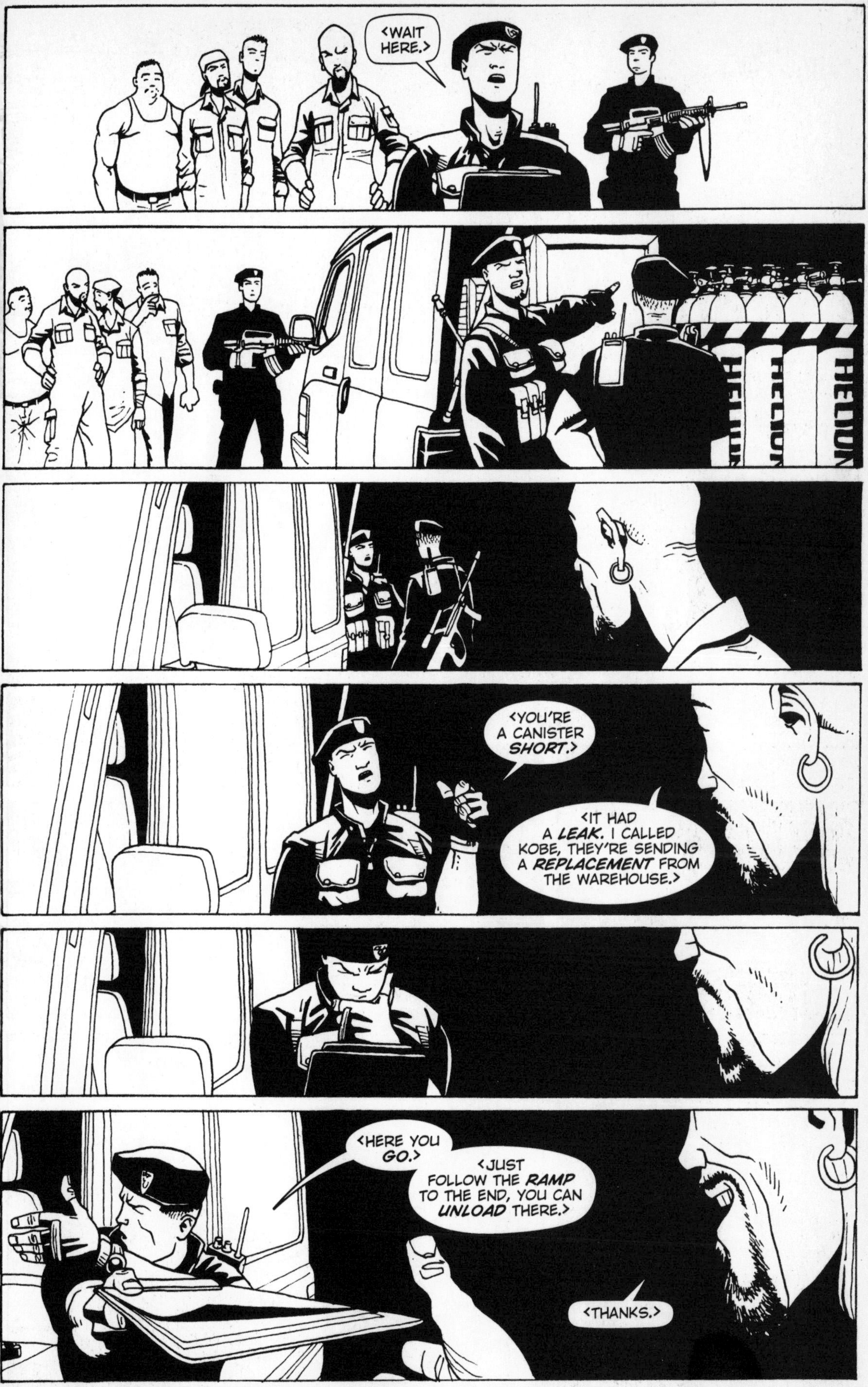
<WAIT HERE.>
HELIUM
<YOU'RE A CANISTER SHORT.>
<IT HAD A LEAK. I CALLED KOBE, THEY'RE SENDING A REPLACEMENT FROM THE WAREHOUSE.>
<HERE YOU GO.>
<JUST FOLLOW THE RAMP TO THE END, YOU CAN UNLOAD THERE.>
<THANKS.>

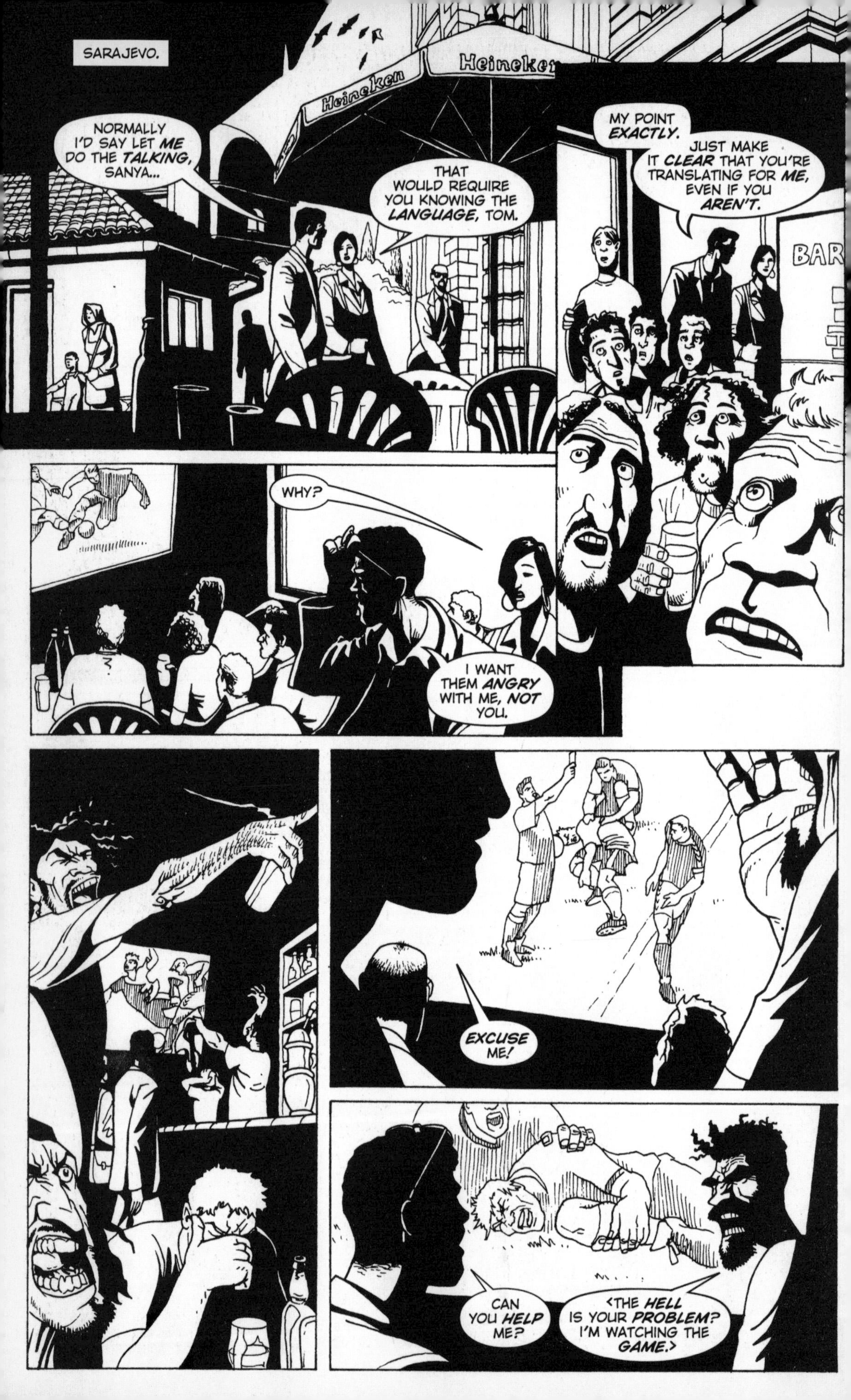
SARAJEVO.
Heineken
Heineken
NORMALLY I'D SAY LET ME DO THE TALKING, SANYA...
THAT WOULD REQUIRE YOU KNOWING THE LANGUAGE, TOM.
MY POINT EXACTLY.
JUST MAKE IT CLEAR THAT YOU'RE TRANSLATING FOR ME, EVEN IF YOU AREN'T.
BAR
WHY?
I WANT THEM ANGRY WITH ME, NOT YOU.
EXCUSE ME!
CAN YOU HELP ME?
<THE HELL IS YOUR PROBLEM? I'M WATCHING THE GAME.>

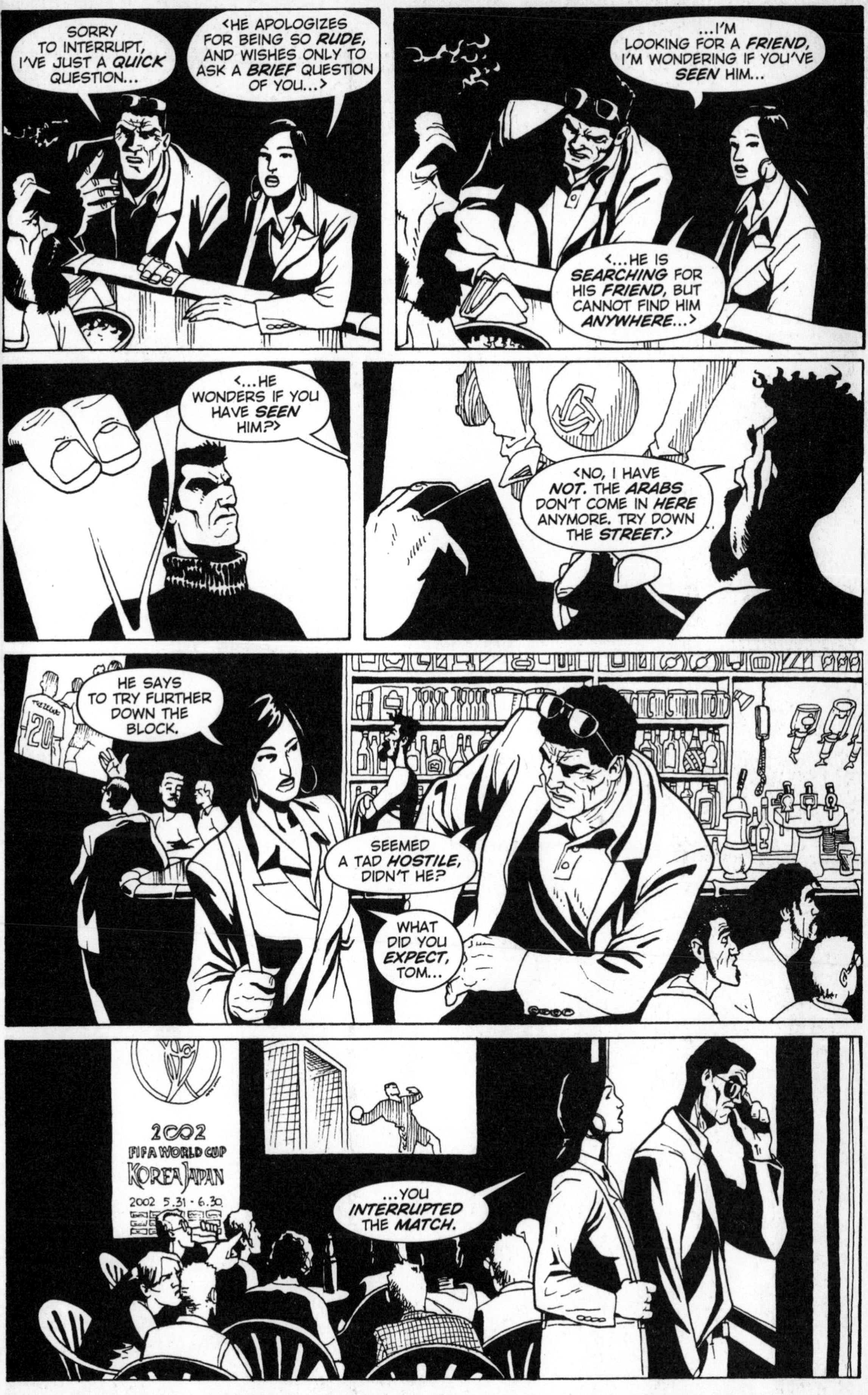
SORRY TO INTERRUPT, I'VE JUST A QUICK QUESTION...
<HE APOLOGIZES FOR BEING SO RUDE, AND WISHES ONLY TO ASK A BRIEF QUESTION OF YOU...>
...I'M LOOKING FOR A FRIEND, I'M WONDERING IF YOU'VE SEEN HIM...
<...HE IS SEARCHING FOR HIS FRIEND, BUT CANNOT FIND HIM ANYWHERE...>
<...HE WONDERS IF YOU HAVE SEEN HIM?>
<NO, I HAVE NOT. THE ARABS DON'T COME IN HERE ANYMORE. TRY DOWN THE STREET.>
HE SAYS TO TRY FURTHER DOWN THE BLOCK.
SEEMED A TAD HOSTILE, DIDN'T HE?
WHAT DID YOU EXPECT, TOM...
2002
FIFA WORLD CUP
KOREA JAPAN
2002 5.31 - 6.30
...YOU INTERRUPTED THE MATCH.

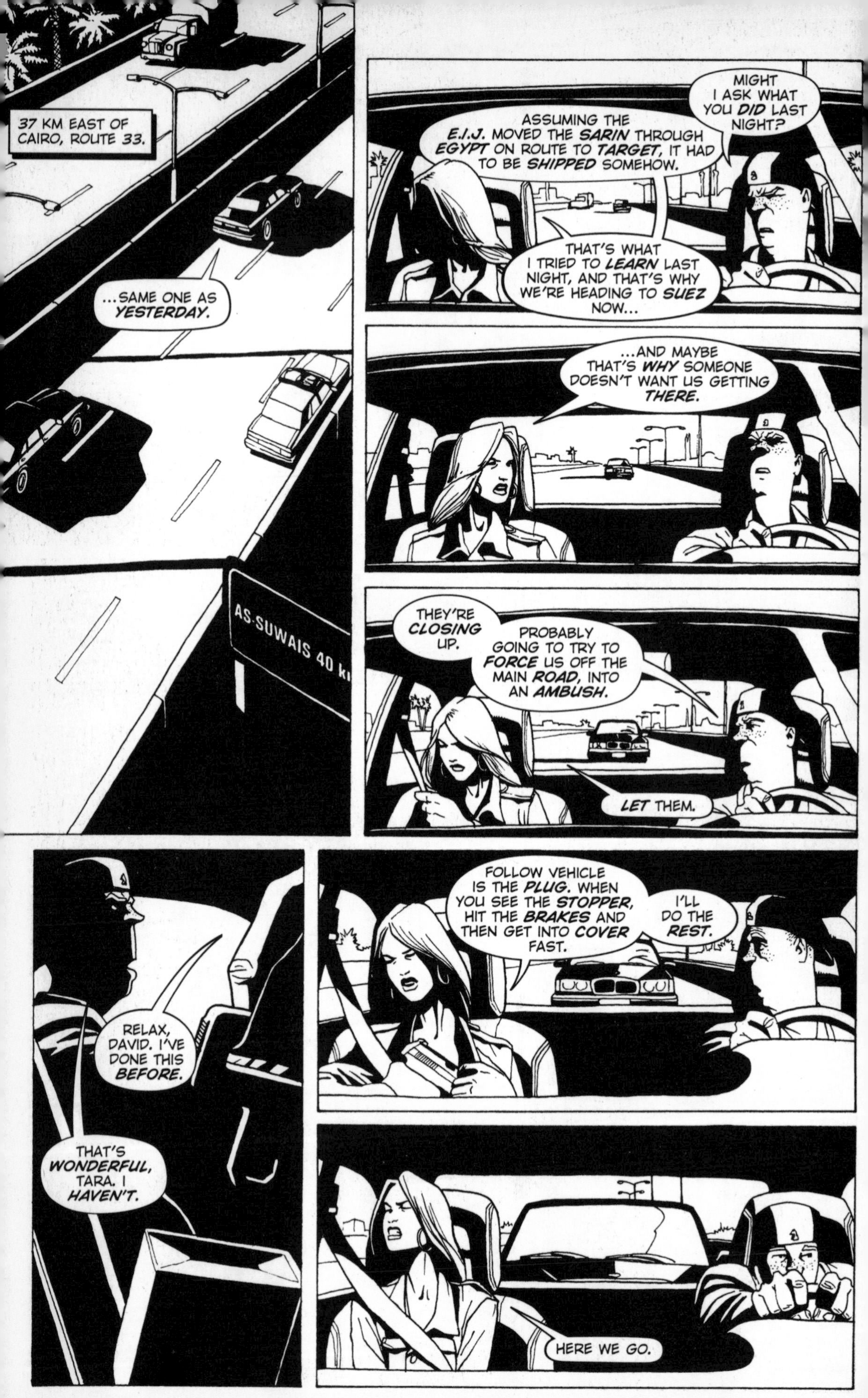
37 KM EAST OF CAIRO, ROUTE 33.
...SAME ONE AS YESTERDAY.
AS-SUWAIS 40 K
ASSUMING THE E.I.J. MOVED THE SARIN THROUGH EGYPT ON ROUTE TO TARGET, IT HAD TO BE SHIPPED SOMEHOW.
MIGHT I ASK WHAT YOU DID LAST NIGHT?
THAT'S WHAT I TRIED TO LEARN LAST NIGHT, AND THAT'S WHY WE'RE HEADING TO SUEZ NOW...
...AND MAYBE THAT'S WHY SOMEONE DOESN'T WANT US GETTING THERE.
THEY'RE CLOSING UP.
PROBABLY GOING TO TRY TO FORCE US OFF THE MAIN ROAD, INTO AN AMBUSH.
LET THEM.
RELAX, DAVID. I'VE DONE THIS BEFORE.
THAT'S WONDERFUL, TARA. I HAVEN'T.
FOLLOW VEHICLE IS THE PLUG. WHEN YOU SEE THE STOPPER, HIT THE BRAKES AND THEN GET INTO COVER FAST.
I'LL DO THE REST.
HERE WE GO.

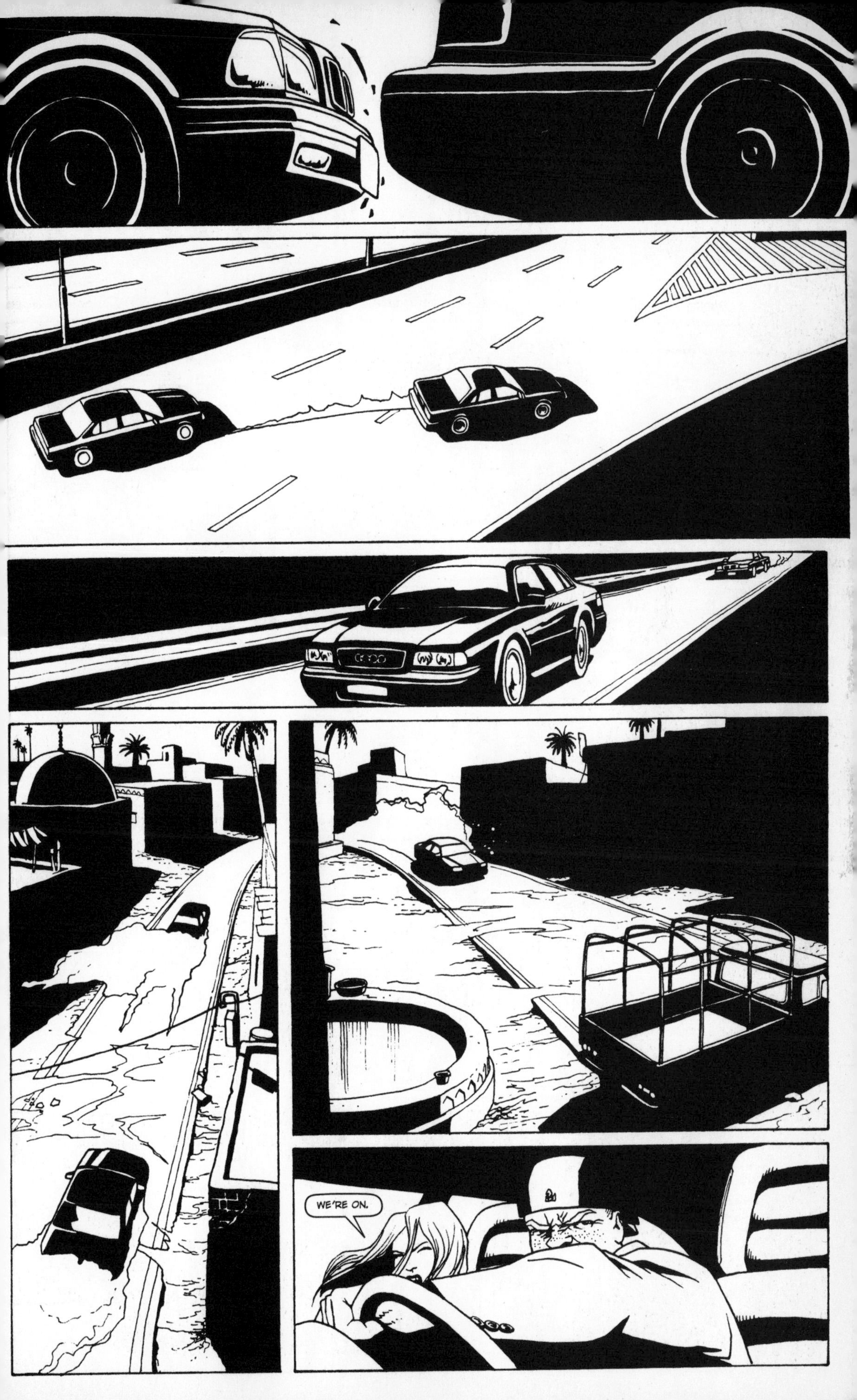
WE'RE ON.

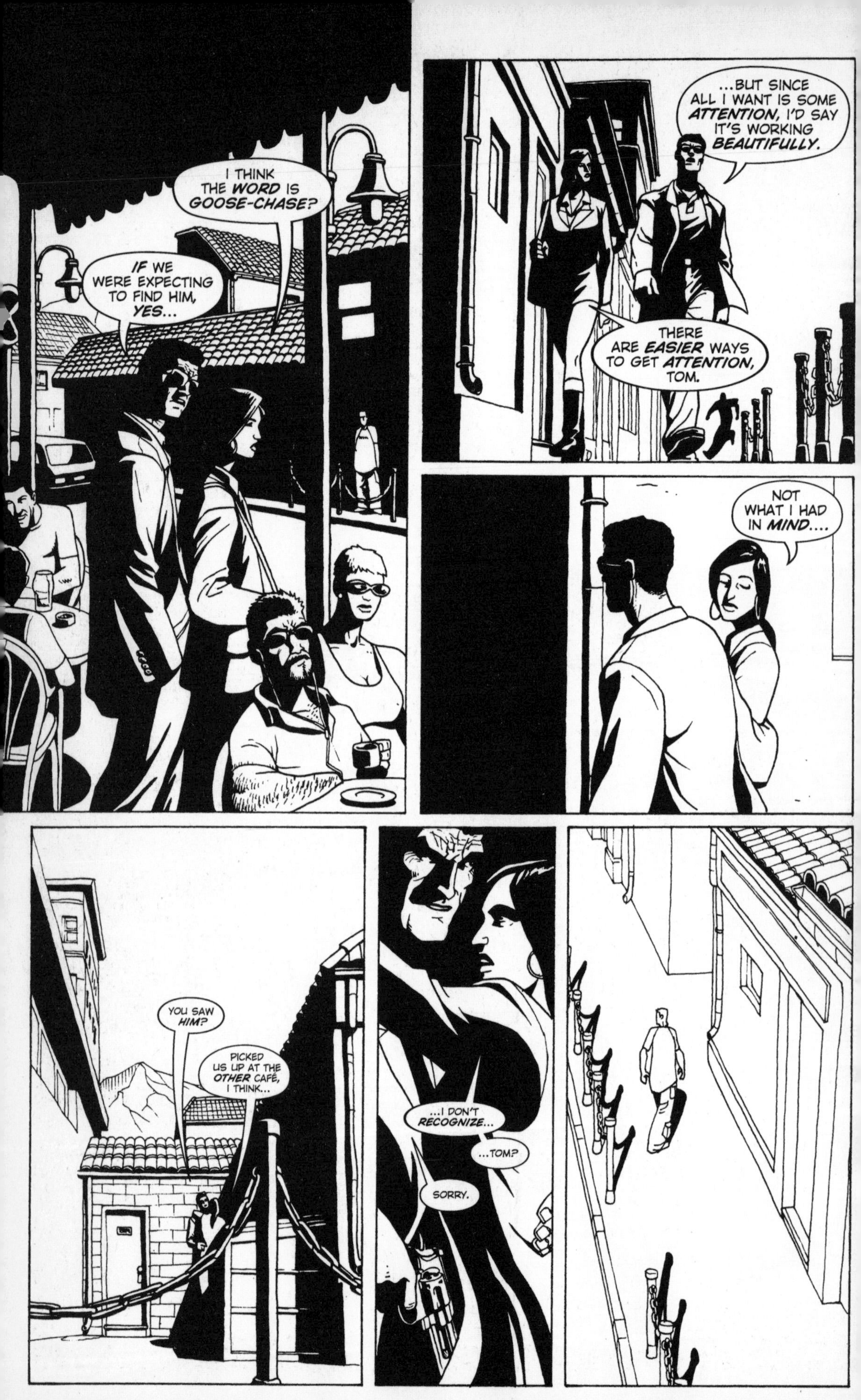
IF WE WERE EXPECTING TO FIND HIM, YES...
I THINK THE WORD IS GOOSE-CHASE?
...BUT SINCE ALL I WANT IS SOME ATTENTION, I'D SAY IT'S WORKING BEAUTIFULLY.
THERE ARE EASIER WAYS TO GET ATTENTION, TOM.
NOT WHAT I HAD IN MIND....
YOU SAW HIM?
PICKED US UP AT THE OTHER CAFÉ, I THINK...
...I DON'T RECOGNIZE...
...TOM?
SORRY.

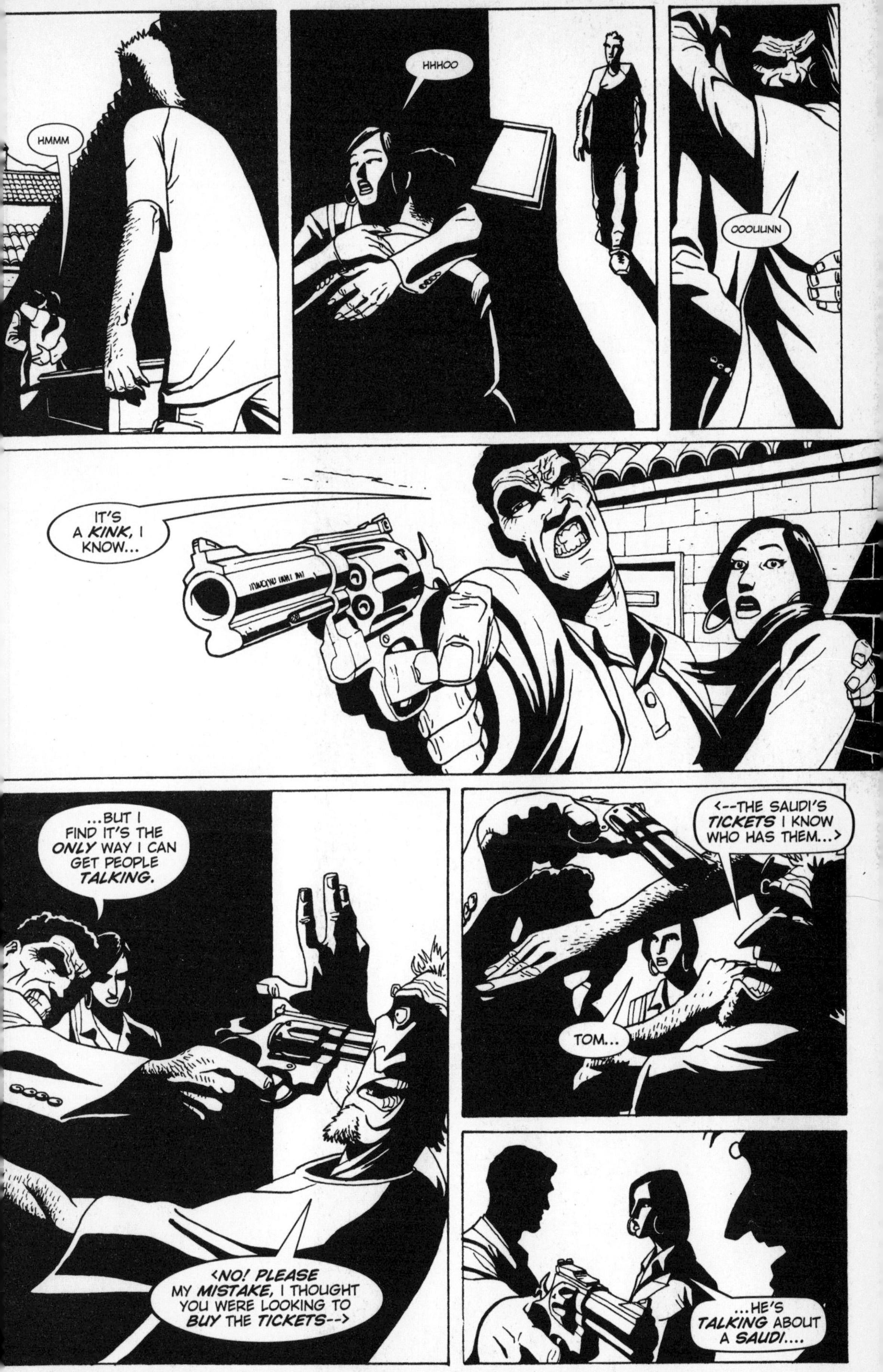

HMMM
HHHOO
OOOUUNN
IT'S A *KINK,* I KNOW...
...BUT I FIND IT'S THE *ONLY* WAY I CAN GET PEOPLE *TALKING.*
<NO! PLEASE MY *MISTAKE,* I THOUGHT YOU WERE LOOKING TO *BUY* THE *TICKETS*-->
<--THE SAUDI'S *TICKETS* I KNOW WHO HAS THEM...>
TOM...
...HE'S *TALKING* ABOUT A *SAUDI*....

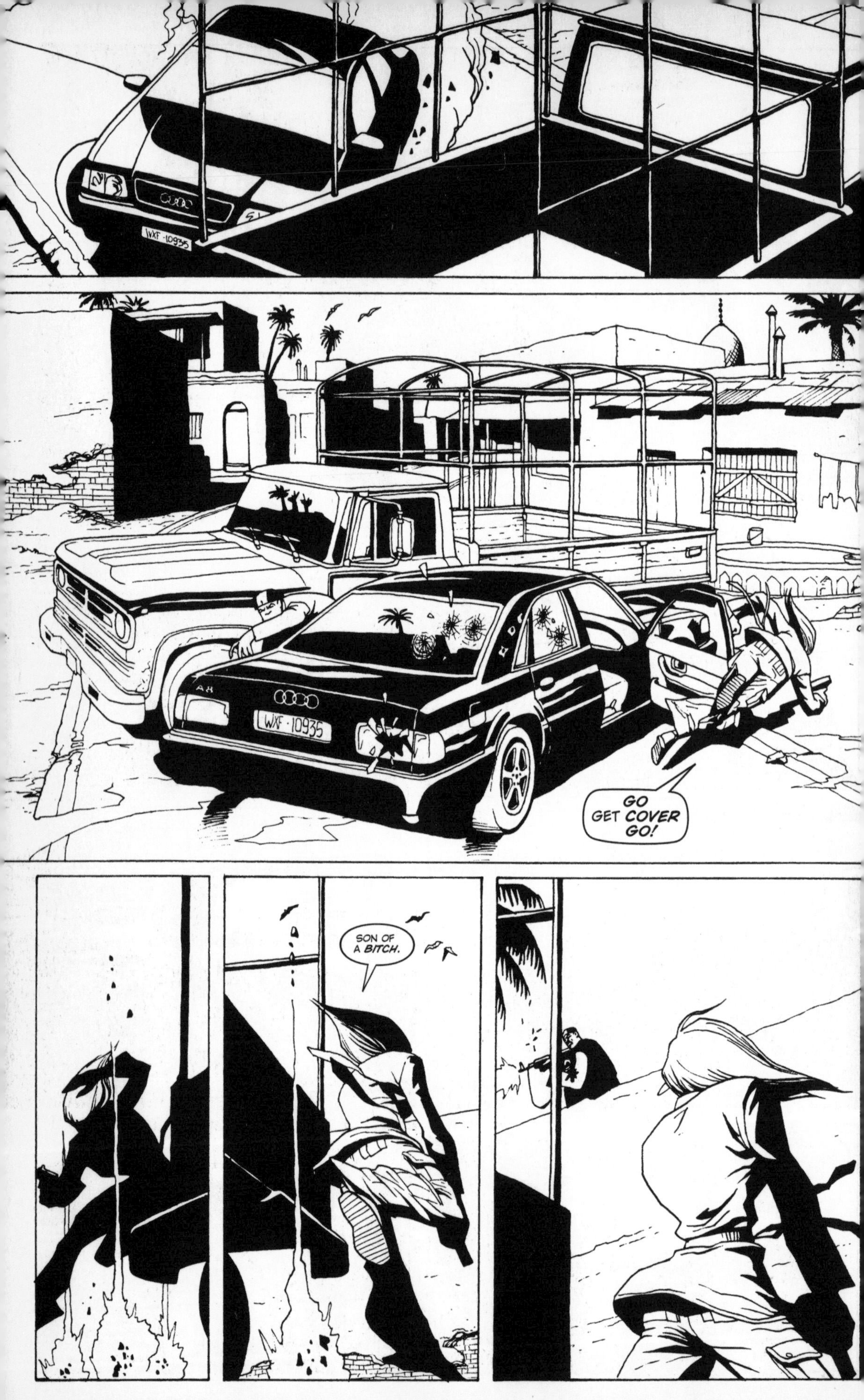
GO GET COVER GO!
SON OF A BITCH.

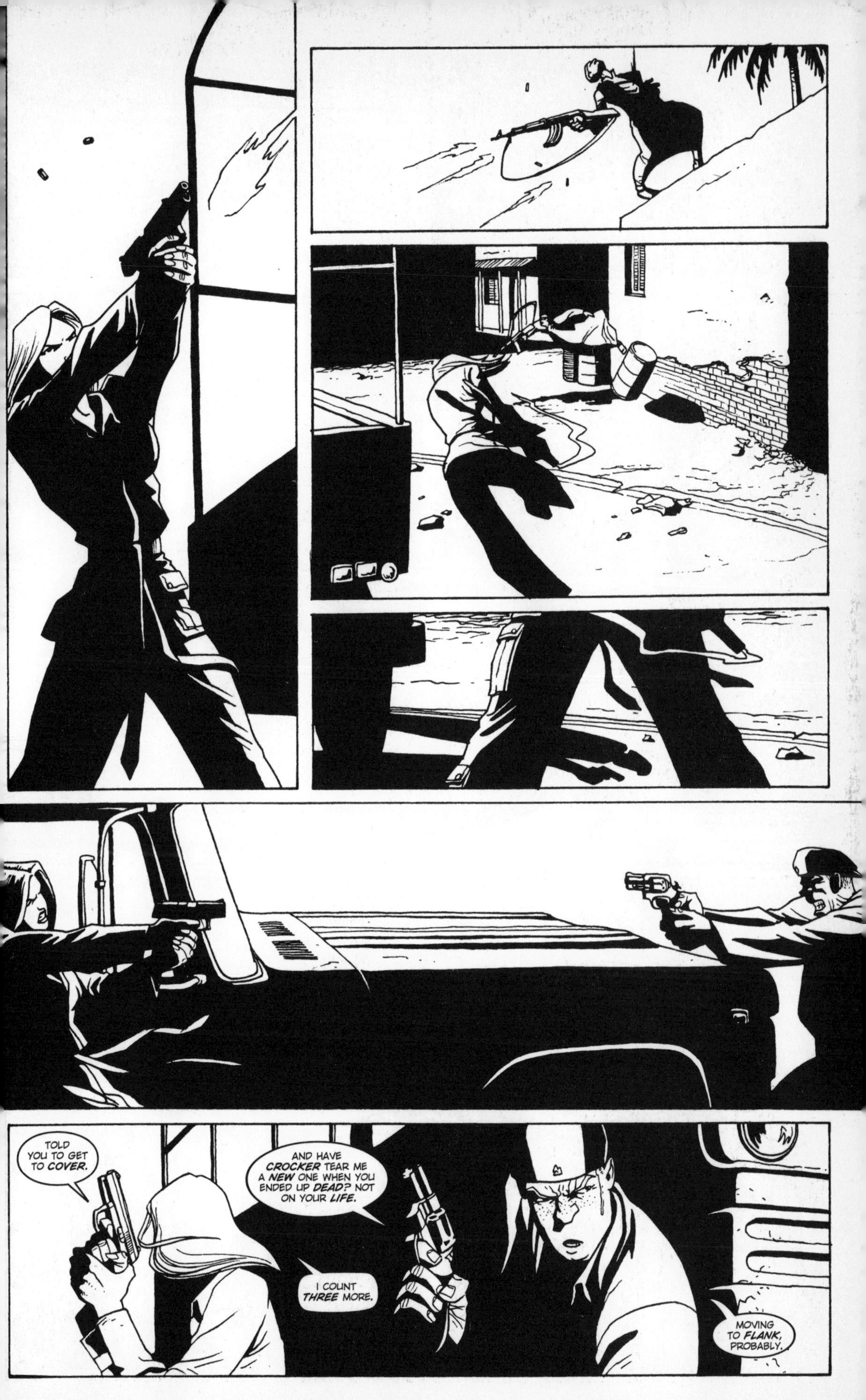
TOLD YOU TO GET TO COVER.
AND HAVE CROCKER TEAR ME A NEW ONE WHEN YOU ENDED UP DEAD? NOT ON YOUR LIFE.
I COUNT THREE MORE.
MOVING TO FLANK, PROBABLY.

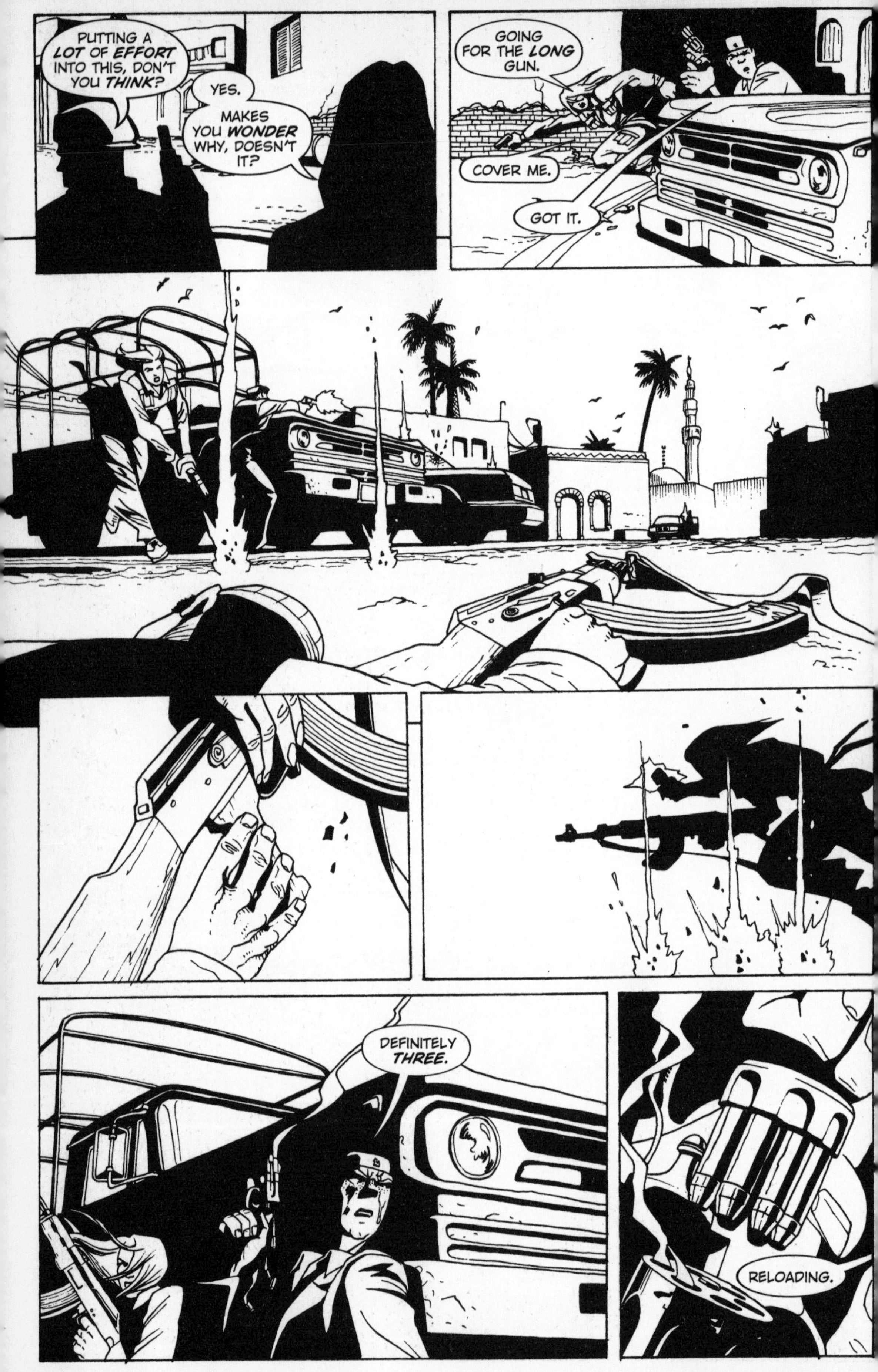
PUTTING A LOT OF EFFORT INTO THIS, DON'T YOU THINK?
YES.
MAKES YOU WONDER WHY, DOESN'T IT?
GOING FOR THE LONG GUN.
COVER ME.
GOT IT.
DEFINITELY THREE.
RELOADING.

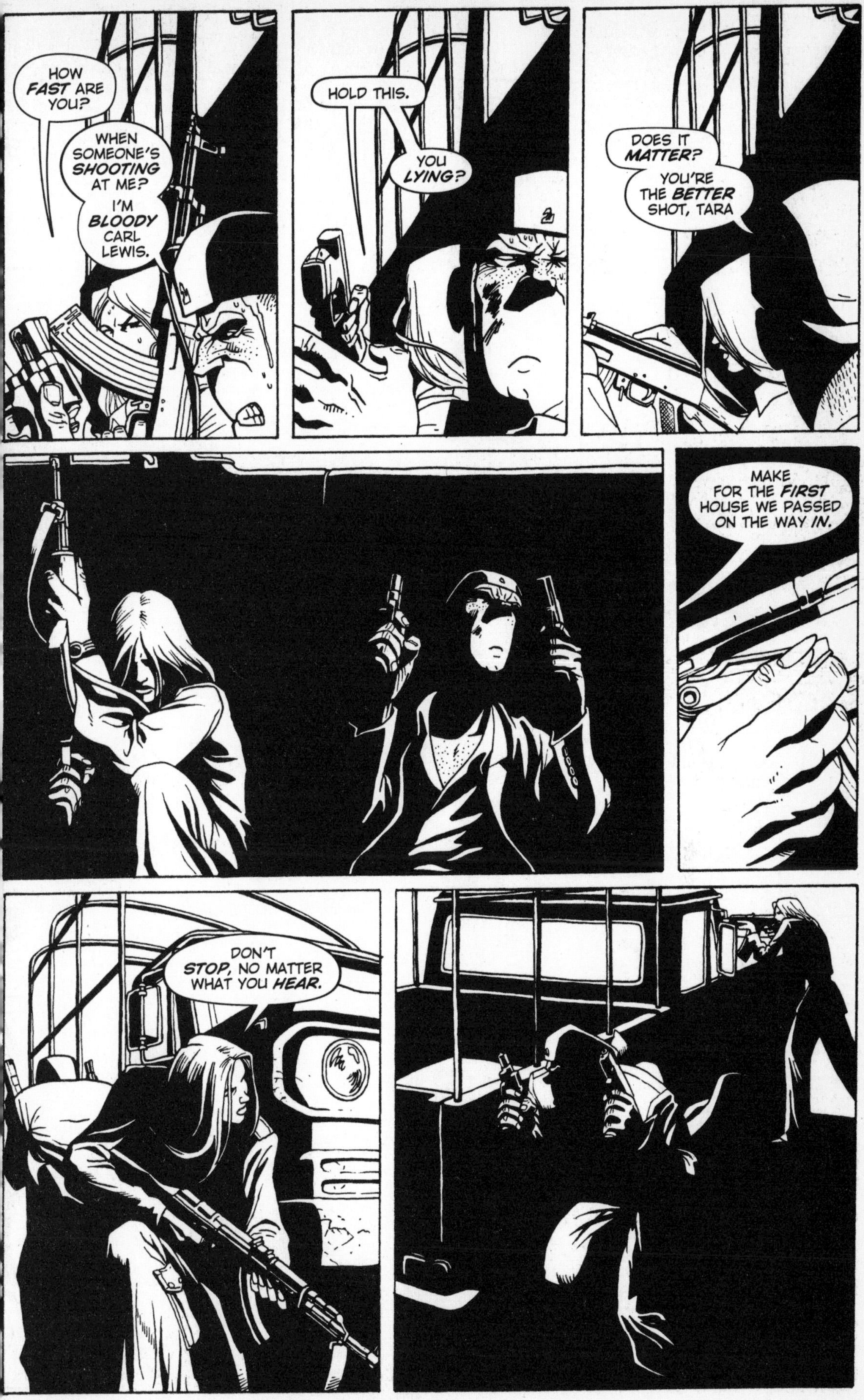
HOW FAST ARE YOU?
WHEN SOMEONE'S SHOOTING AT ME?
I'M BLOODY CARL LEWIS.
HOLD THIS.
YOU LYING?
DOES IT MATTER?
YOU'RE THE BETTER SHOT, TARA
MAKE FOR THE FIRST HOUSE WE PASSED ON THE WAY IN.
DON'T STOP, NO MATTER WHAT YOU HEAR.

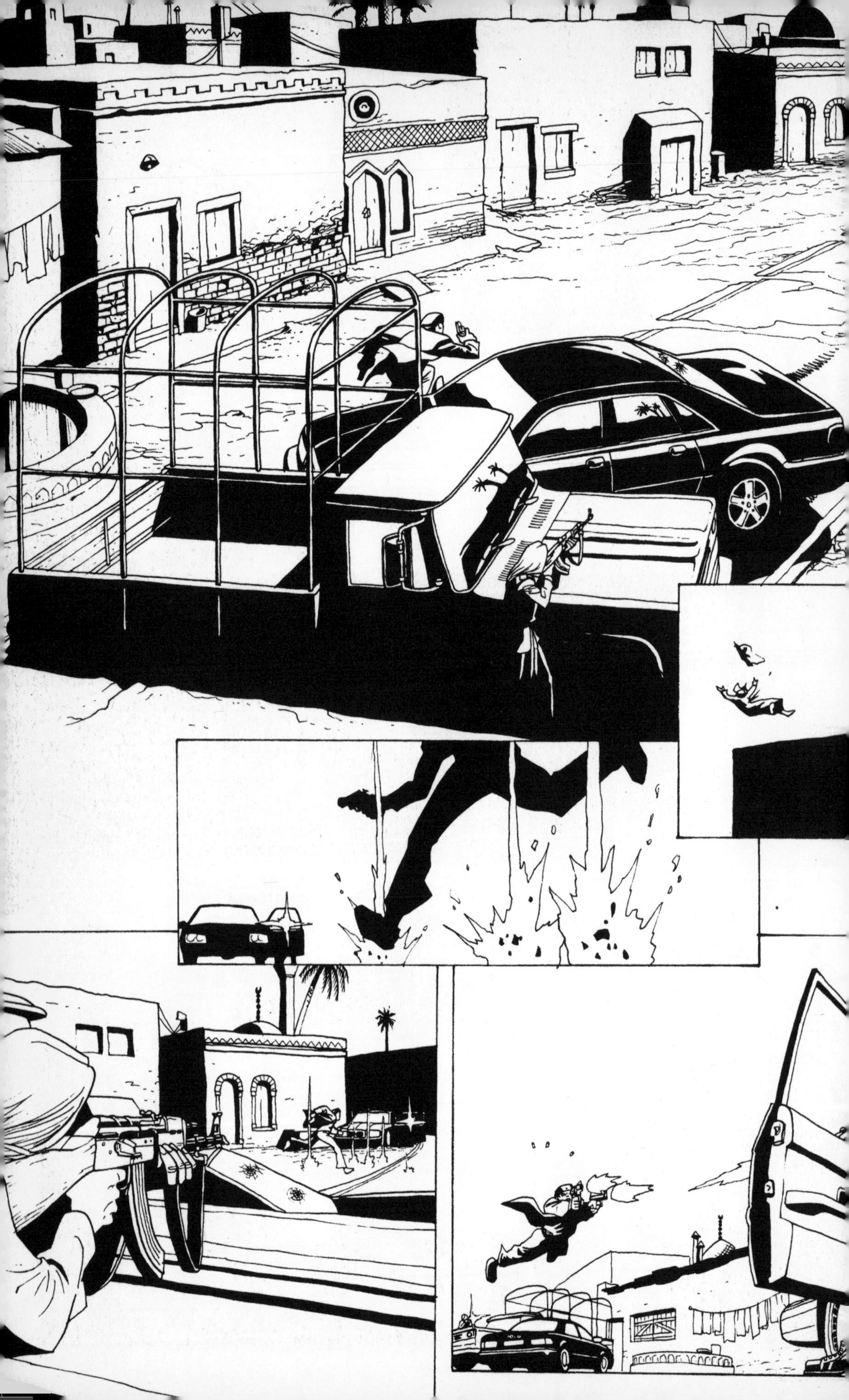

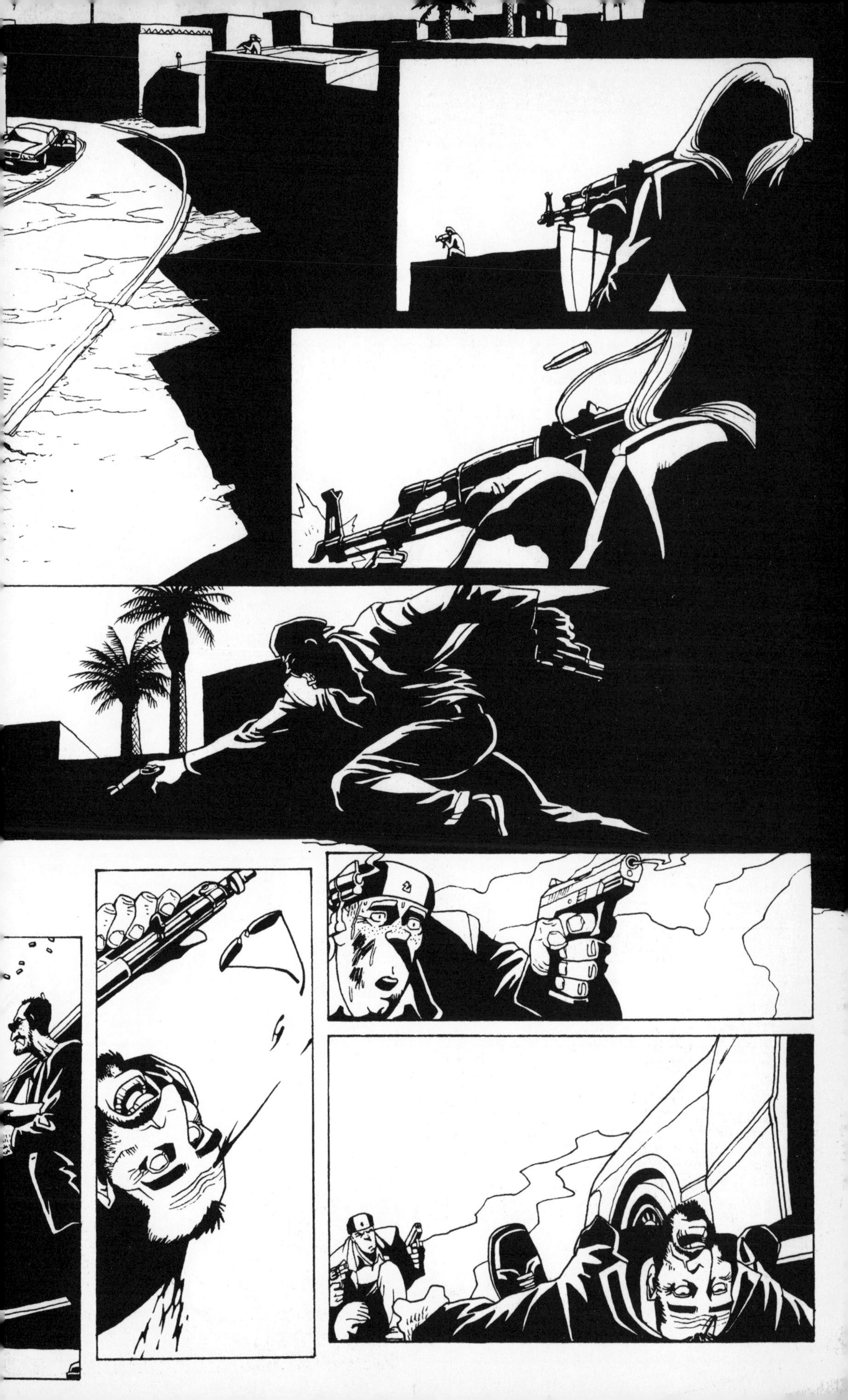

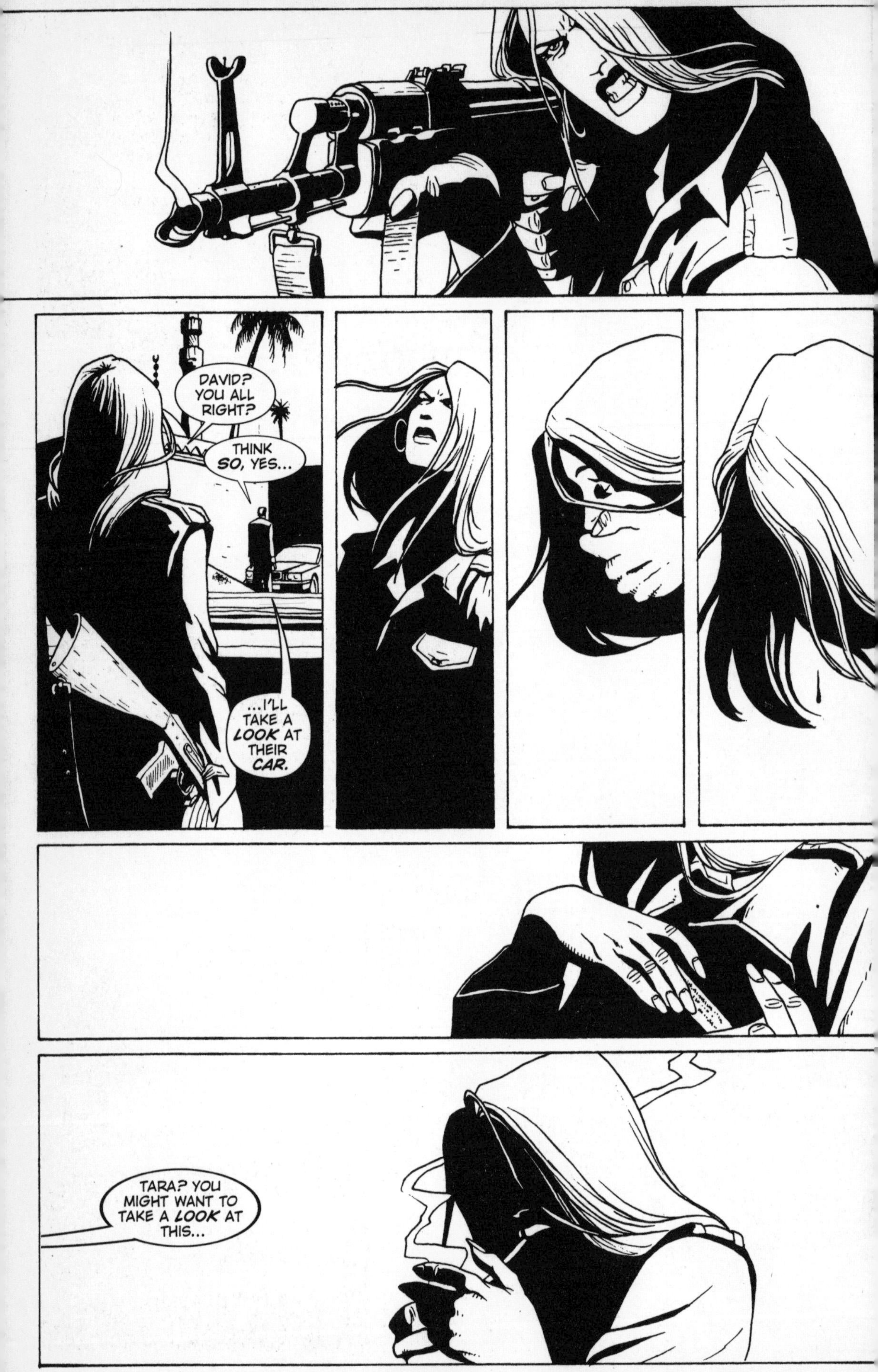
DAVID? YOU ALL RIGHT?
THINK SO, YES...
...I'LL TAKE A LOOK AT THEIR CAR.
TARA? YOU MIGHT WANT TO TAKE A LOOK AT THIS...

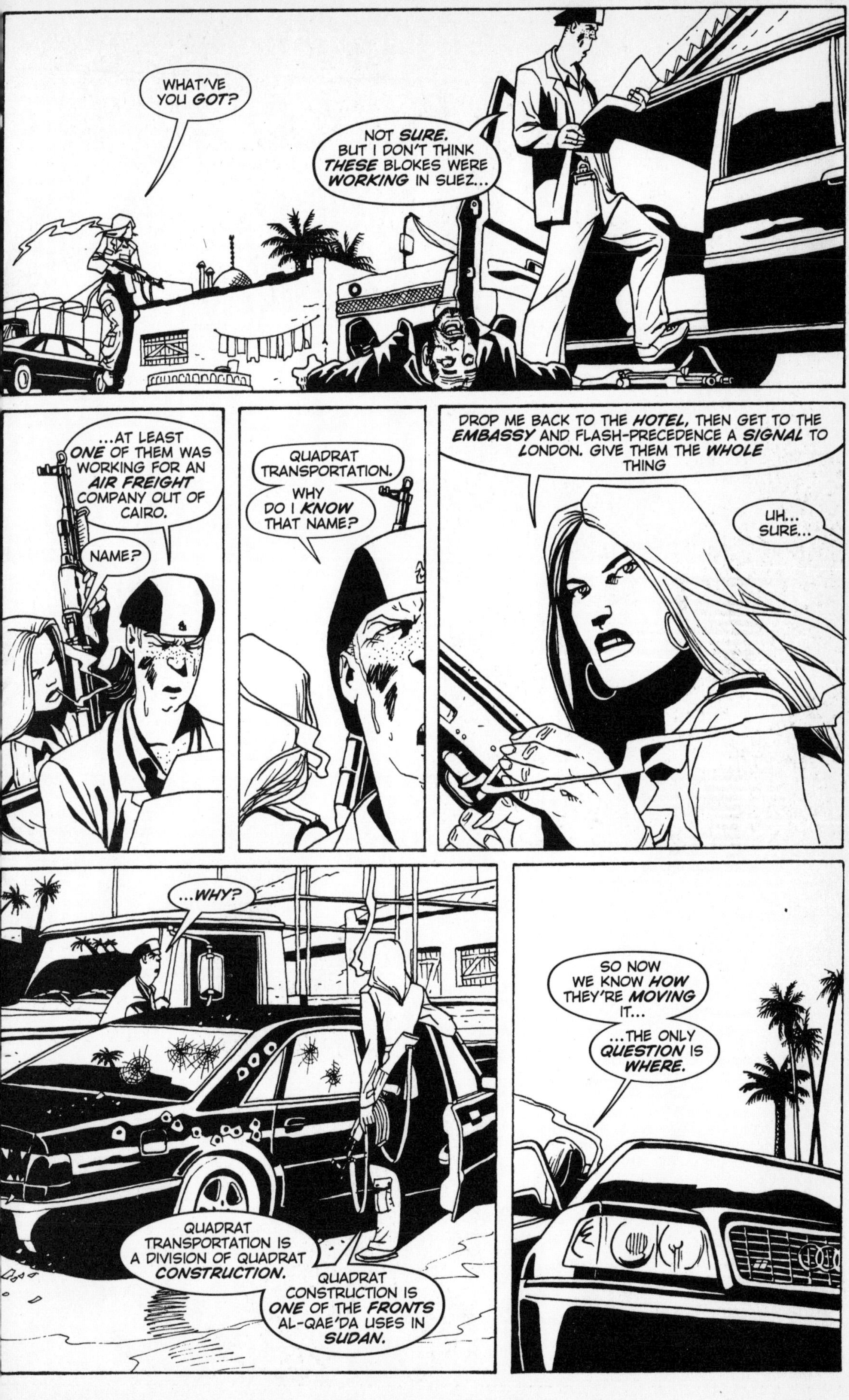
WHAT'VE YOU GOT?
NOT SURE. BUT I DON'T THINK THESE BLOKES WERE WORKING IN SUEZ...
...AT LEAST ONE OF THEM WAS WORKING FOR AN AIR FREIGHT COMPANY OUT OF CAIRO.
NAME?
QUADRAT TRANSPORTATION.
WHY DO I KNOW THAT NAME?
DROP ME BACK TO THE HOTEL, THEN GET TO THE EMBASSY AND FLASH-PRECEDENCE A SIGNAL TO LONDON. GIVE THEM THE WHOLE THING
UH... SURE...
...WHY?
QUADRAT TRANSPORTATION IS A DIVISION OF QUADRAT CONSTRUCTION.
QUADRAT CONSTRUCTION IS ONE OF THE FRONTS AL-QAE'DA USES IN SUDAN.
SO NOW WE KNOW HOW THEY'RE MOVING IT...
...THE ONLY QUESTION IS WHERE.

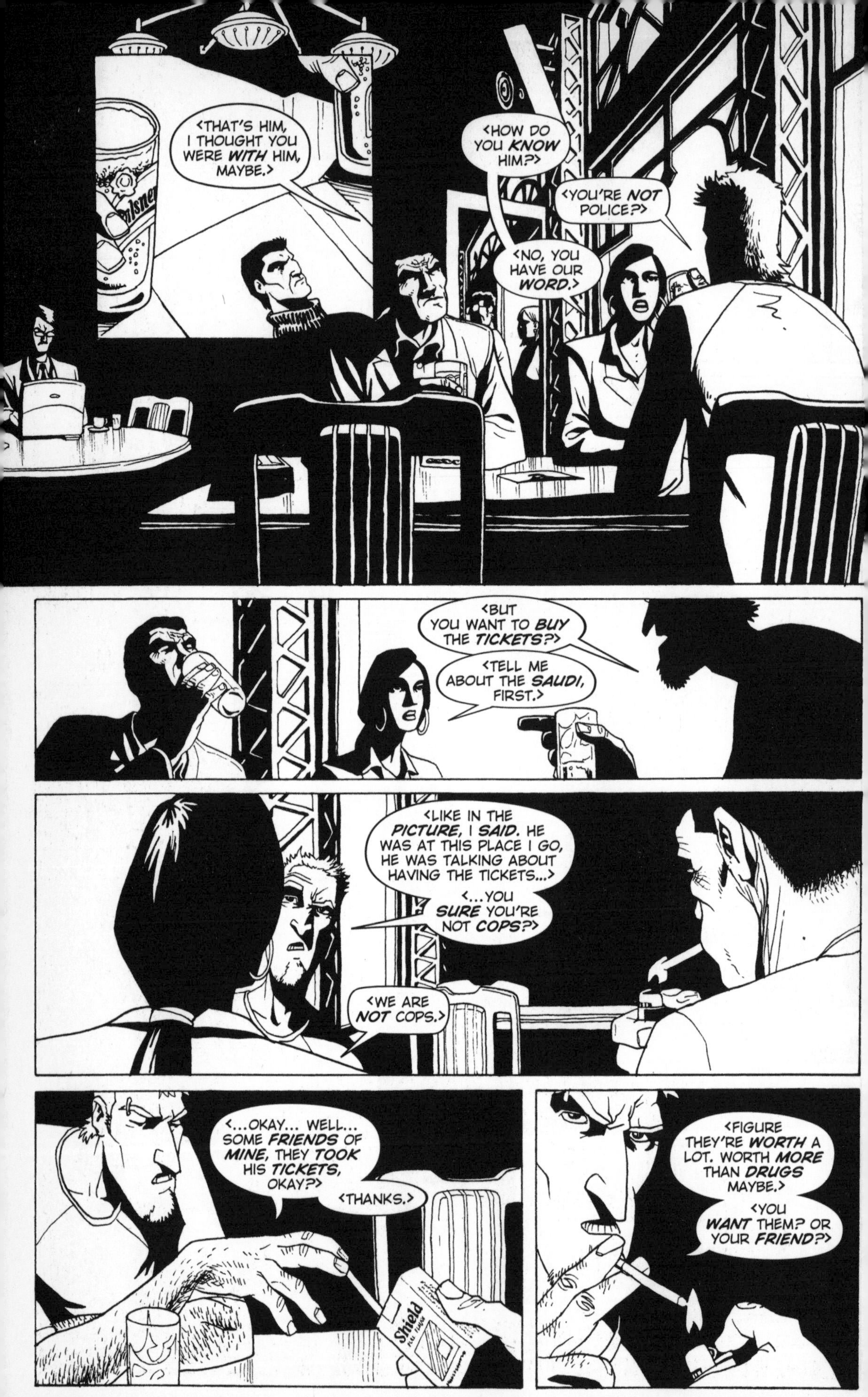
<THAT'S HIM, I THOUGHT YOU WERE WITH HIM, MAYBE.>
<HOW DO YOU KNOW HIM?>
<YOU'RE NOT POLICE?>
<NO, YOU HAVE OUR WORD.>
<BUT YOU WANT TO BUY THE TICKETS?>
<TELL ME ABOUT THE SAUDI, FIRST.>
<LIKE IN THE PICTURE, I SAID. HE WAS AT THIS PLACE I GO, HE WAS TALKING ABOUT HAVING THE TICKETS...>
<...YOU SURE YOU'RE NOT COPS?>
<WE ARE NOT COPS.>
<...OKAY... WELL... SOME FRIENDS OF MINE, THEY TOOK HIS TICKETS, OKAY?>
<THANKS.>
Shield
<FIGURE THEY'RE WORTH A LOT. WORTH MORE THAN DRUGS MAYBE.>
<YOU WANT THEM? OR YOUR FRIEND?>

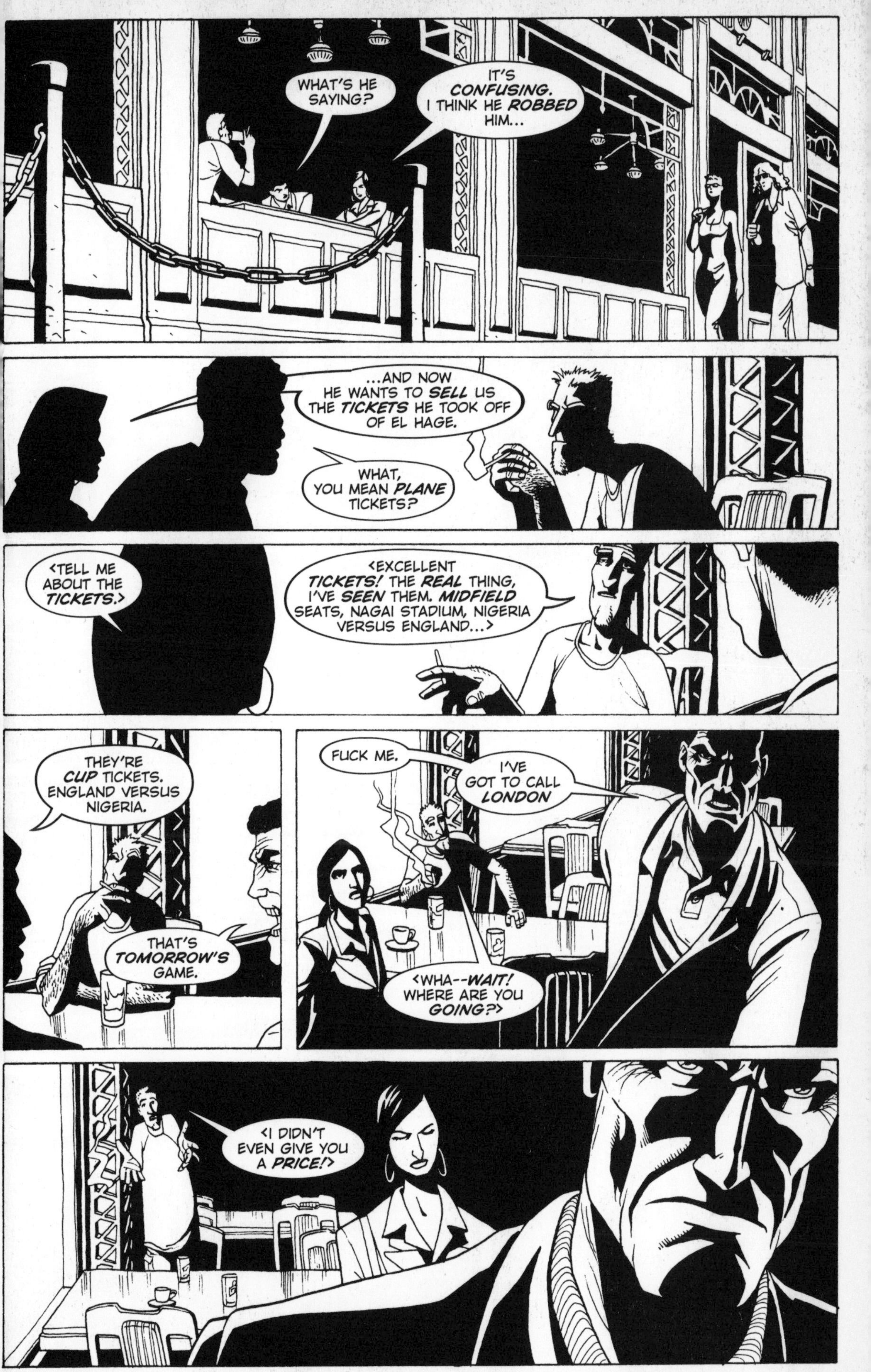
WHAT'S HE SAYING?
IT'S CONFUSING. I THINK HE ROBBED HIM...
...AND NOW HE WANTS TO SELL US THE TICKETS HE TOOK OFF OF EL HAGE.
WHAT, YOU MEAN PLANE TICKETS?
<TELL ME ABOUT THE TICKETS.>
<EXCELLENT TICKETS! THE REAL THING, I'VE SEEN THEM. MIDFIELD SEATS, NAGAI STADIUM, NIGERIA VERSUS ENGLAND...>
THEY'RE CUP TICKETS. ENGLAND VERSUS NIGERIA.
THAT'S TOMORROW'S GAME.
FUCK ME.
I'VE GOT TO CALL LONDON
<WHA--WAIT! WHERE ARE YOU GOING?>
<I DIDN'T EVEN GIVE YOU A PRICE!>

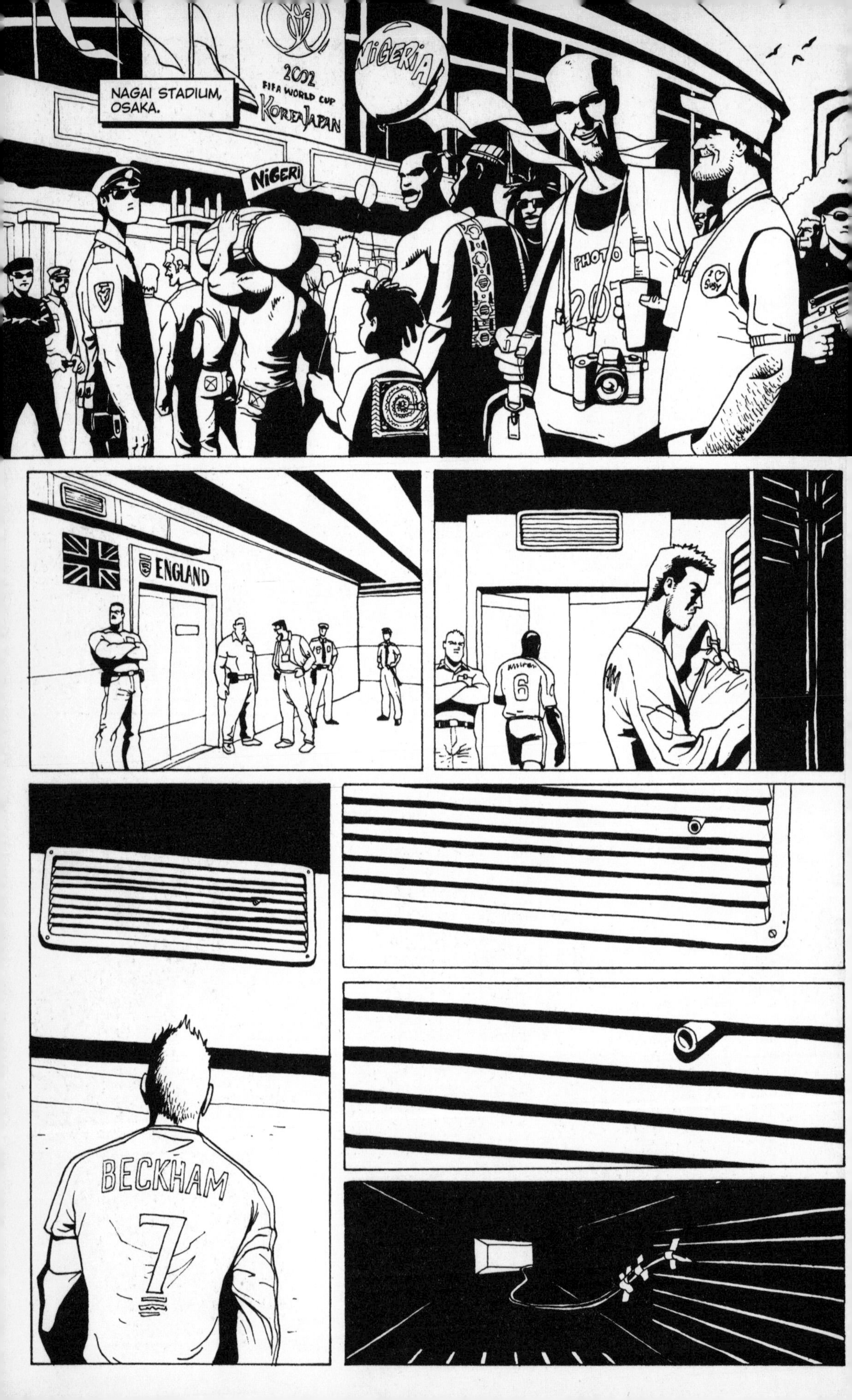

NAGAI STADIUM, OSAKA.
2002 FIFA WORLD CUP KOREA JAPAN
NIGERIA
NIGERI
PHOTO
ENGLAND
BECKHAM
7

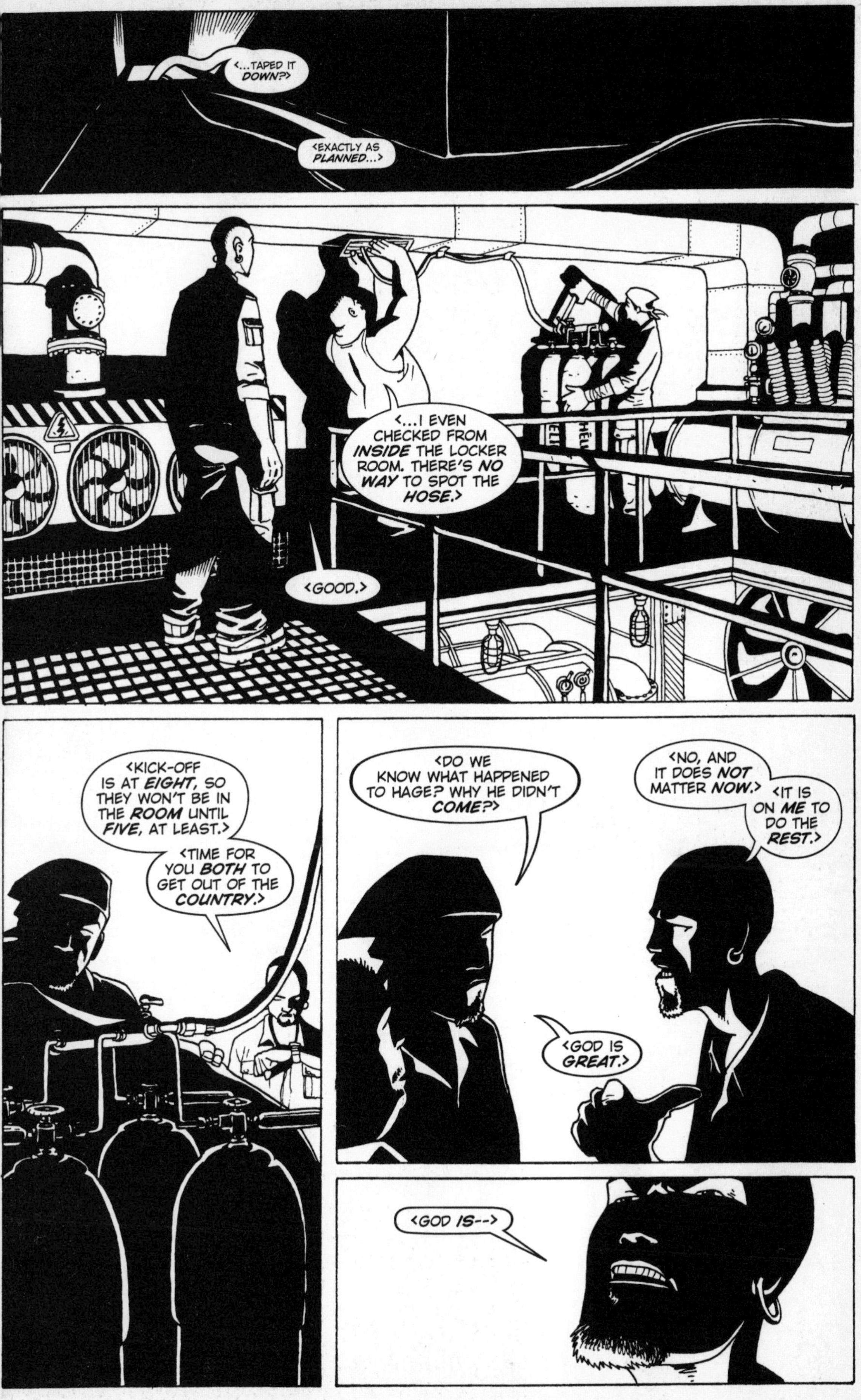

<...TAPED IT DOWN?>
<EXACTLY AS PLANNED...>
<...I EVEN CHECKED FROM INSIDE THE LOCKER ROOM. THERE'S NO WAY TO SPOT THE HOSE.>
<GOOD.>
<KICK-OFF IS AT EIGHT, SO THEY WON'T BE IN THE ROOM UNTIL FIVE, AT LEAST.>
<TIME FOR YOU BOTH TO GET OUT OF THE COUNTRY.>
<DO WE KNOW WHAT HAPPENED TO HAGE? WHY HE DIDN'T COME?>
<NO, AND IT DOES NOT MATTER NOW.>
<IT IS ON ME TO DO THE REST.>
<GOD IS GREAT.>
<GOD IS-->

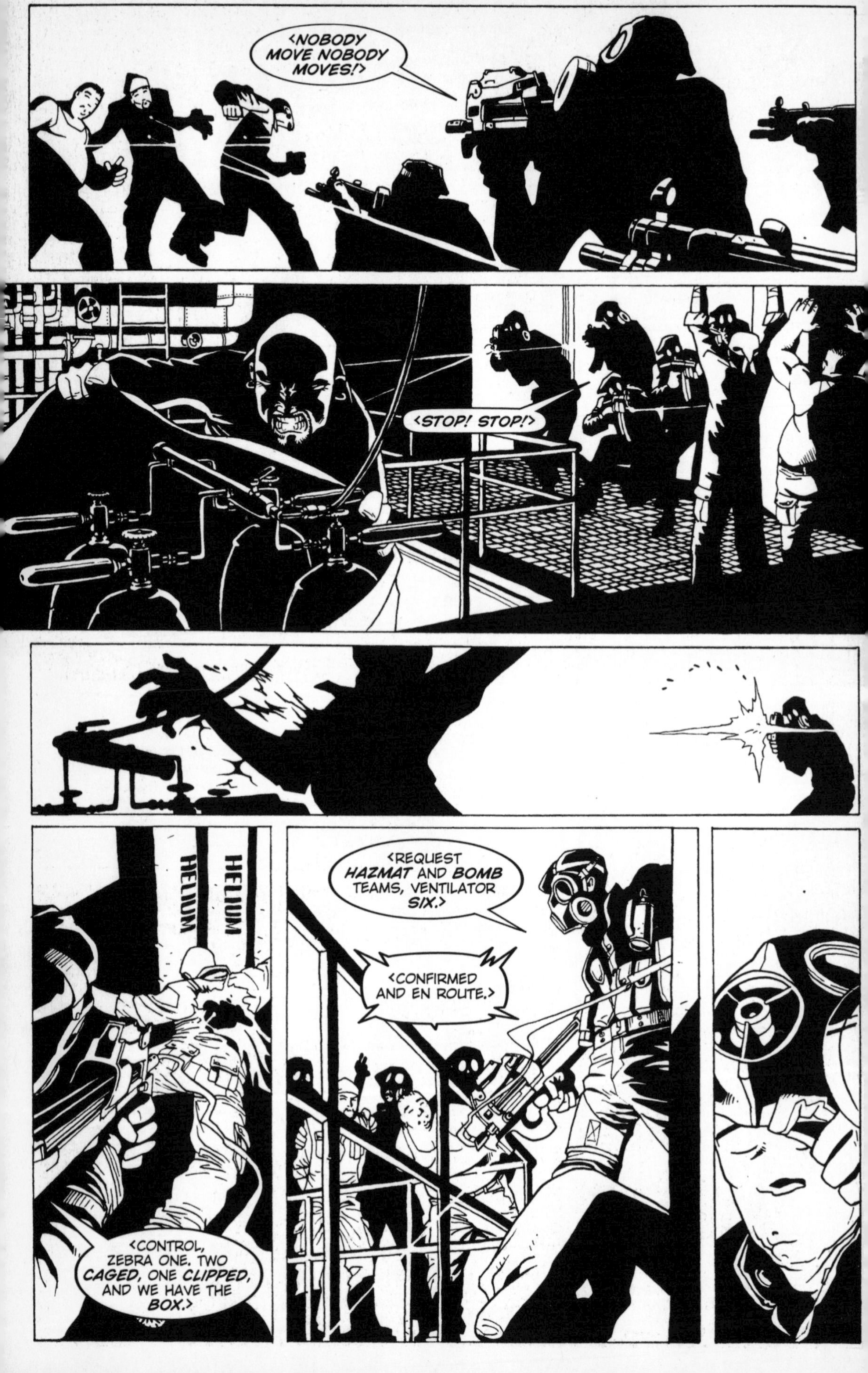
<NOBODY MOVE NOBODY MOVES!>
<STOP! STOP!>
<CONTROL, ZEBRA ONE. TWO *CAGED*, ONE *CLIPPED*, AND WE HAVE THE *BOX*.>
<REQUEST *HAZMAT* AND *BOMB* TEAMS, VENTILATOR *SIX*.>
<CONFIRMED AND EN ROUTE.>
HELIUM
HELIUM

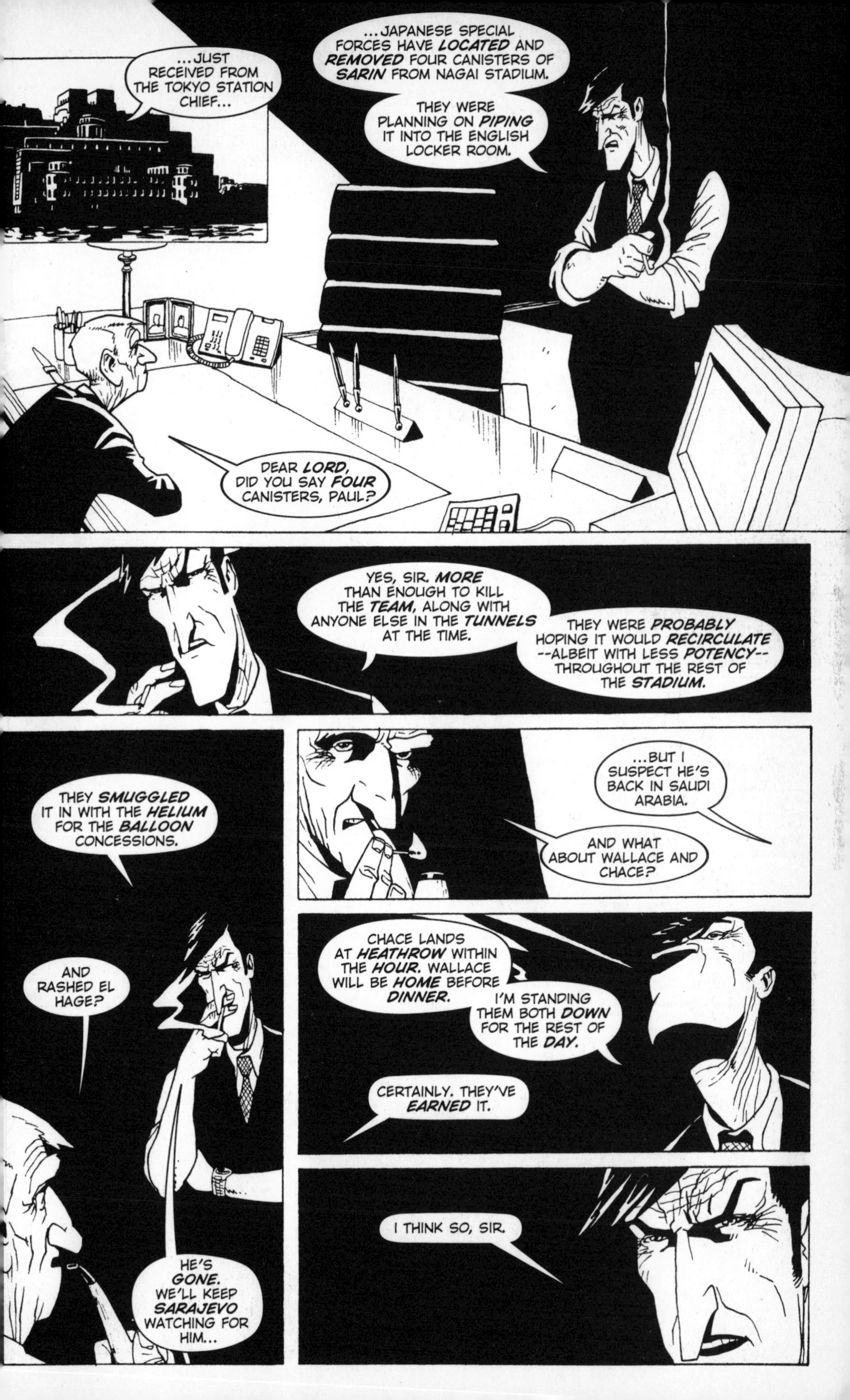
...JUST RECEIVED FROM THE TOKYO STATION CHIEF...
...JAPANESE SPECIAL FORCES HAVE LOCATED AND REMOVED FOUR CANISTERS OF SARIN FROM NAGAI STADIUM.
THEY WERE PLANNING ON PIPING IT INTO THE ENGLISH LOCKER ROOM.
DEAR LORD, DID YOU SAY FOUR CANISTERS, PAUL?
YES, SIR. MORE THAN ENOUGH TO KILL THE TEAM, ALONG WITH ANYONE ELSE IN THE TUNNELS AT THE TIME.
THEY WERE PROBABLY HOPING IT WOULD RECIRCULATE --ALBEIT WITH LESS POTENCY-- THROUGHOUT THE REST OF THE STADIUM.
THEY SMUGGLED IT IN WITH THE HELIUM FOR THE BALLOON CONCESSIONS.
AND RASHED EL HAGE?
HE'S GONE. WE'LL KEEP SARAJEVO WATCHING FOR HIM...
...BUT I SUSPECT HE'S BACK IN SAUDI ARABIA.
AND WHAT ABOUT WALLACE AND CHACE?
CHACE LANDS AT HEATHROW WITHIN THE HOUR. WALLACE WILL BE HOME BEFORE DINNER.
I'M STANDING THEM BOTH DOWN FOR THE REST OF THE DAY.
CERTAINLY. THEY'VE EARNED IT.
I THINK SO, SIR.

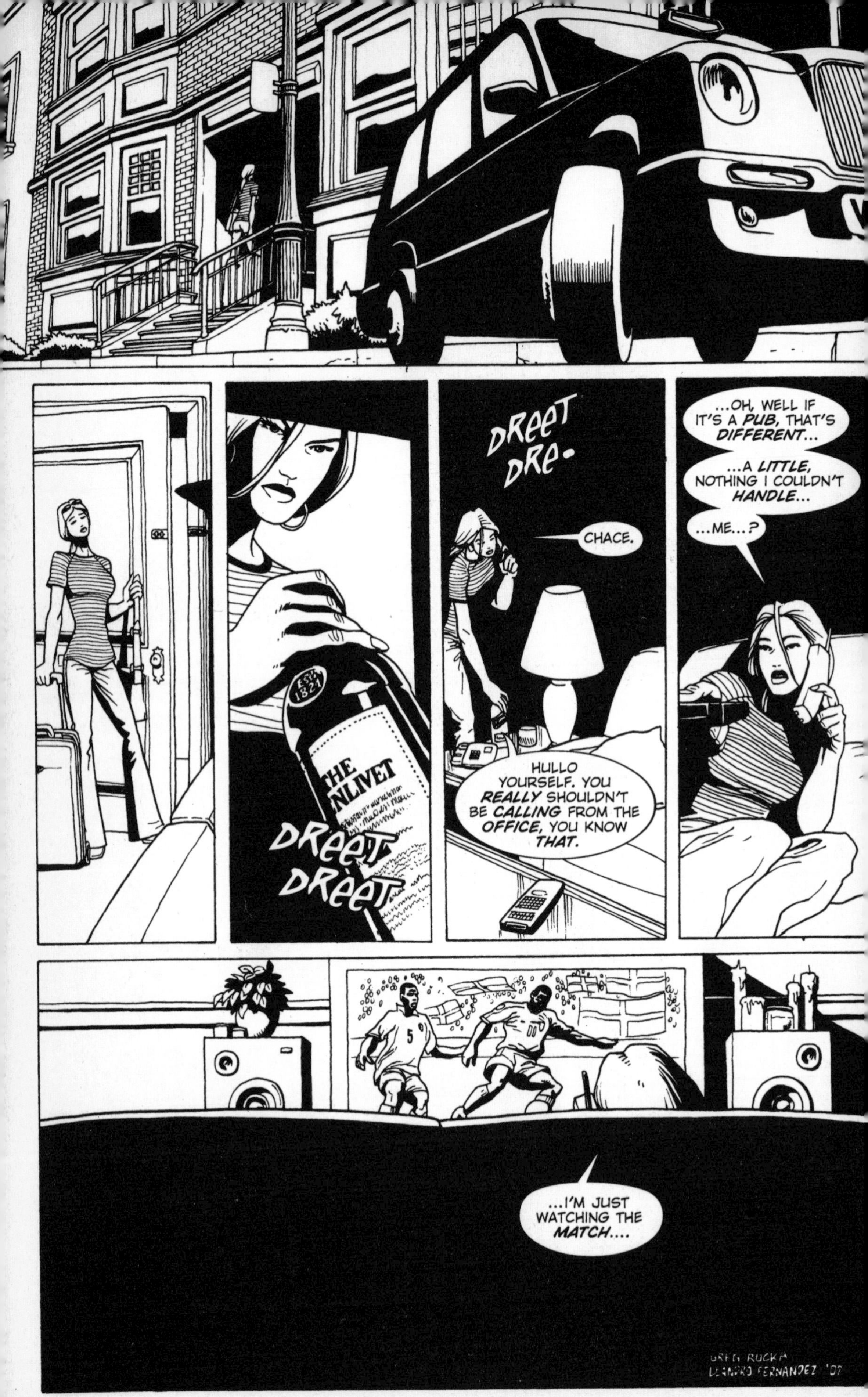
DREET DRE•
CHACE.
HULLO YOURSELF. YOU REALLY SHOULDN'T BE CALLING FROM THE OFFICE, YOU KNOW THAT.
DREET DREET
...OH, WELL IF IT'S A PUB, THAT'S DIFFERENT...
...A LITTLE, NOTHING I COULDN'T HANDLE...
...ME...?
...I'M JUST WATCHING THE MATCH....
GREG RUCKA

PRODUCTION GALLERY

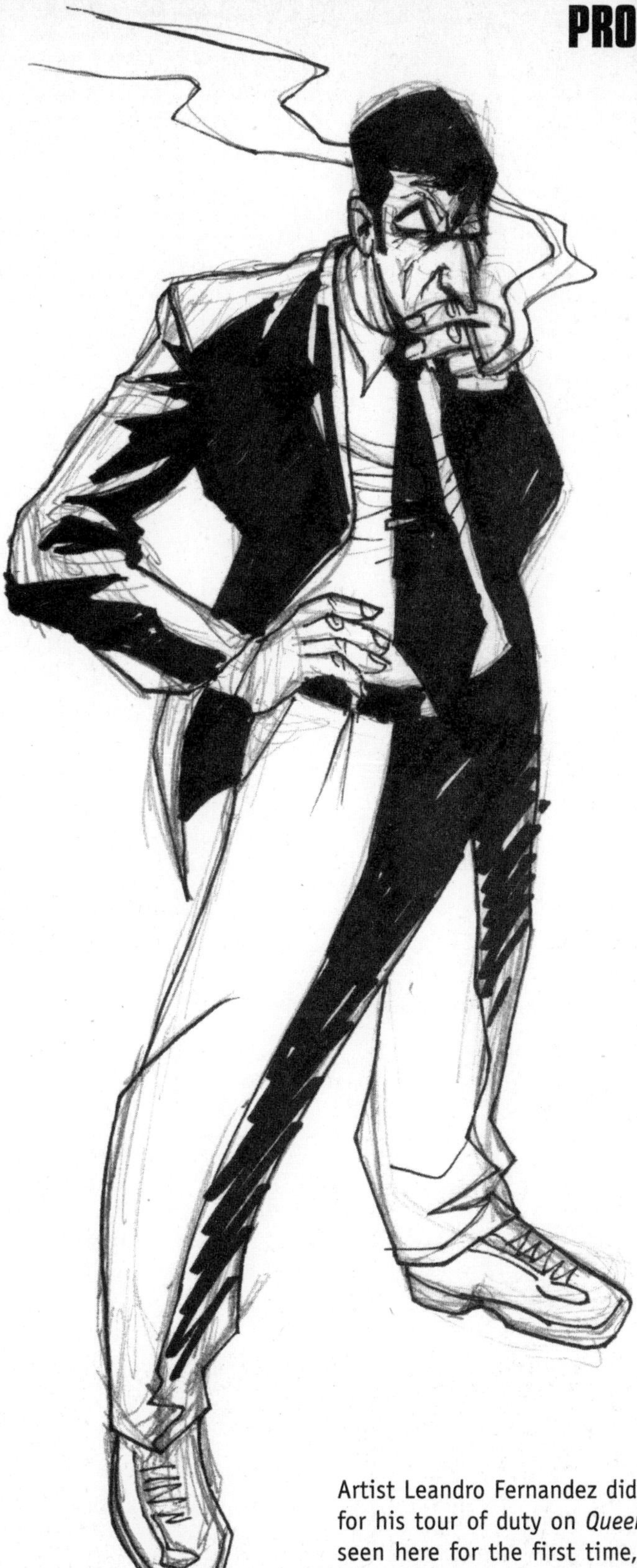

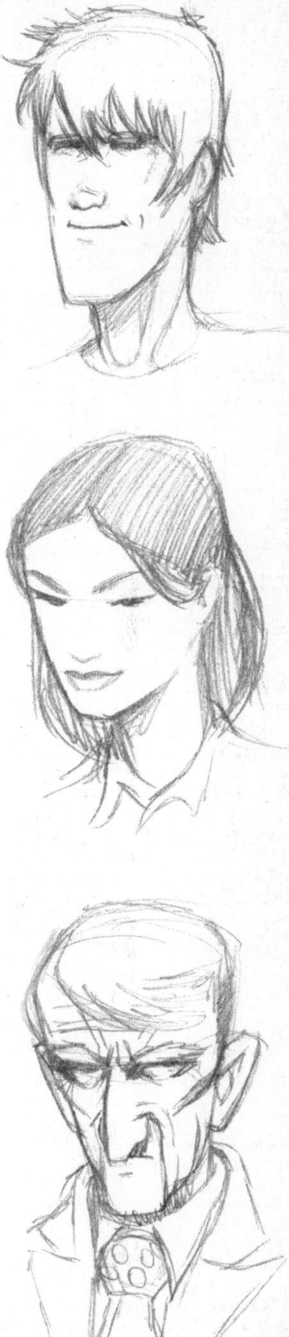

Artist Leandro Fernandez did extensive preparatory work for his tour of duty on *Queen & Country*. The material is seen here for the first time, and ranges from character sketches and cover designs to a look at his pencilled pages.

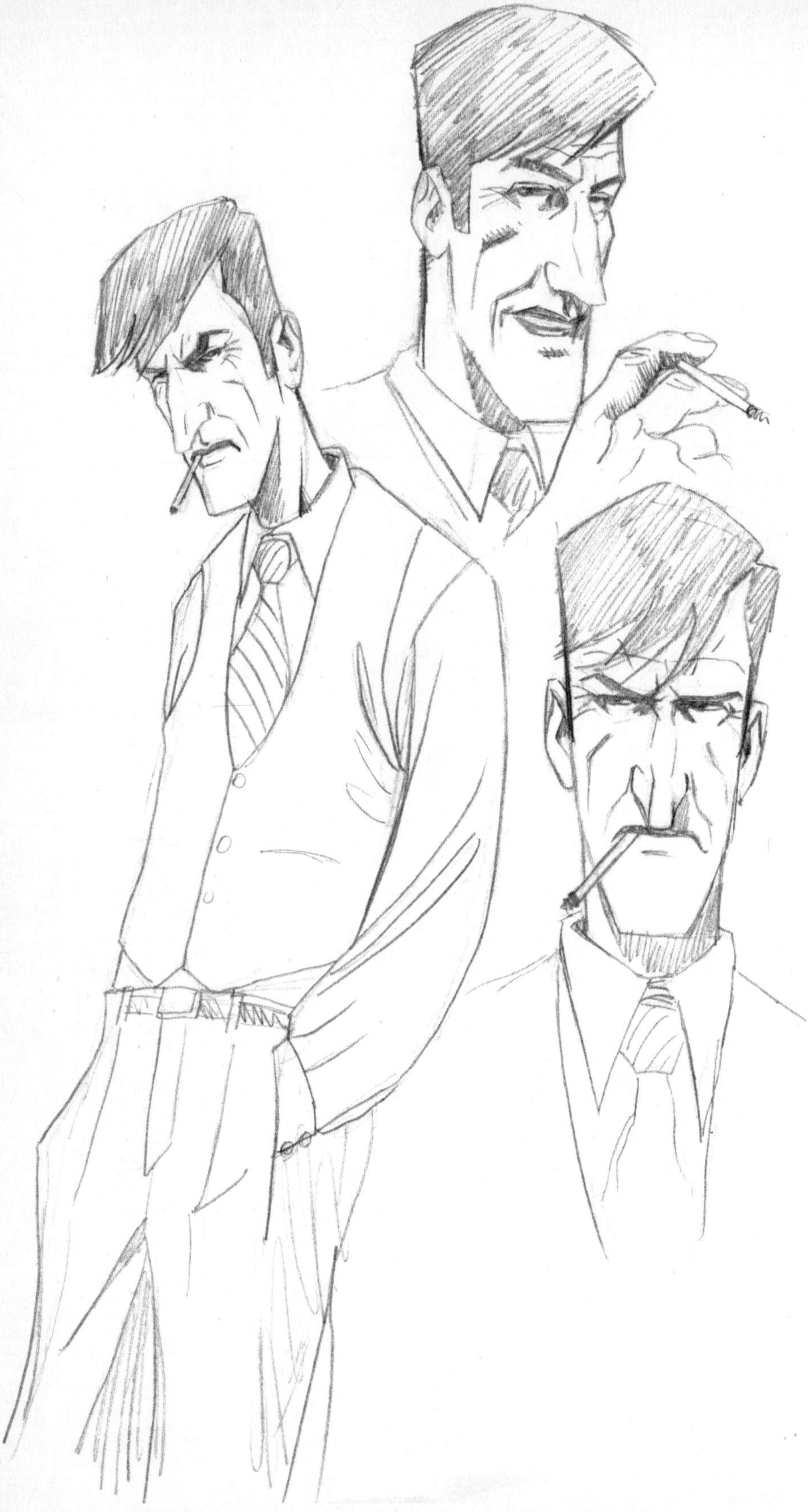

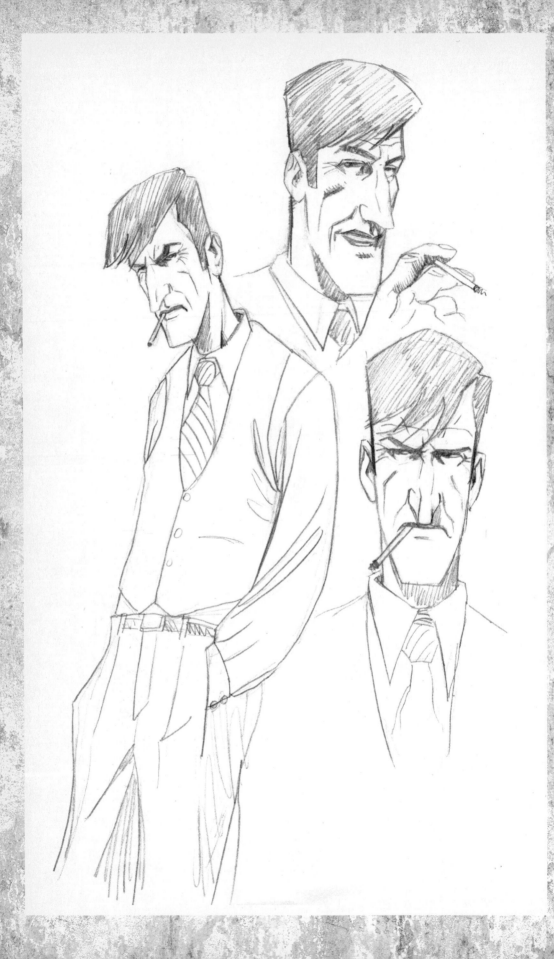

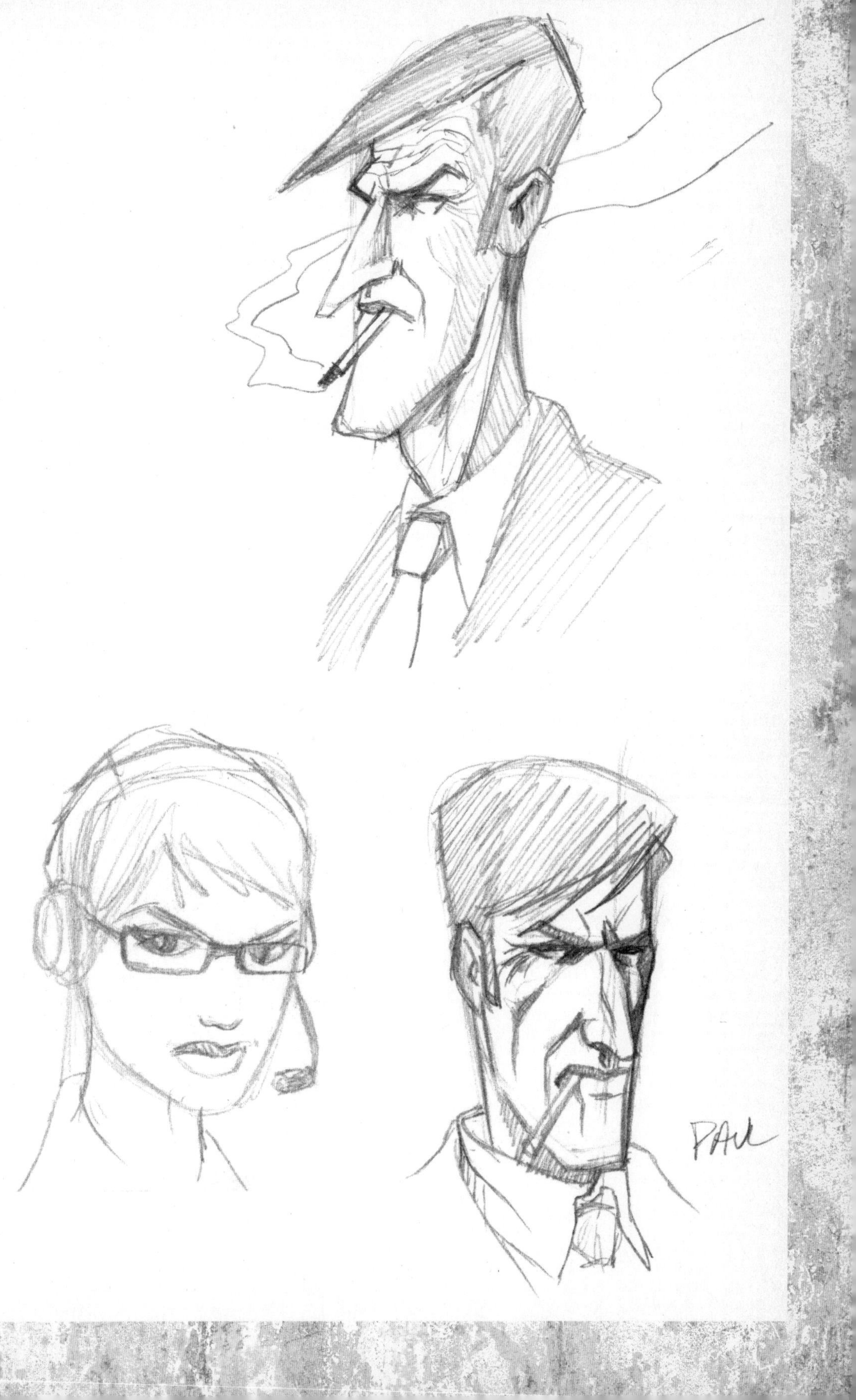
PAUL

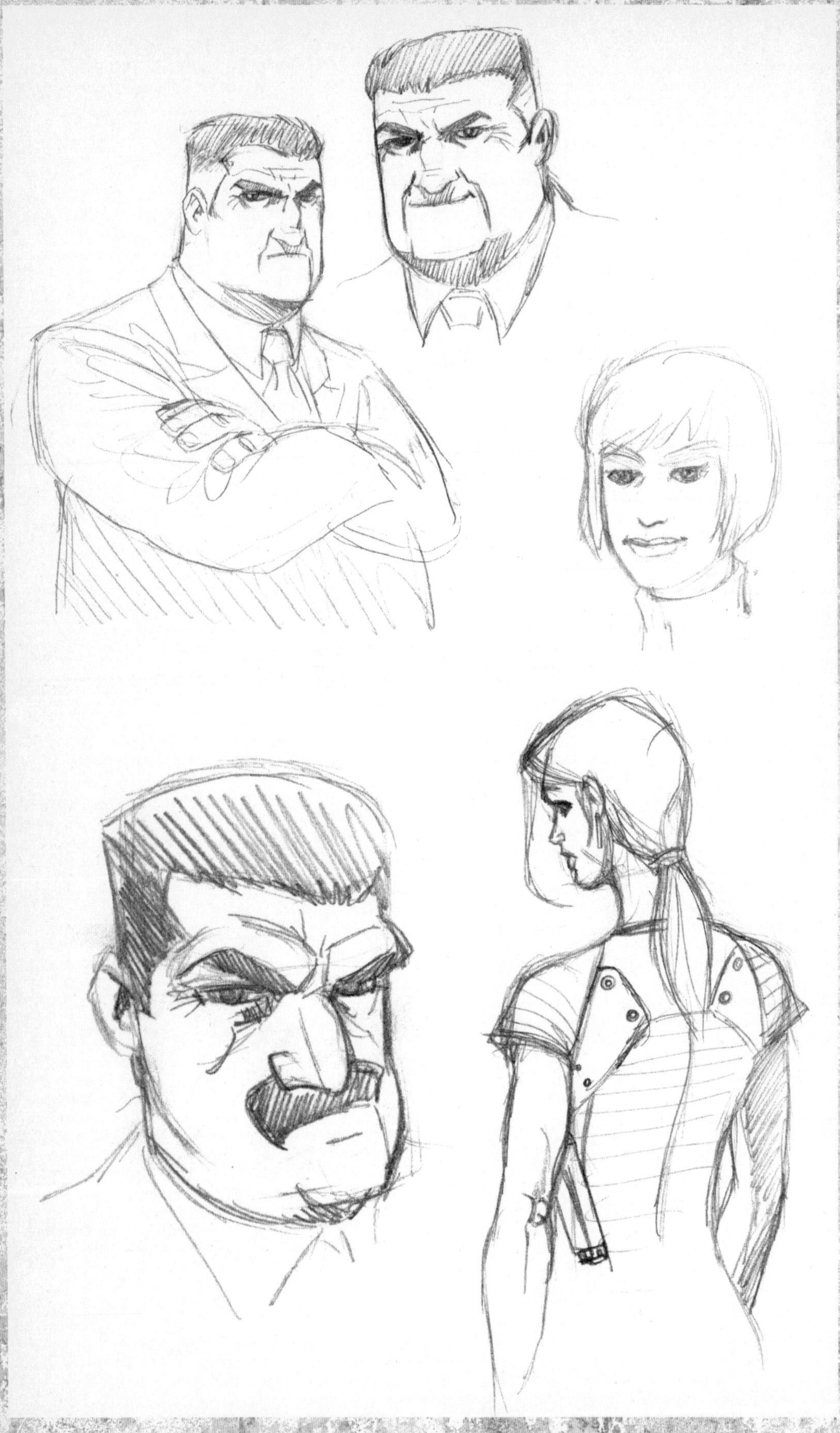

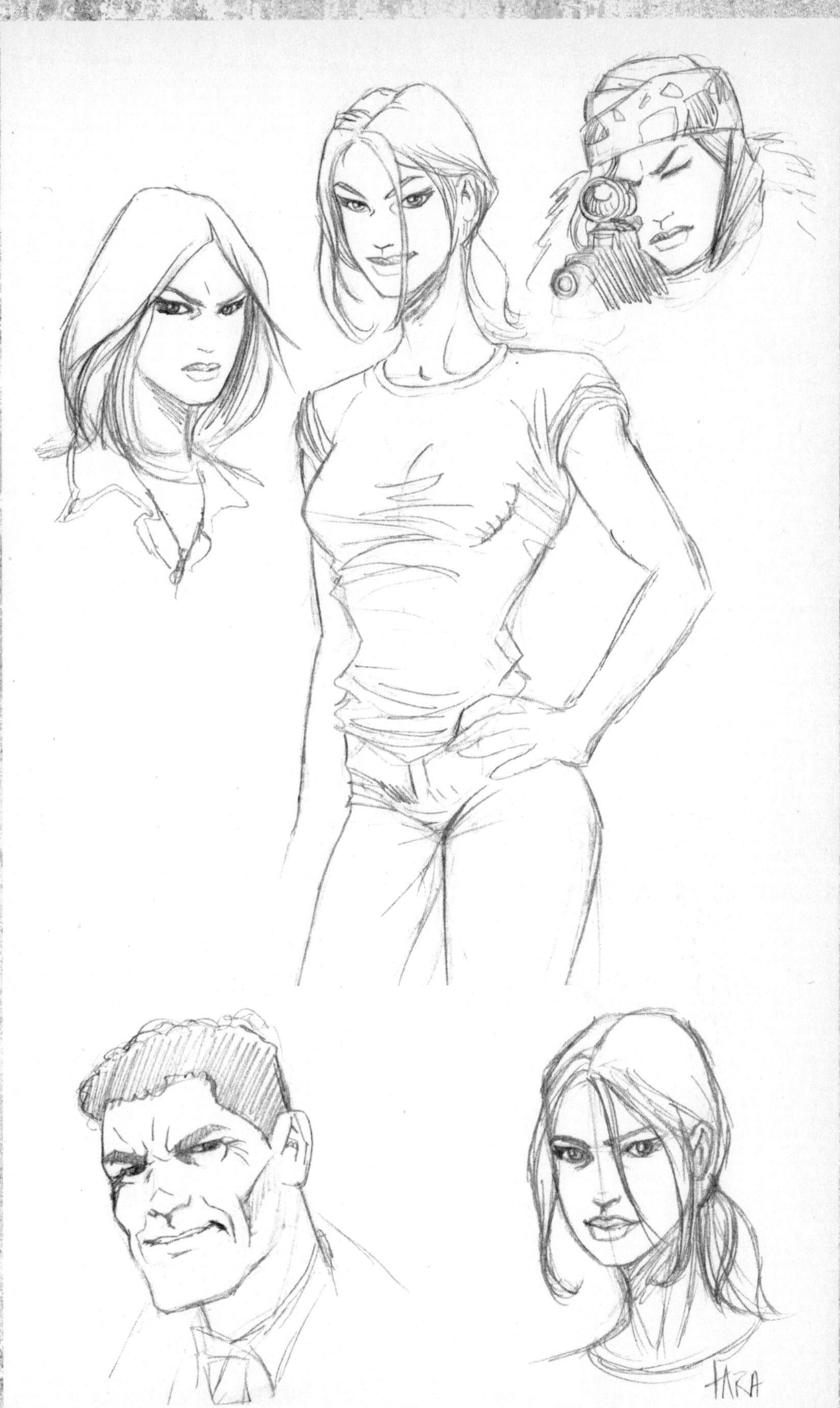

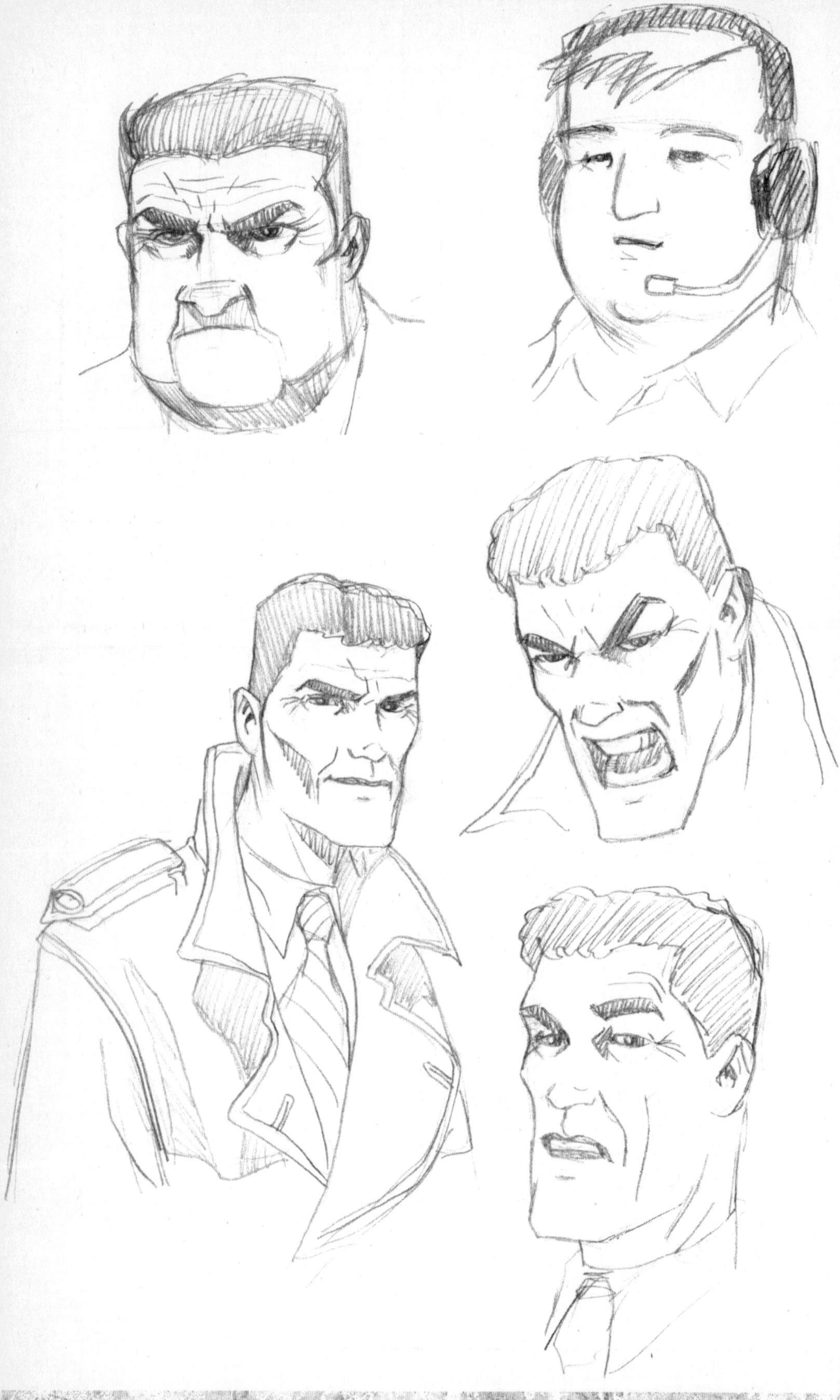

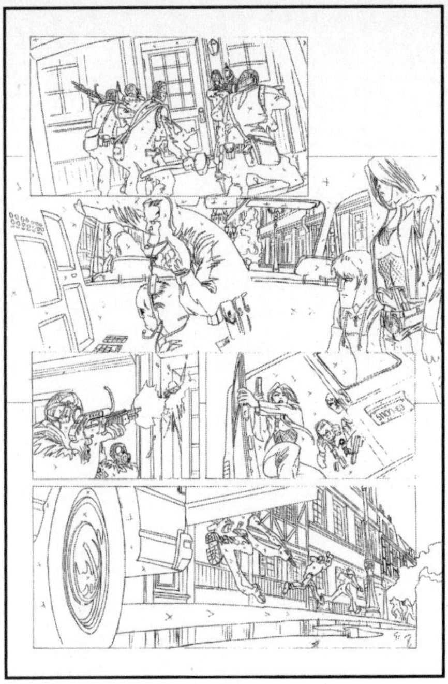

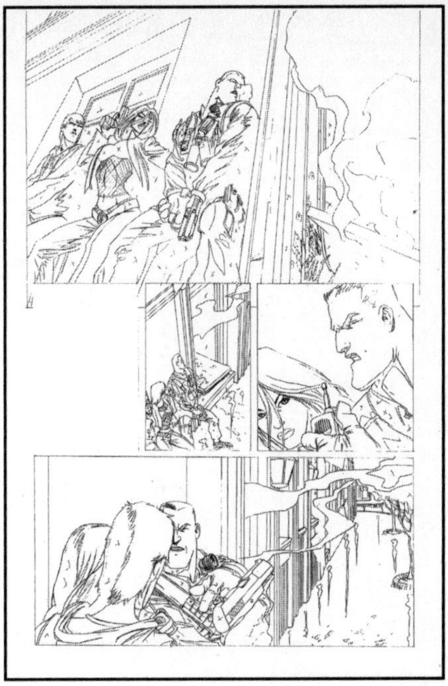

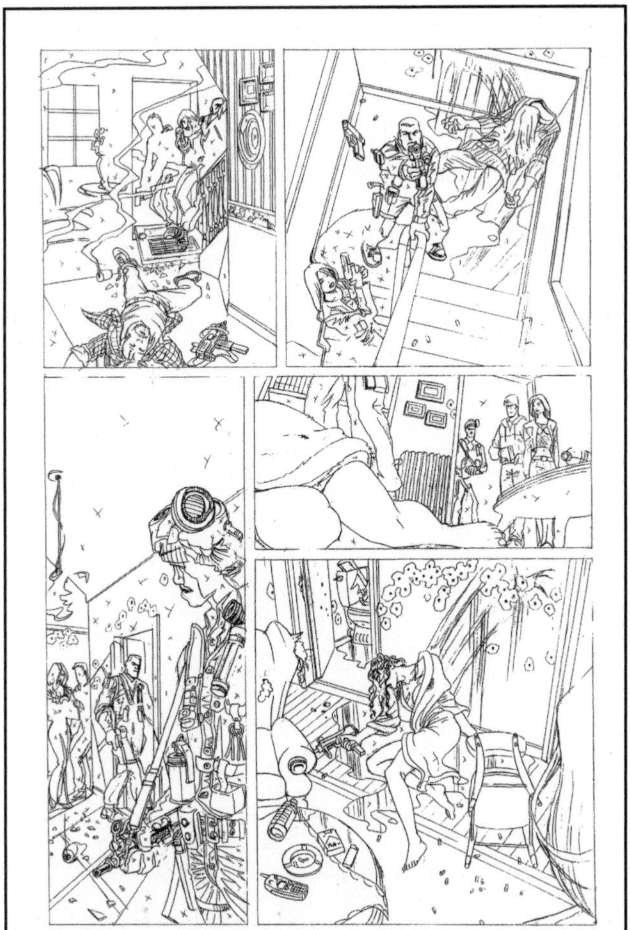

A look at how Leandro maps out his pages.

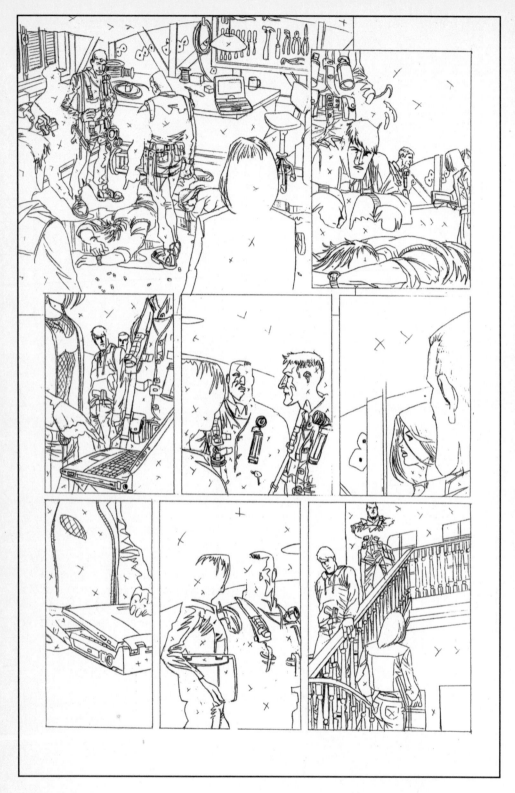

Note in this sequence from chapter 1 how the blacks are planned for early on, but left open until the inking.

Planning for a quiet scene requires just as much planning as a complicated action scene. All the characters must be placed properly and the panels designed in such a way to create the illusion of movement, even if the characters are just standing around talking.

QUEEN &
COUNTRY

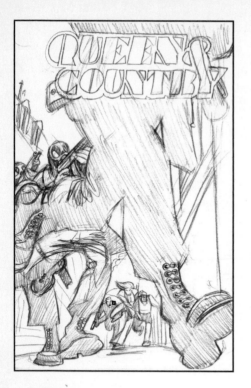

Leandro's cover roughs show not only a work in progress, but an assured designer's eye that knew exactly want it wanted to see.

QUEEN &
COUNTRY

QUEEN &
COUNTRY

The cover to issue #10 (chapter 3) was tested out at different angles.

QUEEN & COUNTRY

QUEEN & COUNTRY

QUEEN & COUNTRY

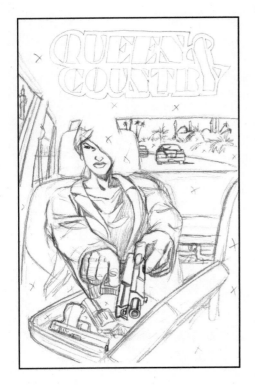

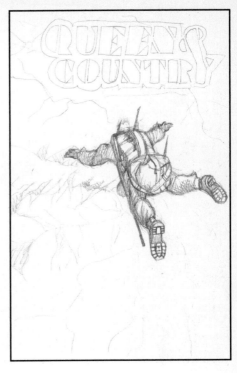

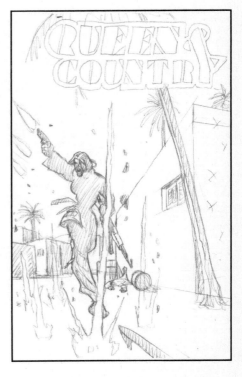

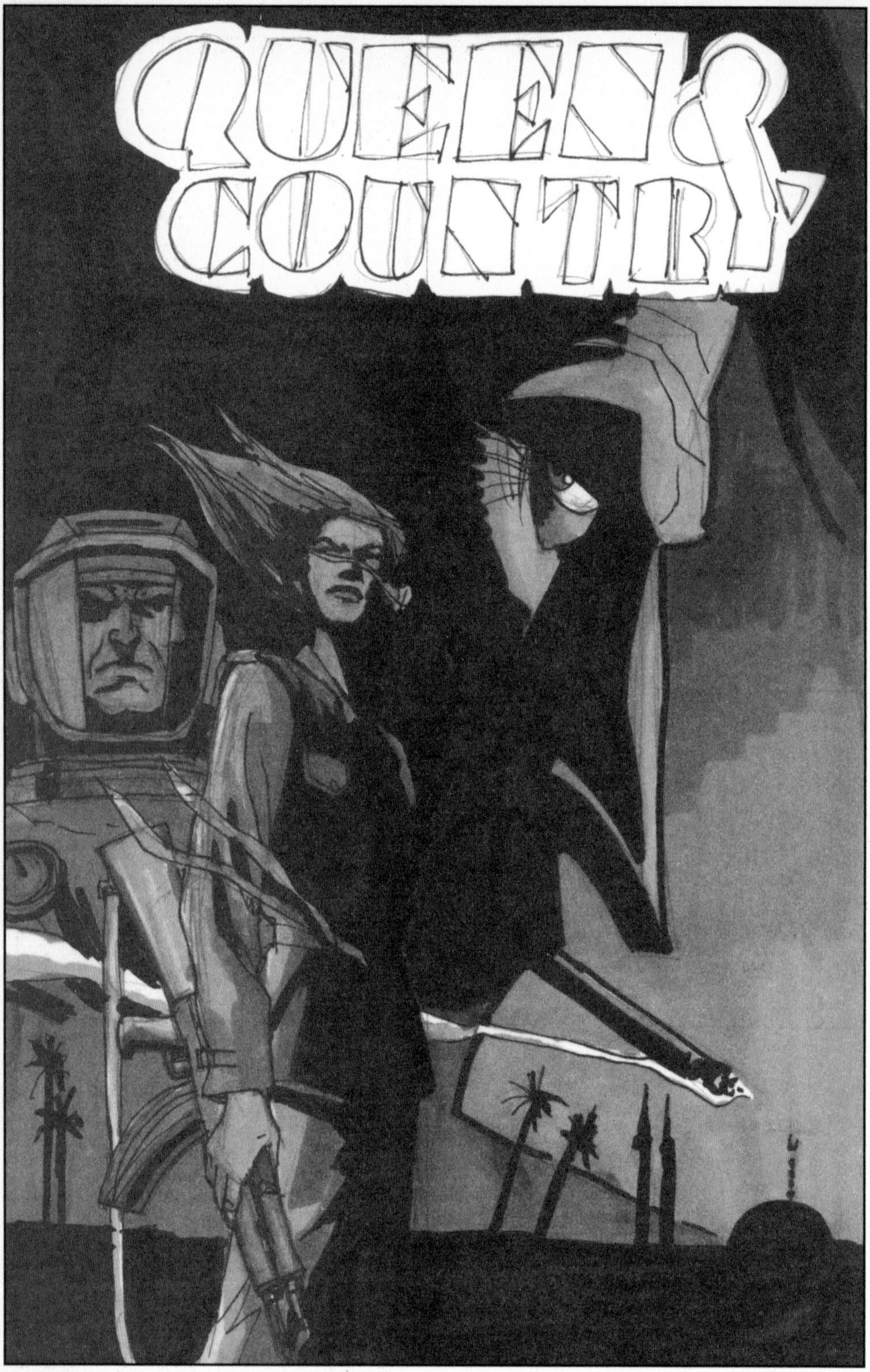
QUEEN &
COUNTRY

The cover for this collection went through several permutations before we landed on the final version.

The image to the right was taken out of the running due to its unintentional resemblance to Durwin Talon's cover for *Queen & Country, Vol. 2 – Operation: Morningstar.*

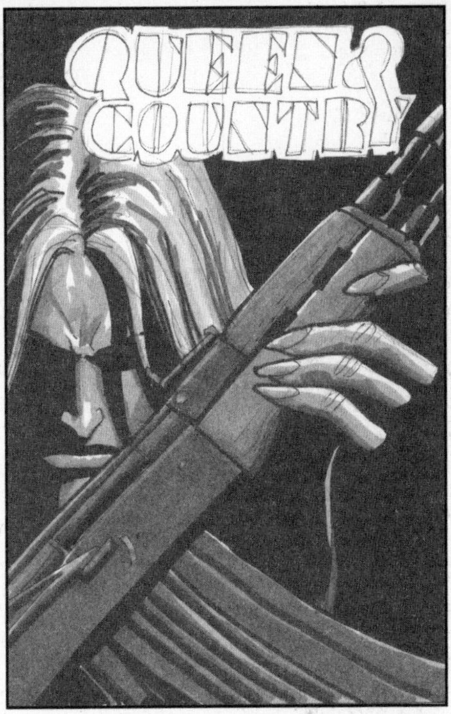
QUEEN &
COUNTRY

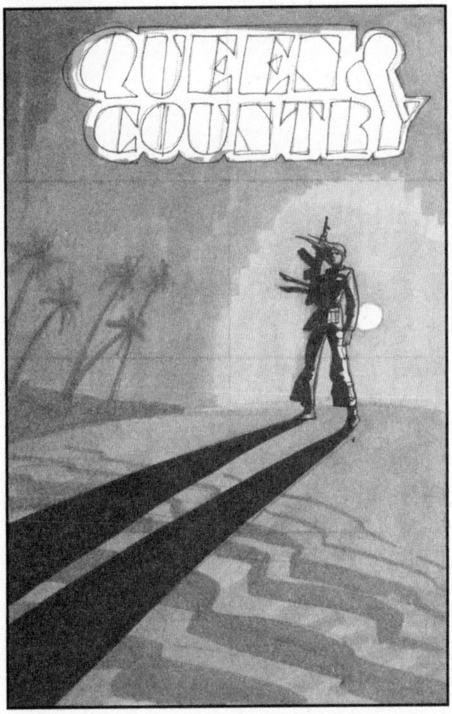
QUEEN &
COUNTRY

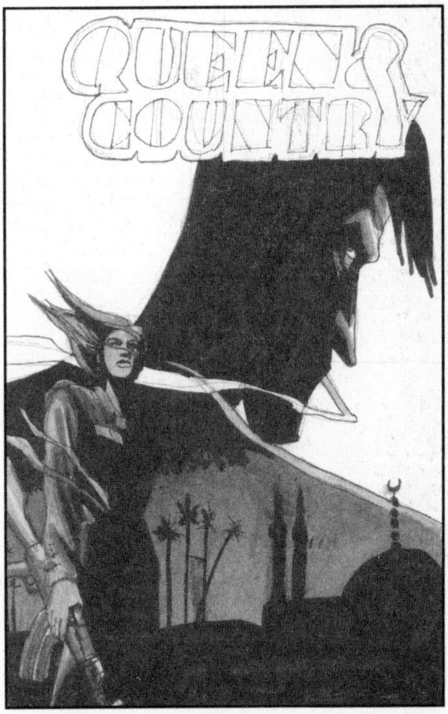
QUEEN &
COUNTRY

Photos taken at San Diego Comic Con International in 2002, just a couple months after the serialization of *Crystal Ball* began. It is also the convention where Greg Rucka and Steve Rolston won their Eisner Award for *Queen & Country* as Best New Series.

(Right) Behind Leandro and Greg is Greg's wife, Jen Van Meter *(Hopeless Savages)*, and she's speaking to Judd Winick *(Pedro & Me)* and his wife, Pam Ling.

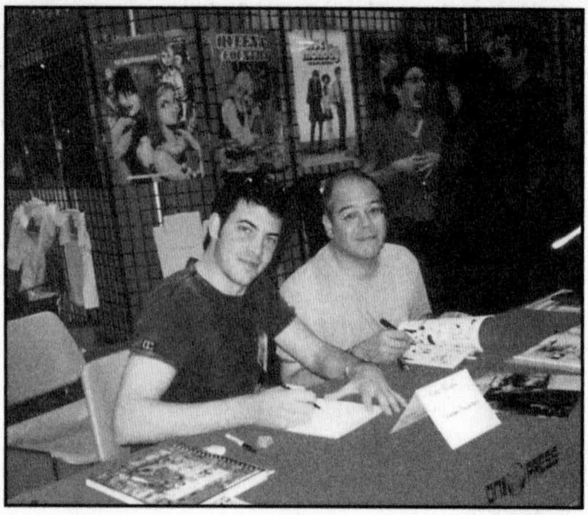

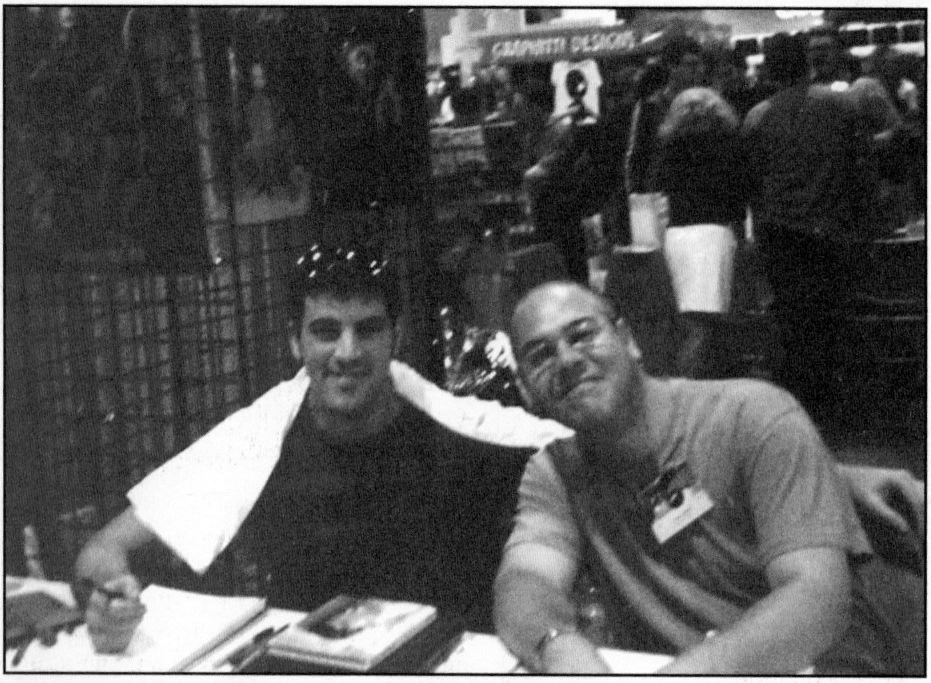

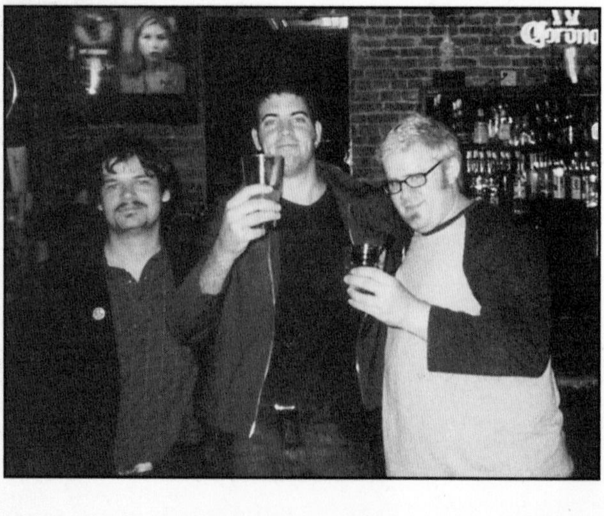

(Left) Leandro is flanked by writer Ivan Brandon on the left and one of *Queen & Country*'s editors, James Lucas Jones, on the right. You decide which one has already had too many.

GREG RUCKA

Born in San Francisco, Greg Rucka was raised on the Monterey Peninsula. He is the author of several novels, including four about bodyguard Atticus Kodiak, and of numerous comic books. He has won two Eisner Awards for his work in the field, including one for *Whiteout: Melt* (Best Limited Series, 2000) and one for *Queen & Country* (Best New Series, 2002). His most recent writing credits for comics include *Ultimate Daredevil & Elektra*, the original graphic novel *Wonder Woman: The Hiketeia*, and a much-anticipated tenure on the monthly *Wonder Woman* title. Greg resides in Portland, Oregon, with his wife, Jennifer, and their son, Elliot. His next novel, *A Fistful of Rain*, is due in 2003, and he is planning a miniseries about an expedition to climb Mt. Everest to be drawn by Scott Morse.

LEANDRO FERNANDEZ

Leandro Fernandez is part of a vibrant comics scene in Argentina. He began his career at the age of 15 as a pupil of artist Marcelo Frusin (*Hellblazer*), and he later assisted Eduardo Risso (*100 Bullets*) and studied graphic design at the university level. He did some work for a comics publisher in Italy and a few odd jobs for Marvel Comics before landing the gig on *Queen & Country*, which instantly attracted the attention of fans of sequential art the world over. He immediately followed with a two-issue run on *Spider-Man's Tangled Web* and is currently working on more comics projects to hit the stands in 2003.

En memoria de mi padre. – Leandro Fernandez

Other books from Greg Rucka and Oni Press...

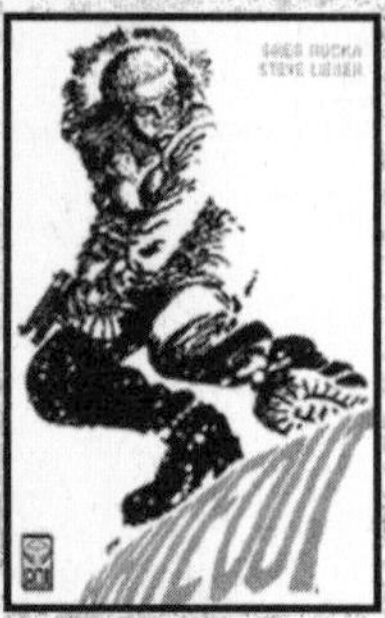
GREG RUCKA
STEVE LIEBER
WHITEOUT

Whiteout™
by Greg Rucka & Steve Lieber
128 pages, b&w interiors
$11.95 US
ISBN 0-9667127-1-4

"Whiteout's well researched, well written and expertly rendered. Don't buy it for those reasons, though. Buy it because Carrie Stetko's mouthy, freckled and cool..."

– Kelly Sue DeConnick, artbomb.net

"Greg Rucka is not a lesser writer. As an author, he thrives in political, moral and emotional complexity."

– Warren Ellis, creator of **Transmetropolitan** *and* **Global Frequency**

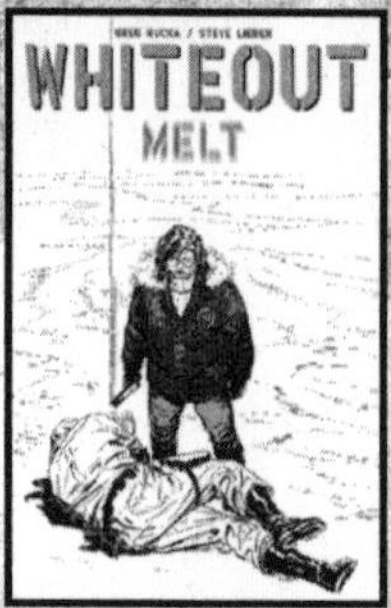
GREG RUCKA / STEVE LIEBER
WHITEOUT
MELT

Whiteout: Melt™
by Greg Rucka & Steve Lieber
128 pages, b&w interiors
$11.95 US
ISBN 1-929998-03-1

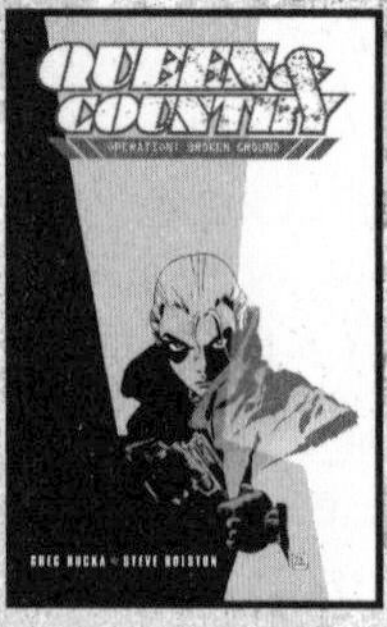
QUEEN & COUNTRY
OPERATION: BROKEN GROUND
GREG RUCKA • STEVE ROLSTON

Queen & Country™
Vol. 1 Operation:
Broken Ground
by Greg Rucka, Steve Rolston & Stan Sakai
128 pages
black-and-white interiors
$11.95 US
ISBN 1-929998-21-X

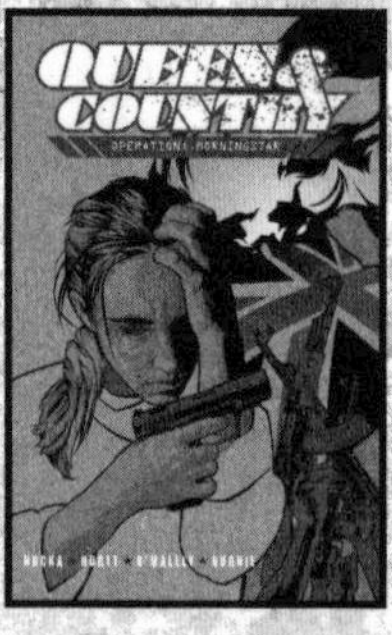
QUEEN & COUNTRY
OPERATION: MORNINGSTAR

Queen & Country™
Vol. 2 Operation:
Morningstar
by Greg Rucka, Brian Hurtt, Bryan O'Malley, and Christine Norrie
88 pages
black-and-white interiors
$8.95 US
ISBN 1-929998-35-X

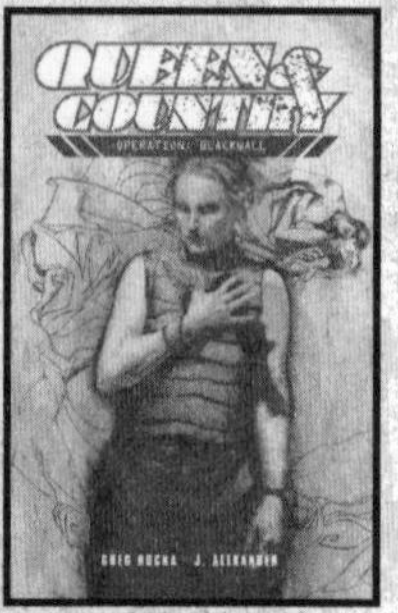
QUEEN & COUNTRY
OPERATION: BLACKWALL

Queen & Country™
Vol. 4 Operation:
Blackwall
by Greg Rucka & J. Alexander
88 pages,
black-and-white interiors
$9.95 US
ISBN 1-929998-68-6

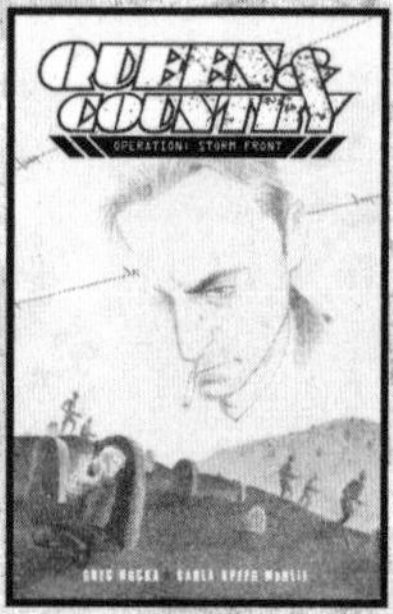
QUEEN & COUNTRY
OPERATION: STORM FRONT

Queen & Country™
Vol. 5 Operation:
Storm Front
by Greg Rucka & Carla Speed McNeil
152 pages,
black-and-white interiors
$14.95 US
ISBN 1-929998-84-8

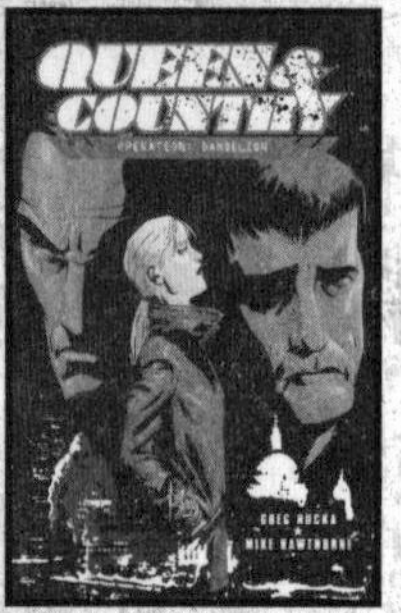
QUEEN & COUNTRY
OPERATION: DANDELION
GREG RUCKA
MIKE HAWTHORNE

Queen & Country™
Vol. 6 Operation:
Dandelion
by Greg Rucka & Mike Hawthorne
112 pages,
black-and-white interiors
$11.95 US
ISBN 1-929998-97-X

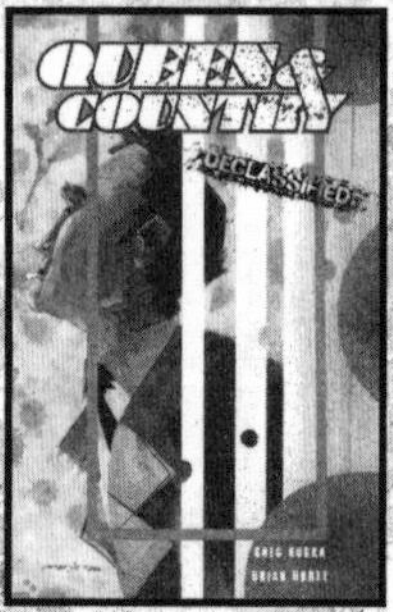
QUEEN & COUNTRY
DECLASSIFIED
GREG RUCKA
BRIAN HURTT

Queen & Country™
Declassified
Vol. 1
by Greg Rucka & Brian Hurtt
96 pages
black-and-white interiors
$8.95 US
ISBN 1-929998-58-9

AVAILABLE AT FINER BOOKSTORES EVERYWHERE.

For a comics store near you, call **1-888-COMIC-BOOK** or visit **www.the-master-list.com**.
For more information on more Oni Press books go to: **www.onipress.com**